Eileen

A Still and Bitter Grave

ANN MARSTON

All Best
Wishes,
Ann Marston

FIVE RIVERS PUBLISHING
WWW.FIVERIVERSPUBLISHING.COM

Published by Five Rivers Publishing, 704 Queen Street, P.O. Box 293, Neustadt, ON N0G 2M0, Canada.

www.fiveriverspublishing.com

A Still and Bitter Grave, Copyright © 2016 by Ann Marston.

Edited by Lorina Stephens.

Cover Copyright © 2016 by Jeff Minkevics.

Interior design and layout by Éric Desmarais.

Titles set in Minion Pro designed by Robert Slimbach in 1990 for Adobe Systems and inspired by late Renaissance-era type.

Text set in Noto Serif designed by Google and are intended to be visually harmonious across multiple languages, with compatible heights and stroke thicknesses.

Published in Canada

Library and Archives Canada Cataloguing in Publication

Marston, Ann, author

A still and bitter grave / Ann Marston.

Issued in print and electronic formats.

ISBN 978-1-988274-09-6 (paperback).—ISBN 978-1-988274-10-2 (epub)

I. Title.

PS8576.A7593S85 2016   C813'.54   C2016-902519-5   C2016-902520-9

Dedicated to the memory of the Edmonton Municipal Airport, the first licensed municipal airport in Canada (1929 - 2013). *Requiescat in Pace*

CONTENTS

Part One – The Dream

CHAPTER ONE

Spring - 1993

THE DREAM *came back to haunt my sleep again. The vast, familiar expanse of rocks and trees and lakes flowed peacefully beneath the wings like an unrolling Chinese scroll painting. The fall colours on the trees reflected in the lakes against the hard, brilliant blue of the early autumn sky. All the well-known landmarks came into view exactly on schedule and slid behind as the next one moved up over the horizon. The note of the Pratt & Whitney Wasp Junior engine was loud and smooth and confident. I was happy, smiling to myself as I thought of what awaited me when I reached home late in the afternoon.*

Then, in the space between one heartbeat and the next, everything changed. The note of the engine rose to a tortured scream. The ordered view outside turned to chaos as the natural arrangement of sky above trees and lakes spun together and changed places with no pattern, no sense, no sanity. Fear escalated to terror. The aircraft answered to none of the control inputs. Elevator, aileron, rudder—all useless. I had no control. None. The aircraft was dying—dead—and I with it.

From a long way off, I heard her call my name. The

rocks and water filled the windscreen and my own voice whispered softly amid the shriek of the wind around the broken aircraft and the clatter of failing structure. "I'm sorry. Oh, God, Judy. I'm so sorry—"

I came gasping and twitching out of the nightmare, bolt upright in the tangled morass of quilt and sheet, the echoes of my own strangled cry still ringing in the silence. My heart pounded like a badly timed engine as I breathed in great, ragged gulps of air. Sweat soaked my hair, ran in streams down the sides of my neck, down my chest. It seemed to take a long time to get my lungs under control, but once I did, my heart rate slowed toward normal.

Surprised, I found myself still fully dressed, on the sofa in the family room rather than in the bedroom. For a moment, it confused me, then I remembered the fight Glynnis and I'd had the night before. This one so terribly bitter and acrimonious, one of the nastiest quarrels we'd ever had. I'd ended up here after she stormed off to bed.

I went quietly into the bedroom so I wouldn't disturb her. She slept curled on her side, her tawny hair sprayed across her cheeks and throat. The Seconal-induced sleep had erased the tiny, petulant lines around her mouth and between her golden eyebrows. I stripped out of my sweat-sodden clothing and reached for my bathrobe, then padded barefoot back to the family room.

The family room. A room for the family I didn't have, and perhaps never would. The huge picture window faced back out over the promontory and the water. A full moon hung just above the horizon and reflected off the gentle swell of the ocean at flood tide. It bathed the room with a faintly ashen silver glow. My own reflection wavered in the window against the background of ocean and moon. It looked wan and remote and unreal. About the last thing I needed to see right now was the pale ghost of myself, so I turned away and went into the kitchen without turning on any lights and opened the fridge. I wanted something stronger to drink than the orange juice I took out, but I was flying in the morning and the company was adamant about their *twenty-four hour bottle to throttle* rule. I drank the juice straight from the carton until my stomach started to feel tight.

That damned dream was enough to scare me white. And tonight, the sudden vision of death....

But it hadn't always been like that. The dream, like the marriage, hadn't always been a nightmare.

I shut down that line of thinking, put the carton back into the fridge and went back to the family room. The pallid shadow of myself appeared again in the window. I scrubbed my hands over my face and turned away.

Jesus, is this what it all comes to? How did everything go so flat and stale and sour? What happened to me? Only a couple of years ago, I thought I had it made. I had everything I'd ever dreamed of having. Where did it all go?

The effects of the dream were already beginning to dissipate. The adrenaline rush from the terror ebbed and left in its place a cold, uneasy lump of formless dread, a nebulous, undirected sense of foreboding. I thought of Glynnis, still oblivious in sleep, and my eyes stung suddenly.

Dear heavens, what was to become of us?

I stumbled across the room to the recliner chair in the corner. This was my chair. It faced away from the television, toward the fireplace in the corner by the window. Close at hand were the shelves that housed my books and the flying magazines I subscribed to and read thoroughly as soon as they arrived. The books were an oddly assorted collection of fiction and non-fiction, most of them with aviation themes. I had everything from a complete collection of Nevil Shute's works to a variety of coffee table books on aviation, from technical texts on aerodynamics and aircraft design to biographies of famous aviators. Long ago, Glynnis had said with mild exasperation that I would buy anything that had a picture of an airplane on the cover; that I was still a little boy bewitched by airplanes.

Perhaps she was right. Most little boys go through a stage when they want to become policemen, or firemen, or cowboys, or pilots. Obviously, some of us never outgrew that, or there would be damned few policemen or firemen in the world. I never outgrew wanting to be a pilot. Now, at thirty-three, I was Holiday West's youngest captain. Colin James Fraser, boy prodigy of the airways. It was something I used to be proud of, but lately during this past year, I just couldn't seem to work up the energy. It had become a sour achievement.

The tattered fragments of the nightmare hovered at the edge of my mind. I still didn't want to think about it, still didn't want to examine it or try to sort it out.

I didn't want to think about the fight Glynnis and I'd had last night, either. But the memory was there, fully realized, in my mind.

"I hate you," she'd shrieked. "I hope you crash and die. I hope you lie in the dark and die!"

I stared at her. We had said some terrible things to each other over the past year, but she had never been so vitriolic, so malicious. I took a deep breath. "Does that mean you want a divorce?" I asked fighting to keep my voice even.

"I'd sooner kill myself and you than let you divorce me,"

she cried. "I'll never give something of mine to someone else. Never, do you hear me? Never!" She spun and reached for one of the paring knives in a wooden block by the sink. I grabbed her hand before she could reach one. The last time she'd done that, she'd brought the blade down on the back of her own hand hard enough to drive the tip clear through her palm, screaming, "See what you made me do?" I had no wish to go through the inquisition at the emergency room again. A paring knife through the back of a hand is not easy to pass off as an accident. So this time, I held her wrist tightly and turned her back to face me.

"Glynnis, don't—"

"You're hurting me," she yelped. She tore herself away and stumbled sobbing out of the kitchen toward the bedroom. I heard the door slam moments later. There was no use in trying to talk with her now. I went into the family room and sat down on the sofa, watching the restless movement of the ocean in the glimmering dark, and wondered what I was going to do.

The bitter realization that my life was a shambles didn't exactly come as a revelation, one of those bolts from the blue you're always reading about. Nor did the scales suddenly fall from my eyes. Over the past year, it had just become painfully obvious I could no longer hold the broken pieces together, that everything around me was crumbling to ruin, and it was just as apparent that I didn't seem to give a damn if it did.

I sat slouched into the sofa cushions and stared down at the beginnings of a soft roll of flab at my waist. I hadn't worked out in the dojo for months, and it showed. No energy. No enthusiasm. No longer any pleasure to be taken in the precise and graceful movements of *kata* or *kumite*. Not anymore. I was flaccid and limp, without animation.

And speaking of flaccid and limp... I glanced down at the male flesh that lay as if exhausted against the top of my thigh. How long since Glynnis and I had made love? Months? Since Christmas? A cynical smile turned down the corners of my mouth. No, we hadn't made love at Christmas. We'd fucked. The last time we'd made love was so long ago I couldn't even remember it. Perhaps we'd made love in that first breathless year or so of our marriage, before I began to realize what a ghastly mistake we'd made. But certainly not many times since.

Now there was a truly devastating thought. But certainly one that had a melancholy ring of merciless truth to it. It didn't exactly paint me as the hero of my own life.

I looked at the clock on the mantel. It was a gold and crystal anniversary clock Glynnis had picked up years ago on one of her shopping binges. Anniversary of what, I never figured out. But it kept perfect time and boasted a pleasant and melodious chime marking the hours, the half hours and the quarters. Right now, it was telling me that it was twenty past four. In about four hours, I had to strap on a Boeing 767 and aim it through the sky at Orlando, Florida, by way of Los Vegas and Houston. I had to be at the airport an hour early, and it took an hour and a half to drive there at this time of year, even at the ungodly hour of six in the morning.

How long would it take before my fitful dissatisfaction with the rest of my life spread to my job, to my flying? The answer to that one shocked and startled me.

It already had.

My hands trembled as I realized the implications of that. I clenched my hands into fists on my knees. Unenthusiastic and unsatisfied pilots were pilots who began to make mistakes. Perhaps only small mistakes, but enough small mistakes all too often added up to a disaster, not only for the pilot but for all who were unfortunate enough to place their lives in that pilot's hands.

Safety slogans are universal in aviation. Nearly every safety information bulletin board I'd seen carried the slogan: *Three mistakes equals an accident. Don't make the first.* Nobody needed an accident.

Accidents....

And I was back in the nightmare, feeling the broken airplane limp and unresponsive around me, controls useless, as the world tilted and spun dizzily outside the windscreen. The vividly clear and detailed view of the rocks and water loomed up ahead of me, each ripple on the water, each vibrantly coloured leaf sharp and distinct. Then, again, as everything burst into light and noise, a woman's voice calling my name and my own voice crying out in pain to Judy.

My wife's name was Glynnis. I knew nobody called Judy. A long time ago, I had dated a woman named Julie, but the name I called out in the dream was Judy. The name the woman called out was my own—Colin.

That wasn't the only disturbing thing about the dream, apart from the terror of the crash. In the dream, I knew with the same certainty that I knew my own name that the aircraft I flew and crashed and died in was a de Havilland of Canada DHC-2 Beaver on amphibious floats. But I had never flown a Beaver, never done any float flying at all. Except for reading articles about the aircraft in flying magazines, I knew nothing about them. But in the dream, I knew the Beaver as well as I knew the 737 I had flown for five years, or the 767 I had flown for only this last year.

I shuddered and clenched my hands into fists again to control their trembling. The dream hadn't always been a nightmare. Once, it had been something I looked forward to, something that had given me pleasure. Then, about a year ago, it had changed. By then, my life was already beginning to fall apart. In a twisted way, I suppose it made sense that the dream would turn to a nightmare at the same time my life seemed to be turning into one, too.

Not for the first time, I wondered if I was losing my mind. Maybe I needed a psychiatrist. Maybe I was skidding helplessly into insanity.

Or maybe I just needed a good, swift kick.

The mantel clock chimed five o'clock. Outside the window, the moon had slid below the surface of the ocean. I dragged myself out of the chair and padded to the bathroom and the shower to rinse and scrub away the stink of the sour nightmare sweat.

Glynnis hadn't moved since I left the bedroom. The thick quilt blurred the outlines of her slim body, rising with the mound of her hip, descending steeply into the valley of her waist. I dressed without turning on a light. Then, my tie hanging unknotted around my neck, I stood by the bed and looked down at her.

Watching someone sleep has always seemed to me to be an act of mild voyeurism. The sleeper is completely unguarded and defenceless. Entirely vulnerable. All the artifices and subterfuges of wakefulness are gone. Faces are relaxed and clear of thought. In the face of my sleeping wife, just barely delineated in the glow of the yard lights filtering through the drapes, it was easy to see the face of the beautiful girl I'd fallen in love with almost six years ago. The woman was still lovely, even without make-up, but the face was curiously bland and characterless.

She owned the face of a lovingly handcrafted doll to be carefully and meticulously dressed in velvet and lace and displayed behind glass. Glynnis had always been beautiful. When did I finally realize that she had always been vain and foolish and selfish as well?

She had her career. She had been a model—an actress. Now she ran her own agency and training school for models and did well with it. Her face had never been splashed all over the big fashion glossies. She had done a lot of those energetic, life-style commercials the beer companies were so fond of, but they had not led to the glamour and excitement of the top model jobs or the fabled land of the movie or television contracts she had been so sure of when first I met her. For a while, she blamed me because the contracts had never materialized. She had wanted to live in New York or Los Angeles. My job was based in Seattle. She never could, or never would, face the cold, hard truth that the contracts had not been offered because being beautiful wasn't enough. She had a little talent, but it wasn't enough talent to overcome her obdurate and inflexible need to have it all her own way. Nobody wanted to work with an actress or model who was too wilful and intractable to take direction.

In that obscuring light, in this introspective mood, I could take that objective look at my wife. Did I love her? Now I could say that I did not. How can you love anyone who is incapable of loving or giving anything of herself? Had I ever loved her? Oh, yes. I had loved her very much indeed, or I'd thought I did, which pretty much amounted to the same thing. Even now, the face and body should have been enough to produce a powerful and explosive physical desire. But did I still desire her? Right now? No. I did not.

And now I was certain she didn't love me, and probably never had.

But last night when I asked her if she wanted a divorce, she had shown in no uncertain terms that she did not wish to discuss it. Another *see what you made me do* response.

Where did we go from here?

I finished knotting my tie and left.

A busy airport terminal never sleeps. Even at quarter to seven, it was crowded with people lined up at the ticket counters, the check-in counters, the security check-throughs. Throngs of people milled around in the concourse, filling the restaurants, coffee shops and news stands. More crowds waited for boarding in the holding rooms by the gates. I was always mildly amazed that so many people had the need to go so many places on the same day. But that was what kept me employed. Off the streets and out of the bars, as Delaney Braedon my first co-pilot used to say, all pilots know if nobody wanted to fly, we'd have to go out and find a real job, and work for a living.

Morg Hannarhan, my first officer, met me as I entered the Ops Office. He was chewing on the first of three sticky doughnuts that lay on a paper napkin on the counter before him. I'm a little over six feet, but Morg, even with his casual slouch that makes his uniform looked as if he slept in it for the last week, towered several inches over me. He was hardly ever seen without a doughnut or a Danish or a packet of cookies from the galley. The only effect all that sugar had on him was to curl his hair and broaden his smile but never his waistline. He had a reputation as one of the most imperturbable and unflappable first officers on the line. Outside the airplane, he appeared to have all the grace of a grounded pelican, but on the flight deck, he had a swift, deft, almost delicate touch. He wasn't quite the pilot that Delaney Braedon, my previous first officer had been—Braedon had been one of the best first officers on the line, but she was gone, quit and gone back to corporate flying was the rumour.

"A hundred and seventy-eight souls, Skipper." Morg licked the sugar from his fingers. "We're gonna bulge at the seams today. A flock of conventioneers. Gonna be an interesting flight."

"Who's in the cabin?" I asked.

"Marilee and her usual crew, and a new one. Cindy or Suzie or something."

I nodded absently. A good cabin crew. "What's the weather?"

"The gods smile upon us. If you'd ordered it yourself, you couldn't get better."

"Fuel?"

"Half a sec—"

That restless lump of undirected foreboding in my belly made me frown at him and snap, "Haven't you had enough time?"

He glanced at me, one eyebrow arched in surprise, but didn't snap back. Instead, he reached out, lazily pulled the forms across the counter and showed me his pre-flight calculations. We would be off the ground with an all-up weight of just over 231,000 pounds. It looked good. I should have apologized to him, but he turned away to complete his paperwork, and the opportunity passed and was gone.

The flight went smoothly enough for the first leg. Marilee

brought coffee to us soon after we levelled off. When I asked her how it was going in the back, she smiled.

"No problems, Captain," she said. "Tina had her ass pinched once and sort of accidentally spilled coffee down the jerk's shirt. We're coping. We're just serving breakfast and coffee. No liquor."

Morg smiled dreamily. "One of these days, I'm going to pinch Tina's ass, myself," he said. "Reminds me of that old cigarette commercial. So round, so firm, so fully packed. Yes, indeed."

Marilee swatted him lightly across the back of the head. "Don't be a sexist pig, junior," she said, only half in jest. "You never know what might turn up in your coffee."

I had stopped listening to their by-play. Like a video tape, the nightmare replayed itself inside my head. When it came to the part where the rocks and water loomed preternaturally clear in the windscreen, something scalding hot and wet splashed over my knee. I swore, then looked down to see the crushed remains of the styrofoam cup in my clenched fist.

Marilee rushed off to get a napkin to mop up my trouser leg, and Morg looked at me curiously, that eyebrow raised again.

"You okay?" he asked.

I flexed my fingers. "Yeah," I said. "Sure. Just didn't get much sleep last night. Cramp in my hand, that's all."

He nodded, but the thoughtful expression didn't leave his face.

I made the mistake on the departure out of Orlando. If Morg hadn't said something—a mild and casual reminder in an offhand tone—I would have flown right through our assigned altitude and intruded on someone else's airspace.

It was a serious mistake and it chilled me. I had never in my life made an error like that. It left me thoughtful and uncomfortable. Mistakes like that kill people.

We got back to Seattle in the early evening. Some time during the last leg of the flight, the unsettling lump of nebulous dread had finally dissipated, leaving a miasma of despair in its place. I almost wanted the nervous energy of the fear back. At least it hadn't left me feeling so dead and numb inside.

Brett Murphy, the Chief Pilot, was still in his office, swamped in the ever-present paperwork. He looked up as I knocked on the open door and came in.

"I swear to God, Fraser, you must be psychic," he said with a grin. "I just pulled your file. I was going to tell Lucy to write you a note to see me tomorrow about your check ride."

"Am I due again?" I asked.

"By the end of the month," he said. "I can book you for early next week. That okay?"

I sat down in one of the dark grey swivel chairs in front of his desk and turned so that I could see the busy ramp through the window. "That's not what I came to see you about," I said. I hesitated, unsure of how to put it. But the only way to say it was straight out. "I have to put myself on the inactive list. I'm grounding myself before I make one hell of a large smoking hole in the ground. I made a bad mistake today. I don't want to make another."

He didn't say anything. Instead, he shuffled through my file for a moment. Finally, he looked up and met my eyes. "You've got three months' vacation time coming. Do you want to take it now?"

"I was thinking of a six month leave of absence, if I can get it," I said. "I'm burned out. I have to get away for a while and think."

"Take the three months to start, Colin," he said. "If you need more time after that, I'll arrange it."

"Thanks, Brett. I appreciate it." I stood up.

A tall man in a dark suit stepped into the doorway. "I'm looking for Captain Fraser," he said. "They told me I'd find him in here."

"I'm Fraser," I said.

"Captain, I'm Sergeant Steinway, Highway Patrol. I'm afraid I have some bad news for you. Your wife had an accident this morning driving into the city. She lost control of her car. I'm afraid she's dead."

It suddenly became very dark in the office and the solid ground dropped right out from under me. The next thing I knew, I was sitting in the chair again, my head down on my knees. I felt nauseated and weak and light-headed. For one chilling instant, I was certain she had done it purposely as a childish, vindictive *You'll be sorry when I'm dead* trick.

"What happened?" My voice sounded rusty, hoarse. A stranger's voice.

"We're not sure, sir," Steinway said. "It looked as if she pulled out to pass a truck and somehow she sideswiped it. Her car flipped. They think she must have been travelling at close to a hundred when it happened. We haven't found the truck, and the only witness didn't get the license number."

I nodded, still numb. *"See what you made me do?"* I whispered to myself

"Sorry?" Steinway said. "I missed that."

I shook my head. "Nothing," I said. I looked up at him. I

didn't know what to say. My chest was so tight, so painful, I could hardly breathe.

And under it all was the horrid little flicker of relief that it was all over now, all finished, all done. No more fights, no more tearing each other to bits. It was over. Over and finished and done with.

Then my mind emptied and all I could think of was I had to go home. I had to go home before my mind snapped.

Chapter Two

1965 – 1976

I have always dreamed of flying. When I was a child, I dreamed of floating suspended and entranced above the mountains, fields and coves of my small world, or moving through the air as gracefully and effortlessly as the clouds of gulls that swirled over the beach behind our house. I can't remember a time when the dream wasn't with me. The dream didn't come to me every night, but it came often enough to become an integral part of my life.

As I grew and matured, so did the dream. By the time I was six, I flew my dream landscape in a machine contrived with a lot of imagination from my father's old wooden swivel chair on casters, complete with ratty maroon cushion, and wings made of slabs reminiscent of the leaves my mother occasionally put into the dining room table to give her more room to spread out her artwork. When I dreamed, I felt warm and safe and loved. In the morning when I awoke, the good feeling lasted most of the day.

That ungainly contraption of pure imagination eventually gave way to machines fashioned after pictures of jet fighters in magazines and space ships in books I took from the library. And as the dream developed and matured, the landscape below me gradually firmed and became steady, a landscape of trees and hills and lakes.

We lived in a small town called Brindle Falls on the coast of Oregon. Our house was the last house on the street, which ended at a yellow barricade on top of the low cliff above the pale gold sand of the beach. The house backed onto that same cliff and at low tide, I had half a mile of back yard to play in. Yellow broom and blackberry brambles grew thickly around our wild and uncultivated back garden. Neither of my parents had any horticultural ambitions or pretensions. Our front lawn got mowed occasionally, usually long after it was due, but that was the total extent of my father's compliance with the conventions of yard work.

My mother, a classic Black Celt with her midnight black hair and vivid dark blue eyes, moved with all the unconscious grace of a young deer. I can hardly ever remember her not smiling or laughing. She hummed to herself a lot and sang old Gaelic songs to me. My father was red-headed and green eyed. He was tall with a good breadth of shoulder and chest, and narrow at the waist. He, too, moved with grace and precision, but it was the grace of a natural athlete, balanced and explicit. He was a quiet, reserved man, but I never saw him pass where my mother was without some gesture of affection—a tender touch to her shoulder or hair, or simply a gentle trailing of his fingers along her back. To me, he showed his love by listening gravely when I chattered to him and being willing to slow his long stride to match mine when he took me with him for walks along the beach.

I looked very little like either of them. Unlike either of my parents, my hair was very blond when I was a child, and as I grew gradually darkened to something closer to light brown, and my eyes were an uncertain grey that tended to shade toward green. I had none of their grace, either in body or movement. By the time it was three, it had become apparent that I would be tall like my father, but without his athletic build.

There were no other children living on our street, and I was an only child, so I had very few playmates when I was very young. Not until I started school did I discover that my parents weren't like the parents of other children. My father didn't get up early and leave the house every morning after breakfast to return just before dinner. On the rare occasion that he did get up early, he was just as likely to tuck me under his arm and take me on an exploration trip along the tidal pools below our house. We both sat on our heels and watched as tiny crabs scuttled across the wet sand, and my father always carefully explained to me something about their habits. From him I learned the differences between the wide variety of mollusca and other shellfish along our shore. He showed me how the great, pulpy bulbs on the kelp plants kept the seaweed upright and swaying in the water. On a day when huge waves thundered onto the sand, higher than ever before, he explained to me how hurricanes and tsunami half way around the world affected our secluded cove, which taught me we weren't as remote and apart as we thought. He gave me to understand that people, like continents, were not isolated, but affected by the loves, hates, agonies and triumphs of those around us.

Other mornings, my father slept late. He spent a lot of his time in the little room he had built into the wide, old fashioned screened veranda that surrounded all four sides of our house, producing interesting and staccato rhythms on his old typewriter. I learned my alphabet on the keyboard of that battered and ancient machine. I was only occasionally allowed into that room, an intriguing place of many books and fascinating papers scattered in a careless welter across the desk, and always faintly redolent of my father's pipe tobacco. He very frequently worked late into the night. I remember often waking up in the summer to the pearly grey light of dawn with the sound of the typewriter still faintly echoing from his study. From time to time at fairly regular intervals, the study produced a large brown envelope, and my father and I walked down to the post office where I was allowed to lick the stamps that sent it out into the mysterious reaches from which it seldom returned. There were always smaller envelopes for me to carry importantly back to my mother. I found out later that my father wrote an excellent series of police procedural novels under a pseudonym. Under his own name, Ian Fraser, he wrote historical books about North America and Britain that were both scholarly and popular.

My mother spent only a little more time in the traditional housewife role of cooking and cleaning than my father spent on yard work. As soon as my father disappeared into his tiny study, she dressed in jeans and an old shirt and, with me by the hand, took her easel, paint box, brushes, sketch pads and a haversack full of peanut butter sandwiches and apples, and set off for some corner of a cove, field or woods. Sometimes, I was entrusted with the care of the canvas carry-all containing the paints, brushes and sketch pads. But most often, I lugged the haversack. Once settled, she was fully capable of sitting by the hour, capturing imagery rather than images. I loved the paper she used. It had such a gloriously thick and rich texture between my fingers. I particularly remember one painting of a clump of vine maple, salt-bitten and wind-scoured, clinging tenaciously to its rocky crag. It was a delicate study, fragile and lovely as a soap bubble. I asked her solemnly if it was supposed to be the soul of the tree. She laughed in delight and hugged me, ruffling my hair as she told me gravely that it was obvious I would grow up to be a poet. That watercolour, carefully framed behind glass, still hangs in my bedroom, entitled *The Spirit of the Maple*. In the corner is her flowing signature—*Aislinn*.

Most of the time I spent with my mother on these expeditions was passed in watching the gulls, or dreaming of exploring the bewitching canyons and cliffs among the clouds. If an airplane wandered over, I watched it wistfully until it finally vanished in the distance. Sometimes, I merely watched my mother as she sketched and painted. I thought her very beautiful.

In walking to and from school each day, I had to pass the airport. Little more than a broad expanse of pasture with two or three ramshackle buildings that served as hangars, it was home to five or six small single-engine aircraft. Very quickly, I fell into the habit of stopping on my way home from school to look at the airplanes and talk to anyone who might be around. By the time I entered second grade, I was a confirmed airport brat. It was about that time, too, that my dream began to change. No longer was I simply hanging free in the sky or surrounded by an imaginary contraption made up of familiar but incongruous parts. Nor was I in something out of the magazines I read avidly. I became aware there were metal wings out there, above and behind me, supporting me in the living flow of the air. I accepted this knowledge without question, as one does in dreams.

But in all the years I dreamed about flying, I never once shared the dream with my parents. There had never seemed to be any need to do so. Far from being nightmares, the dreams had always left a residue of pleasure and quiet elation that lasted well after the dream faded upon waking.

In the early spring when I was ten years old, a crowd of men with heavy machinery descended upon the airport. They worked throughout the summer for an audience that consisted of most of the children in Brindle Falls and a good many retirees. The earth movers—the bulldozers, scrapers, graders, electric shovels, and front-end loaders—were fascinating to watch. They spent the first part of the long summer industriously chewing up the pasture from which the handful of little aircraft had fled in panic like a covey of flushed grouse. Then during the second part of the summer, the paving machines, the huge rollers and graders put the airport back together again. While they did that, another horde of heavy equipment gouged out three large holes in the ground. Presently another swarm of men arrived and began to build frameworks of steel girders over the foundation holes.

That was the most exciting summer of my life up to then. I spent every moment I could watching the new airport take shape.

Presently the construction crews packed up and moved on, leaving behind two freshly paved runways with markings bright and crisp in new paint, an office-cum-terminal building, and two cavernous hangars. The day after the equipment and crews departed, the little aircraft returned in ones and twos like geese returning in spring. Three days later, a scheduled Pacific Northwest Airlines Convair landed, the first regular link Brindle Falls had ever had to Portland, and from there to the world beyond.

I was there, sprawled in the shade of a caragana hedge, to watch the Convair land. I was highly aware it was a momentous event. I knew then I would be an airline pilot when I grew up. I wanted to be one of those men in their neat blue uniforms, gold rings on their sleeves and gold wings over the pockets of their tunics, who stood smiling with dignity and careless grace beneath the wing while the photographer from the paper snapped their picture with the huge, square paddles of the propeller blades behind them.

Eventually, it became apparent to my mother and father that I wasn't going to outgrow my enchantment with aircraft, and would probably learn to fly when I became old enough. They were never really sure how to take my single-minded determination to be a pilot. Although they had never tried to steer me toward any particular profession, clearly aviation was something that had never entered their heads as a serious possibility. Neither of them had any more than a vague idea of exactly what it was that pilots did. It was almost as if they weren't quite sure if it was a laudable or even respectable ambition for a young boy. But with time, they became resigned to the fact that I would fly, and because they loved me, they accepted it and began to offer encouragement.

In spite of getting a jump start on education by learning how to read early, I was never an exceptional student. I progressed stolidly through grade school, remaining somewhere in the top third of my class, without distinguishing myself except as an avid and voracious reader with catholic and eclectic tastes in literature. I had, of course, read almost everything my father wrote, almost as soon as it was published. And I read everything I could lay my hands on even faintly concerned with aircraft, aviators and aviation in general. In due course, I landed up on the threshold of high school and puberty at approximately the same time.

Brindle Falls Airport was now home to a small air taxi and flying school. At fourteen, I managed to land a job as a ramp rat, mostly through persistence and pestering. Nav Harty, the owner, probably hired me out of sheer self-defence as anything else in order to put an end to my constant querying. But I worked hard and he had to admit I earned my keep. I opened a savings account at the bank and deposited a little more than three-quarters of my pay every month. That was my flying lessons money, and I watched it grow, pleased and satisfied with myself.

I entered high school exactly like millions of other young teenagers. I discovered girls and survived my first kiss, a rather traumatic incident under the bleachers on Sports Day. The only sport I went out for was karate which was taught by the gym teacher, a third dan black belt in Shōrinji-ryū. The karate helped cure me of an unfortunate tendency toward clumsiness brought on by a body that had sprouted too quickly for me to keep up with. Tuesdays, Thursdays and Saturday mornings between 6:00 and 8:00 a.m., I worked on the karate. After school and on weekends, I washed and fuelled aircraft, fetched and carried for the engineer, answered phones, made bookings, swept hangar and office floors, washed windows, tidied work shop shelves, kept parts inventories, made endless pots of coffee, and dispatched flights. Conscious of the fact that airlines preferred to hire pilots with university degrees or some post-secondary education, I applied myself to my school work with diligence for the first time, and my marks rose accordingly to stand near the top of the class. I didn't have a lot of spare time but I think I was as happy then as I've ever been in my life.

Somewhere in the midst of all this frantic activity, my flying dream changed again. In it, I knew I held the horn of a control yoke lightly in the fingers of my left hand. My right hand was closed around the knurled black knob of a throttle. Right beneath the ball of my thumb was a chip in the plastic, worn smooth with age. It fitted my thumb comfortably and naturally. My feet rested on rudder pedals and I was vaguely aware of instruments on the panel in front of me, although I seldom looked at them. My body moved easily and intuitively to compensate for the small oscillations of the aircraft in very mild turbulence. I was conscious of happy contentment. I was doing exactly what I wanted to do——the only thing I wanted to do.

On my sixteenth birthday, two things happened that had a greater impact on my life than anything before or since, the first in an obvious way, the second more subtle and insidious. The first was taking my first flying lesson. The second was my parents told me I was adopted.

CHAPTER THREE

1976

MY BIRTHDAY fell on a Saturday. I was up at five, as usual, just before the pale, golden dawn. I'd dreamed of flying again that night and felt light and eager to tackle anything. By five-thirty, I was on my bike, my *gi* rolled and slung around my shoulder, heading for the gym at school and my karate class. I was working on my brown belt, the last level before the black belt. After two hours of painstaking and sometimes painful practice of *kata* and *kumite*, Sensei Mashite informed me he was ready to arrange for me to do my brown belt exam.

By eight-thirty, I was on the ramp in front of the Goldwing hangar, making sure the four Cessna trainers were fuelled and ready to go, and checking the Aztec because Nav Harty had a charter for a run to Eugene. Saturdays were always busy days. The three instructors and four trainers were booked solidly from nine on with no breaks until evening. I had barely finished with the trainers when the first bunch of students arrived, signed out the aircraft, and left to fill the air with noise and commotion. At nine-thirty, Nav and his passenger got into the Aztec and took off in the wake of the Cessna 150's and headed for Eugene.

I was busy all day. I ate my sandwich and apple in the hangar that smelled of fabric dope and engine oil as I scurried around finding parts for the engineer who was doing an annual inspection on a beautiful old J-3 Cub. When he landed at three, Nav found me on a ladder, pouring fuel into the tanks of a visiting Cessna 180.

"Soon as you're done, see me in my office," he said without smiling, then turned on his heel to walk away without listening for my reply.

He was sitting behind his desk when I came in, a lean, ropy, taciturn man with glittering anthracite eyes and a big hooked nose. On the desk in front of him lay a white paper sack. He pushed it at me with a flick of his forefinger. "Picked that up for you in Eugene," he said. "Happy birthday." Still no smile, but for him, that was usual. He seldom smiled and even less frequently laughed. Those who earned one of his smiles felt as if they were the favoured recipients of a coveted award. In nearly three years, I had earned exactly two of them.

Surprised, I picked up the sack. It contained a book, about nine by twelve, and maybe an inch and a half thick, beautifully bound in black leather. In the centre of the front cover, embossed in gold leaf, were the words *Pilot Log Book*. And in the lower right hand corner, again in gold leaf, my name. *Colin James Fraser.* I opened it reverently. Inside, the pages were neatly ruled into columns for recording the date, type and identification of aircraft, name of first pilot or instructor, name of second pilot or student, a remarks or route column to record the exercises you did on the flight or where you had gone, and columns to enter flight times for dual or solo, single or multi engine aircraft, day or night, or instrument time. Enough pages to record thousands upon thousands of hours. Chances are I'd never need another log book. It would take decades to fill this one. I ran my fingers over the smooth, flawless paper, speechless, too stunned to even thank him. He must have seen my reaction plainly in my face and my stance, though. He just grunted, then got to his feet.

"Don't smudge the damned thing up with greasy fingerprints," he said. "Go get the Stearman out of the hangar. Wash up first. Don't want fingerprints on the fabric there, either. Move it, boy. You're wasting time."

I came out of my trance and got my feet back down on the ground with a thump. "Yessir," I muttered. I left the book on the corner of his desk and ran.

The Stearman was Nav's own airplane. A relic left over from World War II pilot training days, it had two open cockpits and a big, mean radial engine. Nav used the husky old biplane for his own pleasure, often taking it up to aerobat around the sky. In a fit of loquaciousness one day, he'd told one of the instructors that it kept him on his toes, kept him sharp and honest, and the flood of adrenaline kept him from fossilizing before his time.

Taking the Stearman out of the hangar was always a precise and ritualistic procedure. The aircraft had to be carefully towed out onto the ramp where it gleamed in the September sunshine. Then the canvas cockpit covers had to be stripped off, neatly folded and stowed in a special locker in the hangar. God might forgive the ramp attendant who folded the covers sloppily and left wrinkles in them— but Nav never would. And finally, the control locks on the rudder and elevators had to be removed and stowed on top of the cockpit cover locker, lined up exactly parallel with the top.

When I had finished the ritual to his satisfaction, Nav came out of the office. He wore an ancient brown leather bomber jacket, worn to the softness and suppleness of velvet, and a leather flying helmet. A second helmet dangled from his left hand. This he tossed carelessly to me. I managed to get my hands up quickly enough to snatch it out of the air as it sailed past my head.

"Put that on and get in," he said.

The grin that spread itself across my face nearly hurt. "Yes, *sir!*" I said and scrambled up onto the rough wing-walk on the lower wing, pulling on the helmet as I moved.

"Not there," he said as I started to climb into the front cockpit, the passenger seat. "You're in the back here."

I stared at him.

"Jesus Murphy, boy," he said in disgust as he climbed up onto the wing beside me. "If you're just gonna stand around gawking all day, we're never gonna get this lesson started."

"Lesson?"

He didn't reply; he simply waved me into the rear cockpit.

It took me maybe all of five seconds to get myself strapped in with the complicated five-point harness. He checked it, grunted in approval, and showed me how to work the battery operated intercom system. Then he got into the front cockpit and beckoned the engineer to come and swing the prop.

Strangely enough, after nearly ten years of being an airport brat, and three summers of working as a ramp rat, this would be my first flight ever in an airplane. I had never been off the ground at all except in my dreams. I should have been quivering with agitation as the engine fired, sputtered, then caught and roared as one of the engineers swung the prop. But I wasn't. All I felt was an oddly calm excitement and exhilaration, a sense of the inevitability and fitness of this, as if it was happening exactly as it should.

As we trundled sedately off the ramp to the taxiway, Nav told me to put my hands on the sides of the cockpit and keep them there until he told me different. Obediently, I placed my hands on the coaming and put my feet flat on the floor without being told to do so. The stick came back hard between my thighs as Nav pulled his stick full back and the Stearman began to move.

In the grass just off the end of the runway, he paused to do the engine run-up and the final check on the engine gauges and the flight controls. Then, with a careful look to make sure there were no other aircraft on final approach, he taxied out onto the runway, smoothly fed in the power and pushed the stick full forward. The tail came up as the aircraft accelerated down the runway. As it lifted off, I glanced over the side of the cockpit coaming and watched as our shadow detached itself and moved away. For a moment or two, I forgot to breathe.

We climbed swiftly. Then the left wings dipped as Nav began a turn to the north. The town fell away below and behind us and the wings levelled. I looked up and ahead to where the blunt, round nose of the Stearman hung against the sky above the horizon, watched to see how the upper and lower wings lay parallel, above and just below the flat line of the ocean against the sky. And I listened to the full-throated bellow of the engine.

The wind through the flying wires between the wings sounded like the long, sustained musical note of a cello in the lower register. The air moved around and over me and I felt it rippling my cheeks as I grinned widely. This was more than worth waiting for. I don't think I had ever before felt so completely happy. I was vastly content just to sit and watch, feeling the aircraft flying.

Suddenly, the nose came down to steady itself just below the horizon. The note of the engine quietened and smoothed as Nav reduced power. His voice came over the intercom.

"Your airplane, kid."

I goggled at him.

"You have control." He raised both hands above his head, indicating I should take the controls. Gingerly, I put two fingers and a thumb onto the stick and stretched my feet forward until they touched the rudder pedals. Nav made a thumb's up signal with his right hand. Then he talked me through straight and level flight, climbs and descents, and finally, a few turns. When he finally gave me a heading to fly and told me to find him an airport, it astonished me to discover we had been in the air a little over an hour. I was elated and grinning like an idiot. Nav had only to tell me and show me a manoeuvre or technique once before I understood what had to be done and why. With a few minutes' practice, I could do it with reasonable accuracy and precision. Up until then, I had always harboured a small and secret doubt, a tentative misgiving about my ability to learn this awe-inspiring skill.

I felt at home in the aircraft, as if I'd spent a lifetime in one. It was only much later that I realized how realistic and true to life my dream actually was. As if I'd known from birth what it was like to fly, but had merely forgotten the simple mechanics of the skill.

On the ground again, I helped Nav refuel the Stearman, reinstall the control locks and the cockpit covers, and push the aircraft back into the hangar to prevent the sun and salt air from damaging the paint or the fabric. He took me back to his office and showed me how to fill in the log books.

First the aircraft log, which was worn and getting ragged with use and age, then my own, which was pristine.

Date: September 18, 1976; type flown: Boeing B-75 Stearman; Ident: N75NH; First pilot: N. Harty; Second pilot or student: self; Remarks/Route: Lesson 1, straight and level flight, climbs, descents, turns; Flight time: 1.4 hours dual.

"No charge for this flight, boy," he said when I asked. "We'll work something out for the rest. I want you to do most of your training with me in the Stearman."

"Nav?" The question came out before I could stop it. "Why the Stearman? And why me?"

He looked at me, an odd expression in those black eyes. Finally, he said, "Because you're going to make one helluva pilot, boy, and that airplane will make you work at it. Hard. It won't let you get complacent or cocky or lazy. It'll keep you humble and alert and scrambling. It will keep you alive."

All I could do was thank him. I turned to go back to work.

"Colin?"

I turned.

"You're a natural, kid. You learned more today than most students learn in five hours. In my whole life, I've only had two other students who could do that. And both of them were sons of pilots who had spent most of their lives flying with their fathers. I think it's going to take me a while to figure you out." He gave me a precisely measured second of his smile, the smile that transfigured his face and made me feel as if I'd won the lottery and been elected president of the world. Then he sat down and gave every indication of forgetting me. I went back to work.

Nav's three instructors waylaid me in the hangar just

before I was ready to leave. They gave me a crudely drawn card showing a widely grinning cartoon pilot in a Stearman. The caption was: *How can you spot a happy Stearman pilot?* On the inside, it said, *By the bugs in his teeth.* All three of them had signed it. I left the airport amid much laughter and back-slapping and headed for home, completely, blissfully happy.

My parents were in the living room when I got home. It didn't surprise me to see the dining room table laid for a formal meal. About the only time my mother ever bothered to put a tablecloth on the table and set it with the good china and silverware was for family birthdays, Thanksgiving and Christmas. Several wrapped packages sat on my chair and beside my plate. My mother got up from the floor beside my father's chair where she had been sitting cross-legged with a book, and came across the room to hug me.

"Happy birthday, Colin," she said. She had to reach up now to kiss my cheek. "Come and see what we have for you."

My father got up and drifted over. He stood with his arm around my mother's shoulders as I attacked the gift wrapping on the parcels. The largest parcel produced a leather flying jacket. One of the others turned out to be a knee board for holding maps and flight planning sheets.

"I asked Nav Harty what you might like," my father said diffidently as I admired the jacket and the knee board.

"Thank you," I said, stroking the soft leather of the jacket in awe. "This is great. Just great."

The meal was a merry one. After it was over and the mess cleared away, I took my presents to my room to put them away, then returned to the living room. My parents were both on the couch. My mother beckoned me over to sit beside them.

"Colin, there's something we have to tell you," she began. I looked at her quickly and a sudden cold clutch of fear closed around my heart. My beautiful and serene mother looked distressed. I glanced at my father. He, too, looked troubled.

"What's wrong?" I asked.

My mother took my hand and pressed it to her cheek. "Nothing's wrong," she said. "Don't look so scared. It's just that we have something to tell you and we think you're old enough now to handle it properly."

"Handle what properly?"

"I suppose the best way to say this is to come right out and say it," my father said. "We, your mother and I, thought it was time to tell you you're adopted, Colin. It's not easy for us to say that because we've all but forgotten. Right from the start, you were our own. We couldn't have loved you any more than we do."

All I could do was just sit there staring at him. It was, of course, something that had never even once crossed my mind.

"Adopted?" I repeated weakly.

"We adopted you when you were not quite a week old," my mother said. "We took you home from the hospital. In cases like that, they never tell the adoptive parents much about the natural parents. All we know about yours is that both of them died very shortly after you were born. It wasn't a case of them giving you away. Never, never think that you weren't a wanted child. They told us your natural father died in an accident and your mother died a few hours after you were born. That's all we know of them."

"Why tell me now?" I asked.

My father smiled slightly. "You have a right to know this.

You were six months old when we moved here and we never told anyone here we had adopted you, but there was always a small chance that it would come out by accident. It was much better that you found out from us than from someone else."

"I'll have to think about this," I muttered. I got up and went out, down to the beach. I watched the sun paint colours on the clouds that nobody would believe if an artist tried to copy them. I watched the gulls wheeling and gliding above the luminescent ocean and listened to the waves breaking on the sand.

I spent a while wondering what they had been like, those two people I had never known, and never would know. Try as I might, I couldn't think of them as my *real* parents. My real parents were in the house behind me, the house I had grown up in, that they filled with love and warmth and acceptance. There was a lot of publicity about adoptees searching out birth parents these days. It didn't make any sense for me to try to go that route, since my birth parents were dead.

For some reason, what my mother had said about not being given up for adoption made a big difference. I hoped I was old enough at sixteen to realize that children are not always given up for adoption because their parents didn't want them, but because the mother wanted the best chance for the child. But, it made a difference to know I hadn't been rejected.

I thought about the little boy who trotted along holding his father's hand and exploring the tide pools, and the small boy who watched his mother paint beautiful pictures. I thought a lot about the nature of love. Finally, I smiled and went back into the house.

I didn't know then it would eventually matter a great deal to know more about the two people who had given me life.

Three weeks later, I soloed, and a week after that, I was out in one of the 150s practicing steep turns and constant radius turns against a brisk wind. A thick bank of cloud hovered on the western horizon, threatening to turn the day misty grey with rain, but I still had plenty of altitude to practice upper air manoeuvres.

Eventually, I grew bored with the exacting precision of the turns. I was contemplating returning to the airport when it seemed of its own volition, right in the middle of a steep turn, my hand reached out and pulled the throttle right back to idle. At the same moment, I yanked back on the yoke and put my left foot on the rudder pedal all the way to the floor.

The little airplane reared back into a stall, then snapped over into a spin to the left within the space of one breath to the next, startling me badly. I had never practiced solo spins. I had, in fact, only done them once, and that was with Nav sitting in the other seat, carefully guiding me through the manoeuvre. They can be damned scary as the world seemed to rotate around the nose of the aircraft, which looks as if it's pointed straight at the ground.

Suddenly, I found myself grinning, even laughing aloud, as I popped the column forward and pushed the right rudder pedal all the way to the floor. It took almost a full rotation for the spin to stop. I centred the controls, then eased out of the resulting dive, glancing to either side to make sure the yellow-painted, fabric-covered wings of the little Cub were level.

My heart gave a hard lurch in my chest. Yellow Cub? No,

that was wrong. The aircraft I flew was a white Cessna 150 with red trim. Wasn't it?

Taking a deep breath, I looked out again at the wings. White metal. As they should be, registration numbers painted on them. I relaxed, then thoughtfully turned the little 150 toward home.

Yellow Cub?

Where on earth did that come from?

I had seen pictures of Piper J-3 Cubs; there was even one belonging to the druggist in the hangar for its annual. They were classics, all of them far older than I. But I had never flown one. Why was I seeing one? Then something odd occurred to me out of nowhere. Might it have been something from my dream?

CHAPTER FOUR

1978 – 1985

EVENTUALLY, I finished high school and entered Mt. Hood Junior College. I had decided to do my first two years in Brindle Falls for two reasons. First because I could save a lot of money by living at home instead of in residence or taking an apartment in Portland, and second because I wanted to work with Nav Harty for as long as possible. I had finished my commercial license by the time I graduated from high school. I wanted to do my Instrument Rating and multi-engine training with him, too.

I was twenty when I left home to finish college in the city. By then, I was a little over six feet tall, about an inch taller than my father. I had been a little worried that I would grow too tall to fit comfortably into the cockpit of the Cessna 150 trainers I flew working for Nav as an instructor. I had enough charter time under my belt so that I could also work as a multi-engine and instrument instructor, too. I hoped I could get a job that would help pay my way through my last two years of college.

Armed with a letter of reference from Nav, I spent the first weekend after enrolling in State at the airport, and landed a job instructing at the Flying Club. I was a bit younger than most of the other instructors who seemed to be mostly in their early to middle twenties, but I was tall and the years spent in the *dojo* and hauling airplanes around in Brindle Falls had given me a man's shape to match my height. I thought I looked older—more mature at any rate—than twenty.

Nothing much happened during the next two years. I fell in love a few times, fell out of love just as often. Summers I spent in Brindle Falls working for Nav and his expanding charter service. The town was growing, too. Timber, dairy farms and fishing kept the economy moving. They were good years then.

By then, too, the dream had become so integral a part of my life, it hardly seemed worth making note of the changes. It grew as my knowledge of flying grew. The aircraft around me took shape, developed all the little quirks and foibles that make one airplane different from another. It was comforting and reassuring. It was uniquely mine and nobody could take it away from me. As long as I had the dream, nothing could hurt me.

I graduated with a B.Sc. in physics at twenty-two, eager to make my own way in the world. Now I needed a job that would support me full time. I had almost fifteen hundred hours and an Airline Transport Pilot License. However, finding an airline, rather than a flying school, that would hire me proved to be more difficult.

By tradition, airline jobs have never been easy to get. With a lot of other aviation jobs, most of the time it's been a matter of showing up in the right place at the right time with the right qualifications. Pilots flying charter or corporate usually get into it because a friend told them of the opening. The jobs seldom have to be advertised.

Once a pilot gets some decent time in his logbook, he

starts looking at the airlines. The resume gets composed, put together in such a way as to make any chief pilot think he'd be a fool to turn away this paragon of aviation skill, knowledge and potential. However, chief pilots are graduates of the system, too, and know all the tricks and artifices ten times better than any neophyte wannabe who comes knocking on their door looking for the left seat of a Boeing 747 and a six figure annual income.

The average airline receives a couple of thousand resumes a year. Most of them go into the bottom file drawer where they eventually turn yellow and brittle with age, then get thrown out. Some, a very few, get a little closer consideration. Maybe, out of two thousand applicants, two hundred get letters granting them interviews. Out of that two hundred, perhaps twenty get hired. It was a tough and remorseless process of elimination. The airlines are fussy because they can afford to be. It's simple supply and demand economics.

My resume went out right along with the rest. In the meantime, I managed to land a job with a good outfit in Portland, doing charter and medevac work. In two years, I worked my way up from mail runs in the Navajo to the left seat of the Lear 35. In that two years, I had one interview with Delta and another with Northwest. Both times it was thanks, but no thanks. Don't call us. We'll call you. It was about what I expected.

Any time I managed to get a couple of days off, I went home. My mother, as serene and beautiful as always, still spent a lot of her time painting in remote corners of the countryside. The brown envelopes still came out of my father's study with the same regularity. Brindle Falls still considered them an offbeat, curious and eccentric couple, and weren't surprised that their son had gone into something as hare-brained as flying. After all, what else can you expect from people like that? However, at least now it was usually said with an amused, tolerant or fond smile.

Whenever I was home, I usually managed to borrow Nav's Stearman for a couple of hours. He was right about that cumbersome old beast. It kept me honest and it certainly kept me humble. Like a cantankerous human being, it was uncannily able to detect any flaw in technique and magnify it to the point where you knew it could kill you if you didn't sharpen up and fix it in a hurry.

I had just climbed out of the Stearman one crisp early November day when Nav strolled over to meet me. Without speaking, he helped me reinstall the control locks and cockpit covers and push the aircraft back into the hanger. He watched me as I got some cotton waste and polished a few oil streaks from the engine cowling. It was too late in the season to pick up many bugs, for which I was thankful. Bugs stick like glue and they're sheer murder to clean off an aircraft without scratching the paint job.

Finally, Nav said, "Coffee?" and headed toward his office. I got two cups from the battered silver urn in the engineers' office, loaded his with sugar and cream, and followed him.

"You still looking to fly the heavy iron?" he asked.

I nodded and grinned. "Oh, yeah."

"Go see Brett Murphy. He's Chief Pilot, Holiday West. Charter. Runs 737's, a couple of 727's and an old turbo-prop or two. Good outfit, and you won't be just a goddam bead on a string shuttling back and forth over the same piece of sky every day."

I called Murphy as soon as I got back to the city. I mentioned Nav's name and Murphy suggested I drop around to talk after lunch. For the rest of that morning, I did a little fast research on Holiday West Airlines. I found out it was a good, solid little outfit. Not flashy, but of good reputation. Since incorporation, it had grown slowly but surely, weathering the hard times and expanding cautiously in the good times. It was efficiently run by people who knew what they were doing. It had been around since the early fifties, flying DC-4s and 6s. It graduated to a DC-8 and a 707 around the middle sixties, then eventually to the equipment it operated now. It specialized in holiday charters, everything from delivering cruise ship passengers to and from the point of departure, to tours both home and abroad, to ski holidays and sports charters. From what I could gather, its pilots weren't paid spectacularly well, but they were happy. Nobody had ever had occasion to question the quality of their maintenance. The aircraft looked good and flew well. The outfit kept a fairly low profile. Any advertising they did was aimed directly at travel agencies and tour packagers. The name of the airline certainly wasn't a household word, but it sounded like the kind of outfit I could be very happy working with for the next twenty or thirty years. Once a pilot hires on with an airline, he's usually there for his career. The seniority list is too big a factor to be ignored when contemplating a move to another airline.

I managed to hitch a ride to Sea-Tac, and had no difficulty finding Holiday West's hangar. The receptionist in the office told me I was expected and directed me to a seat while she spoke briefly on the phone.

Brett Murphy turned out to be a lot younger than I expected him to be. Most chief pilots of airlines running large aircraft tend to be in their late forties or early fifties. Murphy looked about thirty-five or thirty-six. Certainly not yet forty, anyway. He tended slightly toward chubbiness and his hair was almost exactly the same shade of red as my father's. He stood up behind his desk as I entered the office toting my log book and a copy of my resume, and leaned forward to shake my hand in greeting. I wore CoastAir's standard uniform of grey flannel slacks, navy blue blazer, white shirt and regimental tie. He had no difficulty placing it or me immediately.

"Air ambulance?" he asked, looking at the beeper on my belt.

"Yes, sir," I said. "And Lifeguard flights."

"What are you flying? The Lear 35?"

"Yes, sir. Sometimes the Citation, but mostly the Lear."

"Nice airplane. I always liked Lears."

"So do I."

"You'd be a fool not to." He held out his hand. "Let's see your logbook." I handed it to him and he opened it to the current page. The last entry was my flight in Nav's Stearman. He frowned a bit then looked up thoughtfully. "That's Nav Harty's Stearman," he said.

"Yes, sir, it is," I said, surprised he recognized it. "Nav taught me how to fly. I did most of my training with him. Private, commercial, Multi IFR and Instructor."

He nodded, then turned to the first few pages in the book. "Nav trained you in the Stearman?" he asked.

"Yes, sir."

"Must have been one hell of an interesting course."

"It was. I enjoyed it, though."

He nodded and continued leafing through the book. Finally, he closed it, handed it back to me, and leaned back in his chair. "Nav taught me how to fly, too," he said. "You were probably still missing your mouth with Pablum at the time. He let me fly that old bird of his once." He gestured toward the logbook. "I'm impressed. Nav is one pilot I've got a whole hell of a lot of respect for. He didn't take on many students, and he expected a lot from those he did. If he still lets you fly that old Stearman, it tells me you haven't become complacent or lazy."

"That's hard to do in a Stearman."

"It is if you want to live. How old are you, Fraser?"

"I was twenty-five last month. September 18th."

"That's pretty young."

"Yes, sir. But time has an uncanny way of rectifying that defect."

He grinned. "Good answer," he said. "Are you married?"

"No, sir."

"Girlfriend?"

"Sort of between them, sir. I'm seeing a girl now, but it's not really serious. I was sort of engaged to a girl in college, but it didn't work out."

"Ever had an accident flying?"

"No, sir."

"Driving?"

"No, sir. No violations, either. Driving or flying."

"Where do you want to be in twenty years?"

"You mean, what are my career goals, sir?"

He smiled. "I don't want to read the bullshit you put in your resume, kid. I want to know exactly what you really want out of your career."

I thought about it for a few minutes, then I grinned at him. "In twenty years, Captain Murphy, I think I want to be pushing for your job. Until I get it, I plan on being the best line pilot you ever had."

He laughed. "That's the first time anyone's ever given

me that answer," he said. "You're honest, Fraser, and I like that. We run this outfit a little differently than most," he went on. "We don't carry any career first officers. We move a man up into the left seat on merit as often as we do on seniority. If a man can't upgrade, he's history. Once trained, I expect all my first officers to be able to handle the airplane almost as well as the captain. When you're a first officer, every captain you fly with will hand me a report on you. A bad report in itself doesn't mean much because we recognize the possibility of personality conflicts. Even three or four bad reports won't mean much unless I see a pattern developing. If three captains complain about the same thing, then you and me go round and round a few times about it. If the problem isn't cleared up, you're history because I can't afford screw-ups in my airplanes. By the same token, the first officers hand me reports on the captains, too. You know that old joke about the three things every first officer has to learn?"

I ticked them off on my fingers. "Nice landing, sir. Must have been a gust, sir. I'll take the ugly one, sir."

He smiled without humour. The joke was about as old as aviation. "You will also learn to say, excuse me, sir, but I think you're too high, or too fast, or too slow, or whatever damn-fool thing might be wrong. If you don't, the captain is liable to come down on you with both feet, then I drop on you like a load of bricks and broken glass."

"That's fair."

"You wanna believe it. Have you taken any courses on team management, cockpit resource management or cockpit communication? No? You will. Plenty of them."

It suddenly occurred to me that he was talking as if I'd already been hired. I just sat there and nodded dumbly as he outlined the pay scale, the benefits package, the training schedules — all the administrative details. I wasn't sure if I should say anything or not.

"Any questions?" he asked at last.

"Just one," I said slowly. "Does this mean I'm hired?"

"Yes," he said. "Conditionally. I want twelve first officers. We're hiring twenty people right now. If you do okay in training, you're on line. If not, well...."

I understood. "When do I start?"

"We'll be sending the bunch of you to Boeing to check out on the '37 in the middle of February. Report here for training on the 16th of January. You'll be in class for four weeks before you go to Boeing." He got to his feet and held out his hand. "Congratulations, Fraser. Welcome aboard, and good luck."

I scrambled to my feet to take his hand. "Thank you, sir." Then, "Captain Murphy, how much weight did Nav's recommendation swing?"

"A fair amount," he admitted. "Over the years, I've learned to listen to him. He's sent me a couple of other pilots. They turned out to be some of the best pilots I have."

"I won't let him down," I said fervently. "I won't let you down, either."

"I hope you won't. I'll see you back here after the New Year."

"Yes, sir. You will. You certainly will."

That night, the dream changed again. For the first time, I knew that I flew a de Havilland of Canada DHC-2 Beaver on floats. It was a hard working, rugged little airplane, built especially for getting in and out of short, rough strips, or small lakes in the bush country on skis, wheels or floats. I was especially fond of this particular bird, found it to be a friendly little beast. I was completely content to be flying it. Beneath us lay a vast wilderness of rocks and trees and lakes. I was happy. I was going home to the warmth and love that waited for me.

Chapter Five

Early Winter 1985

When the beeper on my belt went off, it didn't matter what I was doing, who I was with, or where I was; it meant I had to drop everything and run. It made no difference whether I was in the middle of a meal or making love to a woman, when that beeper went off, I had twenty minutes to get to the airport and get the airplane ready to fly. I was never sure until I got there whether it was a medevac, which is short for medical evacuation, or a Lifeguard flight. Most of the Lifeguard flights we did were organ donation flights. It was a hell of a way to make a living. The only woman I ever went out with who didn't end up hurt and angry when I had to take off running was Julie, and that only because she understood. She was a transplant team nurse, and spent a lot of time in the cabin fidgeting while the co-pilot and I aimed the airplane at the organ to be harvested.

Lifeguard flights were rewarding when we had time to stop to think about what we were doing. We carried the team of doctors and nurses who were going to save someone's life through an organ transplant. In a way, too, it could be depressing. Lifeguard flights usually meant somewhere a young and otherwise healthy person had just been declared brain-dead. It said something for bereaved parents or spouses that they could consider someone else at a time like that.

As soon as consent was given by the donor's next of kin, the call went out to people who were awaiting heart transplants, or kidneys or livers, and a frantic race against time began. The recipient patient was notified. My beeper went off. I met the harvesting team at the airport and within twenty minutes of the donor being declared brain-dead, we were in the air and streaking for some city anywhere in continental North America. Optimum time for transplanting a heart is four hours. That means the heart had to be inside its new owner and beating, being nourished by new and living blood, within four hours of being taken out of the donor body. There is no such thing as best economy cruise when you're flying Lifeguard teams. It's max cruise all the way. The only aircraft that had priority over us was one that had declared an in-flight emergency. We had precedence over even Airforce One, the President's aircraft, if it came to that. It could be heady and exciting work, not to mention a bit breathtaking. It was work I enjoyed doing. If nothing else, it most certainly prevented any pilot from going stale because he was in a rut.

Around Christmas, it always seemed to get busier. Medevacs increased, and so did Lifeguard flights. Julie was a pretty, pint-sized transplant team nurse. On occasion, she could be wryly cynical about her job. She told me once it became so busy at Christmas because the idiots insisted on loading to the gunnels on booze at Christmas parties, then cheerfully and merrily went about the business of bashing into everybody else with their vehicles. While alcohol soaked organs weren't great prospects for transplants, most often the victims of the happy drunks weren't intoxicated.

Those organs made fine transplants. She had given me a down-turning smile full of black amusement and said, "Deck the ghouls with boughs of holly."

I worked a rotating schedule. Twenty-four hours on call, twenty-four hours off. Most of the time, it wasn't bad, but sometimes I flew two flights in my twenty-four hours on call. Crew fatigue was something Ralph Cotter, the Chief Pilot, kept a close eye out for. When you had to go everywhere at top speed, there was no room for error caused by a tired pilot who wasn't as sharp as he should be.

As soon as the letter from Holiday West arrived, confirming my interview with Captain Murphy, I handed in my notice to CoastAir. I made my resignation effective at the end of December. That gave them almost six weeks to get my replacement trained and it gave me two weeks of much needed holiday before I started training. During that six weeks, though, I probably worked harder than I'd ever worked before.

The company tried to make it a policy that all medevacs and Lifeguard flights went out with two pilots, but the Lear 35 is certified for single pilot IFR flight, and occasionally, we just didn't have enough pilots on hand to send out two fully qualified Lear pilots. I was senior pilot, so several times, I went out alone, which put a double work load on a pilot. A few times, I took Bill Jacobs along. Bill was a competent IFR pilot. He flew the Navajo or Cheyenne, though. He didn't know the Lear, but he could do the radio work and thereby take a load off me. I recommended that he be transferred to the Lear when I left, so they assigned him to me as my co-pilot for the six weeks I had left with the company. I don't think poor old Bill realized quite what he was getting into until then.

As Christmas came nearer, we became unusually busy. On

December 21st, I was in Cincinnati in the early morning, and Dallas-Fort Worth in the late afternoon on medevacs. They were just routine patient transfers, though, and not emergency flights, which was a little less wearing on the nerves. The weather for both trips had been the pits, coming and going, and I had no co-pilot. I got home about midnight, and simply tumbled into bed. Just before I fell asleep, I realized that I had stood up a girl for a movie date. I wondered briefly if she would ever speak to me again, decided it didn't really matter, then rolled over and went to sleep.

Almost as soon as I closed my eyes, the familiar landscape of rocks, trees and lakes began unfurling below the wings of the old Beaver. The broken wilderness rolled gently past, the small lakes reflecting the incredible blue of the sky. Autumn colours glowed richly against the outcroppings of black and grey rock. Beneath me and around me, the aircraft rocked gently in the slight burble of moving air.

Contentment filled me, spilling over into a grin I could feel. I was exactly where I wanted to be, doing exactly what I wanted to do. Luck like that needs to be appreciated.

The phone rang at quarter after three. I fumbled around until my groping hand encountered the phone, managed to connect the receiver with my ear, and mumbled something incoherent into it, still not quite awake yet.

"Colin? It's Cotter."

"Umph?"

"Look, I know you just got in a while ago, but we've got a trip to Edmonton. Eighteen-month old girl needs a kidney and it's a rare match. Can you go?"

"What time is it?"

"Oh three twenty."

Three hours sleep. I'd flown on less. "Can you get me a co-jo?"

"How about Jacobs?"

"He'll do. I'll be at the airport as soon as I can." I thought for a second. "Where the hell is Edmonton?"

"Canada. Straight north of Montana."

"I guess I can find it."

It took me five minutes to get dressed, another ten to get to the airport. Jacobs was already there, glumly studying a weather print-out. Edmonton had two airports: the International, twenty-five miles south of the city, and the Municipal which apparently sat smack in the middle of the city. Both were forecasting marginal conditions. We wanted the Municipal, a seven-minute trip to the hospital by ambulance.

I located a set of Canadian approach plates while Bill went out to count the wings and kick the tires. I was relieved to find that Edmonton Municipal had an Instrument Landing System. Precision approaches were so much easier than non-precision approaches off a non-directional beacon. They also meant you could come down lower on the approach looking for the runway so there was less chance you might have to declare a missed approach and perhaps go somewhere else. There was nothing more frustrating than galloping madly across the continent only to find you couldn't get into the airport because of bad weather. The weather briefers assured me if conditions at Edmonton didn't get any worse than forecast, we shouldn't have a lot of trouble getting in.

When the harvesting team arrived, Bill and I were in the cockpit beginning the start-up routine. Six minutes later, we were in the air.

We had the sky pretty much to ourselves at that time of night. Bill had programmed the R-Nav for a direct flight and we climbed quickly to get over the Rockies. We never saw them, of course. We were in cloud from about eight hundred feet off the deck until we popped out on top at 15,000 feet. We went right on up to 25,000 before levelling off. I switched on the autopilot and sat back to monitor the black boxes.

"I don't know about this job," Bill said as he stared through the windscreen at the star-scattered black sky. "Is all this midnight tearing around normal?"

I grinned. "Absolutely," I said. "You can't say you weren't warned. Hey, it's a great way to build a lot of good jet time."

"That's true." He sighed and shook his head. "But my wife's going to kill me. We were right in the middle of something very important when Cotter called."

I laughed. "Serves you right. A bit late for it, wasn't it? You're going to have to learn to direct those basic urges to a more unconventional time. Afternoon delight."

"What does it do to your sex life, Fraser?"

"What sex life? I've been at this for two years, and I don't have a wife who feels obligated to put up with my weird schedule."

Julie Tremayne came forward and knelt between the seats. She reached up with both hands and ruffled my hair and Bill's. "Hey, Sports," she said. She sounded horrifyingly cheerful. "This must be the early-to-rise part of the old saw, wouldn't you say? Like early-early."

Bill looked at me sourly. "Do you want to pitch her out the hatch, or shall I do it?"

"If you open the hatch now, it's going to get awfully bleedin' cold and noisy in here," I said.

"There's that about it," Bill agreed.

"You'll have to pardon him," I told Julie. "He just discovered sexual frustration is a non-taxable benefit of the job."

"Poor baby," Julie commiserated and Bill made a face at her, then grinned ruefully. She, like the rest of the team, got pretty pumped on an organ run. Some of them reacted to the anxiety by becoming tensely silent. Julie chattered and bounced. I had heard other team members say she was the best there was at her job, though. We had been dating off and on for six months. She was energetic, playful and loving in bed, but wanted no part of any emotional commitment, and, maybe because I was already beginning to verge on being too straight and stodgy, that bothered me. She was fun to be with and I suppose you could say that we were very fond of each other, but the relationship was a dead-end one for both of us. About a month ago, we had drifted out of the affair almost as casually as we had drifted into it.

"Hey, Colin, they tell me you're abandoning us for the big time," she said.

"I'm getting out of this racket while I still enjoy flying."

"Airline?"

"Charter airline. Holiday West."

"Boeings," Bill said. "737's. Lucky bastard."

Julie cuffed him lightly across the back of the head. "Don't spill your sour grapes tonight, Jacobs," she said and laughed. Then to me, "They're not local, are they?"

"Seattle," I said.

"Will you be based at Sea-Tac, then?"

"I think so." I yawned hugely and excused myself.

Julie chattered on for a while, then went back to the cabin to check out her equipment again. I must have been more tired than I thought. I found myself drowsing as we bored our way north and east. I didn't worry about it too much. Bill would wake me when he needed me, and it was good practice for him to fly the jet. He was fully checked out on it now, anyway.

Once, I looked down at the instrument panel and serenely scanned the instruments that told me I cruised at 6,000 feet at 110 knots. When I looked back, startled, I realized I had half fallen back into the dream that had been interrupted by Cotter's phone call. Crew fatigue is the legal term for it now. I was tired. Too many hours in the air in too short a time span. I told myself I had to be especially alert for mistakes, then dozed off again. I came back with a start when I caught myself reaching out to adjust a mixture control that wasn't there.

As we crossed the border into Canada, we were handed over to Calgary Area Control. I heard Bill say, "Calgary Centre, Lifeguard Six Eight Tango is with you, flight level two-five-zero," and the Canadian reply, "Roger, 68 Tango. Report the Calgary VOR." I came more awake as we crossed the VOR and were cleared down to 13,000 feet. Fifteen minutes later, we were handed over to Edmonton Area Control Centre.

"Do you want to do the landing or the approach?" Bill asked. It made good sense to have one pilot do the approach on the gauges and the other one do the landing. The transition from instruments to visual flight can be difficult sometimes, and if the weather is down to close to minimums, there's not a lot of time to make it. What we usually did was have one pilot fly the approach while the other monitored the altitude and looked out the window into the splodge looking for the first glimpse of the runway. When he saw it for certain, he called it, and took control for the landing. It worked well and saved a lot of shredded nerves.

"I'll do the approach," I said. "You need the landing practice. We'll trade off on the flight home."

Area Control cleared us down to 10,000, then 8,000. We crossed the Edmonton VORTAC at 4,500 feet and were given vectors to intercept the ILS for Runway 34. Both Bill and I had a copy of the approach plate clipped to the yoke in front of us. He set the radio frequencies and talked to the controller while I flew the airplane.

We were still well up into the splodge when the Horizontal Situation Indicator told us we were on the glide slope and localizer for the runway. Bill lowered the gear and set the flaps, peering forward through the windscreen. The city lights below us set up an eerie glow in the cloud. It made it feel as if we were in the centre of a translucent glass globe.

At six hundred feet above the ground, Bill said quietly, "Runway visual. I have control."

"You have control," I said and sat back, putting my hands in my lap. I looked up. We had just passed the downtown hi-rises of the city centre. Our nose was pointed directly at the approach lights leading to the runway. Beyond the black space of the airport were a couple of miles of more city lights. Residential neighbourhoods. It was a heck of a place to put an airport. When they said it was in the middle of the city, they weren't kidding.

Some of those lights out there on the edge of the city seemed to waver, blink out, then come back on, as if the city were shrinking, then growing again. I rubbed my eyes. I must have been a lot more tired than I had thought, but there should be a chance to rest while the team harvested the organ. I hoped.

The wheels touched the ground gently. Bill was getting pretty good with the airplane. His landing was much better than mine would have been, tired as I was. I picked up the flashing red lights of the ambulance on the west side of the field. It was still hours before dawn in Edmonton. Up here, this far north at this time of year, the sun would not rise until well after 0800 and set shortly after 1600. It must be cheerless place in the winter.

Bill found the taxiway and turned off toward the ramp. I watched as we taxied past a white, bow-shaped terminal building that arced in a convex curve away from the ramp, topped with the angular glass and steel of a tower cab. A cluster of old hangars lay grouped beyond the terminal building, all looking ghostly in the reflected light of the blue taxi lights and the regular white flash of the beacon. How odd they'd have such an old-looking terminal building at an airport like this, I thought.

Bill stopped by the ambulance and shut down. Customs clearance was a swift formality. It didn't even slow the team down as they tumbled out of the Lear and into the ambulance.

"Better see about refuelling," I told Bill. "I'll check the weather. I think that big white building over there on the other side of that hangar is the terminal. The weather office should be there."

"What white building?" Bill asked.

"That one——" I turned, then felt dizzy and disoriented and a little scared. My mouth went dry and for a moment, I forgot to breathe. There was no white building. There was no old blue hangar. Just an ultra modern brick and glass terminal building with several white jetways thrusting out onto the concrete ramp, a 737 snugged up against one of them.

But I had seen a white building. I *had* seen it. I had seen lights in the windows. And a sign that said, *Welcome to Blatchford Field, Edmonton, Alberta, elevation 2241.* And I had seen an old hangar painted a bright blue in the landing lights.

But they weren't there now.

"I guess I was looking at the jetways," I said a little hoarsely. I took a deep breath and tried to get a firm grip on myself. It wasn't easy. I felt a bit sick and wobbly. "Well anyway, see if you can get some fuel. I'll go check the weather."

It was bitterly cold on the ramp. The last weather sequence we had been given by the controller put the temperature at minus 28 Celsius, nearly minus 20 Fahrenheit—cold in any language—with a north wind of almost 20 knots, bringing the wind chill factor down to something that just didn't bear thinking about. My leather jacket was not sufficient to keep out the biting chill, but the cold served to wake me up. I found the General Aviation door into the terminal building, found the weather office. It was empty except for a man pushing a vacuum cleaner. He told me that the weather briefer might be upstairs talking with the Duty Manager.

The Airport Manager's office was upstairs, near the closed restaurant and lounge. There were two men in the office, talking and drinking coffee. One of them stood up as I approached the counter.

"Need some help?" he asked.

"I'm looking for the met briefer," I said. "We're a Lifeguard flight out of Seattle, heading back in an hour or so."

The other man got to his feet. "I'll go down with you," he said.

But I hardly heard him. I was too busy staring at a picture on the wall behind him. It showed the curving white terminal building I had seen, with an old DC-4 parked on the ramp in front of it. It was exactly the building I had seen as we taxied in. Beneath it was the legend, *Blatchford Field, Edmonton, Alberta, 1962*. I felt a little lightheaded and woozy again.

"What's that?" I asked, gesturing at the picture.

The Duty Manager glanced back, then smiled. "One of Pacific Western's old DC-4's. The Airbus to Calgary."

"No, not the aircraft. The building."

"That? Oh, that's the old terminal building."

"When was it torn down?"

"I'm not sure. Sometime around '74, probably. This building opened in '75. It's right where the old one used to be."

I cleared my throat, then took a deep breath to steady my voice. "I guess the old one was around for a long time, was it?"

"I think the old one went up just before the war, but I'd have to check on that for you."

"Don't bother. It doesn't matter. When did it become the Municipal Airport rather than Blatchford Field."

"I think it was '78. They changed the name to Edmonton Industrial Airport in about '63, then to the Municipal. I can check if you want."

"No, that's okay," I said. "Don't bother, thanks anyway."

It really shook me. I have never been tired enough before to hallucinate, and I wasn't sure even now that I had been hallucinating. I had seen the building clearly, even down to the white shingles on the walls facing the taxiway. I'd swear to that. But how could I see it if it had been torn down almost ten years ago?

It made no sense. But I *had* seen the building in the photograph. I had. Even down to the sign on the front.

How very odd. And stranger yet, it didn't really frighten me. Just puzzled me. I told myself that it was probably because I was too tired to sort it out properly.

It wasn't until we were nearly back to Seattle that I realized that I had been half into my dream again, and the old terminal building was part of the dream. It was the first time since I spun the 150 in Brindle Falls that the dream had interfered with my waking life. And it started me wondering if it was really just a dream. I skittered away from the idea, but couldn't shake it off completely. What if by some monstrous coincidence it was a memory? But if it was a memory, was it mine or someone else's?

Chapter Six

Winter 1985 - 1986

THAT TRIP to Edmonton was the last flight I did for CoastAir. Cotter added up my airtime and discovered I was seven hours over limit for the month, so he sent me home. He said to come back just before I went to Holiday West and finish up any leftover paperwork. Then he held out his hand and smiled.

"I'm glad to see you moving up, Colin. But I'm really sorry to lose you. You're one of my best pilots. One of the best I've ever had."

I thanked him and went home to Brindle Falls. I was exhausted. My mother gave me one speculative glance, then put me to bed ten minutes after I walked in the door. I slept for sixteen hours. If I dreamed at all, I can't remember it.

When I finally dragged myself out of bed and got dressed, it was the afternoon of Christmas Eve. The sound of my father tapping industriously away at his typewriter came softly from the study, so I didn't go in to disturb him. My mother was nowhere in sight. I wandered through the house but couldn't find her. The Christmas tree with its eclectic assortment of ornaments sat in front of the living room window kitty-corner to the huge stone fireplace where it had been erected every year since I could remember. Something about the room was odd and different, though, and it puzzled me until I realized suddenly what it was. All the books were in the book cases. There were no magazines lying around. The small tables weren't piled high with the clutter of half-finished sketches, brushes, paint and water pots. The surfaces of the tables actually glowed in rich, warm wood tones. The rest of the house was the same. No clutter, no mess. My parents had always been clean, but neither of them was what you could call a neat-nut. I grew up in a welter of organized clutter. This tidiness was odd and somewhat unsettling.

I tracked my mother down on the beach behind the house. She sat on a bleached and silvered log in a tumble of rock, dressed in the inevitable jeans and a heavy Irish-knit fisherman's sweater. She held her sketch pad on her knees and was working at a sketch of a piece of driftwood on the littered sand. Even in charcoal with no colour, she deftly and easily captured the cheerless damp chill of an Oregon December.

"I like that one," I said. "Another of your mood studies?"

She looked up and smiled at me. "Very likely," she said and raised her cheek for my kiss. "Feel better now?"

"I'm a new man," I assured her.

She laughed. "The resilience of youth," she said. "He arrives looking like December, sleeps nearly twenty hours, and rises looking like April."

"Green and all wet?" I asked innocently.

She hardly bothered to glance at me. Just smiled benignly. "You're still an impudent brat, aren't you?"

"It's the way I was raised. The atmosphere of abandoned irreverence."

"It's the in thing now, is it?" She jabbed gently at the paper with her charcoal and a shred of desiccated bark clinging to a crevice in the driftwood came to life. "To abuse one's parents?"

"Wasn't it always?"

"Of course it was."

"What happened to the house?" I asked.

"You mean the air of painful neatness?"

I smiled. "Painful is a good word for it. Yes."

She made a quick, seemingly random series of lines on the paper, then smudged her hand lightly over them. The surf ripples on the sand around her tortured and twisted driftwood came alive with texture and suggested movement. I had watched her do something like that too many times to count, and still found the process fascinating and uncanny. When I was very young, I had thought the enchantment was in the charcoal or the brushes. It took me years to figure out that the magic was in her hands, or more accurately, in her eye. My mother had never looked at anything the way other people did.

"It's a trifle disconcerting, isn't it?" she said. She frowned at her drawing in concentration, then added another swift line to it and smudged it a bit. It became a wisp of dried and brittle seaweed trailing from the driftwood.

"Just a little," I agreed.

"We sold out to the establishment, your father and I did," she said. "After all these years of bohemian living, we've seen the error of our ways."

"Uh huh. Sure you did."

She laughed. "Actually, it's a lot less dramatic. You know

Mrs. Knowles next door? Well, her husband died a few months ago, and she's finding it very difficult to make ends meet on just his pension. In a fit of Christian charity, I asked her if she could perhaps help me with the housework for a couple of hours a day. She has been very efficient and very patient with us. I have a cup of coffee and a chat with her when she comes in, then I flee in panic. I can't stand to be around when she's in. It makes me tired just to watch her. We nearly had to restrain her forcibly this morning from making up your bed with you in it."

I laughed. "I appreciate it. Has she succeeded in organizing you?"

"Oh dear, I hope not. Passive resistance is a difficult thing to overcome, even for a fanatic like her. Your father and I are holding our own."

"Flower child," I said.

She put down the sketch, finished now, and smiled. "Will you be coming with us to Midnight Mass tonight?"

Nominally, we were Catholic, members of Our Lady of the Shores Parish, although about the only time we ever attended Mass was Christmas Eve and Easter Sunday. I attended Catechism classes long enough to make my First Communion and Confirmation. My parents had a comfortable and comforting faith that they didn't find difficult to live by. It was something that hadn't quite taken with me, although I found the formal Christmas Eve Mass beautiful and soothing.

"I suppose so," I said. "Mother...." I sat beside her on the smooth, worn log. The chill of it seeped quickly into the backs of my legs through my jeans.

She looked at me, then reached out to put her hand to my cheek. "What's troubling you, Colin? Can I help?"

"I don't know. I'm not sure. On both counts."

"Something about your job? The new one?"

I shook my head. "No, there's no problem there. It's what I've been aiming at all my life. Ever since I can remember."

She laughed. "I suppose I'm not the first mother to have a fledgling leave the nest and quite literally take wing and fly. It always startled me when I realize the old metaphor is the prosaic truth in your case."

"Just another instance of a mother's love being unable to make her errant off-spring see the error of his ways."

"Not only are you still impudent, you're still an owl. So, if it isn't the job, is it a girl?"

I laughed. "No, not a woman. My love life isn't very complicated. I was too busy for that."

She smiled but said nothing.

"Mother, do you believe in reincarnation?"

She looked at the horizon, grey sea and grey sky. There was only the slightest touch of silver in the midnight of her hair. She must have been getting close to fifty now, but she was still as slim as a girl, and just as beautiful as ever. Her profile was serene and contemplative. A stray breeze ruffled her hair and drifted a strand across her cheek. She tucked it back behind her ear, then turned to me.

"I don't know," she said. "Sometimes I think I do."

"You think you do?"

"It's a seductively comforting belief when you start growing older, when you suddenly realize you're not young anymore."

"Intimations of mortality," I said, misquoting Tennyson.

"Exactly. And then, too, sometimes I think that we can't possibly learn everything we need to know in one lifetime. So there has to be a second chance to come back and learn it. Possibly even a third chance. It would depend on how much you needed to learn. You might be allowed to return if you still had something to learn."

"Or maybe something to finish?"

"Yes, perhaps to finish something important that was left undone. My grandmother used to talk about old souls. She meant partly the same thing as kindred spirits, but she also meant souls that had come back often enough to wear off the rough edges, to become mellow and kind and wise, with all the rawness and harshness polished out."

"I've never heard that one before."

"It's an old Celtic concept. I think your father must be an old soul. Perhaps I'm one, too, I don't know. You might possibly be one, but it's too early to tell. You're still too full of the brashness of youth."

"That's a form of reincarnation, I suppose," I said slowly.

"I suppose it is." She laughed. "Then again, sometimes as I get older, I find myself thinking, next time around, I'll do this differently. But that's probably just orneriness creeping up on me."

"You've always been ornery," I said and grinned.

"Long years of practice, that," she said, smiling. "Why do you ask?"

"I'm not sure." I wasn't ready to tell her about my dreams. Not yet. And I didn't want to tell anyone about the eerie experience in Edmonton. I didn't want her to think I was losing my mind.

"I've heard some people say that *déjà vu* is a manifestation of a previous incarnation," my mother said. "There's some interesting literature on it. Some of it is sheer spiritualistic nonsense, of course, but some of it is quite serious. If you're interested, you should check out the library."

"The Search for Bridey Murphy," I said facetiously.

She laughed. "That, too," she agreed. "Here, help me pack up this stuff. It's high time we rescued your father from the concrete jungles of the big city police beat and fed him."

"Another Sergeant Brooker mystery?"

"I think so. Ian's getting awfully tired of that man. It's about time to kill him off or retire him honourably on a pension."

"Millions of fans would mourn. Ralph Cotter, my boss, collects them. Remember him? I think you met him last summer. He's got them all. I never did have the nerve to tell him hard-boiled detective writer Fraser Endicott was really my father, mild mannered historian, Ian Fraser."

"Better he shouldn't know," my mother agreed. "Leave the poor man his illusions."

I gathered up her things then took her hand to help her to her feet. She came up easily, lithe and supple. She didn't let go of my hand as we walked to the house. She hardly seemed to notice that, these days, she didn't quite stand as high as my shoulder.

"Colin...."

"Um?"

"You will tell me if something is really wrong, won't you?"

"Nothing's wrong. Really. It's just a really weird dream I had the other night. But it was probably a case of being over tired and eating far too much pizza before bedtime."

I had a good Christmas and New Year at home. I spent a lot of time out at the airport with Nav Harty. I got a couple of hours in on the Stearman. I don't know if I put the heavy old biplane through its paces, or if it put me through mine, but I thoroughly enjoyed myself. I slept well. I don't remember dreaming at all.

Nor did I dream when I returned to the city. I survived the classes and I survived the conversion to the Boeing 737. The Turbo Football they called the sturdy and stubby little jet. I heard a tall tale about some hotshot test pilot doing an eight-point hesitation roll in one during an airshow. As I got to know the aircraft, I began to believe it was perfectly capable of performing the highly complex and flashy aerobatic manoeuvre. I also decided that I definitely wasn't the pilot to attempt to duplicate the feat.

"Ladies and gentlemen, this is your captain speaking. Please fasten your seat belts. We are about to experience some violent turbulence. Yah-hoo!" Certain to make an impression on both the passengers and the powers-that-be in management.

My uniforms arrived. Tunic and slacks of a light navy blue, three gold rings on the sleeves, caps with the airline device in gold above the shiny visor. I bought a navy blue wool overcoat in a military cut for cold weather. I was ridiculously pleased with myself when I looked in a mirror. Except for the giddy smile on my face, I was the image of the heroic and dignified men who had stood under the wing of that Convair so many years ago.

It crossed my mind only briefly that, after working so determinedly for the whole part of my life that I could remember, perhaps nothing could be as good or wonderful as the dream image of a goal. It certainly didn't occur to me to wonder what happened to a man who no longer has to really stretch to reach a goal. Where did he go from there?

I went to bed the night before my first flight as a real, live airline pilot almost too keyed up to sleep. This was it.

A Still and Bitter Grave

This was what all the work and effort and strain had been aimed at.

When I finally slept, I dreamed. Again, I flew the small aircraft over the vast sprawl of wilderness. I was happy. I was working at a job I loved, and I was flying home to the love and the warmth that was the other half of me, to the best part of my life, the part that always made the circle whole, the golden circle complete. But somewhere there was a tiny edge of apprehension—a faint shadow of fear that now, especially now that everything was so very good, without a lot of care, something could go terribly wrong.

73

CHAPTER SEVEN

1986

I MET Glynnis at one of those parties that just seems to happen spontaneously. It was at the home of a Western pilot I knew vaguely, some sort of a house warming, I think. Somehow, it collected a mixed bag of airline personnel from all over, flight crew, cabin crew, a few counter reps, and grew to the point where it overflowed out onto the patio and lawn. Glynnis was standing with a dark drink in her hand, her mouth curled faintly in detached amusement as she listened to a pair of flight attendants who were very nearly flying without benefit of aircraft, bemoan the lack of young, single, good looking pilots. Glynnis looked both aloof and remote. I had seen her arrive on the arm of one of our senior Boeing 747 captains, a man I knew was married, and certainly not to her.

She had that too-carefully constructed casualness of the professional model in one of the glossier magazines, like the girl who says, "Don't hate me because I'm beautiful." Julie used to say the woman should have wiped the canary feathers from the corners of her mouth before she spoke. Glynnis's hair was a tawny colour, sun streaked to many tones of toffee, gold and russet, and done in a way that suggested she stood in the perpetual embrace of a cool ocean breeze. From where I stood about ten feet from her, her skin appeared to have a flawless, almost textureless, perfection. Her make-up had been applied with a careful, meticulous and practiced hand to give the impression of unadorned naturalness. Like everyone else, she was dressed casually in jeans and a shirt, but the jeans were obviously tailored to fit her exactly without being skin tight, and the shirt was pure, shimmering silk in a jewel tone blue that set off the colour of her hair and skin as well as it was designed to do.

I suppose I was watching her too intently. As she turned away from the stews, her gaze met mine briefly before she looked away. The eyes were an odd shade of sherry brown, almost shading toward amber. Her gaze slid past me as if I were just another and slightly taller potted plant, and finally found Captain Sievers. When she moved, it was all of a piece, like a dancer or a star gymnast, totally conscious of the oiled and articulated grace of her own body. She took Sievers' arm and smiled up at him. Whatever it was in that smile, it fairly crossed Sievers' eyes. He put his arm around her, his blunt, competent hand resting on her delicate hip. She leaned into him a little and her claim of ownership couldn't have been made any plainer if she'd clipped a leash to his collar.

"I've seen that expression before," Grant Bevin said at my elbow. He was looking in the same direction I was. "Poor old Sievers looks like a bull my granddaddy used to have on the ranch. That ol' bull was meaner 'n sin. Tried to stomp and gore every man or animal came within a mile of it. Come after my granddaddy one day. Granddaddy took a quick hop, skip and jump behind a pine tree and that ol' bull, he ran spang head on into that tree. Crossed his eyes and wobbled his knees, it did. Looked just like Sievers."

"Pole-axed," I agreed. "Who is she?"

"Her name's Glynnis Alexander," Bevin said. "I hear her daddy swings a wide cat back east. She's here filming a commercial. Says she's working her way through college. She also seems to be working her way through the seniority lists of a few airlines." He grinned. "Or so I hear."

"Collecting pilots? She a wing-nut?"

"So I hear. Just another airplane groupie."

"She managed to collect you yet?"

Bevin's ugly face lit with his famous smile. There were rumours about how that smile had already cracked the little plastic hearts of more than a few flight attendants. "Nope," he said. "I'm not pretty enough. And I'm too far down the seniority ladder."

His seniority number was eight higher than mine. I might have been a bit prettier, but not a whole lot. "We should be devastated," I said.

"Amen," he said and raised his glass. "I'll buy you another. What are you drinking?"

"Ginger ale. I'm flying tomorrow."

About half an hour later, I literally bumped into her and Sievers again as I was searching for a way out. Sievers glanced at me over his shoulder as I apologized and started to move away. I heard the girl murmur something, then Sievers' voice came after me. "Oh, Fraser...."

I turned and smiled. "Yes, sir?"

"Fraser, have you met Miss Alexander?" he asked. "Glynnis, Colin Fraser. He's one of our first officers."

"Only a lowly three-striper," I agreed cheerfully. "How do you do, Miss Alexander."

"Glynnis, please." She had a controlled, smoky contralto voice. It wasn't unexpected. She held out a hand that featured very long fingernails painted pale frosty peach. Her grip was firm, dry and warm. "With a name like that, you should be wearing a kilt and a claymore."

"I left them at home with the sporran and the *sgean dhu*," I said straight-faced.

Something flickered through the amber-sherry eyes. I didn't know her well enough even to begin to interpret the look. She let go of my hand and leaned back against Sievers. He looked at me with that uncomfortably tense expression of the thoroughly hooked prey. I had met his wife and he knew it. I felt embarrassed by the blatant trophy tag Glynnis had hung onto him.

"I was just on my way out," I said. "Good night, Captain Sievers. Good night, Miss Alexander."

I went to Mexico City early the next morning. Captain Dawson was the answer to a co-pilot's prayer. He wasn't stingy with landings. Under his watchful eye, I managed the take-off from Sea-Tac and the landing at Benito Juarez, then slipped back into my humble co-jo slot for the return trip. We got back to Sea-Tac just before midnight with a crowd of returning cruise passengers who were sunburned, peeling and probably completely broke, judging by the startling variety and sheer volume of souvenirs stuffed into the overhead bins. The cabin attendants, run off their feet satisfying the demands for food, drinks, pillows, coffee, juice and magazines, weren't sorry to see the last of the herd. Those women worked hard enough to exhaust plough mules, and they still managed to look fresh and glamorous and dainty. Dawson and I waited until the stampede abated and the dust settled before we gathered up our brain bags and trudged up the jetway.

Dawson's wife picked him up at the door. I began the long trek to the parking lot. I hadn't walked a hundred feet when a sleek little sports car pulled up beside me. The top was up against the typically unfriendly Pacific Northwest wet spring.

"Colin. Get in." It was Glynnis Alexander's voice. It surprised me that I recognized it.

"My car's not far," I said.

"I didn't ask you where your car was. I told you to get in."

I stooped and peered intently into the car through the open window, looking puzzled.

She frowned. "What are you looking at?"

"Nothing. Just wondering if you'd suddenly sprouted four gold rings on your sleeve or something, the way you're ordering me around."

Unexpectedly, she laughed. "Please get in," she said. "I'll give you a lift to your car."

"Miss Alexander, I've had a long day. I'm tired, I'm grubby and I'm going home to climb into the shower. I'm perfectly capable of tottering the distance between here and the parking lot. Thank you, anyway."

"You'll never get there if you stand around arguing with me."

"You're absolutely right. I won't." I straightened up and began walking. I wasn't sure why she roused so much disapproval in me. It certainly wasn't my job to safeguard the morality of senior captains—or anyone else for that matter.

She was waiting for me when I got to my car, standing by the door of the lethal looking little Kharman Ghia sports car. She had surprised me again. I wondered how she knew which car was mine.

"You're not at all impressed by the fact that my father could buy half the airplanes out on that ramp out of his petty cash, are you?" she said curiously.

"Not particularly," I said and slung my flight bag into the back seat of my car, a five year old Ford that suffered greatly in contrast with her car. But it was mine, and it was almost paid for. "Could he?"

"Yes. And he could buy a thousand of you, too."

"No, he couldn't. There aren't a thousand of me. Only the one."

"You're an arrogant bastard, Fraser."

"That's not very complimentary to my parents."

She bit her lip, then raised one hand, palm out. "I'm not sleeping with Carl Sievers, you know."

"That's none of my business in any event," I said. "A low seniority first officer hardly goes around questioning the behaviour of a senior captain." Even I could hear the disapprobation in my voice; it bothered me. I'm not usually so judgmental.

"You think I'm a spoiled brat, don't you?"

She had pretty much hit the nail right on the head with that remark. Not only a spoiled brat, but big trouble, too. I turned to her. In the harsh light of the magnesium overhead floods, the flawless beauty of her was almost breath-taking, but I felt no desire for her. I've admired other lovely things without feeling any passion for possession, too.

"Look," I said. "I'm a poor, dumb co-jo earning next to nothing. My opinion can't matter in the least to you."

Glynnis frowned and for the first time, she looked as if she were constructed out of ordinary mortal flesh and bone and blood instead of priceless porcelain, ivory and amber. She looked up at me. Those eyes were really something else. "It shouldn't, should it?" she said quietly. "But for some reason, it seems it does. Good night, Colin." She climbed into the little car and roared off into the misty night. I went home and went to bed.

I saw her again six weeks later. She was standing at the Delta ticket counter, surrounded by expensive luggage, dressed in a smart and elegant green suit, her hair pulled back severely from the perfect oval of her face. The ticket agent handed her a boarding pass and began the prolonged task of tagging the luggage and heaving it without ceremony onto the baggage belt. Glynnis put the boarding pass into her purse, turned, and saw me. I had to walk right past her to get to the stairway to the ops room. I couldn't very well pull a sudden 180 turn to avoid her. She stepped out of the line to meet me. Her smile was incandescent.

"Why, hello, Colin," she said.

I nodded to her. "Flying to New York?" I asked.

"I'd rather be going to Colorado with you."

"How—?"

"I asked Carl."

"Have a nice flight home," I said and started to go. She stopped me, her hand on my arm.

"Men don't usually ignore me like this," she said. "You make me feel fat, frumpy and frowsy."

"You are certainly none of the above, Miss Alexander. But I learned very young not to play with fire."

"You intrigue me, Fraser. You really do." She walked along with me as I began weaving through the crowd.

"I don't see why. There's nothing special about me."

"Oh, I wouldn't say that. Carl thinks you're going to be one of the youngest captains on the line very soon."

I stopped and stared at her. "He told you that?"

She laughed. "So I finally succeeded in capturing your attention. Yes, he said that. He said you're young and you're hungry and you're exceptionally good. I think you worry him but he wouldn't admit that. I like ambition in a man, Colin. I've got a lot of it myself. Have a good flight." Then, before I knew what she was doing, she stepped close, reached up to pull my head down and kissed me full on the mouth. Her tongue moved briefly against my lips, hot and wet. Five seconds later, she was lost in the crowd.

I suddenly had a pretty good idea why Sievers looked a little pole-axed. I stood for a moment, disoriented, then realized I was going to be late and hurried through the crowd.

The next time I saw her, it was in one of those monstrous electronics discount stores. I had gone in to buy a new needle for my turntable. There was a whole wall of televisions along the back of the store, maybe sixty feet long and ten feet high. Each and every one of them was on. I don't watch very much television. My parents had always refused to have one in the house. They said it killed conversation, stifled the imagination and stultified the mind. Perhaps it did. But that display on the wall was certainly devastating. Mesmerizing. Almost psychedelic. It was akin to being caught in the centre of a light storm. I had the crazy feeling I was being sucked into a vortex of light and colour. Thank God there was no sound.

As I watched, dizzied and blank, the movie stopped and a commercial came on. Four hundred girls in a shiny grey one-piece swimsuit walked in an attitude of pensive grace to the end of a diving board. She had a superb figure. She raised eight hundred arms, four hundred heads still bent, and sprang into the air in slow motion. She rose, floating into the air, graceful as a seagull's wing, then landed and rose once more. That's when I recognized Glynnis. Her body arched crisply and cleanly into a professional jackknife dive, then straightened out in time to slice into the blue, blue water with hardly a splash or ripple. A caption I didn't read scrolled across the bottom of the screen.

One Glynnis was overwhelming enough. Four hundred of them were annihilating. I left the store, almost gasping for breath, and found myself on the street, dazzled and blinking like a man coming out of a trance. This was most definitely sensory overload. Two more seconds of that would have burned out every synapse I owned. But the thirty seconds I had been hit with was enough to sear her indelibly into my brain.

CHAPTER EIGHT

1987

WE WERE in Acapulco, and we were stuck. The cruise ship we were supposed to connect with to deliver one load of passengers and collect another bunch for the return flight, had developed a problem after leaving the Panama Canal, and was going to be a day late. Captain Dawson called Flight Ops; Flight Ops called the Executive Office. Word came back down through channels. The cruise operators were willing to pay for waiting time because they couldn't afford to have a whole shipload of unhappy people on their hands. *The Duchess of Eden* would be only one day late. Philosophically, Flight Ops told us to enjoy our unexpected holiday.

Captain Dawson shrugged. "Sounds good to me," he said. "Hit the beach, Fraser. Go enjoy all that semi-naked flesh."

I hit the beach. There was some sort of a film crew at work when I got there. There seemed to be a lot of frantic activity involving a huge gaudily coloured beach ball, much scampering back and forth and splashing of water, and at least a dozen scantily clad bronzed bodies, half of them female. There was quite a crowd watching. One woman quite close to me said something disparaging to her companion about television commercials, then they turned and walked away. I moved about a hundred yards down the beach, spread my towel, then swam for half an hour. The filming was still in progress when I emerged from the water. I set up my rented beach umbrella, then promptly fell asleep.

When I awoke an hour later, the film crew were packing up, the oversized beach ball had been deflated, and the joyously capering young bodies were still. One of the girls wore a silver grey swimsuit. It did spectacular things for her figure. Either that, or her figure did spectacular things to the suit. She turned and looked straight at me and my heart gave a curiously painful thud in my chest. It was Glynnis Alexander.

Towelling the bright, tawny hair, she left the film crew and walked toward me. "Are you following me?" she asked, smiling.

"Hardly," I said. "What are you doing here?"

"That should be obvious. I'm working. Didn't you see?"

"I didn't pay much attention, to tell you the truth."

"You're not doing nice things to my ego. I saw you as soon as you arrived. I wanted to impress you with how hard I was working, and you didn't even notice me?"

"Sorry. No."

"God, Fraser. You really are bound and determined to shatter my self-image, aren't you?"

"I'm a cad and a bounder and a curmudgeon," I agreed helpfully.

"You're far too young to be a curmudgeon. Yet. Have you got a car here?"

"I rented one at the airport. Why?"

"Because you're going to drive me back to my hotel, then you're going to take me out for dinner."

"I can afford a burrito and a Coke."

Glynnis rolled her eyes skyward. "Then how about a drink?"

"I'm flying in the morning."

"Coffee or iced tea, then." She sighed. "The hell with it. I'll buy dinner."

For some reason, that stung badly. "It's okay. I've got a credit card." I gave her what I hoped was a sardonic smile. "It's not even maxed out."

She laughed and sat down on the blanket beside me. Fine grains of sand like crystalline sugar powdered her feet and ankles. She brushed them off, then turned to look at me.

"I meant it, you know," she said.

"What, that you'd buy dinner?"

"If you can't. No, I meant what I said about not sleeping with Carl Sievers."

"I meant it, too. It's none of my business."

"No, it wasn't. But that didn't stop you from going all stuffy and moralistic and maybe even judgmental anyway."

I started to protest, then shut my mouth as I realized that, unfortunately, she was right. When they catch you at it, you can't really yelp in protest.

She sighed and brushed off more sand. "I don't know why I feel I have to explain this to you. I was using Carl as protective colouration that night. There was a man who was getting a little too intense, wouldn't take no for an answer. He wouldn't listen when I told him to go drown himself. I thought that if he figured I was all wrapped up in Carl, he'd bug off and leave me alone. It worked. It turned him off completely. But it turned you off, too, didn't it?"

"It was a good act."

She gave me the full impact of those wide amber-sherry eyes. "It was one hell of a good act, Fraser, because I'm one hell of a good actress."

"Did Sievers know it was an act?"

She burst out laughing. "Of course he knew. Poor Carl. He played along but he was so uncomfortable." She got to her feet and held out her hand to me. "Come on. Feed me before I start gnawing on your ankle. I'm starving."

So I drove her back to her hotel. She wanted to go up to her room to shower and wash the salt out of her hair before we went out. I stood by the window and looked out at the ocean, then turned as she spoke my name.

She had come out of the bathroom wrapped in a towel, another towel turbanning her hair, a cliché out of dozens of mediocre movies.

She walked toward me, head bowed in that pensive attitude I had seen duplicated four hundred times in the electronics store. A tiny gold bird in flight on a thin gold chain nestled just below the hollow of her throat. The beat of her pulse caused it to glint and flash in the strong late afternoon sunlight pouring through the window. Her legs gleamed below the white of the towel. With one hand, she held up the towel above her breasts while the other hand stretched out to touch a button on the wall. The drapes slid shut with a muted whir and a soft swish. Glynnis still had not looked at me.

I stood there, my mouth dry, while my heart made a creditable effort to tear itself right out of my chest. The tawny eyelashes lay long against her extraordinary cheekbones. For a long moment, neither of us moved. Then she let the towel drop to the thick carpet at her feet, stepped forward to put her arms around my neck. She had to come up on tip-toe to place her mouth on mine and she made a soft little sound of great need in the back of her throat.

The next hour isn't very clear in my mind. I remember her body gleaming pearly and golden in the subdued light that filtered through the drapes. I remember how her mouth tasted faintly of honey and almonds, and how her lips and tongue felt like fire and ice together as they moved across my body. I remember how one breast loomed huge and sharply defined, etched faintly with a delicate tracery of blue veins, against the light and seemed to fill my whole field of vision as I kissed the other. Her bones below the almost translucent tanned skin felt fragile as a bird's beneath my hands.

There was an unexpected steel-spring strength and resilience in the fine webbing of muscular structure to that exquisite body. She held me with incredible power and energy, then her quick intake of breath, held for a long, eternal moment, and finally let out in a wordless cry of completion that sounded almost like a sob of agony as her eyes went wide and blind and her mouth twisted fiercely in fulfillment. Then my own cresting surge moments later and the obliteration of any conscious thought for many long seconds after.

She sighed deeply and contentedly as she settled herself into a warm curl against my chest, her breath moving softly against my throat. Her body was faintly misted with a film of moisture and felt slick and smooth beneath the palm of my stroking hand.

I couldn't believe this had really happened. Girls like Glynnis just didn't fall into bed with men like me, except perhaps in fairy tales. I've never heard anyone rave about my looks, and certainly nobody has ever accused me of being a world class lover. My experience was limited enough and not once had it ever been like this first time with Glynnis.

Glynnis moved languidly in my arms. She sighed and then made a soft, purring sound in the back of her throat. When I turned my head to look down at her, I found her drowsy and somehow blurred eyes staring back. If the phrase *drowning in a woman's eyes* was more than just an evocative image conjured up by some hopelessly romantic writer, then I certainly felt myself going down for the third time.

She smiled and raised herself on one elbow so she could look down at me. "Is it against the rules to tell you I think I'm in love with you?" she said in a tone I hadn't heard from her before. There was a catch in her voice, a touch of breathlessness. "I think it happened when Carl introduced us and you made that silly crack about the sporran."

I was lost then. Hopelessly, utterly, irretrievably lost. I drew her back down against me, kissed that yielding mouth, made love again to that slender and supple body. This time, the word she cried out at the end was my name.

Six months later, she took me home to New York to meet her father.

I had never been to New York before, at least into the city. There were several other cities I knew only by their airports. I'd flown into JFK several times, but never made it farther than the terminal. I quickly decided that I didn't really want to come back to the city all that often, either. It was too big, too noisy, too crowded. It was a confusing and incomprehensible jumble of streets, buildings and people. Glynnis knew her way around. She organized a taxi and the luggage and before I knew it, we were on our way to some place with a name I didn't catch. I was unaccountably nervous. I hadn't felt like this since I'd been hauled up in front of the principal in fourth grade for breaking a window. That was an accident; this wasn't. Glynnis didn't seem to notice. She cheerfully pointed out all the sights to me, one after the other, obviously as familiar with New York as I was with Brindle Falls.

The cab finally pulled up in front of an apartment building that came right out of a movie set, compete with uniformed doorman who tipped his hat and murmured, "Good afternoon, Miss Alexander, nice to see you back," as we passed. I felt uncomfortably like Johnny Hick, combing the hayseed out of his hair. But I was a pilot, and that meant I was supposed to be able to adapt quickly to a new situation. So adapt I would, no matter what. Onward and upward in the best tradition of the intrepid aviator.

Glynnis linked her arm through mine as the elevator whisked us up to the rarefied atmosphere of what would probably turn out to be a penthouse suite like Roz Russell's in Aunty Mame.

"Nervous?" she asked.

"Nope," I lied bravely. "Just abjectly craven."

Glynnis's father met us in the foyer. I noted absently and with dismay that I had been correct in my assumption of what the apartment would look like. What the hell was a boy from Brindle Falls doing in a place like this?

Glynnis hugged my arm tightly against her side. "Daddy," she said brightly, "this is Colin Fraser. Colin, my father. Isn't he beautiful, Daddy? I think I've outdone myself this time, don't you?"

Mr. Alexander offered his hand. "How do you do, Colin," he said formally. "I've heard a lot about you."

His grip was firm and brief. "I'm very pleased to meet you, sir," I said. He looked to be somewhere in his middle fifties, not tall but erect and at ease. He had some of his daughter's grace, a double portion of poise. I found out later that he was actually seventy-two. He certainly didn't look it.

We had dinner. It was the first time in my life I had been served a meal by a maid. I wondered if I could ever become accustomed to living like this, decided reluctantly that I couldn't. You had to be born to it.

"I believe I've met your father, Colin," Mr. Alexander said as the silent woman in the black dress and white apron removed the salad plates and began to serve the main course.

"When was that, sir?"

"Several years ago when he changed his publisher. John Trent is a good friend of mine. He invited me to lunch to meet Ian because he knew I'd always admired his books." He smiled. "All of them."

"Books?" Glynnis repeated, looking up with interest. "I didn't know your father was a writer, Colin, darling."

"More than just a writer," Mr. Alexander said, smiling. "Colin's father is Ian B. Fraser. He's also Fraser Endicott."

"Colin. You never told me."

"You didn't ask. My father doesn't advertise the other name."

"He should," Mr. Alexander said. "All of his books have a wide following."

"They filmed a made-for-TV movie out of one of his detective books, didn't they?" Glynnis asked. "I think I tried out for a part in it. I didn't get it. They said I was too young."

After dinner, Mr. Alexander suggested that Glynnis go somewhere and powder her nose or something. With a sinking heart, I realized I was in for a good grilling. Glynnis said she'd go and visit a girlfriend for an hour or so and vanished to leave me alone with her father.

We settled into chairs in his study. It was a much larger and more comfortable room than my father's study. The walls were lined with beautifully bound books which looked as if they had been read often. He offered me a cigar, which I refused.

"May I ask how old you are, Colin?" he asked.

"I'll be twenty-seven in September, sir."

He nodded thoughtfully. "You knew Glynnis is thirty-two, almost thirty-three, didn't you?" he said. "She's a little more than five years older than you are, although I wouldn't say she's a lot more mature."

I hadn't known that. I had thought she was about twenty-four or twenty-five, but I didn't say so. It was something it had never occurred to me to ask Glynnis, and she had never volunteered the information. When I thought about it, I supposed it wouldn't make any difference.

"Are you in love with her?" he asked.

"Yes, sir."

"She wants to marry you."

"I know. I want to marry her, too."

He studied the tip of his cigar for a moment. "Glynnis was a late child, Colin. I'm afraid we spoiled her rotten, her mother and I. We spoiled her two brothers, too, but Michael and Robert are made out of sterner stuff as it turns out. She's not an easy person to live with. She's used to having things her own way."

I smiled. "Are you warning me off, sir?"

He returned the smile. "No. I don't think you're the type of man I could warn off. I'm simply stating the facts as they are without embellishment. I think you might be the man who could handle her. I certainly hope you are, anyway."

"I love her, sir."

"I think she loves you, too. It's difficult to tell young people today that the heady flush of chemistry and infatuation doesn't last forever. In fact, it evaporates damned soon. I believe you've got the strength of character to build a lasting relationship. I sincerely hope for both your sakes that my daughter has."

I said nothing, but if he had deliberately set out to make me decidedly uncomfortable, he had certainly succeeded.

"How do you feel about the fact that her family has a lot of money?" he asked.

"I don't know," I said truthfully. "It wasn't something I thought much about when we decided we wanted to get married."

"I didn't think it would be. My will divides most of my estate between my two sons. I've made provision for Glynnis, but the settlement will go to her children, if any, upon her death, or revert to her brothers if there are no children."

"That's fair," I said. I smiled. "I wouldn't know how to handle a lot of money if it came my way."

"Your father must be fairly wealthy, Colin. He's a very successful writer."

He had startled me. I had honestly never thought about that. It was something that had never been mentioned when I was growing up, nor was there any reason to mention it since I'd grown up.

"That never occurred to me, sir," I said slowly. "We... I mean, my parents have always lived fairly simply."

"They were very wise, then." He sat back and smiled again. "If you were going to ask formally for my daughter's hand in marriage, young man, I hereby tell you that you have my blessing."

CHAPTER NINE

1987

MEETING GLYNNIS'S father was the hard part, and I thought I'd survived it fairly well. The next step in the courtship ritual was the easy part—taking her home to meet my parents. Glynnis was in Los Angeles looking around for a West Coast agent to represent her when I phoned home to make arrangements for the visit. I had never called prior to going home before, but then, I'd never brought a woman out to meet my parents before, either.

I managed to catch my mother at ten in the morning. She sounded breathless as she answered the phone.

"Mother, it's me."

"Colin? I must have known it was you or I wouldn't have run all the way up from the beach."

"Running keeps your figure trim and neat. Didn't you know that?"

"There are less strenuous ways. Did you call just to make sure I got my exercise for the day?"

"That, too. Actually, I called to say I'll be out to see you on the weekend."

"You called just for that?"

"Well, no. I'll be bringing someone with me."

She laughed delightedly. "A girl? Colin, that's wonderful. What's her name? What's she like?"

"Her name is Glynnis Alexander and she's a lovely person."

"I take it this is serious. The meet-the-family ordeal?"

"I guess so. Barbaric, isn't it?"

"As always. But on the other hand, why shouldn't she suffer the way I had to before I married your father, and very likely the way her mother did. The sins of the mothers, you know."

"Don't sound so gleeful about it."

"Don't worry. You father and I won't regale her with amusing anecdotes of your youthful escapades. We're a little more civilized than that, even if we do insist on this barbaric ritual. We'll save the hoary old tales to tell to the grandchildren."

"Oh, good God."

She laughed again. "What does she do, Colin?"

"She's a model. An actress. She does TV commercials."

There was a short silence before she replied. "That's not what one could call a usual occupation," she said. "It must be very interesting."

"She's good at it, and she's a nice girl. You'll like her."

"Of course we will," she said warmly. "When will you be here?"

"We'll fly up Saturday morning. We'll try to be there about eleven. I'm going to borrow a friend's Seneca."

"What on earth is a Seneca?"

"A little twin-engine airplane. I showed you one once."

"You know I do well just to tell the difference between an airplane and a seagull, you obdurate owl."

"It's a cinch, Mother. A seagull has feathers. A Seneca has rivets."

"Of course. Never mind. You can show me a Seneca again when you get here. Your father and I will be there at the airport at eleven on Saturday morning."

Glynnis was still in Los Angeles. I flew down in the Seneca on Friday evening and landed under unusual gloriously clear blue skies.

She met me in the general aviation area, effervescing with happiness. She had found an agent, she told me, and he was going to see about getting her some commercials and maybe some real television work. She was excited to the point of bubbling over about it. When we left Los Angeles on Saturday morning. It was so smoggy we could hardly see the ocean from altitude.

Glynnis had never flown in anything smaller than a commercial jet. She wasn't really enthusiastic about the Seneca, a small six-seater twin. After an hour when we didn't fall right out of the sky every time she moved, she began to relax but she was very quiet and introspective.

"Nervous?" I asked.

"A little," she admitted. "How do I look?"

She wore jeans and the same sapphire-coloured blouse she had worn the first time I met her. Her hair was pulled up into a loose knot on the top of her head and secured with a barrette almost the same colour as the shirt. "You look fine," I said. "Beautiful, in fact. Do you want to try flying this thing for a while?"

She looked at me, horrified. "You're joking," she said.

"It's easy," I said.

"No," she said. She folded both hands in her lap and sat very straight. "I don't want to. You're the pilot. You fly."

It was five past eleven when I put the Seneca's wheels down onto the runway at Brindle Falls. My father's ancient and venerable station wagon was parked by the hangar. He, my mother and Nav Harty stood in the shade of the terminal building on the ramp as I taxied in. They waited until I had shut down, then came forward to meet us.

My mother stepped forward to hug Glynnis as I introduced them. I saw it disconcerted Glynnis for a moment before she collected herself and returned the hug. My father smiled as he shook her hand and bent forward to kiss her cheek, and Nav, being Nav, merely nodded gravely in acknowledgement of the introduction.

"I had Mrs. K make up the spare room," my mother said as we collected Glynnis's suitcase and walked toward the car. "You should be quite comfortable in there, Glynnis. The room has a beautiful view of the ocean out toward the back of the house."

For the rest of the morning, I watched with amusement as my mother brought out the full arsenal of her charm to put Glynnis at ease. Even my father got in on the act. It seemed to work. Glynnis admired the house, made some complimentary remark on the long shelf in the bookcase that held all of my father's books. She perhaps chattered a little too much and a little too quickly about making television commercials, but she was nervous. More nervous at meeting my parents, it seemed, than I had been at meeting her father. When we were alone for a moment, I asked her why she was so nervous.

"My father might be rich," she said fervently. "But your father is famous. There's a big difference, you know."

I hadn't known, I guess. Not really. My father was simply ... my father, accepted as being a popular writer.

All in all, though, I thought the day didn't go too badly. By the time bed time rolled around, Glynnis had relaxed. My mother showed her to her room, then said good night and joined my father in their bedroom. There was no question of my slipping down the hall to Glynnis's room, or of her coming to mine. Not in my parents' house.

The weekend seemed to be going fine. My parents obviously liked Glynnis, and she seemed to like them. There was only one incident that bothered me. I didn't realize at the time that it would be too prophetic of our future relationship.

On Sunday morning just before lunch, Glynnis, my mother and I were sitting in the living room while my father finished up something in his study. We were talking idly of nothing in particular while a tape of mixed classical selections played softly on the stereo. In a lull in the conversation, the opening bars of the second movement of the William Tell Overture spilled exuberantly into the room.

Glynnis looked up and smiled. "The Lone Ranger rides again," she said.

My mother and I looked at each other. The corners of her mouth twitched in amusement. "She'll fit right in," she said and I burst into laughter.

It was a family joke. I had been maybe twelve. My mother had been listening to William Tell when I came home from school. I had burst into the house, hollering "Hi-ho, Silver!" at the top of my lungs. She informed me in mild exasperation that was only half-feigned that the definition of a true intellectual is someone who can listen to William Tell and not think of the Lone Ranger, and she had thought I'd had a better upbringing than that. Just then, my father came out of his study to turn down the volume and said, "Hunh. That plenty loud, *Kemo Sabe*."

So I laughed now, and my mother smiled. Then I noticed that Glynnis had gone white, her mouth compressed into a thin line.

"Sorry," I said and put my arm around her stiff and resistant shoulders. "It's an old family joke. I couldn't help laughing."

My mother smiled and explained it to Glynnis who laughed politely, but was still very pale. She didn't say much during lunch. When we were finished, she asked me to take her for a walk along the beach. She still looked a little pale and set.

We walked for almost half a mile before she spoke. She turned to me and I was shocked to see the naked anger on her face.

"How dare you," she cried. "How *dare* you laugh at me like that in front of your mother. Who do you think you are, anyway?"

"Glynnis—"

"Nobody laughs at me like that, Colin Fraser, you bastard. Nobody, do you hear me?"

"I'm sorry," I stammered. I didn't know what to say. I honestly couldn't see what she was so upset about. "Really. I wasn't laughing at you. I was only laughing because it was funny."

"It wasn't funny. You embarrassed me."

"I'm sorry."

"And your mother laughed at me, too. It's bad enough she doesn't like me, she doesn't have to laugh at me."

I stopped walking and stared at her in surprise. "What do you mean, she doesn't like you?"

"She doesn't think I'm good enough for you. Not smart enough."

"Glynnis, that's ridiculous. She likes you. And she wasn't laughing at you."

"Don't tell me she wasn't laughing at me. I *know* she was. I could tell, damn you."

"Please, Glynnis—"

"Don't treat me like a child, Colin," she cried and stamped her foot. I had never in my life seen anyone stamp their foot in anger. Somehow, it didn't seem to have the hoped for effect in soft sand. It cost me a real effort—all the self-control I had—not to laugh again. I could feel the laughter twitching at the corner of my mouth, but I held it back. Just barely.

"And where the hell were you last night?" she went on. "I needed you to make love to me. I waited for you for two hours and you never did come into the bedroom."

I didn't feel like laughing any more. "I didn't come because we were in my parents' house."

"Fuck your parents. Are you ashamed of sleeping with me? Is that it?"

I looked down at her. The lovely mouth was twisted into an ugly and angry line. This was a side of Glynnis I had never seen before. I wasn't certain that I ever wanted to see it again, either. I waited until I was sure I could control my voice and that my own anger wouldn't show before I spoke.

"I'm not ashamed," I said quietly. "But when I'm in their house, I live by their rules."

"You're afraid of them."

"No. It's only common courtesy."

"Something I lack, is that it?"

"Glynnis—"

Her eyes widened suddenly, and she began to cry. She stumbled helplessly forward and into my arms, her heartbroken sobs shaking her body. "I'm sorry," she wailed in a choked and hopeless voice. "Oh, God, I'm sorry, Colin darling. It's just that I'm so damned nervous and your mother makes me feel so... so completely and totally inadequate and awkward. I don't think she likes me at all."

I held her, kissed the top of her head, stroked her hair. "It's all right," I told her. "She likes you."

"No, she doesn't. She disapproves of me because I do commercials. I heard her say she's never liked TV."

"That doesn't mean she doesn't like you. I don't like TV either. I hardly ever watch it. But I love you."

She raised her head. Her tears made her eyes look larger and more radiant than ever. Her lips parted as she reached up, pulled my face down to hers. Her mouth was hungry and demanding on mine. Her body pressed into me and I tasted the salt of her tears on her lips.

"Make love to me," she whispered urgently. "Oh, please. Make love to me now. Right here. I want you. I need you so badly, darling. Oh, please..."

Only a little distance away was the crag crested by the salt-bitten vine maple my mother had captured in watercolour so many years ago. Beneath it was a sheltered corner surrounded by rock, warmed by the sun. I took her hand and led her behind the rocks. She was still crying as

I undressed her. She didn't stop until I was deep inside her and she clung to me as our tempo echoed the profound, slow rhythm of the sea on the sand as the tide moved over the beach.

When it was over, I cradled her in my arms as I sat with my back to the sun-warmed rock. She held me tightly, her cheek against my chest. "You're mine, now," she murmured. "She's going to have to give you up, you know. You're mine and not hers anymore."

I said nothing. I had never before really noticed this seeming lack of humour. But she was nervous. She was a little insecure, perhaps. I had never thought about it much, but I suppose my mother with her serenity and natural poise could be a bit awe-inspiring. Eventually, Glynnis would realize my mother wanted nothing more than to love the girl I married as much as I did, to accept her as a daughter.

And that was our first quarrel.

Glynnis had to be back in Los Angeles on Monday afternoon, and I had a flight out to Las Vegas in the morning, so we left Brindle Falls that night after dinner. My parents drove us to the airport. Both my mother and father kissed Glynnis good bye. My mother was smiling as we got into the Seneca, but there was a faint, troubled line between her eyebrows.

Three weeks later, Glynnis and I set the date for our marriage. She wanted a spring wedding. She came back after doing a fashion spread in San Diego bubbling over with plans. She hadn't bothered to consult me before she made them, but I had sort of left it all up to her, anyway.

"I want to be married in Maryland," she told me as we lay together in bed in my small apartment. "My brother is a lawyer in Washington. He's got a lovely place and I've always wanted to be married outside in spring. There's a beautiful lawn and my sister-in-law knows some people who can make the whole place just gorgeous. Oh, Colin, there'll be hundreds of people there. It will be just wonderful."

"I don't know if I want a really big wedding," I said, thinking about the uncomfortable formal morning suit. If ever an outfit was designed for ultimate discomfort, that had to be it.

She snuggled closer to me. Some of her tawny hair drifted across my cheek, tickling. I reached up and brushed it away. She took my hand and kissed the tip of my index finger. "It has to be a big wedding, darling," she said. "I've got so many friends I have to invite. Don't you?"

"A few," I said. "But I don't know if they'll be able to afford the trip out to the East Coast." I grinned. "They're mostly broke first officers, just like me. They'll have to deadhead in, if they can get the time off."

"Don't be silly." She propped herself up on one elbow, her hand curled into a fist to support her head as she looked down at me. "And I thought I'd ask Judge Beeton to marry us. He's an old friend of my father. My godfather, actually."

"I sort of thought we'd be married by a priest," I said. "I'm Catholic, you know."

"You haven't been to church since I've known you."

"I know. But I think my parents would like it, too, if we could be married by a priest."

"I'm not Catholic." She frowned. "Will a priest marry someone who isn't Catholic?"

"I think so."

She shook her head. "I still want Judge Beeton. It doesn't

matter, Colin. Married is married, whether it's by a priest or by a judge. Besides, I don't think I want to be married by a priest. It's all superstitious nonsense anyway, that church business."

I gave in on that point. She was right. Married was married.

"And I want to honeymoon in England and Scotland. I've always wanted to go to Scotland. We can spend a month or two there."

"I don't think I can get a month off work, Glynnis. Probably more like two weeks. Besides, I can't afford a couple of months in England. I've got some money saved, but not an awful lot."

She sat up and looked down at me. "I want to go to England," she said, her jaw set. "If you can't afford it, I've got lots of money of my own. You can just tell that stupid airline you need a month or two off."

"It doesn't work like that. I'm a junior first officer. I don't go around telling the airline anything."

"Colin, don't be difficult."

"I'm not being difficult. I'm trying to be practical. One of us has to be."

"Don't you go getting all stuffy on me again." She lay back against me, reached down to stroke the top of my thigh. "Darling, a girl only gets one honeymoon. I want mine to be perfect."

"We can make two weeks just as perfect as two months," I said. "Look, that's final. Two weeks. I can't take any more time than that off. Not if I want to keep my job."

The hand on my thigh stopped stroking. She turned over in the bed and curled into a tight little coil, her back to me.

"If that's the way you're going to be about it," she said remotely.

"Glynnis, we're not going to fight about this, are we?"

"I'm not fighting."

I sighed. "I'll see what I can arrange."

My dream changed again that night. From somewhere came a jittery, almost breathless premonition of danger. It made me hold the control yoke more firmly and reach out to the throttle, thumb tucked into the little notch, to make sure it didn't slip back. I searched the horizon, looking for any sign of an approaching threat, but there was nothing out there except clear blue sky and a multi-coloured tapestry of autumn foliage, blue lakes and grey rocks.

Chapter Ten

1988 – 1991

How do you chronicle the death of a marriage? The sad, slow process of disillusionment that inevitably leads first to low-grade despair then finally to apathy? Exactly where in a failed marriage can you say, "This is where we went wrong. This is where it all started." Was there some point in that first two or three years where either Glynnis or I could have done something, some clever magician's trick perhaps, and made it work and work well?

There was no cataclysmic event that sent us onto the rocks. She wasn't unfaithful, nor was I. By the time I got around to suspecting that she might be, I didn't care anymore. It was the hackneyed old cliché of ending "not with a bang but a whimper."

It's hard to say exactly what I expected of my marriage. God knows I'd seen enough of other people's marriages to realize that my parents had an exceptional relationship. I don't think I was naive enough to believe that Glynnis and I would have the same sort of marriage. Perhaps the naivety comes into it because I believed we could use the same foundation—love, respect, friendship, trust and tolerance—to build something different but that would work for us as well as my parents' marriage worked for them.

Part of it was that I didn't really know what Glynnis needed or wanted from the marriage. I thought I knew when we first married, but the more I got to know her, the more I realized I didn't know her. I didn't know what she wanted out of life, besides a career in Hollywood. As for what she wanted out of her marriage, I realized I had no idea at all. Her requirements seemed to change from day to day. From the start, she was reticent, almost secretive, about her activities and resisted any intimacy except the physical intimacy of the bedroom. I thought that would change after we married, and when it didn't, it confused and frustrated me because I wasn't sure how I should handle it. Or how she wanted me to handle it. Eventually, I sorted out what worked, and that was carrying on as if everything were completely all right.

We were married on the fifteenth of May and spent three weeks honeymooning in England and Scotland. We had glorious weather for it, contrary to pessimistic predictions of typical wet English springs. We spent our days wandering more or less aimlessly among the small villages, the downs and moors, rather than the cities. Our nights were spent in small country inns with quaint names where we made love as insatiably as honeymooners were supposed to. We couldn't seem to get enough of each other. There were even quite a few times when we stopped on our rambles through the soft, hazy country to make love behind a hedge along some quiet lane.

Presently, we left Heathrow under a warm English early summer sun and arrived back in Seattle on a wet, dreary Sunday afternoon. On Monday morning, I went back to work. I was glad to get back and I was eager to be flying again.

The first two years of our marriage were a constant whirl of separations and reunions, and that seemed to keep the magic of being together alive. Her career seemed to be moving along nicely, and mine was becoming solid.

She spent a lot of her time commuting between Los Angeles and Seattle. Filming commercials kept her fairly busy and she got a small part in a television series that unfortunately was cancelled after only a few episodes, then a minor part in another sitcom that didn't last much longer. I suppose we were happy. I just know that I loved my wife then, and I was proud of her.

Maybe part of the problem was that we couldn't spend a lot of time together, in spite of the excitement of our reunions. My job took me away for sometimes two or three days at a stretch, and she could be on location for two or three days, too. There were weeks when our schedules just didn't coincide and we hardly saw each other. But we spent every minute we could together. An airline pilot gets a fair amount of spare time due to the regulations governing the limits on flight time and duty time, so I commuted back and forth as much as Glynnis did. I made silly jokes about how I might become the first airline pilot to make history by racking up more than a million passenger miles.

I didn't like Los Angeles. I guess I'll always be a small town boy at heart. I spent long hours exploring the city when Glynnis was working, but the novelty didn't take long to wear off. I started staying in the apartment and caught up on my reading while she was out.

She moved in a circle of actors, screenwriters and production people many of whom prided themselves on being avant-garde and ultra sophisticated. When Glynnis wasn't working, there were always parties at her friends' places. These were usually always loud, boisterous affairs where everybody talked at once, voicing some of the strangest, wildest ideas I'd ever heard, and nobody ever listened to anyone.

Somehow, her crowd just didn't seem like real, three-dimensional people to me. I met a few people I liked, ones who owned a superbly wry sense of humour, but too many of the others were more like self-absorbed cardboard cut-outs. It made it hard to take them seriously. Sometimes I wondered if they took themselves seriously. Maybe it was all a monstrous joke, and I was the only one who wasn't in on it. It gave me something to muse upon while I listened to the chatter.

I discovered that Glynnis took them very seriously indeed when I mentioned my cardboard cut-out theory one night after a particularly chaotic party. She exploded like a string of firecrackers going off around my ears.

"Those are my friends," she cried. "Don't you dare criticize something you don't know a damn thing about. If anyone's phony, it's those stupid, one-track minded pilots you hang out with." She stayed angry and upset with me for three days about that.

By the middle of our second year of marriage, I was no longer going down to L.A. during my time off. Our reunions were still wild enough, and thoroughly satisfying.

Eventually, I began to catch her out on small lies. At first, I let them go and told myself that they were just small things and not important. Things like the price of a new blouse or jacket. Or she'd lie about the reason she didn't take the car in for servicing when I asked her to. Small things. White lies, I told myself. Not important.

Then I caught her in a big one. She told me she was going to Aspen in Colorado to shoot a commercial. The day she was supposed to be there, Grant Bevin mentioned offhandedly that he had seen her at the airport in Las Vegas. She had just come off a flight from Los Angeles and walked right past him without seeing him.

"They're shooting a commercial out there," I said and managed to keep my voice casual. "One of those boy meets girl, girl meets car, girl gets car things."

"Let's hope it's a Ferarri or a Jag," he said and grinned. "If it was me, I'd find it a lot easier to pretend to make love to a Jag than a Ford or a Chev."

"I think it's one of those four-wheel drive muscle machines."

"That shouldn't take a lot of acting talent," he said, grinning. "I wouldn't mind one of them parked in my garage, to tell the truth."

"Vehicle or female actor-type?"

He considered that judiciously for a moment, then: "Both, I think."

Glynnis came home at two in the morning. I was waiting for her. I put down the book I was pretending to read when she came into the bedroom. She barely glanced at me, a frown drawing the perfect golden brows together above her extraordinary eyes.

"What are you reading now?" she asked as she began to undress.

"An old one by Spencer Dunmore."

"Airplanes?"

"Yes."

"Christ, don't you get enough of that at work?"

"Obviously not." I took a deep breath to steady myself. I didn't want to broach the subject, but I had to know. "How was Las Vegas?"

She went very still for a moment, then pulled her sweater off over her head. "What Las Vegas? I was in Aspen filming that damned feminine protection commercial."

"Grant Bevin said he saw you at the airport in Vegas this afternoon."

She turned and met my eyes squarely. "He's lying," she said flatly. "I was in Aspen."

My heart began to beat painfully hard in my chest. "Why would Grant lie?" I asked, my voice sounding calmer than I expected.

"How the hell would I know?" She yanked a filmy blue nightie out of her drawer and slipped into it.

"Glynnis, please don't lie to me. You were in Vegas when you told me you were going to be in Aspen."

"I wasn't—"

"Why are you lying?"

"I'm not—"

"Glynnis—"

"All right," she shouted. "All right. I went to Vegas to talk to a producer about a regular part in a series. A good one. Second billing. Okay? I didn't tell you in case it didn't work out. Okay? Are you satisfied now?"

"You didn't have to lie about it."

"Okay, I'm sorry. Get off my case, Colin."

"I wasn't on your case. I just thought I had a right to know where you were. You're my wife."

"Yes, I'm your wife. Not your chattel, for Christ's sake."

"Okay," I said, relieved that the Vegas trip was about only a television part. Time to drop the subject. "Let's forget it. Did you get the part?"

"No," she said bitterly. "They gave it to a twenty-two-year-old bimbo with silicon tits like a bitch in whelp."

She got into bed and lay with her back to me. I turned out the lamp and put my hand on her shoulder. "Not tonight," she said indistinctly. "I've had a hell of a long day and I'm tired." She sounded as if she might be crying, but she wouldn't let me comfort her. She never did. Not then, not ever. She always took her hurts into a private place and nursed them in solitary, like a cat. She wouldn't let anyone near her then, especially not me.

We drifted into our third year of marriage and strayed farther apart. When we talked, we spoke of inconsequential things, trivialities. She didn't want to hear about my job. Anything to do with flying bored her. She seldom talked about what she did anymore, and finally asked me why I had to pry into her business all the time. She said that if she thought I should know something, she'd tell me. Rebuffed and hurt, I stopped trying to get her to talk about her job.

That summer, I found a 1946 Stinson 108 for sale. Glynnis didn't want to go with me to look at it, so I drove out alone. The old fabric covered tail-dragger was basically sound, but needed a lot of work. The engine was an old Franklin six cylinder putting out 165 horsepower, and had recently been overhauled. The fabric was good Ceconite, but the paint was sun faded and peeling in areas. The interior was pretty ratty and the instrument panel was sparse. But the price was right, so I bought it. Now I had a hobby. Something to do in my spare time that would keep both my mind and my hands occupied. I stopped going down to Los Angeles. Glynnis's only reaction seemed to be relief.

Our visits to my parents had been getting shorter and farther apart. Glynnis never became convinced my mother liked her, and I finally came about to thinking she was right, although I could never see any sign of it from my mother. I went home a few times by myself when Glynnis was in Los Angeles, but eventually even these visits stopped. I wrote, and I called regularly, but it wasn't the same as seeing them. It just didn't feel right to go home without my wife.

The only time it seemed that Glynnis and I could connect on some common ground and communicate at all, was in bed. It was the only area of our life that was still good. When I made love to her, it was just as it had been at the beginning of our marriage. There was tenderness and love and sharing. She murmured to me and clung to me, all heated and yielding. In the warmth and comfort of the afterglow, we held each other and talked of the future, when she was secure in her career, when I had made captain. We spoke of the possibility of starting a family in a year or two, when things were more settled.

We passed our third anniversary. Somewhere in there, we had developed the habit of quarrelling. She was incredibly sensitive to anything that could be even faintly construed as criticism and blew up at the smallest thing. I couldn't hold my temper any longer. We said terrible, cruel, unforgivable things to each other during those fights. When you each know the other's vulnerabilities, it's a simple matter to deliver that killing blow—the *nipon* it's called in karate. The fatal strike.

The bitter quarrelling finished any residual intimacy there might have been left. Bed became a place only for sleeping. On the rare occasion that we made love, it was either a perfunctory application of the proper frictions to relieve mutual tensions, or it was sometimes another battlefield for a second round of the quarrel. There was no more shared afterglow.

By now, Glynnis was getting fewer and fewer calls for commercials. There were never any parts suitable for her in television series any more. She complained bitterly about younger actresses who were willing to use the casting couch to get the good parts. She once said, "I could have had that part if I could give head like that bitch."

Shortly after Christmas, she gave up the apartment in Los Angeles and came back to Seattle for good. She moped around the apartment for two months, snarling any time anyone came near, then suddenly went into a flurry of activity. She was gone all day, came home in the late evening with a grim and determined set to her chin. When curiosity finally got the better of me and I asked what she was doing, she gave me the first real smile I'd had from her for a long time and merely said, "It's a secret. I'll tell you soon."

The last week in March was a busy one for me. I spent it hop-scotching over half the country in 737 sized leaps. When I got home, I was met at the door by a wife who was smiling and happy and radiantly beautiful. Glynnis grabbed me as I walked through the door and danced us through a few circles and swirls. Then she kissed me with enthusiasm and ardour. We left a scattered trail of discarded clothing all the way to the bedroom. She was passionate and fervent, fierce and tender by turns. Then finally, in subsidence, warm and close and soft. The way it always used to be.

"To what do I owe this returning hero's welcome?" I asked at last with some amazement.

"Wait'll you see." She got up and trotted out to the living room. Most women do not look their best trotting naked when seen from the rear. Not Glynnis. Her buttocks were round and firm as apples. There was no suggestion of looseness in her thighs or waist. From the back, she still looked eighteen. She returned with a small cream coloured business card and climbed back onto the bed as she handed it to me.

I looked at it. It was expensively embossed with raised dark brown print. It read, "Glynnis Fraser Agency and School of Modeling. Professional Training. Mannequins. Fashion Spreads. Television." Then her name, "Glynnis Fraser, President."

My first reaction was hurt and disappointment that she hadn't let me in on her plans at all. Not that I could have been much help, I suppose, but it hurt that she wouldn't trust me enough to tell me. I beat that down when I remembered how happy she was. It had been a long time since I'd seen her happy. And this agency and modeling school idea of hers just might work very well for her.

"This is great," I said with all the enthusiasm I could manufacture. "It's a terrific idea, Glynnis."

"Oh, Colin. I've got such wonderful plans. I've got a couple of the kids coming up from L.A. to teach. I know some camera people who want to help, too. I've been to the papers and the TV and radio stations about an advertising campaign. I rented an office and studio. It's all set to go on Monday morning."

"What about money? All this must have cost a mint."

"Money." She waved it aside as if it didn't matter. I guess

to an Alexander it didn't. "I asked Daddy. He advanced me enough to get it started."

That hurt, too, for a moment. But that was just my pride. My income wasn't exactly in the high six figure bracket, and wouldn't be for a long time, either. If her father wanted to lend her the money to start a business venture, that was between the two of them.

"And Colin?" Glynnis laughed happily and snuggled against me. "I bought a house."

I sat up suddenly and stared at her. "You what?"

"I bought a house. Wait 'til you see it. It's so beautiful. It's big and it's right on the beach so you'll have the whole ocean as a back yard again. You'll like that, won't you? It's about twenty miles up the coast. It won't be hard to get into the city or to the airport. You'll love it. I know you will. It's got an enormous fireplace and all sorts of windows looking out over the water. And trees. It's got lots of trees."

"A house on the water? Dear God. How much did it cost?"

"It was cheap for what it is." She pulled me down again and snugged her forehead into the hollow of my throat. "It doesn't matter how much it cost." She chuckled, a warm, furry sound in the dark. "Let's just say it wasn't a million."

"Good God, Glynnis—"

"It's okay. Really, Colin. Daddy said he'd give us the down payment. He said he'd always meant to do that as a wedding present anyway, but we never wanted a house before now. The mortgage will be small enough for us to handle. Really, it will." She kissed me, pressed hard against me. Her hand went to the top of my thigh. "Don't be angry with me, Colin. Please? Wait until you see the house. I know you'll really love it. I know you will."

We drove out to see it the next morning. It was in a development called Trestle Beach Estates, about twenty-five houses set on lots that were anywhere from three to ten acres in size, scattered along a narrow, winding paved road. The house Glynnis pulled up in front of was on six acres, set deeply into the trees on a promontory above the beach. It was big and it looked to be entirely constructed out of stone, redwood and glass. Attached to the house was a garage that looked big enough to hangar the Stinson.

"There's even a little grass strip about half a mile north of here where you can keep that silly little airplane of yours," she said as she unlocked the door. "Come in and look at this."

The house was furnished. It looked rather too much like a spread in a glossy magazine, but that was probably because no one lived here yet. It was tastefully done in soft colours and warm wood tones with brass accents. The sheer size of the rooms got to me at first, but the proportions were pleasing. Glynnis showed me the living room, the family room with its massive fireplace, the formal dining room that would have fit into any baronial manor anywhere, and the master bedroom, all vast and thickly carpeted, and a den with another fireplace and three walls of built-in bookcases just waiting to be filled with my books. The gleaming oak and chrome kitchen boasted a glowing hardwood floor. There were three full bathrooms and a powder room off the family room. One of the extra bedrooms had been made up as a guest room with a daybed piled high with colourful cushions and pillows, and a television set in the corner.

"Now, look here," she said and opened the door to a third bedroom, a cryptic smile on her face.

It had been done up as a nursery. A frilly, lacy bassinet, a crib, a white chest of drawers, a changing table. Disney characters on the walls. A wryly smiling clown with a lamp-shade hat. I turned to Glynnis in delight and astonishment.

"You're not pregnant, are you?"

She laughed. "No, not yet. But I thought perhaps soon now, before we both get too old to enjoy a child. What do you think?"

I put my hands to either side of her head and cupped her face gently between my palms. "Maybe we can make a fresh start here," I said in a sudden rush of tenderness for her. Right then, I wanted nothing more than for the words to be true.

"Maybe," she agreed gravely. "I think we can."

Our fresh start lasted only a little more than six months. I tried hard. I think Glynnis did, too. When we made love, it was almost the same as it had been at first. In the tranquility and quiet of the afterglow, we talked as we had before, laughed softly together. Perhaps we really did make a start on piecing together the broken fragments of our marriage.

Three months after we moved into the house, she became pregnant. When she told me that she was expecting a baby, her eyes and face glowed, and her smile was softer than I'd ever seen it before. She began humming silly little tunes as she moved around the house, and spent a lot of time simply standing in the doorway of the nursery, smiling. She seemed very happy, as happy as I was. I hadn't realized how much I wanted children until then. To my delight, I found I was looking forward to becoming a father with eagerness and excitement.

Then a little over four months after she told me she was pregnant, she began to bleed. Two of the instructors from the agency rushed her to the hospital, but there was nothing her doctor could do to save the baby.

I had been on my way back from Colorado Springs when they took her to the hospital. The message reached me as I walked off the airplane. I made it to the hospital without killing myself, and ran to the obstetrical ward. But by the time I got there, it was all over. Her doctor let me in to see her.

I burst into the room and Glynnis looked up from the hospital bed, her face almost as pale as the pillow beneath her tawny hair. Then she turned her head away. "Go away, Colin," she said tiredly. "I don't want to see you right now. And I will never, ever, ever go through this again, do you hear me? Never."

I stood there helplessly for a moment, then turned and left.

She would not let me comfort her. Like a cat, she withdrew to be by herself with her hurts. If she felt pain at the loss of the child, she never once let me see it after that first few minutes in the hospital. She didn't want to talk about it, refused to listen the one time I tried to tell her how I felt. The sense of loss carried over into my dream, hovering in the back of my mind as I searched for any signs of more danger. But I saw nothing, and thought perhaps the loss of a child was certainly danger enough.

Glynnis and I had almost lost the art or the habit of intimacy, if we'd ever had it in the first place. When she was released from the hospital, she hurled herself into her work with renewed vigour and determination. Her agency didn't thrive as quickly as she thought it should. It was a harsh, competitive business she had thrown herself into. The competition was fierce, and tough, and cut-throat. Glynnis and her friends knew the one side of it, the side in front of the camera, but they didn't know the back side, behind the cameras. They didn't know the side of finances and paperwork and fighting for a fair market share. Glynnis learned quickly, but it took all her time and energy. She had nothing left for me. She fell back into the habit of reticence. She told me little or nothing of what was happening and discouraged me from even enquiring by snarling and snapping. She became irritable and waspish all the time. Approaching her was like trying to get close to a devil's club stem.

I tried to be understanding because I thought I knew what she was going through. But I had bad days, too, when I came home in a foul mood. On those days, trying to cope with Glynnis's tight secretive taciturnity and hair-trigger temper was too much for my frayed patience. Sometimes it was hard to say who blew up first.

Three days before our fourth anniversary, I came home to find the house full of workmen. They had removed all the Disney characters from the nursery wall and were installing pale ash paneling. The nursery furniture was gone. A desk and a file cabinet stood in the hall, waiting to be moved into the room. In one corner, his china face cracked and broken, lay the wry little clown lamp. As I stood watching, one of the workmen kicked it aside so he could fit a section of paneling against the wall.

Glynnis had been directing two workmen who were changing the overhead ceiling light. She bent down, picked up the little clown, and tossed it into a box full of trash. She didn't even look at it.

Chapter Eleven

1991

THE SENSE of danger and loss eased in my dreams shortly after the nursery became a home office for Glynnis. And once again, as they had before, they left me with a feeling of tranquility and deep calm when I awoke in the morning after dreaming. The dreams didn't come often, perhaps two or three times a month, but I welcomed back the feeling of peace. I think I had almost forgotten the sick uneasiness left by the eerie overlapping of the dream and reality that had happened in Edmonton.

By then, Glynnis and I didn't have much of a marriage left. The conversion of the nursery took the last shred of life out of our relationship. We hardly spoke, hardly even saw each other most weeks. She spent all her time at the agency. Most of my spare time was spent at the small grass strip where I worked on the Stinson. Sometimes we met in the bedroom if one of us was up when the other got home. Somehow, before I fully realized it, my life had dwindled to flat, grey neutrality. Only when I flew or worked on the Stinson were the colours vivid and bright and fresh. When the dreams came, it was like a small island of serenity in a sea of low-grade despair.

There was a note in my mailbox one afternoon when I got in after a flight from Mexico. It was from Lucy, Brett Murphy's secretary, asking me to see Murphy as soon as I got in. I wasn't due for a check-ride for another three months, none of the fitness reports from my captains had been bad, and I didn't think I had committed any major or minor breach of the rules. I wondered why he wanted to see me. There was only one way to find out, so I tracked him down in the staff coffee room and showed him the note.

"Your admin goddess tells me you want to see me," I said.

"I certainly do. Let's go to my office. Get yourself a cup of coffee first, if you want."

"Hanging offence?"

He laughed and shook his head. "Not this time. Come on."

I collected a cup of coffee and followed him to his office. He waved me to a chair then closed the door and sat down on the corner of his desk, one leg swinging idly.

"I'm taking you off line for a while, Colin," he said. The breath caught in my throat for a moment. He laughed at my shocked expression. "Relax. I'm sending you on course for conversion to the 757, then you're upgrading to Captain."

I was speechless. I had just turned thirty last fall, and had been with Holiday West only a little over five years. The company was expanding quickly, but even so, being made a captain at that age was an accomplishment to be proud of. "You want me left seat in the 757?" I asked faintly.

"Eventually," he agreed. "We won't get them until at least next year probably, but I want a few of you familiar with the airplane when we get it. In the meantime, you'll move into the left seat of the '37. When we get the '57, you'll probably have to fly right seat with one of the senior captains for a few trips, but you'll have your own airplane."

"I don't know what to say," I said. "I wasn't expecting this."

"Then you're the only one in the company who wasn't," he said. "Go home and take Glynnis out to celebrate."

Glynnis wasn't home when I got there, but I hadn't expected her to be. I took off my tunic and hung it in the closet, then brushed off a fleck of lint from the sleeve above the three gold stripes. They weren't crisp and new anymore. I was a senior first officer now. One of the old hands, a veteran in the right seat of the 737. It seemed fantastic that there would soon be a fourth ring on that sleeve. Twelve to fifteen years was not an unusual period for a first officer to remain in the right seat before upgrading to captain. Five years was an incredibly brief sojourn. And there weren't a lot of captains of large aircraft who were still under thirty-five.

I changed into jeans, joggers and a sweatshirt, and went to the kitchen to make myself a sandwich. Then I jogged the half-mile to the little grass strip where the Stinson stood in an open T-hangar. I hadn't been working on it any more than twenty minutes when Wendell Markham Blakely III, called Skip, turned up. He was ten years old, the son of our neighbours to the north, and gave every indication of becoming a confirmed airport brat. He thought the Cessna 182, the only other aircraft on the strip, was a great airplane, but that my old Stinson was "kinda neat."

"Need some help, Mr. Fraser?" he asked as he propped up his bike out of the way.

"Tell you what," I said as I crawled out from my cramped position under the instrument panel. "You fit in here better than I do. How would you like to install this ADF head?

I'll hold the light and tell you which screws go where and where you attach the wires."

He looked immensely pleased as I boosted him up into the cabin and handed him the tools. We worked for a couple of hours on the avionics until it started getting dark. Then we put away the tools and I lifted him out of the cabin and swung him to the ground. As I had often done, he patted the scrofulous paint of the fuselage.

"She's an ugly old lady," he commented, invoking the required litany and I was amused to hear my own accents in the words.

"But still a lady," I said. "Never mind. Once we get the panel finished, I'll take her in and get her painted. Then she'll be all prettied up again."

"Then you'll give me a ride in her?"

"You bet, Skip. You can be my first co-pilot in her."

"Wow. That'll be soon, huh?" He got his bike and pushed it as we walked together toward the road.

"Pretty soon now. I have to go away on course for a couple of weeks but once I get back again, it won't be long after that. We don't have much more to put into the panel."

He nodded. "Just the ILS head and the transponder now," he agreed. "Then we have to put the seats back into it."

We said good night at the entrance to his driveway and I slowly walked the rest of the way home, enjoying the soft spring evening.

Glynnis's car was in the driveway, parked in front of the garage, when I got home. I found her in the kitchen, seated at the glass and brass table with a cup of coffee and a slice of toast on a plate beside the pile of papers she was going through. I got myself a mug of coffee and sat down opposite her. She didn't look up.

"I'm being upgraded to captain," I said.

"Great," she said and turned a page.

"And I'm doing the conversion to the 757."

"Super." She turned another page and took a small, precise bite of her toast.

"I could talk to the wall, I suppose."

"For Christ's sake, Colin. Can't you see I'm busy? If you want me to admire your pretty little gold star and pat you on your clever little head, couldn't you wait until I'm done this?"

I sat back in my chair and took a careful sip of the hot coffee. "Glynnis..."

"Jesus Christ! What?" She slapped her hand down onto the table. Her coffee slopped over the rim of the mug and splashed onto the papers. "Oh shit," she cried. "Now look what you made me do." She got up and snatched a paper towel, and returned to mop up the spilled coffee. She sat down again and looked at me. "What do you want?"

"I don't know what I want," I said. "I guess maybe I want to know why you wanted to marry me."

"Oh Christ, is this the time to go into that?"

"It's probably as good a time as any."

She sat back and ran her hand through her hair impatiently. She wore it short now, a soft, loose cap of waves that emphasized the lovely cheekbones. "Your timing is truly incredible, you know that?" She flicked the papers with her finger. "This stuff is really important right now."

"Isn't our marriage important anymore?"

"We've been over that—"

"You still haven't told me why you bothered to marry me in the first place. You never seemed to want a husband for any of the reasons other women want one."

She stacked the papers, evened the edges up carefully, and laid the stack to one side. "You're doing your supportive and sensitive act again, aren't you?" she said. "I don't need that. I told you a long time ago that I was ambitious and independent."

"Then why get married at all?"

"I don't know. Maybe because you disapproved of me so much when we first met. Maybe I had to prove that I could make you love me. Maybe because you had a hell of a good body and you looked like you'd be pure dynamite in bed."

"And was I good?"

"Oh, very good. Then."

"Better than Carl Sievers?"

Her mouth became a level line. "Much better," she said.

Her comment was nothing I wasn't expecting, but the stab of pain that tore through me surprised me. "Then you *were* lying that day on the beach."

"I wasn't lying. I was acting. There's a difference." She picked up the papers. "I have to get this contract sorted out before tomorrow morning." She vanished into her office and closed the door.

Thinking was the last thing in the world I wanted to do right then. I went down to the basement and practiced my *kata* and *kumite* for an hour then worked out with the heavy bag until I was exhausted and soaked in sweat. Then I showered and went to bed.

I dreamed that night of the functionally graceful metal wings supporting me in the living flow of the air. Below, the world moved slowly past, unfolding without haste, without rush. Everything was progressing as it should and I was very happy and contented. There was much to be grateful for up here out of the way of the world. This was a simple and uncomplicated act of love between pilot and aircraft, which was right and appropriate. There wasn't anything else I wanted but what I had, here and waiting for me when I finally had to come down.

Next week, I went away on the conversion course, then went through the snowstorm of paperwork required for upgrading to captain. It was the beginning of June when I made my last flight as a first officer with Captain Dawson. The next morning, I was scheduled out as the captain of a flight to Houston.

I was a more than a little self conscious when I showed up that morning with the four gold rings on the sleeve of my tunic, and the gold scrambled egg on the visor of my cap. I passed other pilots I knew who worked for other lines. They grinned widely and congratulated me. It was very likely I was in grave danger of taking myself far too seriously that morning, the hastily manufactured dignity being a flimsy shield against a small and secret fear that perhaps I wasn't really ready for this yet, an unvoiced doubt that I could really handle it.

Delaney Braedon stood leaning over the counter in the ops room when I entered. She was scribbling on a flight planning sheet and every so often she consulted an electronic flight computer. She wore three gold rings on the sleeve of her tunic, and she was one of two female pilots working for Holiday West. She was a new-hire. She hadn't been with the company for more than three months, but she was quickly developing a reputation as being a canny and competent first officer.

She wasn't very big, only about five feet two and perhaps a hundred and five pounds. She wore her curly light brown hair short to fit under the uniform cap. She had a tip-tilted snub nose with freckles dusted across the bridge of it and over her cheek bones, and a small, pointed chin, a look Glynnis's agency called *gamin*. She wasn't a pretty woman at all, but she had a wide, cheerful smile and she used it a lot. It was infectious as a cold bug. When she smiled at you, it was very difficult not to smile back.

"Hi there, Captain Fraser," she said and gave me the smile. "Looks as if you're stuck with me for a while. What do you expect from your first officers, just so I'll know for future reference. Do you want humility, awe or just plain ol' hero worship?"

"Plain old hero worship will do," I said. "You can get down on your knees and kiss the ground before my feet three times daily. What have we got today?"

"Full airplane, Captain. A hundred and three souls. Fair winds and full fuel. Should be a good trip. CAVOK all the way so the pax can watch the scenery." She slid her calculations across to where I could see them. They were neat, precise and correct as far as I could see. I checked a couple of them, just to be sure. She stood patiently until I finished, then said, "Shall I go out and check over the airplane, sir?"

"Please," I replied.

We had a three hour wait in Houston before taking on a load of passengers for Orlando, Florida and Disney World. I let her do the take off and then the landing in Orlando. She handled the airplane well. By the time we got back to Seattle late that night, I thought that we might make a good team. Murphy liked to keep cockpit crews together so they could weld themselves into a good team. Some companies used a shotgun method of scheduling where the same captain very seldom flew with the same first officer more than once or twice in a row. The theory there was that it kept the flight crew alert and communicating properly. Murphy's theory was that if you kept two people who worked well with each other together, you came up with a combination that was safe, competent and efficient. It seemed to work.

I found I liked Delaney Braedon. She was a serious pilot when the occasion demanded. She had a wry, left-field sense of humour that probably saved her a lot of the frustration of being a female in a predominantly male field. She was deferential and respectful in the airplane, but had no hesitation about speaking up when she should.

We put the airplane to bed and walked together out to the staff parking lot. I asked her how she had ended up flying for a living.

"My father was a pilot," she said. "And my grandfather. And my great-grandfather, too. He flew a Sopwith Camel in France in 1917. Just like Snoopy the Dog. I didn't have much choice in the matter, I guess." She grinned. "I just naturally fell into the family profession. There was never anything else I wanted to be. The old story of being too lazy to work for a living and too nervous to steal. Just like most pilots. What happened to you?"

"I was an airport brat who never grew out of it. Sort of nonplussed my parents. My father is a writer."

"I know." She grinned up at me. "I did some research into you for self-preservation purposes. Ian B. Fraser, isn't he? I read all his historical biographies when I was in college. He's one of the few historians who can make history readable and exciting. The others seem to concentrate on indigestible dates and treaties and battles. I would have liked history classes a lot better if someone like him and written the texts."

We reached her car, a battered little Toyota, and I waited

until she had unlocked it and slung her briefcase into it. "Well, I guess I'll see you tomorrow afternoon," I said.

"Should be an interesting flight," she said. "Good night, Captain."

"Good night, Braedon."

"Oh, Captain Fraser...."

It still sounded strange, being addressed as *Captain*. Probably would for a long time. I turned.

She laughed as she got into the car. "I forgot to kneel and kiss the decking, sir. Will you ever forgive me?"

I grinned. "Just see that it doesn't happen again."

CHAPTER TWELVE

1991 - 1992

FROM THEN on, Delaney Braedon flew as my first officer for most of my trips and she turned out to be one of the better first officers the company had as far as I was concerned. A good first officer can make the captain look even better. When he gets a good one, a captain hates to let him, or her, go, and I wasn't about to let Braedon get away without putting up a fight. It didn't take long before we developed into a very good flight-deck team and worked in concert almost as if we had been doing it all our lives.

I finished the work on the Stinson and flew it down to Portland to be painted by a man recommended by Nav Harty who was supposed to understand fabric aircraft. I brought it home again a month later, resplendent in two shades of blue with grey and gold trim. Skip Blakely received his introductory flight and was gratifyingly delighted. I took the airplane to Brindle Falls to show Nav my new toy. He gave it due admiration. I didn't see my parents that trip. They were in Britain on a research trip and would not be home before Christmas.

Glynnis worked harder than ever at her agency. It was beginning to show a profit, and she was making a name for herself. I had to find that out in the business section of the newspaper. She didn't tell me.

Christmas came, then New Year's, and winter began to wane toward spring. The dreams came more frequently now. I looked forward to them and welcomed the sense of well-being they left me with. I might not have been happy with the way my life was going, but I was reasonably comfortable in it. Perhaps it was only sheer inertia that kept me from any attempt at change—a change that might not turn out to be better. Glynnis's temper tantrum when she impaled her own hand with the paring knife was enough to send chills shivering down my spine. I didn't want to chance that happening again.

Then an early spring blizzard came roaring down out of the north like an avalanche falling down a mountain and changed everything.

The freak weather system caught the northwestern states and western Canada completely by surprise. We were on our way from Los Angeles to Calgary with a party of returning cruise passengers. Only fifteen minutes after I called for gear up, the West Coast began to shut down behind us. Seattle, Spokane, Vancouver and Victoria were all calling it zero-zero in wet snow and fog. East of the Rockies, Idaho, Montana, Wyoming, North Dakota found themselves up to the hips in the worst blizzard in forty years. If Montana and North Dakota were down, could Alberta be far behind? We were in the uncomfortable position of heading for an airport that might be closed when we got there, with an alternate that might not be any better.

"This could be fun," Braedon observed calmly as we listened to the chatter on the radio frequency. Nobody seemed to be getting in anywhere on the Coast. The eastern slopes of the Rockies weren't any better. "Suddenly I'm really glad about that extra five thousand pounds of fuel you insisted on, Skipper."

We were only twenty minutes out of Calgary when Area Control called us. "Holiday three-forty-nine, Centre."

"Holiday 349, go," Braedon replied.

"Calgary International just called closed due to runway conditions. Do you want to declare for your alternate now?"

Braedon glanced at me. I nodded.

"That's affirmative," she said. "Have you got the latest actual for Edmonton International?"

"Stand by one, 349." The controller came back a moment later. "Holiday 349, Edmonton International weather, special at 1815 zulu, five hundred overcast, visibility three quarters of a mile in snow and blowing snow, temperature minus ten celsius, dewpoint minus twelve celsius, wind two-eight-zero at two-five gusting to three-five knots, altimeter 29.44. Remarks, drifting snow obstructing some taxiways. JBI Runway 30 is 0.16, Runway 19 is 0.13."

"Okay," Braedon said. "Keep us informed." She looked at me and made a face. "I don't like that JBI. Even with ten thousand feet of runway, it's not going to be fun trying to stop this thing."

The JBI, short for James Brake Index is a measure of braking efficiency. The lower the number, the less effective braking on the runway surface. An index of 0.3 was marginal on anything less than 8,000 feet. An index of 0.2 on a ten thousand foot strip was cutting it pretty fine. Braedon was right. It wasn't going to be fun trying to get the 737 stopped once we got down.

"Better inform the passengers they're going to Edmonton," I said.

She made the announcement while I dug around for the Edmonton approach plates. An hour later, we crossed the Edmonton VORTAC and found ourselves at the top of a stack of aircraft trying to land at Edmonton International. We heard three aircraft in a row declare a missed approach and opt for alternates. One Air Canada 727 asked about the Edmonton Municipal Airport.

"Open," the controller replied. "They're reporting three hundred feet, three quarters of a mile vis in snow and blowing snow, wind 310 at 20.

"We could go there," Braedon said. "They take 737's all the time. Even '27's. Anything bigger is out of luck, though."

The controller's voice came over the speaker. "All aircraft listening this frequency, Edmonton International Airport is declared closed due to runway conditions. Please declare your intentions."

When it came our turn, I asked for the Municipal Airport. Then another Air Canada 727 asked for it, too. Braedon already had the approach charts out. She dialled in the ILS frequency, set the ADFs for the outer marker and the XD beacon north of the airport, while the controller gave me vectors for intercepting the ILS for Runway 34. We caught the localizer faster than I had anticipated. I called for the gear and flaps for the approach.

Braedon was busy. She set number two comm radio to the Municipal Tower on 119.1 mHz, checked the other radios. "Been into Muni before?" she asked, her hand on the flap switch.

"Once," I said. "Seven years ago. You?"

"Lots of times." She glanced at the approach plate. "Decision height is 2387 above sea level," she reminded me.

"Okay. Call altitude starting with a thousand above, and call runway visual."

At Decision Height, she had not called the runway visual. I declared a missed approach, poured on the power and climbed. She raised the gear and set climb flap. A few minutes later, we heard the Air Canada flight acknowledge landing clearance. The controller informed us he'd made it in. We asked for another approach.

"Your airplane," I told Braedon. "Maybe you'll have better luck."

Ragged grey tatters of cloud swirled past the windscreen in front of my eyes as I strained for the first glimpse of the runway. I was thinking about my last visit to Edmonton. I wasn't tired this time. Maybe there wouldn't be any problem. Only a small part of my mind monitored Braedon's approach. So far, it was flawless.

"Five hundred above," I said as the altimeter crawled down to 2837 feet above sea level.

"Five hundred above, roger," she replied.

"Three hundred above," I called. "Two hundred above. One hundred above..." Then the approach lights swam out of the mist of spinning snow. "Runway visual. I have control."

"You have control," she said and let go as I gripped the yoke with my left hand and put my right hand to the pair of power levers between us. She sat back and reset number one comm radio to ground frequency.

The wheels of the 737 touched the runway gently. It pleased me that my touch-down was smooth and perfect. "Reverse thrust," I said as the nose-wheel came down.

Braedon was grinning as she deployed the buckets. "Very sweet landing, skipper," she said. "If I can ever learn to put one down like that, I'll count all the hours I've spent going cross-eyed from studying as well spent."

"Most of my landings are more like abrupt arrivals," I said. "Where are we heading?"

"Terminal ramp would be the best place, I guess. Left on Delta up there." She got on the radio to Ground Control and requested a parking spot on the ramp, and asked if they could call someone to bring a set of stairs to deplane the passengers. "We're strangers in these parts, sir," I heard her say.

Then without warning it happened again. As we taxied onto the ramp, the terminal building materialized out of the mist. It was the brick and glass terminal that was supposed to be there, but there was an eerie double exposure overlay of the old terminal, the bow-shaped white structure with the angular glass tower cab above it, an ethereal, unreal ghost image superimposed on the solid building. I had almost been expecting it, but it sent a small chill rippling down my spine anyway. When I tried to look at it directly, it was more difficult to see clearly than if I used my peripheral vision. I noted with bemused interest that as we turned to park in the southeast corner of the ramp where the controller directed us, the image of the old building changed in proper perspective. Not only that, but the right wing of the aircraft cut right through the corner of an almost transparent old hangar as we swung the airplane around to park. All it would take, I thought far too calmly, to send me into a howling, twitching fit of hysteria would be to look up into the tower cab and see a group of controllers working hard to keep order around the airport. Fortunately, the tower cab was mercifully bare and dark.

The Ground Controller called us, breaking into my abstracted study of the ghost buildings. "Holiday 349,

Canadian Airlines staff will bring out a set of stairs for you. If you talk to them when you get inside, they'll probably be able to give you a hand unloading baggage if you need it."

"Thank you, sir," Braedon said. "We'll keep that in mind."

By the time she finished speaking, the old terminal building and hangar had faded away. The 737 sat by a tall chain link fence. We were a long way from any other hangar.

I didn't have time to think about the eerie experience. For the next few hours, we were far too busy. We got the passengers into the terminal building. The cabin crew, Marilee, Tina and Bonnie, kept them herded together while I called Flight Ops back in Seattle and told them where we were, and Braedon went to organize a baggage unloader if we needed one. Flight Ops told me to hang tight while he made some phone calls. We waited in the Canadian Airlines office for twenty minutes before the call came in.

It took a while to sort it out. Eventually, a bus turned up to take the passengers to a hotel for the night. Flight Ops arranged with Canadian for servicing of the aircraft. Airport management wanted it clear of the ramp for snow removal, so we had it towed to a quiet corner where it sat beside the two Air Canada 727's that had found refuge with us. It was dark when Braedon and I were finally ready to find a hotel.

Marilee had taken Tina and Bonnie and gone with the passengers to make sure they were looked after. Braedon called the hotel to see if they had room for us, too, and I tried to call home to tell Glynnis I was weathered out and wouldn't be back for at least a day. There was no answer at the house, none at the agency, nor on her car phone. She might have been stuck, too, and gone to a hotel for the night. There was no way I could track her down, so I gave up. I wondered if she'd worry at all. Somehow, I didn't think she would.

Braedon appeared at my elbow. "You and me are right out of luck, Captain," she said. "That hotel's full. I called about a hundred others. They're all full of stranded travellers and people who couldn't get out of the city when this mess hit the fan. I found a place way out in the west end that could take us, but we're going to have a good time getting there. There's not a cab in the city can make it here much before two hours."

"I don't feel much like camping out here," I said.

"Me either."

We were standing by the bank of telephones near the main entrance of the building. Suddenly, Braedon seized my arm. I barely had time to grab my flight bag as she pulled me toward the door. A cab had pulled up to discharge a passenger. Smoothly and adroitly, Braedon slithered through the milling crowd with me in tow, and slid into the back seat of the cab as neatly as she had fitted the 737 into the groove on the ILS approach. She grinned at me, winked, and gave the driver an address.

"That worked," she said.

"That was a very efficiently executed manoeuvre."

"You have to be entirely without scruples to get away with it." She laughed. "Or be able to give a darn good imitation of it."

We arrived at a snow-shrouded motel that advertised a pool, and cable TV in every room. She waited until I paid off the cab, adding a good tip, and we went into the office.

It wasn't much of a motel, but it was warm and it was clean, and there was a reasonably good restaurant attached to it so we didn't have to go out into the still howling blizzard in search of something to eat.

We had dinner, which turned out to be better than we thought it would be. After we finished eating, we relaxed over coffee. I found myself thinking about the ghostly terminal building and the old hangar. It was odd but I hadn't really been frightened this time. Just absorbed and interested. Even fascinated. There had been nothing threatening or frightening about the experience this time. It was almost as if it hadn't been happening to me; as if I had watched it happen to someone else.

I looked up as Braedon called my name, and realized it wasn't the first time.

"I'm sorry," I said. "What was that?"

"I asked where you were," she said. "Maybe I should have asked when you were, too."

She had startled me. "When I was?" I repeated blankly.

"Where ever or whenever it was, it wasn't here and now," she said. "You looked a million miles and a hundred years away."

I surprised myself by telling her the truth. "I was a long time but not that long way away," I admitted. "You're right. Maybe you should have asked who I was when you were asking when I was."

She said nothing, merely cocked her head to one side, attentive and curious.

I think I came closer to telling her about the dream, the eerie first trip to Edmonton, and the ghostly terminal building than I had ever come to telling anyone before. I had the strange feeling that she would understand; that she would not think I was losing my mind. But where do you start telling a bizarre story like that? There just didn't seem to be any reasonable place to begin. In the end, I just shrugged and smiled.

"It's nothing," I said. "It's just that there's something about that airport that always sneaks up on me sideways."

"For me, it's like coming home," she said. "I didn't tell you that I learned to fly here, did I?"

"You did?"

"I'm a Canadian," she said. "My father was in the Armed Forces. My mother was an American, so I've sort of got dual citizenship. Dad got posted here when I was fifteen. He was in Search and Rescue stationed at the air base at Namao, just north of the city. I learned to fly at the Edmonton Flying Club. I went down to Vancouver for University. Before I came to Holiday West, I worked for an outfit there called Allgo Oil, flying a Westwind. You didn't know I was a Canadian?"

I shook my head. "I didn't think about it, I suppose," I said.

She laughed. "You would have caught on pretty quick if I'd ever forgotten and said 'zed' instead of 'zee'." She got to her feet. "I'm whipped. Time for bed, I think. Meet here for breakfast at eight?"

"Sounds like a deal to me," I said.

I went to sleep quickly and dreamed of rocks and lakes and trees moving sedately beneath the wings of the Beaver. The glorious fall colours of the trees reflected in the deep blue water of the lakes, and the rocks were the ancient bones of the earth scraped raw by the glaciers that had retreated thousands of years ago. The scars had hardly had time to begin to heal in the centuries since. It was wild and beautiful country but I was glad to be leaving it and go back where I belonged because now, especially now, I was needed. Not just loved, but needed.

And somewhere in the background, a small chill of apprehension stirred once again. What if something were to go wrong...?

CHAPTER THIRTEEN

Late Summer 1992

SPRING MOVED gradually on toward summer again. My dreams became more frequent. They were as pleasant as before, as calming, but on occasion that thread of uneasiness and apprehension ran through them. It wasn't exactly fear. It was more like the almost superstitious dread you feel when you know things are too good to last, that something has to happen to mar a happiness as complete as mine seemed to be.

Glynnis and I had passed beyond the point where we quarrelled very often anymore. We moved through that lovely house on the shore like two strangers. We were almost formally polite to each other. Out of habit more than anything else, we still shared the same bed. I knew I had to make a decision about our marriage, but for the present, it was as if we had entered a hiatus, a wary truce. It was so much easier for both of us just to let things drift.

Things might have continued indefinitely like that if I hadn't taken the flight to Chicago in early summer. That flight was a bad one. Braedon and I earned every cent of our pay cheques for the next year on that one. We had to pass through a cold front that sent line upon spectacular line of cumulonimbus boiling up into the sky to altitudes of well above 40,000 feet. It was early in the year for a squall line that severe. We spent a lot of time making detours around the worst of it. A full-blown thunder bumper is not something any pilot wants to mess with. The violent wind shear created by the updrafts and downdrafts in those monsters was perfectly capable of tearing the wings off an aircraft, ripping it apart and spitting it out in very small pieces. Ice filled the clouds and could collect on the wings and flying surfaces so quickly that even the best de-icing or anti-icing equipment couldn't keep up with it. Ice on the wings can bring an airplane out of the sky like the proverbial shot duck. Another hazard is hail. If you've ever seen what a bad hailstorm can do to the metal skin of a car, then magnify that by a factor of an aircraft's forward speed at impact with the chunks of ice, you can imagine what large hailstones can do to the surface of the aircraft.

We heard several aircraft reporting funnel clouds in the area. The pilot of a Lear 55 cruising at 45,000 feet reported one monster cloud soaring several thousand feet above his altitude. Another pilot in a commuter airline Jetstream called Centre and said he wasn't even going to try to get through the mess and requested vectors back to Casper, Wyoming.

We got vectors around the worst of it. We were well north of the heaviest build-ups, but still I didn't envy the passengers in the cabin back there, or the flight attendants either, for that matter. The turbulence was enough to rattle the fillings out of teeth, and it took both Braedon and me at times to hold the wings level. Sue and Coral back there would be hard pressed to move to attend any passengers who were sick, and there would be enough of those. We had the seat belt sign on, but I knew neither Sue nor Coral could ignore a sick passenger for long.

"We're sure not making any friends back there today," Braedon said during a brief moment of respite.

"Just make sure the seat belt sign stays lit," I said.

"Oh, yeah," she said.

Fifteen minutes later, we popped out into clear air. Behind us, and curving around to the south beside us, the solid wall of black and green cloud looked like a special corner of hell. Lightning flashes lit it ominously with blue light and it seethed and writhed like a live thing in torment. Turbulence still bounced us around, but it didn't feel like being caught in the epicentre of an earthquake any more.

"You'd better go back there and see if there's any damage," I said to Braedon.

She unstrapped and got to her feet. She had to hold onto the back of her seat to open the door behind us. "Oh, boy," she said as she looked back into the cabin. "Looks as if the overhead bins popped. There's stuff all over the place. I'll go see if anyone's hurt."

"Send Coral up here to tell me if there's any real problem."

"You got it, Skipper."

She came back ten minutes later and slid back into her seat. "No real problems," she said. "Half the passengers are puking their guts out, but nobody's hurt and we've got plenty of barf bags. For once, nobody tried to sneak the heavy stuff into the overhead bins. Just blankets and coats and a camera or two. Sue's organizing Dramamine and coffee. The pax are so grateful to get out of that alive, they think you're a saint."

"While Sue's organizing coffee, maybe she could organize an aspirin or two for me," I said.

"Headache?"

"Yes. I don't get them very often but I'm beginning to think someone nailed me with a two-by-four across the back of the head."

"I've got some acetaminophen in my flight bag. Hang on a sec. I'll get you some water." She slipped out and came back a moment later with a paper cone cup of water and two tablets. She handed them to me and strapped back into her seat.

I took the tablets and leaned back. "Your airplane," I said.

"My airplane," she acknowledged and put her hands on the yoke. "Are you all right?"

"I will be. I'll just sit here and rest for a moment."

She grinned. "I can see the headlines now. Heroic First Officer Lands Aircraft When Captain Suffers Concussion. Credited with Saving Lives of Passengers and Grateful Captain. 'Oh Shucks,' Says Modest First Officer. 'T'wern't Nothing.'"

"You could get to be a pain in the butt, Braedon," I said. But I smiled. It was too hard not to.

"Oh, indubitably, Captain, sir."

The air around us was smoothing out comfortably. Coral opened the door behind us. She carried two cups of coffee. She handed one to me and one to Braedon. "I figured you could use this," she said. "Is everything all right up here?"

"The Captain may keel over from concussion," I said. "But don't worry, we're saved. Braedon is in charge. How are things back there?"

"We've just about got things straightened away. It was a real mess for a while. Almost everyone was sick at least once. We're running low on barf bags, but the worst is over."

"Good girl. I'll buy everyone dinner when we get to Chicago."

"You've got a date, Captain," Coral said with a grin. "I've got expensive tastes."

"You would. Thanks, Coral. Say thanks to Sue and Marnie, too."

She grinned again and went back to the cabin.

"Does that dinner offer include me?" Braedon asked.

"I guess so. It would be ungracious of me to exclude the gallant first officer who rescued the passengers, the captain and the ship, and saved the company from bankruptcy."

She made a face at me.

"We're going to be tight on fuel getting into Chicago," I said. "All that dodging around back there didn't do us much good."

Braedon glanced at the fuel gauges and I could see her doing quick sums in her head. "We should be okay," she said. "As long as we don't get stacked up for very long. I purely hate declaring a fuel emergency. It ties you up in red tape until your medical expires. How's your headache?"

"Better, thanks. I'll be okay."

"I don't get to make headlines?"

"Not this trip, Braedon. Better luck next time."

We arrived in Chicago an hour behind schedule, but the fuel held up and we would still be legal when we put the wheels on the pavement. There were a few isolated thunderstorms hanging around as we lost altitude to begin the approach. Braedon was flying. Uneasily, I watched the storm clouds, but they gave no indication of growing, or moving toward us.

Still, I didn't like the look of those thunder bumpers. When she reached out to bring the power back for descent, I put my hand over hers. I had a sudden and certain premonition. Something was very wrong. It was almost as if I heard a voice in the back of my mind shouting a warning at me.

"No," I said. "Hold on a bit. And maintain an extra twenty or so knots." I don't know what made me say it. Perhaps it was simply because those cb's looked dangerous.

Only seconds later, we hit the wind shear. The vertical speed indicator went from a descent of six hundred feet a minute to over fifteen hundred feet per minute. The airspeed fell off twenty-five knots and the airplane lurched sickeningly as it seemed to fall right out from beneath us. My hand slapped against Braedon's on the power levers, shoving them full forward, as the 737 started to fall out of the sky. The engines spooled up slowly and the wings gradually gained lift. When we got it sorted out, we had lost almost eight hundred feet. If I hadn't told Braedon to remain high and fast, we might have gone right into the ground a good couple of miles short of the runway.

Braedon looked at me. "What in the name of all that's holy was that?" she demanded, her face very pale.

"Downburst or microburst, I think," I said a bit breathlessly. Much has been written about thunderstorms and the violent and sudden gusts of wind they can produce. Before meteorologists fully understood the phenomenon, too many large aircraft had flown into the ground without any apparent reason, and too many accidents had been written off as *pilot error.*

"What made you call for extra altitude and speed?" she asked.

"I don't know," I said, still feeling uneasy and unsettled, as if someone I couldn't see were watching me. "I just didn't like the looks of it."

She laughed shakily. "That's the first time I've ever hit

wind shear like that," she said. "I think you just saved us having to explain a badly bent airplane. I owe you one for that. You got us out of that so neatly, I'll bet they didn't even feel it back there."

We called the tower, reported the wind shear, then continued the approach for the landing. It was uneventful. The passengers gathered up their hand luggage and trudged off the aircraft, congratulating themselves for having survived a terrible experience. This would give them good stories to tell for weeks.

Braedon and I put the aircraft to bed, then gathered up Coral, Marnie and Sue and took a taxi to the hotel. I fed everyone a late dinner in the hotel dining room. By the time we finished eating, it was almost ten o'clock. The three flight attendants said they were exhausted and went to their rooms. I said good night to Braedon and went to my room. The headache was threatening to erupt behind my eyes again.

Half an hour later, I knew I wasn't going to get to sleep until I beat the headache into submission with two or three aspirin. I didn't have any with me. I thought one of the Flight Attendants might have some so I climbed into my shirt and slacks and went knocking on doors.

Coral opened her door immediately. She looked surprised to see me. "I just wondered if you had any aspirin," I said. "I forgot to bring some with me and my headache's back."

"Gee," she said. "I don't think I have any and neither does Marnie. I know Sue had some, but I think she gave the last one to a passenger. We ran out on the airplane. Maybe Delaney has some. Why don't you try her?"

"You're right. I think she does have some. Thanks anyway, Coral."

"You're welcome, Captain. Sorry I couldn't help." She shut her door and I moved down the hall to Braedon's door.

Braedon must have just come out of the shower. Her hair clung to her head in damp ringlets and her face shone shiny and clean. She opened the door wider to let me in.

"I just wondered if you had any more of that acetaminophen," I said. "This headache is going to make me go cross-eyed."

"Sit down," she said and gestured to the chair by the writing desk. "I'll get some for you. Two or three tablets?"

"Better make it three. This headache's a bastard."

She looked at me strangely. "You know something? That's the first time I've ever heard you swear."

"I don't do it very often, but you should hear me when I get mad." I smiled. "My father always used to lecture me about how a man who could express his anger without profanity could verbally slice the opposition into ribbons. I guess I never got into the habit."

She grinned. "Maybe it would make you sound more human sometimes if you swore like us lowly common folk, Captain, sir. I'll get the pills."

She emerged from the bathroom with a glass of water and the tablets. I took the tablets, washed them down with the water, then rubbed my eyes. She sat on the bed and crossed her knees. She wore a short terry towelling robe in faded green, belted tightly around her tiny waist. Her feet were bare. Her little gamin face looked concerned.

"Are you going to be all right? You look a bit pale."

"I'll be fine once I get some sleep."

She looked up and smiled briefly. "You know, you're a very strange man, Colin Fraser."

"Strange?" I repeated, startled. "Strange how?"

"Do you realize that I've flown with you for almost a year and I don't know a darn thing about you except that you're probably the best pilot I've ever known, and that thing this afternoon almost proves you've either got a big slice of ESP working for you, or a guardian angel."

I jumped a bit when she mentioned a guardian angel. There was definitely *something* there; something reminiscent of my dreams.

"You hardly ever talk about yourself, do you?" she continued. "But that's not all."

"There's more?"

She shook her head and smiled again.

"You can't leave it there, Braedon. You mentioned it. Now you have to explain it."

"Do you really want me to explain?"

"You'd better before my imagination does it for you."

"Okay. But remember, you asked for this." She looked away for a moment as if to organize her thoughts. When she looked back, there was a faint frown drawing her brows together. "How do I say this? First off, you're a very good looking man, an extremely attractive man, but you don't act like one."

"What's that supposed to mean?"

"Don't go all defensive on me like that. Remember, you asked for this. I mean that most attractive men play on it. They flirt with women, even if they're married. Maybe especially if they're married because they know they're safe. You don't. You seem to freeze into pleasant and friendly neutrality when there are women around. As if you've got an eight-foot fence around you and you've gone and hung no trespassing signs all over it. It's refreshing in a way. It's as if you've got nothing to prove. It can be a bit disconcerting at times. Then there's the way you carry yourself, the way you handle your body. I'd say you've taken quite a bit of martial arts training."

I stared at her, almost too flabbergasted to speak. Finally, I latched onto the one thing I thought I could decently comment on. "You're very observant. I have a second *dan* black belt in karate."

"I thought as much. My brother has a first *dan*. He's got much the same way about him as you have. A sort of casual elegance you could call it, but it shows more on you. You remind me a bit of the hero in one of those old British movies. A gentleman and a gentle man, but with an underlying toughness and resilience and durable competence to you. I'd highly doubt that you've ever got yourself into a real physical brawl, my friend, but I sure wouldn't want to be the man who ever provoked you into your first. You could probably clean his clock very thoroughly for him and end up not even breathing hard."

I had to laugh at that one. She had conjured up an image that I just couldn't fit myself into. I was no dashing hero, and I never would be. I couldn't fit myself into the image of The Scarlet Pimpernel.

"Laugh if you have to," she said, completely unperturbed. "But it's true nonetheless."

"You're a hopeless romantic, Braedon. In the literary sense."

"Yes, I guess I am. Do you want to hear the rest?"

"There's more?"

"There's more. You're a very troubled man, Captain. I can see it around your eyes. You're in a lot of pain, or you've been through a lot of pain, but you're a very private person and you'd probably bite your tongue off before you'd open up and tell anyone about it. If I had to guess, I'd say that a good part of it was an unfortunate marriage."

"Why would you say that?"

"You've never said anything about it, and I haven't heard any hangar rumours about it, and that's strange, too, because you know how pilots gossip. But maybe the old saw is true, and it really does take one to know one. It so happens that I'm one of the resident experts on pilots' unfortunate marriages."

"So am I," I said. It caught me by surprise. I hadn't meant at all to say that.

"Do you still love her, Colin?"

I made a helpless gesture. "I don't know. I don't think so. It's just that I feel so damnably helpless and disloyal talking about her. I think I knew a couple of years after we were married that we'd made a mistake. But I tried to make it work. For a while there a year or so ago, we almost made it work. I think we both tried, but just couldn't do it." It was suddenly a great relief to get it out like this. I'd never talked to anyone, not even my parents, about Glynnis. I didn't know why it was so easy to talk to Braedon.

"No kids?" she asked.

I shook my head. "We agreed to put off having a family until we were both settled well into our careers. Last year, we lost one. She doesn't want to ever try again. But I'm glad we don't have kids now. The way things are, it would be sheer hell on them. How about you?"

"I wanted kids," she said. "Peter didn't. I suppose I'm glad we didn't have any, too. As you say, it would be sheer hell on them. How long have you been married?"

"It was five years last May."

"That's a long time in a bad marriage, Colin."

152

"I know. The first few years were okay, but there's not a lot of joy in it now, I suppose."

"Are you going to divorce her?"

"I've never thought much about it. I guess it just never seemed that bad. It might come to that. I don't know."

"She doesn't sleep around, does she." It was a statement, not a question. "And neither do you."

"No, I don't. I never have. Not once."

"I didn't think so."

"How long were you married?"

"Two years. When we got married, Peter had just graduated in law. I was working as a flight instructor. He thought it was just so damn cool that his wife was a pilot. It was distinctive and unusual and maybe even glamourous. About a month after he was admitted to the bar, I got a job with Allgo Oil, flying right seat in their Westwind. My first trip with them was to Calgary. Three days. Peter nearly had a fit. He said, what are people going to think, my wife up there for three days with six men. I said, that's my job, I'm a pilot, that's what I do. He said, my wife wouldn't. So I decided to stop being his wife. I could see what was going to happen. First, I'd have to give up flying because he didn't think it was proper. Then eventually he'd make me give up everything else I enjoyed that didn't coincide exactly with his narrow little view of propriety. It took me a long, painful year to make that decision. I got out because I knew if I didn't, I'd lose myself."

"How long have you been divorced."

"Do you know the real farce of the whole thing? I was able to get an annulment through the church because Peter didn't want children. But it's been two and a half years. It's almost stopped hurting now. How's your headache?"

"Almost gone. Maybe I'd better go and try to get some sleep."

"That's probably a good idea," she said. "You'd better take a couple of those tablets with you in case you need them later on tonight."

She came to the door with me, a small girl with short, sandy hair curling crisply around her head, and warm hazel brown eyes in the gamin face. I'm not sure why I did it, but I put my hand out to touch that hair. Then I kissed her. It was an odd, uncertain kiss, as hesitant as a first kiss between two young teens on a front porch. Except for our nearly closed lips, the only other touch was my hand in the lively softness of her hair.

I raised my head and looked down at her. Little bit of a thing that hardly came to my shoulder. So much warmth and humour and life in that small, trim body. Then she was in my arms and the kiss was fierce and hungry and needful, and achingly sweet. Her mouth opened beneath mine to admit my questing tongue. She felt so tiny in my arms, but strong and vibrant and alive. There was a curious sense of belonging, of the innate rightness of it. My hand found a breast through the rough fabric of the bathrobe. It felt round and firm as fruit in my palm.

Then quite suddenly, she broke away from me, stumbled back a few steps. "Not a very good idea, Captain Fraser," she said breathlessly.

It took a few seconds for me to regain control and stop myself from reaching for her again. I took a deep breath. "No," I agreed, hanging onto the control for dear life. "Not a good idea at all. Good night, Braedon."

She closed the door firmly behind me and I went back to my room. The tablets worked fine. I went to sleep like falling down a deep well. I dreamed that night. And in the dream, I knew there was something dreadfully wrong. It was a formless, undirected dread, but nevertheless, a solid and real and tangible presence in the cabin of the Beaver. I leaned forward tensely, scanning the endless blue of the sky for the danger I felt was out there. But there was nothing. Only the vista of rocks and water and trees.

Chapter Fourteen

Late Summer 1992 – Late Winter 1993

We left Chicago early the next morning bound for Salt Lake City, then San Francisco, then home to Seattle. There was one awkward moment when Braedon and I were alone in the weather office. We both reached for the weather print-out at the same time and our fingers touched. A tingle like a mild electric shock trembled through my hand. I looked down at Braedon, found her wide hazel eyes looking gravely back at me. A dusky tint suffused her cheeks and heightened their colour as she dropped her gaze.

"I think we had better proceed on the premise that last night didn't happen," she said quietly. "That would be safer for everyone."

I agreed wholeheartedly.

But it wasn't that easy. During the long flight home, I was acutely conscious of her sitting there beside me to my right. She was no longer just Braedon, my competent and efficient first officer. She was Delaney Braedon, a warm and sensitive woman, a woman I had kissed and held, and if she hadn't stepped away, I would have taken her to bed and learned the intricacies and sweet complexities of that small, strong body. That knowledge hung between us like a solid presence in the cockpit. Once an awareness between a man and a woman has been created and acknowledged, it was difficult to slide it back out of the way like a desk drawer you didn't need open any more.

There's not a lot of space on the flight deck of a 737 and there is an implied professional intimacy between a captain and a first officer. There has to be if they were going to work together well as a team. The inadvertent personal intimacy we had created made for a strained atmosphere. I was too conscious of her as a woman, and I could tell she was just as conscious of me as a man. Unless we could manage to put each other back into the proper professional perspective of captain and first officer, it was going to be very difficult to be a businesslike and efficient team again.

We couldn't avoid touching each other in the cockpit. On take-off, her hand had to cover mine on the power levers to ensure they were at full take-off thrust. Each time, my hand tingled under the warmth of hers and she blushed again. I think we were both glad and relieved when we finally walked up the jetway in Seattle and parted in the terminal building.

"See you next week," she said.

"Braedon...."

She shook her head. "Don't, Colin," she said. "Just leave it be. We'll have to sort it out later."

"See you next week, then."

She smiled briefly and turned to go.

I had five days off. I spent them fussing around with the Stinson. Small airplanes are like boats. There's always some small maintenance chore to be done to keep them in top condition. Skip Blakely hovered around happily to help me as I tinkered. I took him up once and we spent an hour exploring the coast. He was barely tall enough to see over the glareshield of the instrument panel, but he was learning to hold the aircraft straight and level, and his turns were becoming crisp and neat. It wasn't easy to manage a good, coordinated turn in an aircraft as old as the Stinson, but Skip had learned how to lead the roll in and roll out with rudder and knew just where the nose should be on the horizon to keep the turn level. One day, he was going to make a good pilot.

The night before I returned to work, Glynnis and I had another quarrel. We hadn't had an argument for a long time and this one was particularly silly. I was sitting in my chair in the family room, reading an article on a new collision avoidance system, when she came into the room and angrily accused me of taking some papers out of her office. Instead of calmly asserting that I never went into her office and she must have merely misplaced them, I threw down the magazine and snarled something sarcastic about how I'd filched them off her desk and taken great delight in jumping up and down on them before setting fire to them. My uncharacteristic reaction lit her fuse and she blew up. The quarrel ended only when she stormed off, white with fury, to her office and I went stomping off to bed.

I dreamed again that night. The almost subtly threatening thread of apprehension that had been becoming more and more apparent in the dream had solidified, become more pervasive. Something was wrong. There was danger near that threatened all I had and loved, but I didn't know what the danger was, or where it would come from. It was disquieting and obscurely alarming.

I awoke still feeling uneasy. Unlike how it used to be when I dreamed, it hadn't been a restful night and I was tired as I drove to the airport. Brett Murphy caught me as I entered the Ops Room and beckoned me into his office.

"You'll be flying with Morg Hannarhan today, Colin," he said.

"Where's Braedon?" I asked.

He made an odd little shrugging gesture and raised his hands, palm up. "She quit. Came into my office just after you two got back from Chicago and told me she'd had an offer from some outfit to fly left seat in a Grumman G-III, said it was too good an offer to ignore and handed in her resignation. She said they wanted her to start immediately."

I made no reply. There wasn't much I could say. I certainly couldn't tell him that her captain had made a wild and unmistakably direct pass at her in Chicago, and that it had probably scared her enough to curl her toes. But Brett Murphy was no fool. He had spent a lot of years reading pilots' faces. He didn't say anything but one eyebrow twitched slightly.

"I'll miss her," I said at last. "She was an excellent first officer. A very good pilot...."

"Almost as good as you," Murphy said mildly and noncommittally. "Don't forget to give me a report on Hannarhan when you get the time."

I found a letter from Braedon in my letter box. She didn't say much, just that she had received an offer that was too good to turn down and that she was going to accept it. She didn't go into detail. All she said about the incident in Chicago was one line at the end of the note. "Neither of us needs more complication, Colin. Take care of yourself." She had signed it only with a scrawled capital D.

I should have thrown the note away. Instead, I tucked it

into the back of my wallet behind my license and medical certificate.

That flight to Chicago with Braedon had been a turning point. Before then, I had been more or less content to drift along in a lifeless and loveless marriage with Glynnis. Probably the only reason we had remained together all this time was sheer inertia on both sides. I don't think either of us had ever given serious thought to divorce. It would have caused a lot of uproar and tension and distress which neither of us wanted. Divorce would be too disturbing when neither of us wanted the difficulties involved. Perhaps the fact that I was Catholic, albeit not a very strong one, had something to do with it. The Church has never recognized divorce and has always discouraged it as a poor solution to marital problems. I had perhaps absorbed more of the philosophy of the Church during my childhood attendances at catechism classes than I realized.

After Chicago, though, I gradually became aware of a growing dissatisfaction, a restlessness I couldn't put down. It took a long time for me to pinpoint the cause.

In going on six years of marriage, I had never once looked seriously at another woman. Somehow I doubt that I would have recognized an opportunity even if one that wasn't completely blatant had arisen. I suppose it could even have been clinical depression, but it was as Braedon had said. I simply allowed myself to freeze into friendly neutrality.

Until that night in Chicago.

What happened there had caught me completely by surprise. It was as if something deep inside me had burst and broken open, almost like a bird breaking out of the constricting and restraining shell of its egg. The realization that I wanted to make love to Braedon hadn't suddenly burst onto me like the explosion of fireworks. Nor, I think, had it been building gradually over the time she flew with me. It had just suddenly been there, full blown and mature, when I reached out to touch her hair.

Whatever else it was, though, it was also a ridiculous reversal of the Sleeping Beauty myth. That kiss had awakened me, it seemed. It gave me an unasked for and unwanted glimpse of how things could be for me with a woman. I had never before held Glynnis up for comparison to any other woman. Now I found myself constantly contrasting her with Braedon, and she didn't fare well in the comparison. Braedon's plain, gamin face with its pointed little chin and dusting of freckles across the bridge of the snub, turned up nose made Glynnis's beauty seem contrived and artificial. But worst of all, she made my wife look shallow and cold and calculating. Braedon's sense of humour and capacity for warm laughter highlighted Glynnis's complete lack of those same characteristics. Where Braedon could laugh at herself, Glynnis became enraged if it even appeared that she had done something ridiculous and thought someone might have seen her. Where Braedon never took anything, even herself seriously, except the responsibilities of her job while flying the aircraft, Glynnis took herself and everything else with grim, humourless solemnity that brooked no levity.

More and more, dissatisfaction and restlessness urged me into uneasy, undirected energy. But I could find no outlet for it. I couldn't maintain enough concentration to work out in the *dojo*. I didn't have the patience for any painstaking work on the Stinson. My attention span shortened when I wasn't flying. I found myself becoming irritated and annoyed at nearly everything Glynnis did or said. I began to prowl the house at night because I couldn't sleep properly.

At the same time, my dream changed. No longer was there any peace or contentment in it. The sense of danger had grown until it reached the proportions of nightmare. I didn't know where the threat came from or even what it was. I only knew that it was near and immediate and it wakened me breathless and shaking with the sour stink of nightmare sweat sharp in the air.

The only place where the jittery sense of vague urgency didn't affect me was in the air. Only when I flew did I feel calm and untroubled.

Our long expected 757's came on line in September. I took a refresher course at Boeing, then flew two trips in the right seat with Brett Murphy as captain, then took over the left seat. Morg Hannarhan moved over with me.

Autumn deepened and became winter. I awoke one morning in February to the first signs of melting snow and hints of approaching spring. Glynnis wasn't home when I got up and made myself some breakfast. I walked down to the airstrip and spent an hour tinkering with the Stinson. Then I took it flying. I spent a couple of hours wandering through the sky, poking into a few mountain passes, then rambling back to the coast. I flew several miles out to sea and found an old freighter tramping its way stolidly down the coast toward San Francisco. I flew low enough over it to see the rust streaking its sides. On the bridge, I could see the tiny figures of some of the crew. They waved to me. I waggled the wings in reply and made my way back to shore. I was almost out of fuel when I landed at the little grass strip again.

Skip Blakely was there when I got back. He helped me fuel up from the big tank sitting atop the spidery platform, then I took him for a short flight. It was nearly dark when we returned. I walked with him to where the driveway of his house intersected the road. We said good night, and I walked the rest of the way home doing nothing more than enjoying the crisp fall scent in the air. Apples and moist earth and turning leaves.

Glynnis was home. I heard her moving in the kitchen as I hung my jacket in the closet and kicked out of my muddy joggers. When I went into the kitchen, she was standing by the counter. She turned. Her face was white and set and anger blazed in the sherry coloured eyes.

"You bastard," she hissed. "You complete and utter bastard. How dare you do that to me?"

I took an involuntary step backward at the unexpected attack. "What are you talking about?" I asked.

"This," she cried. She stepped forward, grabbed my hand and slapped a piece of paper down into it. "I'm talking about *this*, you son-of-a-bitch."

I opened the piece of paper and stared down at it without comprehension for a second. It was Braedon's note. I had completely forgotten about it. Then I knew what Glynnis was referring to. She had picked up immediately on the significance of Braedon's last line about neither of us needing the complications.

"You're sleeping with that bitch, aren't you?" Glynnis's voice grated, raw and harsh. "You're fucking that slut—"

"No," I said wearily. "I'm not sleeping with her or anybody else. Not even with you lately, it would seem."

"Don't you dare lie to me," she shrieked. "God damn you, I can tell. I can tell you've been with someone else."

"You're being stupid." Then I got angry, too. "And just what the hell were you doing going through my wallet? You have no right to invade my privacy like that."

"Your privacy." She laughed shrilly. "Jesus Christ. Yes, I guess you could call evidence of adultery private."

"There wasn't any adultery."

"I don't believe you. Is she good, Colin? Does she writhe and moan and tell you what a marvellous lover you are? Does she beg to have you inside her?"

"Dear God, Glynnis—"

"Because you are, you know. You are good in bed. I should know. I used to be able to turn you on like that whore can now."

"She's not a whore, and don't you dare to call her one," I said softly. "She's a wonderful—a"

"A wonderful what? A wonderful fuck?"

I clenched both fists at my side, then had to turn away abruptly. "She's gone, Glynnis. That note was written a long time ago. She quit and went away because apparently she had a lot more decency and integrity than I did. She didn't want to get involved in a sordid little affair."

"Decency? Integrity? She got her filthy hooks into you, though, didn't she?"

I turned back to her, too angry for caution. "No, she didn't. I wanted her. God, how I wanted her. I wanted to take her to bed and make love to her and never stop. But she walked away from it. I wanted her more than I ever wanted you, and she walked away because she knew it wasn't right."

"You bastard! You rotten, lousy bastard!"

Then she scared the hell out of me. She came at me, fingernails like claws aimed at my face, her mouth twisted into an ugly line. I grabbed her wrists, held her away. She fought like a wild thing, snarling and trying to bite. All I wanted to do was keep her nails away from my eyes. Then she got one hand free and slapped me across the cheek with all her strength. It stung like a burn and infuriated me.

Blind fury exploded in my chest. I caught myself with my hand raised, palm out, ready for the open-handed slap. Shocked and frightened, all the anger draining out of me like water out of a broken pitcher, I stepped back, pushed her away with enough force to make her stumble backward into the kitchen counter. She reached furiously for a kitchen paring knife. I caught her hand and pulled her away.

"I hope you die," she screamed, sobbing. "I hope you crash and lie in the dark and die all alone."

I stood gasping for breath, watching her, still holding her wrist. The thought of what I had almost done left me cold and shivering. I had nothing for contempt for men who beat women and I had just come too close to being one of them

"You should have hit me," she whispered. "Maybe it would make you feel like a god damned man again."

I took a deep breath before I spoke and tried to keep my voice steady and level. I unwrapped her fingers from the handle of the knife and laid it on the counter out of her reach. "Maybe I'd feel more like a man around you if you had ever stopped acting like a spoiled adolescent too wrapped up in yourself to be a real woman," I said softly.

"You're the only man who thinks that way then," she said.

"What's that supposed to mean?"

"Nothing." She rubbed her wrists where I'd held them. "You hurt me, damn you." She turned and stumbled from the room. Moments later, the bedroom door slammed. Hard.

I looked at the doorway where she had disappeared. My wife. The woman I had vowed to love, honour and cherish, until death do us part. My wife, the woman who had made those reciprocal vows that now meant little or nothing to either of us. God help us both. I turned and went to the guest bathroom. I caught a glimpse of myself in the mirror above the marble sink. The outline of her hand was deeply imprinted on my cheek, livid white and outlined in red. It would take a while to fade.

I took a shower, but the hot water couldn't sluice away the bleak despair that flooded in waves through me. I stood under the rush of the needle spray of water and looked at the dismal and hopeless future. It was a dreary shambles and there was no way to set it right; no way to retrieve or save a marriage that had been a ghastly mistake almost from the first, a marriage that had never been based on trust or honesty. Glynnis's lies about her relationship with Carl Sievers had switched off my original reservations about her. Perhaps it was only a pendulum reaction that turned a physical attraction into what I translated as love. But it was far too late to wonder about that.

Her jealous reaction to what she interpreted as infidelity surprised me until I thought about it for a while. Then I knew it wasn't jealousy. It was fury because she thought that something that belonged to her might be taken away by someone else. She would have reacted with the same blind, unreasoning rage if someone had tried to steal her car or her jewellery.

That night the dream changed again. There was pain and fear and death in it. The thread of danger coalesced into the stark, grim reality of death. It brought me out of sleep crying out in terror and sent me to work still introspective and shaky. And later that day, even while the dream of death replayed itself in my mind, Glynnis found death on the highway as she drove to work.

I knew what I had to do. I had to take her ashes home to New York, and then I had to go home to Brindle Falls. As I walked blindly and unsteadily out of Brett Murphy's office, I took the wide gold band off the fourth finger of my left hand and dropped it into the pocket of my jacket.

CHAPTER FIFTEEN

Spring 1993

IN ANY event, it was almost six weeks before I could go home. I hadn't realized the amount of paperwork an accidental death generated, nor the time it took for the wheels of the law to grind slowly out of neutral into gear.

I was a mess, both physically and emotionally. I hadn't been able to sleep since Glynnis died, kept awake by the nightmares that attacked as soon as I closed my eyes. I couldn't eat. If my throat didn't close up so I choked on food, my stomach rebelled and rejected it. I looked at least ten years older. My eyes were sunken and hollow, and I had an unhealthy pallor. Sometimes a tremor I couldn't control began in my hands and lasted for many minutes.

I was, of course, on a monstrous guilt trip. I kept remembering that bitter quarrel Glynnis and I had the night before she died. Then, the next day, even while she had lain dead and I hadn't known it yet, I had been approaching the decision to divorce her. It was foolish and it was irrational, but I couldn't help connecting the quarrel with her accident. She had done that *see what you made me do* often enough. It terrified and nauseated me to think the accident might have been just one more in the series.

First there was the coroner's inquiry. I felt obligated to attend and listened while a witness told of Glynnis's car passing him. He had, he gravely told the Court, been doing a little over seventy miles per hour when Glynnis passed him going "like a bat out of hell." He saw her pull out to pass the semi, then seem to lose control and sideswipe the truck. Her car rolled spectacularly several times before coming to rest on its side in the ditch. The medical examiner reported no trace of alcohol, prescription or controlled substances in her blood, with the exception of acetaminophen. The coroner shook his head wearily, and officially noted her death as "misadventure" due to excess speed and inattention.

Glynnis had been a good driver, and well accustomed to travelling at well over the speed limit. I pondered how she might have lost control of her car at exactly the wrong moment.

I had her remains cremated and took her home to her father. The memorial service was short and private. Her father was there, of course, as well as her brothers, their wives and children, and a few friends. My parents had not been able to make it. They had been in Britain where my father was doing research for a biography of Sir Robert Herridge, one of the Knights Templar who made it alive through Black Friday, and fled the Holy Land back to Northern England. He had, apparently, been the model for Robert of Locksley, the real Robin Hood, or one of them at any rate. My parents had not left an itinerary with anyone. I hadn't been able to contact them by telephone until the morning of the funeral. The few of us laid Glynnis to rest beside her mother. During the interment, her father laid his hand gently on my shoulder as if both giving and taking comfort.

It was Mr. Alexander who took me to the law office. I was reluctant to go, but he insisted upon it. Glynnis had died intestate and I thought that would be the end of it. I knew the model agency would go to her partners as per their partnership agreement. I hadn't realized she had other assets besides the house. As it turned out, her mother had set up a sizeable trust fund for her, which had matured on her thirty-fifth birthday. Mr. Alexander made arrangements with the law firm that had administered the trust to have the money transferred to me, in spite of my protestations.

"I didn't marry her for her money," I told him.

"I know," he said. "But you are her nearest family now. The money should be yours, Colin."

"Can't you take it and maybe donate it to a good charity?"

"If you want to donate it, that's up to you. But it's your money now."

My money now. I looked at all those figures to the left of the decimal point and all I could feel was bewilderment. I tried not to think about it. Later when my head was clearer, I could sort out what to do with it.

Finally, there was the house. When everything in New York was finished, I went back to Seattle and packed the few things in the house I wanted to keep. There wasn't much. A few cartons of books. Two or three of my mother's watercolours. A few other odds and ends. These went into storage. I saw a real estate agent and signed all the papers to put the house up for sale. Then I went to see Brett Murphy and completed all the arrangements to take my leave of absence. When I left his office, I didn't know when or even if I'd be back. I didn't care.

For the first time in my life, I was helplessly adrift, without plans, without a goal, without direction. The really crazy thing was that I had money. Lots of it. The house would probably bring in a small fortune, even after paying off the balance of the mortgage, which was a lot smaller than I had thought it to be. Between that and the money Glynnis's mother had given her, it was more money than I'd ever dreamed of having. But it, too, didn't matter. It wasn't important. All it did was guarantee I could take as much leave of absence as I needed and not have to think about how I was going to support myself.

So, finally, I went home.

The Brindle Falls airport lay somnolently under the early spring sunshine. I flew the old Stinson. I had finished restoring it to factory fresh condition and it was a joy to fly. The only changes I'd made weren't apparent from the outside. I'd put in a full gyro panel, but left the twin venturi tubes attached to the fuselage on either side of the cowling because they looked right there. Besides, they were a back-up in case the vacuum pump ever packed in. I'd also added a modern nav and comm stack. I was pleased with the way the Stinson looked and flew. It was something I'd done with my own hands—an accomplishment.

I approached over the ocean. As I turned onto the base leg for Runway 26, I passed over my parents' house. A welcome sense of peace stole through me, a feeling that had been too long gone. I hadn't been home for nearly three years now. And that absence had felt like a hollow in my heart until now.

I turned final and the sun flashed into my eyes. With the power to the Franklin engine pulled back to idle, it was quiet in the cabin of the Stinson as the runway rose to meet us. I didn't even have to think consciously about the landing. I found the three-point attitude and the Stinson settled softly and gently onto the runway as if she had been doing it all her life and was as glad to return here as I was.

Nav met me as I taxied in. He said nothing, but helped me push the old aircraft into the hangar beside the Stearman. Both airplanes were of the same vintage. Perhaps they'd have a lot to talk about.

"I'll give you a lift home," Nav said.

"Thanks, Nav," I said. "But I'd rather walk. It's not that far."

He studied my face, his brow furrowed in concern. "You sure?"

"I'm sure. Thanks anyway." I started to go.

"Colin?"

I turned.

"Colin, I never had any kids of my own. I always sort of thought of you as my son, you know. I hate to see you like this. Is there anything at all I can do?"

I smiled wearily. "I'll be okay," I said. "I'm just tired. I need a rest, that's all."

"You sure, son?"

"Yes, I'm sure. Listen, you old cross-grained bear, don't you go taking this the wrong way, okay? But I always sort of looked on you as a second father."

That was the first time I ever heard Nav Harty laugh. He put one hand on my shoulder, squeezed it briefly, then turned and walked out of the hangar.

The grass along the side of the road was already turning brilliant green, starred with white and yellow daisies. Buttercups grew thickly in the ditch and morning glory, unfurling new leaves, rioted up the barbed wire fence that separated the airport from the road. I walked slowly and let the sun soak through my leather jacket and shirt into my back. I'd spent nine years walking this road to and from school. They had been happy years then. I needed somehow to recapture them.

The house stood at the end of the street. The only change I could see was that the barricade at the dead end of the street above the low cliff was now painted orange and white with a large reflective patch in the middle. I stood by the front gate for a few minutes and looked at the house. The old fashioned veranda surrounding it saved it from looking like a square, characterless wooden block. It was a low house, only one story, and not very big. But it was big enough to hold all the love that lived in it. There should still be some there for me.

I opened the gate. A large, longhaired cat, very formal in his black tux and white bib and spats, sat beneath the japonica bush and watched me as I walked up the path. That had to be Faversham, the cat who came to dinner as my mother put it. As was proper etiquette with a cat, I nodded to him gravely as I passed, and he blinked solemnly in acknowledgment.

I was halfway to the house when the door opened and my mother stepped out onto the wooden deck above the three stairs. She wore jeans and one of my father's shirts, the sleeves rolled up past her elbows. She waited for me to reach the bottom of the steps then silently opened her arms. I took the steps in one bound and clung to her like a child. Tears stung the backs of my eyes, flooding out to soak into the collar of her shirt. I had no idea why I was crying. It wasn't for Glynnis and I don't think the tears were for me. They were just there and nothing seemed to be able to stop them.

"Come into the house, Colin," my father said. I hadn't heard him approach. His arm fell across my shoulders.

Then, with my mother's arm around my waist and his arm still around my shoulders, the three of us went in together.

I managed to get myself under control once we were in the house. My mother sat me down at the table, then produced a pot of her own rose hip tea and a jar of wild honey to sweeten it. As she poured the tea into the big ceramic mugs, my father lit his pipe.

"I'm sorry we couldn't make the funeral, Colin," he said quietly.

"It's okay," I said listlessly. "Everybody understood."

"Are you all right?" my mother asked. "You look worn out and exhausted."

"I just need some rest," I said. "I've taken some time off work."

"You look so haggard," she said. "Perhaps you should see a doctor."

I shook my head. "No. I'll be okay." I looked at her, then at my father. "When the police came to tell me about Glynnis's accident, I was in Brett Murphy's office. I had just told him I needed some time off and I was starting to think about divorcing Glynnis. God, talk about timing, huh?"

My mother said nothing. I could see that she was saddened by Glynnis's death, but now, for the first time, I could see that she really had not liked my wife very much.

"Had you discussed that with Glynnis?" my father said.

"No. But we'd had another fight the night before. As usual, it was about something ridiculously stupid. But it was the last drop to make the cup overflow, I guess. I just decided I'd just about had enough."

"We're very sorry, Colin," my mother said.

"There's not much anyone can do about it now," I said.

"I sold the house. I don't want it. It was always her house more than it was mine anyway. You don't mind if I stay here for a while?"

"You know you never have to ask," my mother said with something close to reproach in her voice. It made me smile.

I went to bed late that night. My parents were already asleep when I put down the book I was trying to read and went to my bedroom. I undressed slowly. I was tired, but I didn't want to sleep. I knew that virulent dream was waiting for me. But maybe here, here where I had always felt safe and protected, maybe here the dream would let me rest.

But it was there again. The aircraft out of control. The rocky shore of the lake filling the windscreen. The pain, the terror, the despair. The woman I loved more than anything in the world calling my name and the stark, terrible knowledge that I'd never know my child, never see him born, never know how he grew up. My child would never know me, never know how much I loved him.

I awoke shouting. Someone was in the room with me, sitting on the edge of the bed. The dream wouldn't let go. I couldn't stop crying out for Judy. She was still calling me.

"Colin. Colin! Wake up. Colin, wake up. You're all right. *Colin.*"

A woman's hands touched my face, smoothed my hair back from my forehead. It was a long time before I knew it was my mother who sat there, her hair tumbled around her face, an old dressing gown wrapped around her. She must have turned on the light as she came in because it was glaring and bright in the room. My father stood behind her. He looked concerned, worried. Almost frightened. I gulped in several deep breaths then took my mother's hands and squeezed them briefly in what I hoped was reassurance.

"Nightmare," I said breathlessly. "Damned thing has really sharp edges. I'm okay now. Really. I'm sorry I woke you up."

"For a moment there, we were afraid we couldn't wake you up," my father said gravely.

Not waking up. Trapped forever in the endless cycle of the pain, the fear, the despair.... I shuddered.

"It's a recurring nightmare, isn't it?" my father said. "How long has this been going on?"

"Like this? Since shortly before Glynnis died," I said. "But it's just a continuation of something I've been dreaming all my life. It started turning bad off and on a couple of years ago."

"Maybe you'd better tell us about it," he suggested.

"Let's go into the kitchen," my mother said. "It's almost morning anyway. I'll make some coffee and we can talk about it."

They let me take my time about it. Neither of them pressed me to talk. My mother moved quietly about the kitchen as she made coffee. She brought it to the table presently, together with a plate of huge muffins.

"You kept calling for someone named Judy," she said eventually.

"I know." I smiled faintly and made a feeble attempt at a joke. "Don't worry, mother. It's not someone I've been having an affair with."

"Colin!" Indignation rather than shock in her voice. It made me smile and my father laugh.

I drank the coffee, trying to organize my thoughts. "Let's start out in left field," I said at last. "Remember when you told me that I was adopted?"

They both nodded.

"You said we'd moved here when I was six months old. Where did we live before? And was that where I was born?" My birth certificate said I was born in Portland, but I had been told that adoptive parents were allowed to put down the city where they lived when the child was adopted, just as they listed their own names rather than the real parents' names.

"We lived in Portland for about four months after we bought you home while Ian taught school there, before the first book was published," my mother said. "One of the things that the papers stipulated was that your birth be registered here."

"Isn't that rather strange?" I asked.

"We didn't question it," my father said. "We wanted you so much that we did exactly as we were told."

"You were actually born in Canada," my mother said. "In Edmonton. Ian was attending the University there on a one-year fellowship program."

"I was born in Edmonton?"

"Yes. At the University Hospital," my father said.

Somehow, I had been expecting that. Both times I had been in Edmonton, something strange and eerie had happened. "Was it an agency adoption or a private one?" I asked.

"Private," my father said. "We couldn't qualify for an agency there. We weren't Canadian citizens."

"That might make it easier," I said more to myself than to them. "Was it handled through a lawyer?"

"Yes," my mother said. "We never knew who the other lawyer was acting for. From something Alan let slip once, I got the impression it was an older man. Possibly a relative of your natural mother."

"How did you find out about me?"

My parents glanced at each other and I thought for a moment, they both looked a little guilty. "It was rather through the back door," my father said. "Alan Thurlow was in the law faculty. He lived next door to us. He knew we wanted to adopt a child because we couldn't have any of our own—"

"We tried for years," my mother said and placed her hand over his on the table. "We decided together that we had to adopt."

He squeezed her hand, smiled at her, and continued. "Anyway, one day Alan came over and told us that there might be a baby in the hospital available for us to adopt if we were interested. He didn't explain the circumstances, only that he had heard about it through a friend who was a doctor. We told him we were very interested and he said he'd get back to us the next day. He wasn't exactly secretive about it. Just circumspect in the extreme. But it wasn't any more than we'd expected. Back then, private adoptions weren't considered quite as respectable as they are today."

"He came back the next day," my mother said. "It was a little after noon, I remember. He told us the child's guardian was agreeable to a private adoption, and had stipulated that the adopting family be Catholic. Alan said that he would make all the arrangements with the other lawyer. Then he told us the child was a boy, very healthy, and was of a good family." She smiled a little. "I thought that was rather stuffy of him, but I was too happy to mind."

"He had all the papers ready for us to sign two days later," my father said. "That was on a Friday. On Saturday morning, he came over and drove us to the hospital where we picked you up from the nursery. You were only five days old." He laughed softly and shook his head, remembering. "The odd thing was that I thought you looked just like my grandfather. Actually, you still do."

"Tell him about his name, Ian," my mother said. "It might be important."

"My name?" I asked.

"You know how hospitals put identification bracelets on everybody," my father said. "With babies, all it usually says is Baby Boy Smith, or Baby Girl Jones. Yours said Baby Boy Colin."

"We had wanted to call you James, after my father," my mother said. "But somehow, the name Colin suited you, so we didn't change it. We just added James on after it."

"You're sure it wasn't a surname?" I asked quickly.

"I looked in the telephone book," my mother said. "And in the City Directory, too. I was curious. There wasn't a listing in either one of them for anyone with a surname like that. The closest thing I could find was Collins, with two *l*'s and an *s*."

"I thought as much," I said.

"What does this have to do with that terrible nightmare?" she asked.

I told them about the dream then, how it had begun when I was very young, how it had gradually changed over the years until it turned into the chilling nightmare it was now. I told them about the incidents in Edmonton. It took a long time. They listened quietly, without interrupting.

"Remember that day I came home and I asked you about reincarnation?" I asked my mother.

She nodded. "That was just before you started with Holiday West."

"Yes. And the day after my first trip to Edmonton, the first time I saw that old terminal building. I'm sure it wasn't my memory in that dream. I know it sounds crazy, but I think it was his, the pilot's. The man in my dream. His name is Colin, too. I don't know how I know this, but I know he was my natural father. And the woman in the dream, Judy. She was my mother." I laughed without humour. "Either that, or my mind really *has* snapped."

They said nothing for a long moment. Then my father rubbed his chin thoughtfully and knocked the dottle out of his pipe into an ashtray. "It sounds to me as if you'd better plan on another trip to Edmonton," he said. "I think I can find Alan Thurlow's address for you. It would be the best place for you to start looking, wouldn't it?"

PART TWO – THE SEARCH

Chapter Sixteen

1994

I DIDN'T leave Brindle Falls immediately. Once I had acknowledged and accepted the need to discover more about the man in my dreams, the man who had been my natural father, the urgency left me. When it was time, I would go north and look for him. In the interim, I slept long hours without dreams—or at least without dreams that I remembered. I felt almost tottery and fragile, like an ancient convalescent recovering from a long and debilitating illness, floating in a timeless limbo. I spent my days walking the beach and doing the minimal yard-work my parents' home required. The white area on my finger where my wedding band had been disappeared gradually with exposure to the sun. I developed a tentative relationship with Faversham, the cat, who was adamant in his refusal to accept familiarity, but would occasionally consent to having his ears or chin scratched as long as his great dignity could remain intact during the process.

My appetite returned. I ate hugely, then walked off the excess on the beach. I went to the *dojo* where Sensei Mashite still held classes. He was a little greyer now, but just as swift and deft and graceful as he had ever been. I discovered just how far out of shape I really was. I had difficulty keeping up with the green belts. Sensei Mashite expressed disappointment in me and made me work harder than he had ever made me work before. The murderous schedule he set for me would either, quite simply, get me back into shape in record time, or it would kill me.

I spent several hours a week at the airport. I didn't fly much, but spent a lot of time just talking with Nav Harty. I don't really remember what we talked about, but I laughed often and Nav smiled once or twice.

Spring came, then early summer and I healed. Then one morning early in July, I knew it was time. It was almost six months since Glynnis died, and I knew I had mended as much as I was going to here. The time had come to start my search in earnest.

I went to the airport and gave the Stinson a thorough going over, from prop hub to tail wheel, then walked home in the deepening blue dusk and packed what I needed to take with me in an easily carried canvas duffle bag. I left my uniforms hanging in the closet in my room, secure in plastic garment bags so they wouldn't get dusty. My mother was in the living room when I came out of the bedroom carrying the duffle bag.

"Tomorrow?" she asked, concern flickering in her eyes. "So soon?"

"It's time," I said. I put the duffle bag down by the front door, then reached out to take the hand she held out to me.

"What time will you go?"

"I thought I'd leave about seven," I said.

"You're going to fly that flimsy little airplane up there?"

I smiled. "Mother, if I look so good and fly so well after

I've spent forty-six years in the air as that Stinson has, I'll count it a life well spent."

She laughed. "You always will be an obdurate owl, won't you?"

"Quite likely. I suppose it's fate."

"We'll drive you to the airport in the morning."

"I'd rather walk," I said. "It's not far."

Both my mother and my father were up when I left the house in the morning. My mother hugged me, kissed my cheek. I thought I saw the gleam of tears in her eyes. My father hugged me, too. Hard. Then he stepped away.

"I hope you find what you're looking for, Colin," he said.

"I hope so, too," I replied.

"You keep in touch, now," my mother said. "Call us once in a while and let us know how you are. And remember that we love you very much."

"I'll be back when I've sorted it out," I said. I hugged them both, then turned my back on them and began to walk toward the airport.

Nav had pulled the Stinson out of the hangar. It stood gleaming in the early morning sun. I tossed the duffle bag in the back seat. My briefcase containing my maps, approach charts and flight planning sheets was on the right front seat and my headset hung on the rounded control yoke.

"She's all topped up with fuel and oil," Nav said. "I checked the tires for you, too. Everything looks good."

"Thanks, Nav," I said.

"You can use my office phone to check the weather and file your flight plan," he said.

"Thanks."

"How long are you going to be gone?"

"I don't know. As long as it takes, I guess."

"Don't make it too long, son," he said.

I had planned a leisurely trip. The first hop would not be a long one, just to Vancouver in British Columbia to clear customs. Then through the mountains to Edmonton. I might take it in two stages. I could buy Canadian VFR navigation charts in Vancouver. Once I had them, sorting out the best route through the mountains would be easy. The Stinson wasn't exactly what you could call a high performance aircraft. I wanted to keep it down below eight or nine thousand feet where it still had good performance. I could file IFR in it if I had to, but I preferred to stay VFR if I could possibly help it. Planning the trip in meticulous detail would help keep my mind off the enormity of what I was setting out to find. I could deal with that when I reached Edmonton once again.

Nav waited as I did the calculations for the trip and filed my flight plan. Then he walked out to the Stinson with me. He held out his hand.

"Good bye, son," he said. "Have a good flight."

"Good bye, Nav. See you later, hey?"

"You know where you can find me," he said. He turned and walked into the hangar without looking back.

I followed the coast up past Bellingham, then to Vancouver. The weather was beautiful, the sky a pale and clear blue. The mountains off my right wing were still capped with snow and looked achingly pure and clean against the sky.

This was the first time I had ever flown into Vancouver in anything smaller than a Lear, and the first time I had come in VFR. It was a lot more confusing than coming in IFR where all you have to do is read your approach chart, follow the instructions and do what you were told. But I got in without startling any of the Air Traffic Controllers or other traffic, or even myself. Once on the ground, ATC directed me to South Terminal, away from all the heavy iron. I found the Executive Flight Centre and parked my forty-six year old airplane in among the sleek corporate Lears and Citations and Westwinds. It was the oldest aircraft on the ramp, and the only taildragger.

As I climbed out, two men in the corporate pilot uniform of navy blue blazers and grey flannel slacks came out of the lounge area of the hangar. They stood a respectful distance away and waited until I had closed the door and began to walk toward them before they came forward.

"Beautiful old airplane," the older of the two said. He looked to be in his early fifties, enough grey at the temples to give him a distinguished look. "Did you restore it yourself?"

"Yes," I said. "It took me almost five years to do it."

"You sure did a hell of a good job," he said. "Mind if I look?"

"Go ahead." No real pilot touches someone else's airplane without express permission.

The younger man was perhaps a few years younger than I was, still in his late twenties. He grinned at me as the other man walked slowly around the Stinson, examining the fabric and paint work.

"Forty-five or forty-six Stinson?" he asked.

"Forty-six," I said. "It's a straight 108 with a Franklin 165 horse flat six engine."

"We fly that thing over there," he said, pointing with his chin to the Westwind 24. "Faster than this, but I'd bet this is more fun."

I glanced over at the Westwind. It bore a corporate logo

on the tail. When I looked a little closer, I saw it said Allgo Oil Co. and I remembered that Delaney Braedon had said she used to fly for Allgo Oil.

"Been with the company long?" I asked.

"Almost a year," he said.

"Then you wouldn't have known a friend of mine. Delaney Braedon. She flew for the company maybe three years ago."

"Mike would probably remember her."

The other man finished his inspection of the Stinson and joined us under the wing. "God, it's been a while since I saw an airplane like that," he said. "I'm Mike Robinson, by the way. That's Steve Yablonski."

"Colin Fraser," I said. "I used to know a girl who flew for Allgo a few years ago. Delaney Braedon?"

Robinson grinned. "I remember Delaney. She quit to go to work for a big charter outfit down in Seattle. 737's, I think. Hell of a good little pilot. We were really sorry to lose her. I can't remember the name of the outfit she went to work for down there."

"Holiday West," I said. "She was my first officer for a while. And you're right. She was a hell of a good pilot."

"She still with you?"

I shook my head. "No, she's been gone for almost a year. She's flying left seat in somebody's G-III now, I think. I haven't heard from her since she left."

"She sends the wife and me a Christmas card every year," Robinson said. "But I don't know where she is now. She and Marg were fairly good friends. My wife used to think Delaney needed someone to mother her."

"She was sort of a little bit of a girl," I said.

"We all liked her," he said. "Where are you heading?"

"I thought I'd take a swing up through the mountains to Edmonton," I said. "I've got some time off work and thought I'd do some exploring."

He laughed. "I thought all you American pilots took a jaunt up to Alaska when you went exploring."

"I might do that later." I grinned. "I haven't got a big enough supply of bug juice right now."

Robinson glanced at his watch. "We've got about half an hour before our passengers get back here," he said. "Can we buy you coffee?"

"Sure. I'm not in a hurry."

I purchased some VFR Navigation Charts or VNC's in the office and, over coffee, Robinson and Yablonski helped me figure out the best route through the mountains. The Canadian system for marking VFR routes through the mountains was the same as the one I was used to, a series of diamond shaped markings leading through the mountain passes. Some people call them diamond routes.

Given the performance of the Stinson, we decided that the best way to go would be up the Fraser Canyon to Lytton where the Thompson River flowed into the Fraser, then to follow the Thompson River to Kamloops where it split into the North and South Thompson. Following the North Thompson River to the Yellowhead route to Edmonton was a bit longer than following the South Thompson and picking up the Rogers Pass, but the Yellowhead was a broad, low pass. Yablonski said he'd flown it several times in light aircraft and liked it. There was an airstrip on the average of every forty miles so I'd never be more than twenty miles away from a good place to land if the weather came down. He told me the only place I might run into bad weather might be around Blue River, about a hundred and twenty miles north of Kamloops, but usually at this time of year, it was unlikely I'd run into anything really bad.

I thanked them for their help and sat there with the maps after they had left to meet their passengers. It was about three hundred miles to Kamloops. If I left after lunch, I'd have no problems making it there long before dark. From Kamloops, it was another five hundred miles through the passes to Edmonton. I could probably make it through the mountains before it got dark, but it might be easier if I stayed overnight in Kamloops. I didn't want to take a chance on getting caught in the mountains in the dark, and it wasn't as if I were in a tearing hurry. I could take my time.

I went to the desk and asked the consciously cute-as-a-bug receptionist about fuelling up the Stinson, then went out to watch the ramp rat as he climbed up onto a ladder and spread a foam rubber mat on the wing before he began pouring fuel into the tank. He was taking pains not to scratch or mar the paint on the wing, and he didn't let the heavy nozzle of the fuel hose rest on the wing. I was perhaps paying a premium price for the av-gas he poured into the tank, but service like that was worth the few extra cents a litre I paid for it. When he finished, he neatly folded the fuelling mat, put it back into his truck, and wiped up a few drops of fuel that had dribbled onto the wing. He grinned as I climbed up and double checked to see that the fuel caps were on tight, then he took the ladder and folded it back onto the hooks on the side of the truck. I went inside to pay for the av-gas.

He came inside a few minutes later. "Your oil is down about half a litre, sir," he said. "You might want to check it again and add a litre at your next stop. It should be okay until then."

I thanked him then asked about a good place to have lunch. He directed me to a place down the road a bit and offered to give me a lift. I refused with thanks and began walking. I saw him go out and insert another set of chocks under the tires of the Stinson.

The flight to Kamloops went easily. Again, I had perfect weather for it. It had been a long time since I had crossed the Rockies looking up at the mountain peaks or flying slowly enough to enjoy the scenery. I flew at 5,500 feet all the way. The route was easy to follow, almost unmistakable. Below me were both a main river and a wide highway. I had to smile as I remembered the joking interpretation of IFR—I Follow Roads.

The Kamloops airport sat with the button of Runway 08 almost on the shore of Kamloops Lake. I had been told that some of the best trout and steelhead fishing in the world was to be found around here. I had never been much of a fisherman, but I had friends who came up this way every year for the fishing and raved about it for the rest of the year. Kamloops itself sat at the northern tip of the Okanagan Desert. The mountains are covered with scrub pine, sagebrush and cacti. It's the second oldest geological region in North America. It hasn't changed much since the last glaciers retreated north all those eons ago. The mountains are weathered and rounded, all the sharp edges eroded away. It looked dry and sere to me, but there was an austere beauty to it that was strange and compelling.

The ground controller directed me to a spot where I could tie down for the night. I secured the aircraft, tying down the wings and tail firmly, then went off to find a taxi, a motel and a meal, in that order.

In the morning, I had a leisurely breakfast, then went to the airport and filed a flight plan for Edmonton Municipal Airport.

CHAPTER SEVENTEEN

THE TRIP through the Yellowhead was a good one. I was relaxed and content, almost happy, as I left Kamloops under a cloudless blue sky and wound my way around the shoulder of the mountains into the North Thompson Valley. There was nothing like flying a forty-five-year-old airplane to get back to the fundamentals of flying.

Not more than twenty miles north of the city, the country changed. It was no longer dry, desert country. The low, rounded old mountains were covered with pine, spruce, fir, poplar and aspen. This was cattle and timber country I was overflying now, open range country a lot of it. One by one the little towns slipped away under the wings. Heffley Creek, Louis Creek, Barriere, Little Fort, Clearwater. Tiny little towns, most of them hardly big enough to qualify for the designation. Nearly every one of them contained a lumber mill, the dead cones of the slash burners marking where the towns lay just as surely as grain elevators on the prairies mark the towns there.

At Clearwater, the highway and the river began to bear more eastward than north. I crossed Avola, then Blue River, then Valemount. Valemount was in the middle of the Rocky Mountain Trench. The Trench looks as if some playful giant had built himself a range of mountains, then ran the heel of his hand right down the middle to smooth out a broad, deep valley that stretched farther than the eye could see north and south. It was there I met the only other aircraft I saw on the whole trip through the mountains. As I came out into the valley, I looked up to see a Navajo coming down the Trench from the north. He was about a thousand feet higher than I was. He waggled his wings to show me he'd seen me, and I returned the gesture. Seconds later, my radio, which had been tuned to the Flight Service Enroute frequency, came to life.

"Stinson at Valemount, this is Navajo Fox Charlie Delta Delta." The voice was female. "If you're heading north, we can give you a pirep if you want one, friend."

"Delta Delta, Stinson November 328 Yankee. I'm heading east to Edmonton, thanks anyway."

"Okay, 28 Yankee. Have a nice flight."

"Will do. And you have a good flight, too."

The Navajo was already out of sight to the south.

I left Highway 5 at Valemount and picked up Highway 16. It disappeared into a narrow cleft in the mountains. As soon as I turned the corner, I came face to face with Mount Robson, the highest point in the Canadian Rockies. That mountain was really worth looking at. It soared to almost thirteen thousand feet, and it was one of the most impressive looking chunks of granite and snow I had ever seen. It stood high and broad, and almost isolated in its wide valley, towering above the surrounding peaks. Trailing from its summit like the pennon from a castle turret was a long streamer of cloud. It made me in my Stinson feel very small and insignificant and transient, and it made me wish I had brought a camera with me.

As soon as I crossed the Great Divide, I picked up the Athabasca River which eventually flowed into the MacKenzie River and then into the Arctic Ocean. The glacier melt in the river had given it an odd colour, almost a bright turquoise. It led me to Jasper.

Just past Jasper, the mountains seemed to show more sheer rock cliffs than they had before. I was still at 5,500 and more than 3,000 feet above the valley floor. I glanced out my side window and there on the rock cliff, just at my eye level, stood five mountain goats. They stood on the impossibly sheer face of the cliff and calmly watched me go by. You had to wonder how they got there, and how they managed to get back down to the grassy valley floor without needing a parachute.

I passed a wide valley that branched off to my right. It led to the Columbia Ice Fields where three great rivers arose, the Columbia that flowed west, the Athabasca which flowed north and the Saskatchewan that flowed east. I decided you tend to miss a lot when you do most of your flying at altitudes above twenty-five thousand feet.

Only a few miles past Jasper, two rock buttresses curved around to flank the river and the highway like an old castle gate. Once through there, I was out of the mountains. The country was suddenly rolling foothills, thickly timbered but giving quickly over into prairie and aspen parkland.

I passed over the Jasper-Hinton airport, a long, narrow strip of pavement sitting in isolated splendour on the top of a butte, and checked my fuel gauges. The Stinson's range was five hundred miles, but I had almost a quarter tank in each wing. I'd picked up a pretty good tailwind through the mountains, so when I did a groundspeed check, I decided to forego refuelling at Edson and continue on to Edmonton, only another hour and a quarter from Hinton.

Just to the east of Edson, getting into the real prairie country, I saw an oil well, the pump nodding and dipping. It looked like a patient, stodgy long-neck bird with a big beak bobbing up and down unperturbed by its isolation.

Eventually, the smudge of the city showed up over the horizon. I consulted my Flight Supplement, then descended to 3,500 and tried to figure out which of the little towns below was Spruce Grove, the VFR reporting point for entering the Advisory area. I switched one radio to pick up the Automatic Terminal Information Service and the other to 118.8, the VFR Advisory frequency. I listened to the ATIS, reset my altimeter, then pressed my push-to-talk button to activate the microphone.

"Municipal Advisory, it's Stinson November 328 Yankee, three thousand, five hundred, over Spruce Grove, inbound for landing with the ATIS."

"Two Eight Yankee, Edmonton Advisory, roger. Report to the Tower, 119.1 over the West City Limits. What was your point of departure, sir?"

"We're out of Kamloops on a VFR flight plan to Edmonton."

"Roger."

Over the west city limits, the tower cleared me for the left base for Runway 30. I descended to thirty-two hundred, found the airport and slotted myself in behind an Air BC Dash-8.

I steeled myself for dealing with visions of a thirty-year-old airport, but nothing untoward happened. I landed, turned off onto the taxiway, and taxied past the terminal building, which was the modern brick and glass structure, to the Avitat hangar. There was no sign of the old bow-shaped white terminal building, no sign of the old hangars. This was just another airport today. The terminal ramp contained two Canadian Airlines blue and white 737's snugged up against the jetways, an Air BC BAe 146 by the other, and a few Time Air Dash-8-300's. The usual assortment of light twins, singles and corporate jets crowded the ramps in front of the Avitat and Skyharbour Fixed Base Operators, and a gaggle of light singles was parked almost everywhere you looked. It wasn't a really big airport, but it looked like a busy one. I had been here twice before, but I had never really seen it. One trip had been at night, the other had been in the middle of a blizzard, not exactly conducive to sightseeing.

I parked where the ramp rat with the martialling batons indicated I should, then climbed out and stretched the kinks out of my back as he slipped a pair of chocks under the right main wheel.

"Do you need fuel, sir?" he asked.

"Please," I said. "Hundred low lead, I guess."

"Will you be staying long?"

"Probably a while," I said. "At least a week, anyway. Any chance of keeping it in the hangar?"

"You can ask at the front desk, sir," he said and pointed at the building just to the south east of the hangar.

I made the arrangements with the girl behind the counter to hangar the aircraft, handed her my credit card, then asked about rental cars and a hotel.

"There are car rental booths over in the terminal building, sir," the girl said. "And the Edmonton Inn, right across the street there, is a good hotel. I'll get one of the guys to give you a lift over to the terminal if you'd like."

"I can walk, thanks," I said.

I got my duffle bag, my briefcase and headset out of the Stinson, then walked over to the terminal building. I rented a Sundance at the Thrifty counter and found it in the bottom level of the parking garage. I locked my stuff in the trunk and went back into the building to the Airport Manager's Office upstairs. The woman behind the counter smiled at me as I walked up.

"Can I help you, sir?" she asked.

"I don't know if you can or not," I said. "Are you the Duty Manager?"

She smiled again. "For my sins. What can I do for you?"

"I'm just up from Seattle, and I'm sort of interested in the history of this airport. I wondered if you had anything— any literature—you could let me have to read on it."

"I think I've got just the thing around here somewhere," she said. "We're sort of proud of our history. This was the first licensed municipal airport in Canada. It's been here since 1926. Just a minute. I'll see what I can locate for you."

She came back with a thin booklet bound in a blue cardboard cover. "This was published almost ten years ago, but it should give you some information," she said. "If you need more, you might try the Aviation Museum downtown, or the Aviation Council in the General Aviation Centre just east of this building."

"What I'm really interested in is what it was like here in the late fifties and early sixties," I said.

The Duty Manager laughed. "Well, that was a bit before my time. Let me think. About the only person I know of who might have been around here then is Rich Duggan. He's a pilot with Canadian, and I think he's been around since just after the war. You might try him. I don't have a phone number for him, but they should be able to help you downstairs at the Canadian office."

196

"I'll try him," I said. "Thanks."

It was close two o'clock and I hadn't eaten since I left Kamloops at nine-thirty. There was a restaurant and lounge in the terminal building just down the hall from the Duty Manager's office. I found a table by the window overlooking the ramp and ordered a hamburger and fries. I opened the booklet the woman had given me and began to read. It gave me a general overall history of the airport, but it didn't contain the specifics I wanted. There was a picture of the old terminal building. The caption told me it had been built during the war and torn down in 1974 to make way for the new terminal building, the one in which I sat now.

Interestingly enough, the walls of the Air Harbour Restaurant all around me were hung with old pictures. Most of them seemed to date back to the late twenties and the thirties. Bush pilots, mostly, and bush planes. Old Fairchilds and Gull-wing Stinsons and Norsemen. Beech 18's, Ford Tri-motors and Wacos. Even an Avro Avian. The pilots wore thick, heavy furs and leathers. A lot of them looked to be up to their knees in snow. There was one picture of three Otters, the larger cousin of the Beaver, in formation. The caption identified them as belonging to Wardair. That made me smile. Wardair was running luxury Boeing 747's the last I heard before it was bought out by Canadian a while ago. It was a long way from a brace and a half of de Havilland Otters to 747's.

The Edmonton Inn backed onto the same street as the terminal building. It was hardly worth moving the rental car to get there. It probably took longer to exit the airport parking garage and negotiate the block into the hotel parking lot than it would have taken to walk. I checked in, took a shower and changed, then sat down and picked up the phone book.

There was only one listing for Alan Thurlow, Barrister and Solicitor, and that was an office listing. I could find no home listing. Since it was Saturday, there wasn't much chance I could catch him at his office. I would have to wait until Monday morning.

I had not been expecting to be unable to locate Alan Thurlow. Somehow, it never occurred to me he might have an unlisted home phone number. It left me feeling curiously deflated and at loose ends. What was I going to do until Monday morning? I realized that I had been expecting to find Thurlow immediately, talk with him and solve my mystery all in one fell swoop. Now I knew it wasn't going to be that easy. I wondered a bit morosely what sights Edmonton had to amuse the random tourist.

I flipped through the phone book again. There were several listings for Canadian Airlines. Flight Operations or Crew Scheduling weren't among them, but I knew they wouldn't be. I called the Executive Offices, got a recording, then tried the number listed for Baggage Services. It was most probably located in the Terminal Building.

A woman with a pleasant, melodious voice answered on the fifth ring.

"My name is Colin Fraser," I said. "I'm a Captain with Holiday West Airlines out of Seattle. I need some information and I wondered if you could help me."

The woman laughed. "Don't tell me we've lost your luggage, Captain," she said.

"No, nothing like that."

"Thank God."

"I'm actually looking for one of your pilots, a friend of a

friend. Captain Duggan. Rich Duggan. I wonder if I could speak to someone in Crew Sked who could tell me when I could catch him at the airport."

She hesitated. "I'm not supposed to transfer calls through to there."

"I know," I said. "We don't, either. Look, I'm just over at the Edmonton Inn. If you like, I can come over and show you my company identification. I'm a card-carrying ALPA member."

She hesitated again. "Well, look. I shouldn't say anything, but I know Rich is out of town for a while. He's due back on Thursday. Why don't you drop around and come to the ops office. We're on the main floor by the cafeteria. You might catch him there."

I thanked her and hung up. Then I laughed and shook my head in mild exasperation with myself. That was real bright of me. Exactly what would I have said to Duggan if I had found him? Tell him I was looking for my natural father and I thought his name was Colin, no known last name, and he might possibly have flown out of this airport thirty-two years ago? I think....

Obviously I needed a lot more information before I went to see Duggan. And just as obviously I had to think this thing through a little more before I went kiting off into the blue.

I put the phone book away and went to stand by the window. My room was in the back of the hotel and faced out over the parking lot and the airport. I had, I realized, pinned all of my hopes on Alan Thurlow. I hadn't once stopped to think about what I would do if he couldn't or wouldn't help me. I began to wonder if he had ever known the names of my natural parents. My mother had spoken of a guardian who was possibly a relation of my natural mother's, whom I was beginning to think of as Judy. It was quite possible that this relation had a different last name than Judy and her Colin. But at least it might give me a place to start looking.

But there was no use crossing all those bridges yet. In the meantime, in accordance with good flight planning tactics, it wouldn't hurt to thrash out Plan B and Plan C just in case Plan A came up blank.

CHAPTER EIGHTEEN

I SLEPT late Sunday morning. I got up about ten and wandered down for breakfast at the hotel restaurant. Then, because once an airport brat, always an airport brat, I walked across the back parking lot to the airport and ended up at the Edmonton Flying Club. I remembered Braedon telling me she had learned to fly here. I wondered where she was now. Nobody at Holiday West knew; nobody had heard from her since she left. She hadn't kept in touch with anyone as far as I knew. But where ever she had gone, she was gone forever from my life. I had blown any chance I might have had with her that night in Chicago.

The upstairs lounge at the Flying Club opened onto a balcony overlooking the ramp. In the heat of a summer morning, it was a pleasant place to sit with a cold ginger ale and watch airplanes. The Flying Club was busy. There was a steady parade of Cessna 152's and 172's onto and off of the ramp. It was a fairly good sized operation.

I was leaning on the balcony rail when a Gulfstream G-IV taxied past. There were two very young off-duty instructors standing next to me, arms resting on the rails. One of them said in a tone of wistful longing, "I asked Santa Claus for one of those last Christmas."

The other one didn't take his eyes off the sleek corporate jet as it moved sedately down the taxiway. "That thing's as big as a Dash-8," he said. "Look at those winglets. God, that's a pretty airplane. Highland's new one, I guess."

"Yeppers. Time to update my resume for them, I think."

"Heh. While you're dreaming, ask for Julia Roberts as a cabin attendant, too."

I smiled to myself. Nothing had changed since I was a flight instructor. They still served their time paying their dues and hungered after bigger, faster, sleeker airplanes. Higher, farther and faster. *Real jobs*, they're called. It didn't seem to matter whether you were north or south of the border. Aviation was aviation.

The day passed eventually. I went back to the hotel for dinner, then bought a copy of a Canadian flying magazine and a paperback and took them back to my room. Again, I slept without dreaming.

At eight-thirty in the morning, I called the number listed in the phone book for Alan Thurlow and made an appointment to see him at ten. I got lost twice trying to find his office which was on the south side of the river, but eventually located it in an office block that was part of a strip mall.

He was on the third floor. I gave my name to the receptionist and settled down with a magazine until Thurlow's secretary came out to call me.

The man who rose to meet me from behind the desk was in his early forties. I stared at him blankly. He was much too young to be the man who had arranged the adoption for my parents. He wouldn't have been much more than a young boy himself when I was born.

"You're Alan Thurlow?" I said. "I'm sorry. I was expecting a much older man."

He smiled. "You must be thinking of my father," he said. "Sit down. Mr. Fraser, is it? What can I do for you?"

"I don't know if you can do anything at all," I said. "I suppose I really have to see your father to get the information I need."

"My father died almost five years ago, Mr. Fraser. I've taken over his practice. What do you need?"

I swallowed my disappointment and took in a long breath. This was not working the way I had hoped it would.

"Maybe you could tell me why you wanted to see my father," he said.

I sat back in my chair. "It's a strange request, I suppose," I said. "Almost thirty-three years ago, your father arranged a private adoption for Ian and Aislinn Fraser, my parents. I wanted to talk to Mr. Thurlow to see if I could find out anything about my natural parents. I find myself in a position where I need to know who they were. The only thing I know about them is that they both died very shortly after I was born."

He leaned back in his chair and regarded me thoughtfully. "I remember Mr. and Mrs. Fraser, I think," he said. "They lived next door to us for a year when I was nine or ten. He's a tall, redheaded man, isn't he? And your mother's an artist?"

"Yes, that's them," I said and smiled. "They haven't changed much. If you've taken over your father's practice, would you have access to his old files? There might very likely be something in them that could help me."

He shook his head slowly, regretfully. "I'm afraid I can't help you at all there, Mr. Fraser," he said. "It's not that I wouldn't want to help you. If the information was available, I'd have to go through all sorts of channels to get the consent of the other parties before I could release any of it to you. But in any event, that won't be necessary. It's our policy to destroy all closed files that are older than fifteen or twenty years, depending on the type of action involved, if there's no chance of further action occurring on them. An adoption file would probably have been destroyed at least twelve years ago. There's no way I could retrieve the information."

"Would there be any way I could find out who the lawyer who acted for the other party was? Perhaps I could see him and explain the situation to him."

"That could be almost as difficult," he said. He was silent for a moment, frowning in contemplation. He had a habit of tenting his fingers and tapping his forefingers against his lips when he was deep in thought. Finally, he reached out for the telephone and pressed two numbers. "Cindy? See if you can find me a telephone number for Carolyn Mason, will you? Bring it in here when you've got it." He looked up at me. "Carolyn Mason was my father's secretary for nearly fifty years. When he died, she retired. If anyone can help, she probably could. But she might not remember much about a file as old as the one you want."

"It's worth a try," I said.

"Yes, certainly it might well be worth a try."

The secretary brought in a slip of paper and put it on his desk. She smiled at me briefly as she slipped out again.

"I don't know if I can catch her at home," he said. "She's one of those sprightly old ladies who seem to spend most of their days moving at full speed all the time. She does a lot of volunteer work. Very active." He glanced at the slip of paper, then dialled a number. After a few minutes, it was obvious there was no answer and he replaced the handset. "Not home," he said. "And no answering machine." He tapped his lips again. "Look, what I'll do is keep trying to get in touch with her. I want to explain to her what you need. I can't let her release any information she might remember before we check with the other parties, but I'll have her call you and let you have the name of the other lawyer if she can remember that. How does that sound?"

"It will have to do, I suppose. Thank you."

"I think I can appreciate how you feel. I've got another client right now who's looking for her natural parents. It can be a long, frustrating search, especially if the natural parents don't particularly want to be found. That doesn't really apply in your case, I suppose, but there are still conventions to follow."

"Suppose Mrs. Mason can't remember anything about the file," I said. "Where would you suggest I try next?"

"It was a private adoption, but you might try talking to Social Services. They might do a home study in cases like that, I think. Although they might not have, seeing it was over thirty years ago. They can be quite adamant about not releasing any information without a court order. That's assuming they have any information in the first place. I have a feeling though, that thirty years ago, they stayed out of private adoptions."

"Anywhere else? How about court records? There must have been papers filed at a court house somewhere."

"You're going to run into the same problem there as here," he said. "Records are destroyed after a certain number of years. Especially civil ones."

"Vital statistics probably can't help. My birth certificate shows I was born in Portland."

He looked up quickly. "It does? That's highly unusual."

"My parents said it was part of the adoption agreement."

"It's an extremely unconventional agreement, then," he said, frowning. "I can't see my father arranging something like that, and I can't see your parents agreeing to it."

I smiled slightly. "If you knew my parents, you wouldn't say that. Both of them are completely wonderful people, but you couldn't call them exactly worldly and highly sophisticated in their knowledge of the intricacies of the legal system. All they wanted was a child and they did as they were instructed to get one."

"Highly unusual," he repeated. "But if my father arranged it, then it must have been legally binding." He smiled. "My father was sometimes unorthodox in his methods, but he could draw up a legal contract that was tighter than a miser's purse."

"How about hospital records. They might have records of deaths, mightn't they? My natural mother died shortly after I was born. They might have something on file. It wouldn't be too difficult to trace a woman who had died shortly after giving birth on a given week."

"Same problem of time, I think. No public institution can keep records forever. They'd run out of storage space. You might try, though. I'm very much afraid, though, Mr. Fraser, that you're going to run into that same brick wall almost everywhere. Most hospitals don't keep the files on deceased patients forever, even on microfiche. It's the time factor, in a lot of instances. In others, it might just prove to be the privileged information roadblock. If it *does* turn out to be just that, though, I might be able to help you there. There are ways of extracting information from even the most recalcitrant set of civil servants. It would take time, though."

"Time is one thing I have in plenty," I said. "May I retain you to act for me in this?"

"Most certainly."

I brought out my cheque book and wrote a cheque for a thousand dollars. "This is drawn on my bank in Seattle," I said. "You might have to mail it to them to get it certified."

He smiled. "That won't be necessary. What time frame are we dealing with here? I'm going to need dates that are as exact as we can get them."

"I was born on September 18, 1960. According to my mother, I was five days old when I was adopted, so that would make it the 23rd. All the documentation was completed in those five days."

He smiled faintly. "A miracle of speed for legal papers to get drawn up and executed. Where are you staying in town?"

"I don't have a permanent address yet. I'm at the Edmonton Inn, near the airport. I'll probably look for an apartment. I wanted to spend a while looking around on my own." I slipped in a little white lie. "From something my mother said that your father let slip, I have the impression my natural father might have been a pilot. Aviation isn't a large community. I might be able to find out something there."

"Are you a pilot?"

"Yes. I'm a captain for Holiday West Airlines out of Seattle. I've taken a leave of absence to see if I can find my natural parents." I smiled. "The search for roots, I guess."

"Why don't you leave the hospital and the Social Services Agencies to me," he said. "I'll write a few letters and get them into the mail tonight. Letters from a law firm sometimes have a greater effect than private enquiries. If any information is forthcoming, we should have it within a week. If I think of any other people I should be contacting, I'll write them, too, and provide you with copies of the letters."

We talked for a little while longer. I gave him all the information I had while he made rapid notes. Finally, I got to my feet. "Thank you.". I held out my hand. "It was nice meeting you."

"And you, too, Captain Fraser." His grip was firm. "I must warn you, though, this is very likely going to prove to be a long, drawn out process. You mustn't get your hopes too high for a quick solution."

"I might have hoped for a quick solution if your father was still alive," I said. "But I think you've convinced me of the error of my thinking."

He laughed. "All we can do is our best," he said. "Still, I'll have Carolyn call you when I can get in touch with her. If she remembers the other lawyer, I'll certainly be in touch with him at the earliest possible moment."

"Who knows? We might luck out."

"We might. It would be nice if we did."

But we didn't.

Two hours later I got a call at the hotel from Carolyn Mason. She had a bright, bird-like voice and sounded as sharp as the leading edge of a fighter jet wing. But she didn't have any information for me.

"I'm terribly sorry, Captain Fraser," she said. "I worked with Mr. Thurlow senior for forty-six years, you know. We handled so many cases, so many files. I had to wrack my brains but I do remember a private adoption he arranged for some friends of his, but I honestly don't remember a thing about the file except that the adoptive parents had a Scottish name. I know now it was Fraser, because of your name, but that's all I remember. I must have typed up all the documents and written letters to the other solicitor, but I can't remember who he was. It was such a long time ago, you know."

"Nearly thirty-four years," I said.

"Yes. I do hope you find out about your natural parents, young man. I think it's rather sweet that you're trying. I wish I could be of more help to you."

"Thank you for trying anyway, Mrs. Mason. I appreciate you calling me."

"I wish I could have helped." And she hung up.

I was at loose ends again. I didn't feel like reading, and I didn't feel like tangling with the streets of an unfamiliar city, so I changed into jeans and an old light-weight denim shirt and wandered back over to the airport. I spent a long time studying the pictures on the wall of the Air Harbour Lounge, and eventually sat down at a table near a window and ordered a drink.

The ramp outside was nearly deserted for a while, then suddenly filled up as four or five aircraft arrived within ten or fifteen minutes of each other. Passengers scurried back and forth, then all the aircraft left. Over on the Avitat ramp beyond the terminal apron, the Gulfstream G-IV stood looming large over the smaller Citations and Cheyennes, Navajos and twin Cessnas.

The G-IV was a pretty airplane. I didn't know much about them. I'd never seen one up close before. I wondered if I might be able to get a closer look at it, so I paid my tab and left the terminal.

It was only a short walk to the Avitat hangar. I showed the girl at the desk my pilot license, explained about my Stinson being in their hangar. She let me through the door onto the ramp. I took a long, slow walk around the G-IV. It was a lot sleeker than a 737, and probably travelled at the same speed, if not faster. It was certainly a more luxuriant method of travel. Definitely one pretty airplane.

I was standing there admiring the tall, swept back T-tail when there was a light touch on my elbow. Someone said, "Colin?"

I turned and looked straight down into Delaney Braedon's wide and astonished hazel eyes.

CHAPTER NINETEEN

FOR WHAT seemed like a very long time, Braedon and I simply stood there and stared at each other. Her hair was still the short, undisciplined cap of sandy-brown curls. The breeze lifted several and tumbled them over her forehead and she raised a hand to brush them back. She was dressed in jeans, joggers and a bright yellow scoop neck tee shirt that revealed the dusting of freckles scattered across her collar bones, and it occurred to me that, except for that night in Chicago when she had worn a green bathrobe, this was the first time I had ever seen her when she wasn't wearing the Holiday West uniform. She looked even smaller than I remembered. Her eyes and her smile hadn't changed at all.

Finally, we both spoke at once. "What on earth are you doing here?" she asked, and I said, "Where the hell did you spring from?" Then we both laughed a little self-consciously.

"You first," I said. "What are you doing here?"

"I live here," she said. She gestured to the G-IV behind me. "That's mine. I've been working for Highland Explorations since I left Seattle. I just brought this up from

Arizona yesterday and I came out to arrange for hangarage. We keep both our airplanes here."

"I saw you come in yesterday, then," I said. "I was over there at the Flying Club when you taxied past. I didn't know it was you." I laughed. "I guess I have to call you Captain Braedon now, do I? That's an impressive chunk of iron, that is."

"I like it," she said. "It's not a 737, but it's pretty nice. Kind of a rush to fly. What are you doing here, Colin? This is a long way from Seattle."

"I'm on holiday, I guess you could say," I said. "I have some business here. I flew in on Saturday. My old Stinson's in the hangar here, tucked in between a Westwind and a Citation. Technological juxtaposition."

She smiled. "Are you going to show it to me?"

"If you like."

We went into the hangar where she made the proper delighted remarks and showed the correct reverence for age and dignity to the old bird. When she was done, we walked together back out into the bright sunshine and stood while the silence built up awkwardly between us.

I glanced at my watch. It was only a little after one. "You don't look as if you have to work right now," I said at last. "Could I buy you a Coke or a coffee or lunch or something?"

"If you give me fifteen minutes or so to go in and make the arrangements for this beast," she said. "Then we could go over to the Flying Club and have a sandwich or something. Or to the cafeteria in the terminal building if you'd rather."

"The Flying Club will be fine."

I trailed after her into the office. She spoke with the girl behind the counter for a while. As she was turning away, a man came through the door from the parking lot out front. He walked up to her and put his arm around her shoulders. She smiled up at him and laughed at something he said.

"Colin," she said and beckoned to me. "I'd like you to meet Mark Strang. Mark, Colin Fraser. Colin was my captain when I flew for Holiday West."

Strang removed his right arm from around Braedon's shoulders and held out his hand to me. "I've heard a lot about you, Captain Fraser," he said with a smile. "I fly right seat for the Wee One here, and she's always telling me I'd never get away with half the stuff I do if I flew for the captain she used to fly with."

I took the offered hand. "I didn't realize I was such a martinet," I said.

"I keep telling Mark I don't have nearly as good a first officer as you did," Braedon said demurely.

"That's probably true," Strang said and laughed. "But not all of us can be perfect."

"Don't let her kid you," I said. "She was irreverent, flip and facetious most of the time. But I'll grudgingly admit that she could fly very well."

Braedon made a face at me. "We were just going over to the Flying Club for a sandwich, Mark," she said. "Want to come?"

"I'd love to," he said. "But I'm meeting a flight in about ten minutes. My mother-in-law is coming to stay for a while so she can give Rhona a hand with the baby when it comes."

"You mean she hasn't had that kid yet?" Braedon asked.

"It's due tomorrow," he said. "The first one was early but this one seems to be taking its own sweet time. Must be a girl."

Braedon grinned. "Two demerits for being a sexist pig," she said. "Give my love to Rhona when you see her."

"I will." He held out his hand to me again. "Nice to meet you, Captain Fraser. If you're going to be around for a while, maybe we'll see you again."

"I hope so," I said. "Nice meeting you, too. I hope the baby is on time."

"So do I. Rhona says she's sick of being pregnant again."

As he left, I had trouble sorting out what I was feeling. When he had come in and put his arm around Braedon's shoulders, I hadn't felt jealous, exactly. It was more like a sinking feeling of disappointment and, oddly, loss as if I were missing something I'd never really had. Then when he mentioned his wife and the expected baby, my spirits buoyed considerably.

"Hungry?" Braedon asked.

"Starved," I said. "Let's go track down those sandwiches."

She pulled a bright green identification tag out of the pocket of her jeans and clipped it to the left shoulder of her tee shirt, then led the way back out onto the ramp. Outside, the sun was hot enough to send wavering heat lines radiating up from the pavement.

"Have you upgraded to the 757 yet?" she asked as we walked.

"I have. Shortly after you left, in fact. It's a nice airplane. Now the company's making delighted noises about the MD-80. I was supposed to move over onto them, too, if they arrive in a few years."

She picked up on that instantly. "Was supposed to?" She looked up at me quickly, a slight frown on her face. "What happened?"

"Oh, nothing," I said. "It's just that I've taken a long leave of absence. I might not go back until next spring."

"Is something wrong?" she asked.

We had just walked past the end of the General Aviation Centre and were approaching the Flying Club hangar. Ahead of us, the concrete control tower soared eighty feet into the air, painted white and grey and bright orange, a small, blocky building tucked up against the foot. Behind it stood the brand new Skyharbour Aviation hangar. The outlines of both the tower and the hangar shimmered in the heat waves rising from the pavement.

Then it happened again. Instead of the grey, white and orange tower topped with an octagonal glass cab, I saw a bright blue one, sided with painted wood, standing alone without the small building at its foot. And instead of the new, modern Skyharbour hangar, I saw an old WWII-vintage hangar, painted the same blue as the tower and sided in the same wood. There was none of the double-exposure effect that I saw with the two terminal buildings the last time I was in Edmonton, during the blizzard. What I saw looked as solid and real as the Flying Club hangar we stood beside, or as the orange-striped concrete tower had looked only seconds ago.

On the ramp of the blue hangar stood three aircraft. Two of them were single Otters, painted white and blue. The third was a Beaver. It, too, was painted white with blue trim on the tail and wingtips. A large crest of some kind was painted on the side, just aft of the fuselage door, which was open. It was on amphibious floats and stood very tall on the spindly looking wheels beneath the floats. There was a step cut into the side of the float and a short ladder with two rungs to allow access to the pilot's door under the wing.

The Beaver was the airplane in my dream. It was not just the same type of aircraft; I knew with sudden, concrete certainty it was the exact same aircraft that haunted my dream. If I could walk over and look inside, I knew I would find the small chip in the throttle knob that fit my thumb as if it had been designed just for that. And I would see the same arrangement of instruments in the worn panel as I saw in the dream, even down to the scratches and the gun-tape that mended a crack near where the pilot's left knee would be as he sat in the pilot's seat. I could walk up and find the split in the upholstery of the left seat that rubbed against the top of my right calf. It was the same airplane.

I must have stumbled. When I reached out for something to steady myself, I caught hold of the wing strut of a Cessna 182 and had to hold onto it hard to keep my knees from buckling. I blinked and rubbed my eyes, but the blue hangar and the Beaver didn't disappear. I turned to look back at the terminal building behind me, still holding onto the wing strut. It was the old bow-shaped white building. The brick and glass building had vanished along with the striped tower. The General Aviation Centre and the Avitat hangar were gone. There were no 737s on the ramp, only a couple of Convairs, and in the grass between the terminal ramp and the taxiway, as well as an old Dakota—a DC-3—and a few light single engine aircraft.

The Flying Club hangar was still the same, but it looked almost brand new, the paint crisp and fresh and bright. There were no Cessna 152s on the ramp. Only a row of Fleet-80s, called Canucks, old fabric-covered taildraggers with side by side seating. Even the aircraft I clung to for support had changed. It wasn't a Cessna 182. It was still a Cessna, but it looked like an old L-19.

The air even smelled different. There was no trace of the

slightly acrid odour of burning kerosene. There was a scent of fresh, green growing things nearby, as if the city didn't encroach quite so closely or there were hay fields not far away and from somewhere the faint scent of fabric dope smelling almost like nail polish.

I looked back at the blue hangar and the three white and blue aircraft parked outside it. Similar paint schemes probably meant the same operator. The fuselage door of the Beaver was slid back, wide open. Inside, I could see the shadowy figure of a man.

Suddenly light headed and giddy, and very frightened, I leaned my forehead against my upraised arm and closed my eyes to wait out the dizziness. I was afraid my knees were going to buckle under me and I'd end up sprawled on the tarmac. It had never been like this before. I had never seen anything that even suggested human movement the last two times I had hallucinated these old buildings into existence. And I hadn't even dreamed since that first night at my parents' place when I had gone home after taking Glynnis's ashes back to her family in New York.

Something that felt like a faint tremor in the ground shivered through my body. It was as if the very texture of the air around me changed. I opened my eyes. The grey and orange tower was back. So was the Skyharbour hangar. The aircraft whose wing strut I clung to for support was a Cessna 182. Behind me, the brick and glass terminal and the General Aviation Centre were solid and real again. I breathed a deep, thankful sigh of relief, but I couldn't let go of the wing strut because my knees didn't quite feel steady yet.

Braedon was standing in front of me, both hands gripping my arm. "Are you all right?" she demanded. "Good Lord, Colin, you look awful. What happened? Are you ill?"

"I'm okay," I said. My voice came out sounding like a rusty hinge. "Really, I'm okay now. Just a bit dizzy." I let go of the wing strut, found my knees were willing and able to support me. I straightened up and took a step; I didn't fall down. So far, so good. "I think I need that coffee."

"I think you need more than that," she said, not taking her eyes off my face, her eyebrows drawn together in a frown of concern. "Have you seen a doctor? You look so pale, you're almost green."

"I'll be all right. Really. Don't worry."

She was still holding onto my arm. She bit her lip as she looked up into my face, anxiety in those wide hazel eyes. I tried to smile at her, but it must have come out looking more like a rictus from her expression.

"Really," I said. "I'll be okay. But I'd sure like that coffee."

"Okay," she said finally. "But I think you'd better tell me what's happening."

"Over coffee," I promised.

She nodded. She didn't let go of my arm as we walked to the ramp door of the Flying Club hangar. She made me sit in one of the booths as she went to get coffee. I saw with some bemusement that she had remembered how I took mine, black with no sugar, as she set the two cups down on the laminate top of the table and slipped into the seat opposite me.

"I ordered a couple of open Denver sandwiches," she said. "They don't ruin them quite as often as they ruin other stuff here but the fries are frozen. Is that okay with you?"

"That sounds good."

"You said you had taken a leave of absence," she said. "You obviously still have a valid medical."

"I do." I smiled, a more natural-feeling one this time. "Honest, it's nothing. I just needed some time off."

"Has that anything to do with these dizzy spells?"

"In a way, I guess," I said. "This is only the third time it's ever happened. But I didn't decide to take the leave of absence until Glynnis died."

"Your wife died?" She looked shocked and horrified. "Oh, Colin, I'm so sorry. What happened?"

"An accident. She was driving to work and pulled out to pass a truck. Either it sideswiped her, or she sideswiped it. Her car flipped at close to a hundred." I found I could tell her without the lump forming in my throat. "It happened in February. A while after you left Seattle. I guess that's why you didn't hear about it."

She reached out impulsively and put her hand over mine. "I'm so terribly sorry."

I looked down at her hand. It was small and brown and had a look of strength to it. The fingernails were short and rounded and unpainted, and her fingers were warm and dry over mine.

"Glynnis and I hadn't had much of a marriage for a long time before that," I said. "Probably not for at least three years before she died. I think that might have made it harder when she died. If I had loved her, I wouldn't have felt that nasty flash of relief."

Braedon nodded. "It's a terrible thing to die unloved," she said softly. "I'm really sorry. It must have been horrid for you then."

It was far too easy to tell her things. She listened with everything she owned, leaning forward, her eyes never leaving my face. "Glynnis had never wanted to be loved like that," I said. "She wanted to be admired and worshipped like a movie star, but it seemed she had never wanted or needed to be loved. At least not the way a man loves a woman. I went on the world's most massive guilt trip after she died. We'd had a truly horrific fight just the night before and I had almost decided I was going to divorce her. I didn't know she was dead while I was coming to that conclusion. She had died shortly after I left for Orlando. I didn't find out about the accident until after I got back to Seattle."

"You blamed yourself because you had quarrelled, then decided to divorce her? That's silly, you know."

"I know. But it didn't stop me from feeling that way."

"What about the dizzy spells, Colin? Are they connected with Glynnis' accident?"

I shook my head. "I told you this was the third one. The other two were right here, too. In Edmonton. I had one the first time I was here, almost ten years ago now. The second one was that afternoon we arrived here in the middle of that howling blizzard."

"I remember you looked a little pale then, too."

"Remember at dinner that night when you asked me where I was and when I was?"

She nodded. "And you told me I should have asked who you were too. I remember that disturbed me at the time. Will you tell me about it now?"

I laughed harshly and without humour. "You're going to think my mind has really snapped."

"I don't think so. But I think you'd better tell me."

CHAPTER TWENTY

IT TOOK a long time in the telling. I began with my parents breaking it to me when I was sixteen that I had been adopted, and about the dream, how it had started when I was a child, how it had grown and changed over the years, how I had gradually come to know the aircraft I flew was a DHC-2 Beaver. I told her about the contentment and the pleasure I felt in the dream while flying that old Beaver, and how I knew that I was flying home to someone who loved me very much and was in return much loved. I told her about how the dream had changed to become the nightmare it was now, filled with pain and fear and death. To her credit, Braedon never once let an expression of disbelief cross her face. Her eyebrows twitched once in a frown of concern when I told her about the way the Beaver crashed in the dream and I knew I—or rather the pilot of the Beaver—had died out there in the wilderness of rock and trees and water.

When finally I stopped talking, she was quiet for a while. "You make a very good case for it," she said.

"It scares the hell out of me, sometimes," I said. "I keep wondering if I'm losing my mind."

"I don't think you are," she said. She glanced up at me and smiled a bit ruefully, and it was apparent she was carefully thinking over what she said next. "I'm certainly not going to say *don't be stupid, things like that just don't happen*," she said slowly, "because I've heard of other cases very similar to yours. That's not to say it can't be really eerie and frightening. But really, there's too much evidence strange things like that really can happen."

I took a deep, relieved breath and laughed self-consciously. "At least you seem to believe me. Not many people would, I think."

"I'm not *many people* and I do believe you. I don't think I can explain why, but I do. Remember when I told you in Chicago that I thought you were a troubled man?"

"Yes." It wasn't something I was likely to forget. Having her strip away so many of my defensive layers still stung a bit.

"I said then that part of the problem might have been an unfortunate marriage. But the other part wasn't anything like that. Now I think that I saw some of this around your eyes. At least, I saw something that was causing you pain that didn't seem to have anything to do with the problems a bad marriage could cause."

I laughed softly. "I think I told you then that you were very perceptive."

"I've always seemed to have a sort of sixth sense about people I like," she said, then gave me a self-deprecating grin. "Some of my friends tell me it's downright scary how sometimes I can seem to crawl right into their heads. It used to bother me until I decided that somewhere along the line I must have inherited a witchy gene from some poor ancestress who kept cats and very likely ended up in the dowsing bucket back in Cromwell's merry old England."

I had to smile. "That could be a little startling and strange, too."

"Oh, it could, if I let it," she said. "Maybe I'm just an old soul."

I glanced up at her quickly, a little startled. "My mother used to talk about old souls," I said. "You're the only other person I've ever heard mention the concept."

"My mother used to talk about it, too. She said we have to come back to knock off the rough edges and learn what we need to learn."

Almost my mother's exact words. I nodded. "Maybe I've still got too many rough edges."

"Maybe we all do," she said with another soft laugh. She paused, then: "Here comes a really dumb question. What do you think is going on? I'm not exactly sure how to put this.... Do you think you're haunted by his ghost, or do you think maybe it might be a case of reincarnation?"

I shook my head. "I don't know. I really don't. Somehow, the idea of being haunted by his ghost is a lot less scary than the idea of actually having lived before as him. I don't know what to think."

She looked at me, her head cocked to one side. "Why would the idea of reincarnation be scary?" she asked.

"I don't know. Maybe because I saw him die in my dreams. Maybe because he's too close.... Even given the concept of old souls, it's too damn close. Things like that are probably much more comfortable at a decent distance—like a couple of hundred years, maybe."

"I read a book once about a pilot who dreamed of living another pilot's life. It was set in Australia, I think."

"The Rainbow and the Rose," I said. "Nevil Shute, one of my favourite authors. I read it too, a long time ago. But

this isn't like that. There's no cohesiveness. The only part I know is that last flight. And only part of that. I don't know who the pilot is. I think he may be my natural father. All I know for certain is that his name is Colin, too, because the woman calls my name in the dream. And I know that her name is Judy." I told her what my father had said about the identification bracelet that had been on my wrist when he and my mother had taken me home from the hospital. "They must have changed it when they were told I was going to be adopted," I went on. "Perhaps my natural mother, Judy, had said something about naming me Colin, after my natural father. At any rate, my parents didn't see any reason to change it after they adopted me."

"But why come to Edmonton? Do you think you can find out anything here?"

I told her about my first flight to Edmonton and seeing the old terminal building as solidly as I could now see the shabby cafeteria we were sitting in. I told her about the eerie double-exposure effect I had seen when she and I landed here in the middle of the blizzard. Then I told her what I had seen just an hour ago out on the ramp. I'll say one thing for her; she treated it seriously, as if she believed it had happened just as I said and that I wasn't ready for a straitjacket and a rubber room.

"And when you checked, you found out your double exposure looked just like what the airport looked like thirty years ago?"

"The picture I saw in the Airport Manager's office was taken in 1963. It was exactly the same building I had seen. I don't know about the old blue hangar I saw out there today."

"I remember that hangar. They tore it down when I first

started learning how to fly. That would be about 1980 or so. It was the old MoT and RCMP hangar."

"MoT?" I knew RCMP stood for Royal Canadian Mounted Police. The Mounties were famous all over the world, romanticized in too many dramas to be mistakable.

"Ministry of Transport," she said. "Like the FAA." She smiled. "Or Maker of Trouble, if you believe the new crop of pilots."

I described what I had seen, and she nodded. "That sounds like what it looked like," she said slowly. "I hadn't been flying for very long then. I can't really remember when they tore it down. When I try to remember, it seems as if it was there one day, and gone the next, then when I looked at that big empty spot, it was hard to remember what had been there before. I know they used it as a tie-down area for private aircraft for a long time. That Skyharbour hangar only went up a year or so ago. It's almost brand new."

"Ghosties and ghoulies and long-legged beasties..." I quoted softly. I felt another chill trickle down my back and I shivered. "I don't know what's happening," I whispered, suddenly feeling frightened again. "I don't know and it scares the hell out of me." I looked up at her and smiled wryly. "You're taking all this with remarkable aplomb, I must say. Almost as if you believe it was all real and not a symptom of a deteriorating mind."

"I do believe you," she said. Her smile was just as wry as mine. "Maybe because I've had a similar experience. Not exactly like yours, really. Just a recurring dream where I'm searching for someone who's lost. It doesn't seem really like a nightmare. Only that I'm searching and I'm not frightened because I know I'll find him some day. I'm just sad because we're separated and we can't find each other." She laughed self-consciously. "Maybe not as dramatic as your dreams, but it's been with me ever since I can remember."

"I went to see a lawyer this morning," I said. "I had been hoping he could tell me all about the whole mess. It turned out that the lawyer who handled the adoption for my parents was this one's father, and that all the files had been destroyed years ago. I ran into a solid wall. He thinks he might be able to uncover something, but it's going to take a long time. After what happened this afternoon out there on the ramp, I wonder if I've got a long time. I feel as if I might go absolutely round the bend really quick if I don't find something out soon."

"He couldn't tell you anything?" she asked.

I shook my head. "Nothing."

"What about his father?"

"He told me his father died almost five years ago. I spoke to the woman who had been the old man's secretary. She said she vaguely remembered the file, but she couldn't remember anything else about it. Not even the name of the other lawyer. That seemed to come to a pretty final dead end, too." I shrugged. "Thurlow is going to write a few letters, but he told me not to hold out much hope. It was a long time ago, and private adoptions weren't as well-documented in government agency offices as agency adoptions were. He doesn't even think there might be a home study on file anywhere. Even if there were, back in those days, adoption files were sealed and locked away, and nobody but nobody got to look at them once they were finalized."

"Even now with so many adoptees looking for birth parents?"

"Even now, apparently." I said. "He told me that even birth parents looking for children they had given up for adoption ran into that same brick wall. The files were sealed. You need a Court Order and the written consent of everybody involved to open them."

"So there's not much chance you're going to find out anything there."

"No, probably not, but Thurlow says it's worth a try. It's the only avenue that's open to me."

She looked down at the sandwich she'd taken only one or two bites from, then at my own which had congealed untouched on my plate, then she looked up at me, her eyes suddenly wide and almost startled. "Holy cats," she said. She stood up abruptly. "Come with me. I just remembered something you absolutely have to see. I don't know if it means anything, but it's been puzzling me for a long time."

"What is it?"

"I'll show you. Come on."

She refused to say anything more about it as she led me back out onto the ramp and over to the Terminal Building. I followed her through the General Aviation entrance, then up the stairs and into the lounge area. She stopped in front of one of the pictures on the wall and pointed to it.

"Look at that," she said.

It appeared as if it had been taken on some northern lake in the middle of winter. It showed two men dressed in fur parkas lifting a crate into the open fuselage door of an aircraft. The aircraft fuselage itself filled most of the picture. Behind one of the men was the outer edge of something that might have been a crest, and showing under it were two letters, a P and an E. Another man, also dressed in a fur parka but with the hood thrown back over his shoulders, just on the edge of the picture was doing something near the undercarriage of the aircraft by the skis. He was looking over his shoulder, grinning into the camera. I remembered looking at the picture when I had examined most of them in the lounge. I had wondered if perhaps the aircraft was a Beaver, but it was hard to tell from just the part of it the photograph showed. There didn't seem to be anything unusual about it.

"Look at the pilot," she said and pointed. "Take a good look at him, Colin."

I looked closer. The focus wasn't perfect, and the face was a bit blurred. But I could tell he had a rather ordinary face under the short, wavy blonde hair, clean shaven and rather narrow with level eyebrows and eyes that were set wide and surrounded by laugh lines. He was a man in his late twenties or early thirties, the only lines in his face the laugh lines around his eyes and bracketing the wide mouth. It was a pleasant face, I thought, but I couldn't see much about it that was very special.

"Look harder," Braedon said. She reached out and put her finger over the pilot's hairline. "Does he remind you of anyone?"

Her finger covering the hairline made all the difference. It leaped out at me with sudden, stunning clarity and made me stagger back a pace or two. The face in the photograph was the same face I looked at every morning in the mirror when I shaved. It was my face. Even the approximate age was the same.

"Good God," I said and my voice sounded hollow in my own ears. I glanced quickly at the caption. All it said was, "Loading medical supplies at Mildred Lake, April, 1958."

"How in the hell did you pick up on that?" I asked in a more normal voice. "I looked at that photo two or three times and I couldn't see it."

She smiled. "It was shortly after I came back to Edmonton,"

she said. "I guess you might say you were on my mind a lot back then. It just suddenly jumped out at me one night when I came up here to have a drink with a bunch of friends. I thought the resemblance was a remarkable coincidence. I had to look at it several times before I really believed it and before I knew that it wasn't just my imagination playing tricks on me. It sort of blew me away. He looks exactly like you, Colin. Not just a resemblance, but exactly like you. That could be a photograph of you there, not just someone who looks a bit like you. You yourself."

"I think I need a drink," I said.

She smiled and nodded. "Me, too."

We found a table in a corner overlooking the ramp. When the waitress appeared at my elbow, I ordered a scotch and water and Braedon asked for a light beer. They came quickly and I took a long swallow of mine.

"Is there any way we can find out who took that photograph?" I asked. "It would certainly give me a place to start looking."

"I don't think we need to start there," she said. "Did you take a close look at the airplane in the photo?"

"Not really. It looks like it might be a Beaver."

"It is. But did you take a good look at it?"

I shook my head.

"Dumb question now," she said. "What about the airplane you saw this afternoon out on the ramp. Did you notice anything special about it? Did you see anything that could have been registration letters on it?"

I saw what she was getting at. I closed my eyes and tried to bring up a picture of the Beaver I had seen, but I couldn't seem to see anything on it that might identify it any further than the crest on the side of the fuselage. I didn't recognize the crest, and I couldn't bring into focus any of the words that were written on it. It was just a vague crest with nothing identifiable about it.

"Nothing," I said. "Just a Beaver with a crest on the fuselage. I think it might have contained a buffalo head or something very similar."

"That gives you a one hell of a good place to start," she said. "It could even give you everything you need. The Beaver in that photograph? It's an RCMP machine. That means your father had to be an RCMP pilot."

I just stared at her.

"And another thing," she said. "The last two letters of its ident are PE. Chances are pretty good that the whole ident was probably CF-MPE because in 1958 all Canadian registered aircraft were CF, a dash, and three letters. They didn't go into the C dash F or C dash G and three letter identifications until sometime in the late sixties or early seventies. And most RCMP aircraft have the M and P for Mounted Police somewhere in their identification. The old Otter across the field is C-FMPO, I think. They've been using MP for a long time. It should make it a lot easier to track it down, even if it did crash over thirty years ago. The Accident Investigation Board never throws anything out. Ever. There will be an accident report somewhere. We have a probable ident and we have a date. The pilot's name will be in the accident report."

CHAPTER TWENTY-ONE

FOR A long time, I just sat there and stared at her. She wore a broad, delighted smile, as if she had just produced a rabbit or two out of a hat. She had certainly done that—way more than that. She had opened a door I had almost given up ever finding a key for.

"Braedon, you're an honest to gawd miracle," I said in awe.

She laughed. "All I did was recognize a face in an old photograph." She got to her feet as the waitress approached again. "Quick, pay the lady. I think we can even do better than this. What time is it?"

I glanced at my watch. "About quarter to four."

"Good. Pay up and let's get moving. We don't have a lot of time."

I threw a ten dollar bill onto the table. Braedon took off almost at a run, urging me along with her. We hurried across the ramp and out the door to the parking lot in front of the General Aviation Centre. Her car was a sleek little electric blue Nissan Pulsar. She jumped into the driver's seat, leaned across to unlock the passenger door, and motioned me to get in quickly. By the time we were on the main road that slanted south-east past the airport, she had almost attained escape velocity.

"Where are we going?" I asked as she wove swiftly and deftly past a bus, then took a quick left turn at a set of lights and started north along the south-east side of the airport. A 737 went over our heads, extended gear reaching for the button of Runway 30 just beyond us.

"We're going to see a friend of mine," she said. She looked at her watch again. "I just hope we can catch him before he leaves for the day." She flashed a glance over her shoulder, flipped down her turn indicator for a left turn and slid across the bows of a pickup and into a left-turn bay at another set of lights. What we ended up in didn't look like a road at all, but more like a driveway along the side of some large buildings that might have been a university or a technical college.

"You know government workers," she said as she negotiated the narrow road which had turned into a parking area. "They work eight to four and at two seconds past four, they're gone." We lurched over a series of speed bumps, then over a rounded curb and out onto something that resembled a road far more than the stretch we had just negotiated, but almost as rutted.

A few seconds later, she slewed into a gravel parking lot between two hangars. Over the door of the east building was the same buffalo head crest I had seen on the side of the Beaver. On one side of it were the letters RCMP and on the other side it said GRC. In the motto line below the crest were the words, *Maintien le Droit*. By the time I caught up to her, Braedon was pushing a bell button at the side of the door.

A man wearing a set of stained coveralls opened the door.

"Hey, Braedon," he said. "I was just getting ready to go home for the day. You're lucky you caught me."

"Hi, Billy," she said. "Is Gerry still here or has he gone already?"

"He should be upstairs," the engineer said. "I didn't see him go yet, anyway."

"All right if we go up?"

"Sure. Go ahead." He glanced at me and noted that I wore no security pass as Braedon did. "You're in charge of him?"

She grinned. "More or less. He's an American, but he's probably harmless enough. Thanks, Billy. See you later, huh?" She grabbed my hand and started for the stairs against the hangar wall that led up to the offices on the mezzanine floor, tugging me along in her wake.

"Do you know everybody at this airport?" I asked breathlessly as I hurried along behind her.

"I know an awful lot of them. Or they know me, which amounts to the same thing. Hurry up."

At the top of the stairs, she turned to her right and went to the third door leading off the long landing. There was a man in uniform just rising from behind a desk as she went through the door.

"Hey, Gerry," she said. "Got a minute?"

The man laughed. "Your timing's perfect, Half-pint. How come you're out of breath? Been playing handball against the curb again?"

"Short jokes," she said in a tone of sorely tried patience. "Always short jokes I get from you. Gerry, I'd like you to meet a friend of mine, Colin Fraser. Colin, this overgrown bear here is Staff-Sergeant Gerry Robillard. He's in charge of this flying circus here, or he thinks he is, anyway."

Robillard held out his hand. "Hi there. I'm nominally in charge but everyone knows it's the engineers who run any outfit."

Robillard wore a brown tunic with a broad leather Sam Browne belt over navy blue slacks with a wide yellow stripe down the outside side seams. There was a set of wings on the sleeve of the tunic above two diagonal slashes, and six chevron stripes above the elbow. On the desk behind him was a cap very similar to every police officer's cap I've ever seen, with a yellow band and the same crest as on the front door. If I had been expecting the red coat, Stetson and breeks of the movies, I would have been sorely disappointed. He had the straight, erect bearing of a military sergeant.

"We need to pick your brain a little, Gerry," Braedon said. "Colin has a problem and you might know where we could go to get some information."

Robillard waved us to a couple of chairs and sat down again behind his desk. "What can I do for you, Mr. Fraser?" he said.

"First of all, you can call me Colin." I did some fast mental editing, then said, "I'm an adoptee, Sergeant Robillard. I'm looking for some information about my natural parents. Both of them are dead. I know that for sure but I know very little else about them. About all I really know about them is their first names. His name was Colin, like mine, and her name was Judy. I just recently found out that he may have been an RCMP pilot. I don't have much information, but I think he may have been killed flying a Beaver on floats around the middle of September, 1960. I think the last two letters of the aircraft ident would have been Papa Echo, but I don't know where the accident might have taken place. It might have been around here, or it might have been somewhere else entirely. I have a feeling it was around here, but I have no way of knowing for sure. Is there someone I could talk to who might be able to track down some information on the pilot of a Beaver who might have died around that time?"

He sat back and regarded me gravely. "That was a long way before my time," he said slowly. "I don't have any facts or figures here. The man you want to talk to is Inspector Murchie at K Division Headquarters over on 109th Street. He has records there going back to the Year One of the Originals, I think. I don't know if he can release anything to you, though. It's not exactly the policy of the Force to open its files to civilians, especially on members. But you could talk to him."

"Have you got a phone number for him, Gerry?" Braedon asked.

"Sure," he said. He rummaged around on his desk for a moment, then copied a phone number onto a telephone message slip and handed it to me. "It would sure help if you had a last name to give him," he told me.

I smiled ruefully. "That's part of the information I was hoping he could give me. My parents adopted me privately. They didn't go through an agency and it seems everyone connected with it, all the lawyers, had the sheer inconsideration to die on me since then."

He smiled faintly. "How thoughtless of them."

I laughed. "Indeed. But it leaves me with very few places to turn. That's why I was so glad when I was fortunate enough to discover my natural father might have been an RCMP pilot."

"Well, try Inspector Murchie. If you explain your problem, he might be able to help."

I got to my feet and held out my hand. "Thank you very much, Sergeant Robillard. You've been a great help."

"Not all that much, I don't think," he said, taking my hand briefly. "There's not much sense in trying to call Murchie until tomorrow morning about eight. But give it a try."

"I will. Thank you."

Braedon slipped around behind the desk and kissed his cheek. "Thanks, Gerry."

He smiled at her affectionately. "No problem, Delaney. Don't be such a stranger. Diana was asking about you the other day. She said it was about time you were over for dinner again."

"Tell her next week," she said. "Say Thursday or Friday. I'll give her a buzz."

She kept the Pulsar's speed down below mach values on the trip back around the perimeter of the airport to the parking lot of the Edmonton Inn. "You'll let me know how it goes tomorrow, won't you, Colin?" she asked as I started to get out of the car.

"Of course," I said and hesitated. "I know it's sort of last minute, but would you have dinner with me tonight?"

She bit her lip, then looked up at me and smiled. "That sounds good. Tell you what. Give me an hour or so to go home and change and freshen up a bit, then I'll take you to a really good place. Do you like Chinese food?"

"Love it."

"Great. There's a really good place on the south side. How about I meet you in the lobby here at about six-thirty. I'll drive because I know the city better than you."

We had a very good dinner. We talked about everything and anything except the problem of finding my natural parents. We told each other hilarious and embarrassing things we had done while learning how to fly and teaching other people how to fly. We laughed a lot together. When we finally left the restaurant about eleven-thirty, I felt more relaxed than I had for a long time.

She drove me back to the hotel. I reached for the door handle, then turned to her in the confines of the small car. I wanted very much to kiss her. She read the expression on my face and drew back very slightly. It wasn't much, but it was enough, so I just said, "Thanks for the pleasant evening."

"I really enjoyed it," she said. "Thank you, too. I'll talk to you tomorrow."

I got out and watched the tail lights of the little blue car disappear before I went into the hotel lobby. The only thing I was sure about when it came to her was that it seemed our friendship had survived more or less intact. If she wanted more than that, it wasn't apparent. But I couldn't really expect more than she was willing to give.

The next morning, I called the number Sergeant Robillard had given me and made an appointment to see Inspector Murchie. It wasn't hard to find the RCMP K Division Headquarters building. I could see it from the south-east corner of the airport as I drove down Kingsway Avenue. I found a parking spot designated as visitor parking and left the little Sundance baking in the heat of the already warm July morning. It was going to be like an oven inside when I got back to it.

Inspector Murchie turned out to be a tall, very slender man in his late fifties. His hair was completely grey and cut very short. He was dressed in civvies and wore wire-rimmed aviator glasses and a military moustache. He came out of his office himself to get me and offered me a chair as he closed the door behind us.

I went through my spiel again and explained that Sergeant Robillard had directed me to him, and that I hoped he could help. Murchie sat back in his chair and watched my face closely as I spoke. His expression didn't change much. When I finished, he remained silent for a moment or two.

Finally, he said, "What makes you think your father was an RCMP pilot?"

"That's the strange part, sir," I said. I explained about finding the picture hanging on the wall in the Air Harbour. "I realize it isn't much to go on, but it's about the best evidence I have. I don't know who that pilot is, but whoever he was, in that photograph, he looks enough like me to be me, if you know what I mean. The resemblance is more than just startling. It's uncanny. To look that much like me, he has to be related."

"That's a very flimsy connection."

"I know it is, sir. But if you could find anything on one of your pilots who was killed flying a Beaver on floats about the middle of September in 1960, and if his first name was Colin, wouldn't that add a lot of credence to what I'm saying? Especially if your records showed that his wife's name was Judy?"

"We don't make a policy of opening our personnel files to civilians, Captain Fraser," he said.

"I realize that, sir. I won't ask you to do that, either. If you could just provide me with a last name, it would give me a lot more to go on."

He regarded me thoughtfully for a long moment, then got to his feet. "This might take about an hour," he said. "There's a cafe just down the street. Why don't you go and have some breakfast or a cup of coffee, then come back here at about nine-thirty. I'll see what I can find out for you."

"Thank you, sir," I said, getting to my feet. "I appreciate anything you'd be able to do for me." I shook his hand and made my way back to my car.

I was back in his office at exactly nine-thirty. He had a file on his desk in front of him, and his expression was troubled as he glanced from it to me.

"Fraser, I'm going to do something that's against my better judgment," he said. "And if you ever so much as breathe a word about where you got this information, I'll line you up against a wall and shoot you. Understand?"

My heart gave a painful, expectant leap in my chest. "Yes, sir."

"My daughter is adopted, too. Five years ago when she turned eighteen, she started trying to find her natural mother. It's been a long, painful journey for her. She hasn't been able to find out anything yet. It's very likely that if she does, her natural mother won't want to see her. Patty knows that and she says she accepts it, but it's going to be difficult for her. The only reason I'm going to tell you anything is because I know what my daughter's going through. We love that kid, my wife and I do, and it hurts us to see her doing this, but we can understand why she wants to know."

"Yes, sir," I said. "So can I. I wish her luck."

"Okay. We had an airplane disappear back on September 10th, 1960. It was a Beaver, and it was on floats. The wreckage was never found. The last anyone ever heard from the pilot was when he left a place called Juniper Ridge near the Northwest Territories-Alberta border. There was no mayday call, no indication at all of any trouble. The aircraft just never arrived at Peace River to refuel and it never arrived here in Edmonton."

"It was never found?" I repeated.

"No sign of it. We searched. The military searched. Nothing ever turned up. On the 18th, the search was called off and the pilot was listed as missing presumed dead. He left a widow so we closed it off and listed him as dead because he carried insurance and the widow needed it to live."

My mouth was very dry. I had to moisten my lips with a tongue that was almost too dry to do the job before I spoke. "And the pilot's name, sir?"

"McKenzie. Corporal Colin Ryan McKenzie. According to the file, his wife's name was Judy Maureen, and her maiden name was Scott if that would be of help to you."

"McKenzie," I repeated. Colin and Judy McKenzie. It felt right, as if I should have known it all along. I shook my head in mild amazement. "Thank you, Inspector Murchie. Thank you very much." My voice sounded a bit rusty and hoarse in my own ears.

"There's just one thing more, Fraser."

"Yes, sir?"

"I probably shouldn't tell you this, but you'd find out anyway. Corporal McKenzie's disappearance is still an open file. He had a very valuable cargo aboard that aircraft. Since the aircraft was never found, there was some suspicion in a few quarters that he might have disappeared on purpose with it. There was never much credence given to the suspicion, but because it was there, the file was left open and there is that faint black mark on his record."

"You mean they think he might have been a thief?"

"No, not really. Just that there's a faint suspicion that was never proved or disproved. We'd like to clear his name, but we can't until the aircraft and his body are found."

"What if I can find out what happened to him?"

"Then it would close this file and we could put it to bed, one way or another. Look, I can't tell you anything else. I've already told you far more than I officially should have. But I'm going to give you the name of a man you can go and speak with. He retired from the Force fifteen years ago after nearly forty years' service. He knew almost everyone in this Division, either personally or by reputation. I believe he might have worked with McKenzie. He could probably tell you more about the man than I could."

"I appreciate that, sir."

He wrote something on a memo form and handed it to me. I glanced down at it. It was just the name Tom Riker, and a telephone number. I thanked him again.

"I'd like to know what you find out, if you out anything," Murchie said. "I don't like the thought of any of my men having even that faint cloud of suspicion on their record. I'd like to think I owe it to McKenzie and his widow, and even to his son, to clear his name. Completely clear it, because until this, he had an outstanding record as a good cop and a good pilot."

Chapter Twenty-Two

THERE WAS a message from Braedon waiting for me at the front desk when I got back to the hotel. The desk clerk called me over as I passed and handed me the envelope.

"The lady left this for you, sir," she said. "She asked me to make sure you got it as soon as you got back in."

I thanked her and took it up to my room with me, but I didn't open it right away. I put it on the desk by the telephone along with the memo Inspector Murchie had given me with Tom Riker's telephone number, then lay on the bed, my hands behind my head. Climbing back into the oven of the little car's interior had sent sweat streaming down my body and soaking into my clothing. The air conditioner in the window blew cold air over me and dried the sweat as I looked up unseeingly at the ceiling

I had almost too much to think about. Where did I start?

McKenzie, I thought. Colin and Judy McKenzie. If both of them, or either of them, had lived, I would be Colin McKenzie, too. There would be no Colin Fraser. Perhaps there wouldn't have been a Captain McKenzie instead of a Captain Fraser, either. Ian and Aislinn Fraser might have adopted and raised another child, either a son or a daughter. If it was a son, he would have been James Fraser. I wondered if he would have been like me, and I pondered the age old riddle of nature versus nurture. But what would I be like today? Who would I be?

That Colin McKenzie and Judy had loved each other was obvious if the fact of my dream was to be believed. Had he safely completed that last flight, there was no doubt in my mind that I would have been raised by parents who loved me and would have been loved in return. But I would never have known Ian and Aislinn Fraser.

Colin McKenzie had loved his wife enough to cry out to her in the instant before he died, and to hear her call back to him. He had even loved his unborn child enough to feel grief and regret that his son would never know him. Perhaps he had cared enough so that something of his will—or his love or his spirit or something—had not died with him. Instead, it had reached out and bridged that unfathomable gulf to touch me, I who had been his unborn son at the time of his death. That tenuous thread of his indomitable love, or will, or whatever it was, wasn't strong enough for real communication, only strong enough to cause a dream. Then, eventually, because I had to know his nightmare, the dream he had given me turned to nightmare, too. Only in Edmonton here did the thread seem to be strong enough to give me something more tangible than a dream, to allow me to see what he had seen, and make it as real and as solid as the world he had known all those years ago.

Did he know that his Judy was also dead? Did he know that there was a faint shadow on his name and his record? Was that perhaps one of the reasons he had reached out to draw me inexorably to Edmonton? And if it was, was that thread of his spirit strong enough to show me what I needed to know, or what I had to do now?

Whatever it was in me that was his, it was strong enough to give me his face and his build. It was strong enough to pass on to me his love of flying even after he had died in pain and terror in an airplane. I fervently hoped it would be strong enough to show me what he had to show me if I was going to do what he wanted me to do.

I got up and went to the telephone. I put the call through and waited for a long time as it rang on the other end. When she answered, my mother was out of breath.

"Hi," I said. "It's me. Did I make you run up from the beach?"

"Oh, Colin," she said. "I was out trying to convince that wretched beast Faversham that it was lunch time. Just a minute. I'll get Ian on the extension." I heard her calling out to my father, heard him pick up the other phone.

"Hello, Colin," he said. "Any news?"

"I've found out quite a lot," I said. "Not everything yet, but I think it's only a matter of time now. My natural father's name was Colin McKenzie. He was a pilot for the Royal Canadian Mounted Police. He was a Corporal. He went missing on September 10th, nine days before I was born. The file is still open because the aircraft was never found."

They were both quiet for a moment. Then my mother said, "And your mother?"

"Her name was Judy, just as I thought. I haven't found out much about her yet. I've got the telephone number of a man who knew them. I'm going to call him and talk to him later today. But that's not the main reason I called."

"Ah," my father said. "My son and his ulterior motives."

"Always an ulterior motive. It just sort of occurred to me that it's been too long since I told both of you that I love you very much," I said quietly. "I was just lying here thinking about who I'd be if Colin and Judy McKenzie had lived, and I came to the conclusion that I'm very glad to be Colin Fraser, beloved son of Ian and Aislinn."

There was a long silence on the other end of the line. Then finally, my father said, "Now you've gone and done it, Colin. You've made your mother cry. And me, too, dammit."

"I'm sorry."

"Don't be sorry. They're very pleasant tears. We love you very much, too. Now you go and do what you have to do so that you can come back and get on with the rest of your life."

I smiled. "Yes, sir."

"Good bye for now, Colin," my mother said. "Call us again when you know the rest."

"I will. G'bye."

I put the phone down and reached for Braedon's note. It wasn't very long.

Colin, I might have something for you when I get back this afternoon. I've got a friend doing some investigation work for me. I'm heading out for Vancouver but I'll be back tonight around seven. Meet me at the airport and we'll go and see what Lisa found. Call Area Control to get an actual ETA for us so you don't waste too much time hanging around waiting. The ident is GRHE.

It was signed with a scrawled D"

I frowned at the note. I wondered what sort of investigation work she had this friend doing. What information was she going on? But I'd know when she got back, I suppose.

There wasn't much sense worrying about it before then. I picked up the memo Murchie had given me and punched in Tom Riker's number.

A woman answered the phone. I gave her my name, and when I asked for Riker, she said she was Mrs. Riker and that Tom wasn't home just now.

"I sent him out fishing," she said with a trace of tolerant exasperation in her voice. "Otherwise, I'd never get anything done around here. He's gone up to Slave Lake and won't be back until tomorrow evening. Can I have him call you when he gets back home?"

"If you would, please." I gave her my room number at the hotel. "Tell him Inspector Murchie at RCMP Division Headquarters gave me his name and told me that he might be able to help me with something I'm trying to research."

"I'll have him call," she promised. "If you get him yarning about his days on the Force, you might have a week's worth of listening to do, young man."

I laughed, thanked her and hung up. I took a shower, changed into jeans and a shirt, then went out to the car. Eventually, I found the University Hospital, found a place to park, and even found the Patient Records Department. When I told the woman behind the counter what I wanted, her mouth went small and thoughtful.

"I don't know if I can give you that information, sir," she said.

"Judy McKenzie was my mother," I said. "I'd really like to find out what day she died, and what she died of. All I know for sure is that she died shortly after I was born. Within a day or two. That would make it sometime around the 20th or 21st of September, 1960."

"Those records might be on microfilm," she said. "It might take a while to find them."

"I can wait," I said. "I'm not in any particular hurry. It was thirty-three years ago. Another couple of hours isn't going to hurt."

She glanced up at the clock on the wall. It was almost noon. "If you come back around two-thirty, I might have something for you then," she said. "That is, if the records have been put onto the computer. If they're still just on microfilm, it could take a lot longer." She pushed a piece of paper across the counter at me. "Sign this. It's a next-of-kin release of information form. Just for the record."

I looked at it. It was a standard form to allow the hospital to release information regarding a patient file. I dated it and in the block that asked for the relationship to the patient, I filled in 'Son.' Then I signed it "Colin James McKenzie Fraser." It gave me an odd feeling in the pit of my stomach to sign my name that way. It was a new facet in my own identity, one I was going to have to get used to.

There was a cafeteria on the main level of the hospital. I had a sandwich and a cup of coffee, then sat there thinking of very little for another hour. At two-thirty, I presented myself at the Patient Record counter again. The woman I had spoken with before came forward.

"It was on the computer," she said. "Not the full file, but I think I have what you wanted. Judy McKenzie died at eleven twenty-six on the night of September 18th, 1960, six hours after giving birth to a son. The cause of death was listed as heart failure. We'd call it cardiac arrest now. She apparently had a history of rheumatic fever when she was a child, and that could lead to a permanently weakened heart."

"Is there anything in there about her date of birth?" I asked.

"June 20th, 1934."

So, Judy McKenzie had been only 26 when she died. A little over six years younger than I was now. Far too young to die. "Thank you," I said. "I appreciate the trouble you've gone to for me."

"You're welcome," she said and smiled.

I spent an hour or so looking around the University campus. I wondered how much it had changed since my father had attended for that one year all those years ago. Some of the buildings looked old enough to have been there for almost a century. Others looked fairly new. It was hard to tell. I should have asked them for the address of the house where my parents had lived when I called them earlier. It would have been nice to see that. It made me smile to wonder how much yard there was, and what it had looked like, given my parents' penchant for doing as little as possible in that area. Both of them had always had better things to do with their spare time than compete for the most beautiful yard in the neighbourhood.

I did some more exploring inadvertently on my way back to the hotel. The bridge I had used to cross the river on my way south turned out to be a one-way bridge and I ended up getting hopelessly lost trying to find another going north. By the time I lucked out and eventually found myself on the north side of the river again, I had to stop and get a city map at a service station to figure out how to get back to the hotel. It was six-thirty when I walked back into my hotel room. I looked up the number and called the Area Control Centre.

"I'm looking for an ETA for Golf Romeo Hotel Echo,"

I said. "Gulfstream IV out of Vancouver for Edmonton Muni."

"Stand by one," the controller said, then came back a few minutes later. "We have him arriving at YXD at 0115 Zulu."

I did some fast mental arithmetic and translated that into seven-fifteen local time. I thanked him and went to shower and change again. Sports jacket and slacks this time. I didn't bother with a tie.

I arrived at the General Aviation Centre a little early and was standing looking out at the ramp when suddenly, the whole scene shimmered before me. For only an instant, the old blue tower and hangar were visible, the white terminal building hovering in the background. An old DC-4 trundled by with sedate dignity. I stood in a dimly lit old hangar, surrounded by bits and pieces of airplane parts. I closed my eyes, taking a deep breath, and when I opened my eyes again, everything had vanished except what was supposed to be there, I was back in the modern lounge area of the GAC.

I stood for a moment, staring out the window, my mouth parched. Perfectly normal, I told myself, getting my breathing under control. Whatever was happening, whatever my father might be sending me, this was only a quick glimpse. Hardly more than a few seconds. Certainly not as bad as the last time. I hoped that meant it was getting better, that there would be fewer of these aberrations, and they would become farther apart.

I looked up in time to see the G-IV touch down at the end of Runway 30. Watching the landing helped take my mind off the hallucination—if that's what it truly was. Braedon's touchdown was a very pretty landing, one of those greasers where you had to look out the window to make sure the wheels were rolling. I grinned. I'd have to remember to compliment her on it.

I waited by the window as the passengers deplaned and filed through the office to a waiting cab. I decided I wouldn't tell Braedon about this flash. It wasn't so bad. I didn't want to worry her.

I watched as Braedon and Mark Strang put the airplane to bed, supervising as a ramp rat with a mule pushed it back into the hangar, then they came through the sliding doors. Braedon grinned at me, and Strang smiled in greeting.

"Any news on the baby yet?" I asked him.

He held up a cell phone the size and shape of a brick and smiled ruefully. "Not yet. It's got to be a girl."

"Three demerits," Braedon said. "Get out of here, Mark. Go tell Rhona she has about four and a half hours to produce that kid or I lose two bucks in the preggie pool."

"Yes, ma'am, Captain ma'am," he said. "Nice to see you again, Captain Fraser."

"You look official," I said to Braedon. She wore slacks in a greyed blue and a shirt with four gold stripes on the epaulets on the shoulders, a pair of gold wings pinned over the left breast pocket. "And you made one heckuva neat landing out there. Almost like a real captain."

She made a face at me. "Who needs you?" she said airily, then went through a door to the right of the reception desk marked Flight Planning. I followed and found her on the telephone. I didn't catch most of the conversation, but I saw the expression of disappointment on Braedon's face when she hung up.

"Lisa couldn't get me everything," she said. "She got busy on another project but she promised she'd have it for me tomorrow before noon."

"What's this secret project you've got her working on?"

"I just used my fuzzy, curly little head and thought that if your natural father had died in a plane crash, there would be something about it in the paper. Lisa is an old school friend. She's also a red-hot reporter and has access to all the morgue files down there. She owes me a lot of favours, so I called in a few this morning."

"Would a name help?" I asked.

"You've got a name?"

"Yes. I got it from Inspector Murchie this morning. It's Colin Ryan McKenzie. He was a corporal in the RCMP."

"Hot damn," she said and grabbed for the phone again. I heard her give the name to her friend, then she hung up and turned to me again, a wide smile on her face. "This calls for a mild celebration," she said. "Dinner again?"

"I'd love it."

"Okay, tell you what. I make spaghetti that's only one step removed from sheer heaven, and it just so happens I stuffed all the ingredients for the sauce into the slow cooker before I left home this morning. I have to go home to change anyway, so why don't you follow me and I'll feed you."

"Sounds like a deal."

She lived high up in a tall apartment complex about twenty minutes' drive from the airport. The place was cluttered with books, aviation magazines and safety publications. An open briefcase sat on one of the chairs, charts spilling out of it. She offered no apology for the disorder and I needed none. I felt right at home.

She disappeared into the bedroom, returned a few minutes later dressed comfortably in jeans and a sweat shirt with a stylized drawing of a G-IV on the front. The caption read,

Gee-four, Gee Whiz. Forty minutes later, she had set the table with a huge dish of spaghetti and meat sauce and about an acre of salad. I was hungry enough to do it justice, and it was, as she had promised, only one step this side of heaven. While we ate, I told her what I had found out that day. She listened carefully and marvelled at how things were falling so neatly into place.

I helped her with the dishes when we were finished eating. It was pleasant and cozy in the tiny kitchen. As I reached up to put the serving dishes onto a high shelf, she laughed and said, "That's what I need around here. A little bit of tall."

When we finished, she shooed me into the living room while she wiped the counter and the stove. It had been a long day, and I was tired. I sat down on the couch and promptly fell asleep.

Chapter Twenty-Three

It was dark in the room when I awoke. I lay on my side on the couch, a pillow under my head and a light blanket thrown over me. I twisted my arm around so that I could see the luminous dial of my watch. It was after midnight. I sat up, spilling the blanket to the floor. There was no sign of Braedon in the room.

Feeling a bit like a total idiot, I stood up. It takes a special kind of fool to have dinner with a very attractive woman and then crash out on her couch while she's finishing up in the kitchen. Shows a lot of gratitude, that does. I wondered if I should just leave a note with an abject apology and leave. If she was asleep, I didn't want to waken her.

I heard someone moving on the balcony outside. I went to the window and saw her standing there by the railing, dressed in something long and pale, her hair tumbling around her face. She stood with her back to the window, her arms resting on the railing as she looked out at the lights of the city. In the middle of a dark section, the blue lights of the taxi lights at the airport shimmered in the night.

She didn't turn as I slid back the glass door and stepped out onto the deck. I came up behind her, slipped my arms around her from the back and folded them below her breasts. She put her arms over mine and leaned back against me, tilting her head back so it rested lightly against my shoulder. I bent to find the soft skin of the side of her throat with my lips. Her body quivered and she drew in a long, shaky breath as I kissed the tender spot between her ear and the angle of her jaw, then down the column of her throat to where the collar of her robe blocked my mouth. There didn't seem to be any great hurry. I shifted slightly so that I could kiss the other side of her neck and again, she drew in that quivering, unsteady breath. Finally, she turned in my arms, put her arms around my shoulders tightly, almost fiercely. I reached up with one finger to trace the side of her face, down the line of her jaw.

"This has been coming for a long time," I told her quietly.

"Yes," she said. "A very long time. But it couldn't have happened before. It would have been all wrong that night in Chicago."

"Yes," I agreed. "But it's right now."

"Yes, Colin. It's right."

"Are you sure?"

"Very sure."

"Delaney...." I said her name more to taste it on my tongue than anything else. Then I kissed her and it was better than the kiss in Chicago. If it had felt right then, it was so much more right now. She fit against me as if she had been made to, as if I had been made to conform to her body. She opened her mouth to admit my tongue and we stood like that for a long time, content simply to explore each other's mouths. For one so small, there was a surprising sturdy abundance of breast, a pleasing and exciting incurve to waist and outcurve again to hip. I moved my hand to cup her head to fit her mouth more firmly against mine and one of her hands crept up into my hair to hold us together with strength and passion.

Finally, I lifted my head and looked down into her face, reached up to stroke her hair back from her forehead. Her eyes were closed and her mouth was still imprinted with the shape of mine.

"Can you find the bedroom?" she whispered.

"I'm a pilot," I said and smiled. "I can navigate almost anywhere."

She chuckled softly. "There's no VOR or NDB."

"Trust me."

I led her back into the apartment and closed the door after us. Then, my arms around her, I walked her backwards down the hall, found the room with the big double bed with the blankets already folded back. The robe she wore had one long zipper from throat to hem. It made a soft purring sound in the silence as I pulled it down. Beneath it, her body was bare and quite lovely. I cupped her breasts in my hands, lifted one nipple to my bent head. She shivered and put her hand to the back of my head, pressed me closer.

"I'm going to get a crick in my neck doing this," I said presently.

She laughed. "Short jokes again," she said. She reached out, took my hand, pushed me gently down onto the bed and slowly began to unfasten the buttons on my shirt. When I tried to help her, she pushed my hands away. "No, let me, please." She pulled off my shirt, reached down to undo my belt, then the snap and zipper of my slacks. I rose to step out of the slacks and she let her robe fall to the floor beside them. I turned to her and drew her down onto the bed with me.

We moved without haste into the pleasurable business

of becoming acquainted with each other's body. She liked being kissed in that tender place where the neck joined the shoulders. Kissing her breasts caused great tremors to quiver through her. She discovered all the places to touch on my body that sent shocks like electric currents through me. She shivered under the touch of my fingers, my lips

"Colin? Oh, God, Colin...do you know what that's doing to me?"

I laughed softly. "I certainly hope I do."

Much later, she stirred in my arms, then raised herself on one elbow to look down at me. The apartment was too high up to get much light reflected off the street, but I could see the faint gleam of her eyes and the highlights on her cheeks in the dark. I reached up and stroked my finger down the side of her face.

"Turn on a light so I can look at you," I said.

She reached across me and snapped on the lamp on the small table by the head of the bed. One of her breasts brushed my cheek as she moved.

"There," she said. "Better?"

"Much better." I smiled. "You know, you're an awful lot of woman, Braedon."

She laughed softly. "No more short jokes, Fraser."

"That wasn't a short joke. I'm having a bit of a problem here."

"A problem?"

I had to laugh. "What am I going to call you now? In a situation like this, Braedon hardly seems appropriate. And somehow, Delaney just doesn't sound like a name you call the woman you love."

"Blame my mother for that one. It was her maiden name, but it's been so long since anyone's called me Delaney

I hardly even answer to it any more. Go ahead and keep on calling me Braedon. Or you can call me sweetheart, or darling or even hey you, just as long as you keep on calling me."

"I think I can think of you as Delaney easier than Braedon now. In fact, I think I like it...."

"So, okay. Delaney it is. I'll get used to it again." She curled back down against my chest. "I sat there in the living room for a long time and watched you sleep, you know."

"Do I snore?"

She laughed. "You didn't then. That strained look around your eyes is going away." She reached up and stroked her fingers down my cheek. "In fact, it's nearly gone, did you know that?"

"No. I didn't notice." Her hair tickled my chin and I smoothed it back gently. It smelled of vanilla and some light flowery scent.

"I did. I sat there and watched you sleep and I felt so protective about you. I got the pillow and the blanket and then I stroked your hair back and you smiled. You didn't wake up but you smiled. I had no I idea what I would do if you just got up and walked out of my life again after this was all over. I didn't know how I was going to be able to handle it."

"You walked out on me last time."

"I know. But I had to. If I hadn't, we would have killed anything we might have had right then. I couldn't even stay in the same city with you because I knew you'd come to find me and I couldn't have walked away twice in a row."

"You were a lot wiser than I could have been," I said. "All

I knew then was that I wanted you. I didn't realize that I loved you."

She raised herself on one elbow and looked down at me. The faint light limned the soft lines of her cheek and brow. I ran my finger across her lips, marvelling at their softness.

"I think you had better plan on staying here with me until you finish getting this thing about your natural parents sorted out," she said.

I put my finger on her chin and drew her down to kiss her. "Well, as I see it, there's only one problem that you and I have to solve."

"What's that?"

"We're going to have to sort out where we're going to live after we get married, and then we have to figure out exactly which one of us gets to remain being Captain Fraser."

She began to sputter, then burst into laughter, long peals of mirth that shook her whole body against mine. "Ha!" she cried. "My four stripes against yours?"

"My airplane's bigger than yours," I said mildly.

"Ptui. Mine's more fun to fly."

"You want to fight about this?"

She reached down between us, grasped me gently. "Yeah, I wanna fight."

"You're not fighting fair—"

"This is eminently fair."

"I've been a captain longer. I have more dignity as befits the august position."

She raised herself, straddled me, took me deep into her. "You don't look very dignified to me right now, Captain, sir."

"Neither do you, Captain, ma'am."

She began to move slowly, rotating her hips in lazy, lingering circles, then bent forward and put her nose up against mine. "Just one minute there, Captain, sir."

"Are you calling off the battle, Captain, ma'am?"

"Nope. I'm just clarifying the lines of the trenches here. It occurs to me that if we're going to do battle over who is going to keep his or her four stripes after we get married, you could at least have the decency to declare a formal war and ask me if I'll marry you in the first place."

"Did I forget to do that?" It was getting harder and harder to concentrate on anything but what was going on where we joined.

"You did."

"Oh. Do you want me to get down on one knee?"

"That might be difficult, considering the situation here."

"Well, if you'll stop distracting me for a second or two—"

"If I can concentrate, so can you."

"I am concentrating, but don't think I'm concentrating on what you want me to concentrate on."

"Try." A burble of laughter caught at her voice.

"Okay. Captain Braedon, ma'am, will you do me the great honour of consenting to become my wife?"

"Captain Fraser, sir, I would be delighted." The movement of her hips began to quicken. "Now, let's call a truce for a few minutes and try a little fraternization."

The fraternization was a fine thing, indeed. It had been a long time since making love had been just happy fun.

Presently, I turned out the light again, got her snugged comfortably against me with her cheek on my shoulder and my cheek against the soft curls on the top of her head.

"Colin?" she said sleepily.

"Umm?"

"Remember I told you about that dream I used to have? The one where I was searching for someone who was lost?"

"I remember."

"Well, what I didn't tell you was that I stopped dreaming it a while ago."

"When was that?"

"Shortly after I met you. I stopped dreaming about searching for someone because I knew I'd found him."

Chapter Twenty-Four

We slept late the following morning and made long, slow, gentle love again upon awakening. There was no reason to rush getting out of bed. She didn't have to fly and I had nothing in particular to do until I could get in touch with Tom Riker. Her friend Lisa had said she'd phone when she had put together what we needed. So Delaney and I stayed lazily in bed and held each other and made plans and laughed together.

Just before noon, the phone rang. Delaney reached across me to pick it up. Before she even got it to her ear, I heard the shout. "Six demerits, Braedon. It's a girl!"

With an absolutely straight face, Delaney said, "Congratulations, Mark. You owe me five bucks." She hung up, looked at me and said, "That should confuse the heck out of him," then dissolved into laughter.

At about one-thirty, she sat up suddenly and announced, "I am going to starve in about three and a half minutes. Bacon and eggs and waffles are called for here."

"Need a hand?"

"No. I'm going to do my grimly determined housefrau

act. Bathroom through there, clean towels on the shelf by the tub."

I had the shower at just the right temperature when a cup of icy water splashed onto my back. I howled, nearly jumped right out of my skin, then made a grab for her through the shower curtain and tussled her into the tub. I held her against me, back to belly, kicking and writhing and giggling, with one arm while I reached for the hot water tap with the other, and turned it off. The blast of cold water made us both gasp. She struggled harder and yelped and whuffled and yowled as I held her under the main force of the spray. Her little butt squirming against my belly was beginning to pay unexpected dividends.

"Okay," she sputtered. "I give up. Turn it off before I freeze."

I shut off the water, turned her wet, slippery body to face me. Her hair lay plastered against her skull in dripping ringlets and her eyes were wide with the shock of the cold water.

"You're a cruel, cruel man, Colin Fraser," she whimpered, shivering, her fists clenched beneath her chin.

"I always react violently to an attack on my dignity."

"Don't be silly," she said with some asperity. "How can you possibly be dignified with *that* thing poking out in front of you? So much for the myth of the cold shower."

I put my hands behind her thighs, lifted her so that I could fit us closely and firmly and intimately together. Her eyes went round with surprise.

"Oops," she said and grasped my shoulders as her legs tightened around my hips.

"Yep. Oops."

"You snuck up on me when I wasn't looking."

"I blind-sided you."

"Don't sound so insufferably smug about it." Then: "Colin...?"

"Yes?"

"About this sex/love thing...do you really think it's supposed to be this much fun?"

"I certainly hope so."

"Navigate us back to the bedroom, Captain. I can't see where we're going from here, but I sure know where we've been." And she began gnawing on my earlobe and the side of my throat.

Some time later, she clambered off the bed. "Food," she muttered. "That's what I was going to do before I was so rudely interrupted. I was going to organize some breakfast."

The phone rang while she was stacking the breakfast dishes in the dishwasher. She came out of the kitchen to pick it up. "Maybe it's Lisa," she said.

I watched her face as she spoke on the phone. She didn't say much, and the conversation was short. When she hung up, she sat down opposite me at the table.

"That was her," she said. "She says she's got quite a package for us. Do you want to drive down to the newspaper office now and pick it up?"

"I'm anxious to see what she's got."

"So am I. That's a yes then?"

"That's a yes."

"We can stop by the hotel on the way back and pick up your stuff. There's no sense paying for a room you're not going to be using. And you'd better call that Mrs. Riker and give her this number here. You don't want to miss that phone call."

Lisa Chisyk was a tall, cool Nordic blonde. She was just on her way out of the building when we arrived. She thrust a large manila envelope into Delaney's hands, called something about being in a mad rush to get somewhere, and whirled out the door before Delaney could even reply. Delaney looked down at the thick parcel, shrugged, and handed it to me.

"That's why it takes her so long to do something," she said. "That woman has two speeds—fast and omigawd. Let's get your stuff and go back to the apartment so we can look at that without being bothered."

I gathered up my things at the Edmonton Inn, paid my bill and went back down to where Delaney waited in the car outside the main entrance. The manila envelope was sitting on the front seat. I picked it up and hefted it as I strapped in.

"This feels like the first draft of the Great American Novel," I said. "I wonder what makes it so thick?"

"We'll find out soon enough, I guess."

She cleared an area at the table big enough for us to spread out the pile of photocopies Lisa had put together for us. There was a typewritten note on the top addressed to Delaney.

"She says she found a lot of stuff leading up to the story we wanted," Delaney said, skimming through the letter. "Says she put it in chronological order, so we have to start at the top and work our way through." She pulled the thick pile of paper out of the envelope and placed them in front of me, then pulled her chair around so she could look over my shoulder. "Might as well get started then...."

The first paper was a photocopy of a large, thick headline. "Mine Manager's Daughter Kidnapped. Quarter Million in Ransom Demanded."

"What's that got to do with Colin McKenzie?" I asked.

"I don't know. He was a cop, though. Maybe he was in on the investigation." She pointed. "Look. The date there is almost a week before he died."

The package contained photocopies of enlarged microfilm records. Some of them weren't very clear and we had to strain to make out what they said. The first story didn't have a lot of information, just the bare facts that a girl named Mollie Stevenson had been kidnapped from her school in a place called Juniper Ridge. An hour after her parents, David and Linda Stevenson, had reported her missing to the local RCMP detachment, they had received a phone call demanding a ransom of $250,000 be paid if they ever wanted to see their daughter again.

"Juniper Ridge," Delaney said. "That was one of the big uranium mines that suddenly sprang up out of nowhere around then. Pine Point was another. They made a lot of overnight millionaires. Maybe this David Stevenson was one of them."

"Juniper Ridge was also the place Colin McKenzie departed from the day he crashed," I said.

"So it was... That's interesting."

We turned to the next story. It was just a continuation of the one before. There was no new information in it, just a rehashing of what had gone before. The next day was just about the same. On the fourth day, the headlines were big and black again. The police had laid a trap and captured the kidnappers. Using marked bills as bait, they had followed the kidnapper's directions and put the money into a large suitcase and sent Mr. Stevenson out along a trail into the bush where the kidnappers would contact him and take the money, and at the same time, give him directions to where he could find his daughter. The police, of course, had the whole of the area under surveillance. Mr. Stevenson met the kidnappers, handed them the money, and was given a map to the trapper's cabin where he found his bound and gagged daughter who was frightened half to death but otherwise all right. The police swooped down and bagged the two surprised kidnappers and trundled them off to the nearest cell.

"Can you believe how stupid those kidnappers were?" Delaney asked in amazement. "Drop the cash in the bush. Sheesh."

"Nobody ever said crooks were smart," I said. "If they were, they probably wouldn't have to be crooks."

The next story was dated three days later, September the 10th. Again, the headlines were big and black. *Local Mountie Missing on Flight from Juniper Ridge. Ransom Loot from Stevenson Kidnapping said to be on Board.* Then, in smaller type, *Money on its way down to Edmonton to be used as evidence at trial.* Then: *Corporal Colin Ryan McKenzie, 30, of Edmonton, a popular figure at Blatchford Field, went missing today on a flight from Juniper Ridge to Edmonton....* It went on to give the same details of the flight that Murchie had given me. The Beaver had taken off from Juniper Ridge and was scheduled to stop for fuel at Peace River. It never arrived. There was no hint in the story that Corporal McKenzie might have skipped out with the money. It gave a brief history of his service record on the Force, that he had joined when he was twenty-two and spent five years on detachment in British Columbia and Alberta before transferring to the Air Detachment three years ago. His superior officers praised his record as a good policeman and a good pilot. It went on to mention that McKenzie's wife was expecting their first child at any time. There was a blurred photo of him next to the story. It showed him in a Stetson and a high, tight collar looking grim, serious and uncomfortable and probably a lot younger than thirty.

"If the higher-ups on the Force had any suspicions about that missing money, they kept it out of the papers," Delaney said.

"I guess it would be something Internal Affairs would investigate on their own. They'd keep it quiet, wouldn't they?"

"I'm pretty sure they would. This was back in the days when all Mounties were supposed to be the next best things to gods, all noble and virtuous and all that. Nobody had exposed any feet of clay, so nobody would be expecting any dirt to be spread."

"A quarter of a million was a fortune in those days. I wonder why they'd send it down on something as slow as a Beaver?"

"Why not? They'd know the pilot was reliable, anyway."

"I guess you're right."

"Hey, look," she said. "They lost another aircraft the same day." She pointed to a small article near the bottom of the page. "A Grumman Avenger water bomber. It went down about eighty miles from Fort Vermilion." The article continued onto the next page, but we didn't have the next page. "That was a bad day for airplanes, wasn't it?"

The article dated the 12th of September talked about the massive air search by police and military aircraft along the route of the proposed flight of the Beaver. There were quotes from police and military spokesmen explaining how the search was being conducted, quotes from pilots flying the search expressing confidence in finding the downed aircraft soon. There was even a quote from a survival expert who voiced the opinion that Corporal McKenzie, an experienced outdoorsman, might very well be found alive and well. Near the bottom was a short paragraph on how his wife Judy was holding up bravely under the strain.

There was only one more article, and it was dated September 18, 1960. It simply stated the search for Corporal McKenzie and his aircraft had been called off, and that a memorial service for him was scheduled for the following afternoon at two-thirty. There were no further articles, and there was no mention at all of the death of his wife.

I stacked the papers, then went over to look out the window. The newspaper articles had given me the circumstances of Colin McKenzie's death, but it hadn't given me much insight into what the man himself had been like. I still knew very little of the man who had been my father.

I had seen two pictures of him. One in the Air Harbour Lounge, smiling widely into a camera, the other a blurred reproduction of an official photograph. The photo in the Air Harbour was very likely a more reliable clue to his personality. But what had he been like? Who was he, besides a *popular figure at Blatchford Field?*

Delaney came up behind me, put her arms around me, rested her cheek against my back. "So now you know what he was," she said quietly. "Now we have to find out who he was. When is Tom Riker due back in town?"

"His wife said some time tonight."

"Colin?"

"Yes?"

"What are you going to do when you find out?"

"I don't know."

"I mean, where does it end? Are you going to have to go out and look for him?"

"I don't know that, either."

"They looked for ten days and couldn't find him back then when it was still fresh. In thirty years, if he went into the trees somewhere, there would hardly be any trace at all left of the airplane. The trees would have grown up again around it."

Fragments of the nightmare flickered through my mind. "I don't think he went into the trees. I think he went into rocks and water."

I felt her shudder against my back. "But if they couldn't find him then...."

I turned and put my arms around her, rested my cheek against the top of her head. "I have to find out who he was, and then I think I'm going to have to go out and find him. I don't think he's going to let me rest until I do."

"To clear that black mark off his record?"

"Partly. I think there's more, though."

"More?"

"I don't know, yet."

She sighed. "The one I feel sorry for is poor Judy. Pregnant and alone and afraid while they went out looking for her Colin. She must have been so frightened, and she must have tried so hard to keep up a brave front. Poor kid."

I had to smile. "She was about the same age as you are. How can you call her a kid?"

"Because sometimes I still feel like a kid. He was all she had, you know. There wasn't anybody else in the world she could turn to. Her Colin was all she had and she was all he had."

I raised my head, held her away, looked down at her, a slow chill crawling down my spine. "Delaney?"

"Umm?"

"How do you know that?"

She looked up at me, startled. "I don't know," she said slowly. "I just—I just know." She frowned, put one hand to her breastbone. "I just feel it, here, and I suddenly feel very close to Judy. Like empathy, you know? And I just know how she must have been feeling then." She laughed shakily. "My witchy ancestress at work again, maybe, shrieking as she went down for the third time." She blinked as the implications of what she had said dawned on her. "Wow. That gives us something else to think about, doesn't it?"

"It does, indeed," I said. "But I don't know if I really want to think about it right now—"

The phone rang. Delaney broke away from me to answer it, then turned and held it out to me. "For you," she said. "Tom Riker."

I crossed the room quickly and took the phone. "Mr. Riker, I'm glad you called," I said.

"Della said you wanted to talk about some research you were doing."

"Yes, sir. I was looking for some information about a man named McKenzie. Corporal Colin McKenzie. He died in an airplane crash in September, 1960. I wondered if you knew anything about him."

"What name was that again?"

"McKenzie. His full name was Colin Ryan McKenzie. He was a Corporal. A pilot in the Air Detachment."

"Yes. Yes, I see. Yes, I did know Corporal McKenzie. I would very much like to talk with you, Mr. Fraser. Unfortunately, we have a dinner engagement tonight, and I will be busy most of the day tomorrow. Would you care to drop around tomorrow evening? Perhaps around seven?"

"I'd like that very much, sir," I said. He gave me his address and I scribbled it down on the back of one of the photocopied sheets on the table.

"If you could hold on just a minute, I think I can find you the names and phone numbers of two other people who might be able to tell you something about him."

"I'll hold." I put my hand over the mouthpiece and told Delaney what he was doing.

"We lucked out?" she asked.

"Could be."

Tom Riker came back onto the line. "Yes, I thought I had something," he said. "The first is a man called Ted Wozoleynko. I believe he might have worked with Corporal McKenzie. He was a pilot with the Air Detachment, too. The other is a man named Rich Duggan. I believe he's a pilot with Canadian Airlines now. They might be able to help you." He gave me the telephone numbers, then chuckled. "It just so happens that I was going over some of my papers connected with that time only a month ago. It's quite a coincidence you happened to telephone now."

"It is odd, isn't it?" I said blandly. "I'm looking forward to meeting you, sir."

But I wondered exactly how big a part coincidence really played in any of this hide and seek search for Colin McKenzie. I had a feeling there might be as much coincidence as was involved when I saw the photograph of the old terminal building in the airport manager's office, or in Delaney noticing the photograph of him in the Air Harbour. I was beginning to speculate about his phantom finger reaching out to touch more than just my dreams. I wasn't sure if that was reassuring or just downright terrifying.

CHAPTER TWENTY-FIVE

DELANEY PEERED over my shoulder as I hung up the phone. She read the two names I had scribbled under Tom Riker's address, then looked up at me and grinned widely.

"Rich won't be back until tomorrow," she said thoughtfully. "He went to Toronto on some sort of course at Flight Safety. But I'll bet you dollars to doughnuts I know where to find Ted Wozoleynko."

I looked at her in mild amazement, although it was getting to the point where little about this mess surprised me. "I get this feeling I should hang you from a key chain instead of a rabbit's foot. You really do know every last pilot at that airport, don't you?"

"I told you I did. I spent six or seven years hanging around it before I went to Allgo. Then after I left Seattle, I came back. Rich and Woz are sort of landmarks around here, though. Rich must have been just a kid when Colin McKenzie flew for the Air Detachment, because I don't think he's much more than fifty now. Woz works for Northern Suppression. He spent umpty-dozen years in a B-26 firebomber, but he's getting a little long in the tooth for that now. He's the chief spotter pilot. And it just so happens he's in town. I saw him come in yesterday. His Aerostar must be due for some work."

"Where would he be?"

"His girlfriend tends bar in a place down on the south side where they play some cool blues and hot jazz. He's always down there when he's in town. If you like blues or jazz, it's the *in* bar in town. Want to try it?"

"I'll buy you a drink. Hell, I'll buy you two."

The place was called Artie's and it looked like an old converted gas station hung with gaudy green and pink neon. It was darker than the bottom of a Welsh coal mine inside. Delaney paused as we entered, and looked around. Then she pointed.

"There he is," she said and led the way through the crowded tables to the long, zinc-topped bar. A big man with a bushy shock of iron-grey hair turned slightly as she slid onto a chair beside him.

"Hey, Woz," she said. "I thought I'd find you here."

"Hey there, Braedon," he said. "You must be out slumming."

"I'm a true jazz aficionado," she said. "I'd like you to meet a friend of mine. Colin Fraser, Ted Wozoleynko."

Wozoleynko reached out a huge hand to me. "Hi there," he said. "What are you drinking?"

"Draft looks good."

He made a sign to the bartender, a blonde woman in her fifties, who drew three glasses and brought them over. She greeted Delaney by name, then moved away to serve someone else.

"Woz, we need to pick your brain," Delaney said. "Do

you remember a Force pilot called McKenzie? It would be back about 1960 or so. He flew a Beaver."

Wozoleynko took a long swallow of his beer. "McKenzie," he repeated thoughtfully. "Jesus, that was a long time ago. Yeah, I remember. He disappeared. They never did find him, last I heard."

"That's him," Delaney said.

He lit a cigarette and turned to look at her. "How come you're interested in a guy who got killed thirty-some-odd years ago, Little One?"

"I'm the one who's interested," I said. "Can you tell me anything about him?"

He swung around to look up at me where I stood behind Delaney. The light in the bar wasn't good. He peered through the gloom at me for a moment, then blinked. "Christ, you look enough like him to be his twin brother," he said. "Wait a minute. That little wife of his was pregnant when he went down. You gotta be his kid, huh?"

"Yes."

"Son-of-a-bitch," he said softly. "How about that?" He took another deep swallow of his beer and laughed quietly. "Yeah, I remember McKenzie. Christ, but he was one hard-nosed bastard. Cost me a promotion and damn near cost me my job, he did." He shook his head and laughed softly again, like a man deep in fond reminiscence. "One hell of a hard-nosed son-of-a-bitch, but oh my sweet Jesus, could that bastard fly."

I beckoned to the bartender for another round as Wozoleynko finished his beer. She brought them quickly.

"Never liked that bastard," he said, gazing thoughtfully off into the middle distance. "I dunno. We just never hit it off. He was senior pilot when I transferred in. He was a little younger than me, I remember. I thought he was a conceited son-of-a-bitch. Anyway, I dinged an airplane, a little Witchita spam can, a Cessna 180. Nothing serious. Just clipped a fence with a wingtip. Crumpled it a bit, busted the nav light, but the airplane was still okay, so I flew it back. It wasn't even ours; belonged to the Flying Club. I had borrowed it for the weekend. McKenzie hit the roof. Told me I should have called the DoT to let them know about the damage so they could go out and take a look at it before I flew it back. I said it was only a nav light, for Chrissake, and told him not to get his knickers into such a goddam twist. He said he was going to have to report me and I said it was only about fifty bucks' worth of damage so it was hardly worth it." He laughed softly in reminiscence. "Anyway, I heard about it from the DoT *and* Division, and I told McKenzie he was a real horse's ass, because that was the second time I got dumped on for bending one and they weren't happy with me even a little bit. One thing sort of led to another, so I invited him out behind the hangar. Surprised the hell out of me when he came out with me."

Delaney grinned and cuffed him gently. "For Pete's sake, Woz, you must have outweighed him by fifty pounds."

"More like seventy-five," he said, nodding. "Christ, I beat the shit out of him, but he kept on getting up every time I knocked him down. He got in a few good licks, too, though. But he just wouldn't stay down until finally I just couldn't lift my arms to hit him again. Then the crazy son-of-a-bitch wiped the blood off his mouth and looked at me and said, 'Goddammit, Woz, you're still a piss-poor excuse for a pilot but you've got one hell of a good left hand.' Jesus."

And for an instant, I felt the blood trickling down my chin

from a split lip, tasted it on my tongue, and I lifted a hand to wipe it away. Then the sensation was gone before I fully realized what it was.

Wozoleynko laughed again and shook his head in what might have been admiration. "Goddam. I'd almost forgot about that bastard. They found out we'd gone round and round together like that. I'll say one thing for him. He took his share of the blame, but I nearly got fired right out the door for beating on a superior NCO. Blew my promotion right out of the water. Probably set his promotion to sergeant back about ten years, too. That must have been around May or June. Early summer, anyway. He got killed that fall."

"You said he was a good pilot," I said. "What do you think happened to him?"

"Christ, who the hell knows?" He signalled for another round. "Back then, it was sort of accepted that if you flew long enough, you were eventually going to buy the farm. But when I think about it now, it was really strange. He was on a milk-run from out of the north. The weather was good. The airplane was in good shape. He knew the route. And like I said, he was one hell of a pilot. Cautious, and he knew that airplane inside and out. Christ, he could make it sit up and beg for cookies. Watching him fly that bird was enough to make you cry sweet tears. Never did see another pilot with his touch."

"They never did figure out what happened," I said.

"No, they never did. There were rumours floating around for a while. There was supposed to be a suitcase full of ransom money on the airplane. A few people wondered out loud if he was sitting somewhere in South America knocking back cold ones on a beach and laughing, but he was an honest cop. I don't think he took off with any money. But it would be interesting to find out where he got to."

"That's what I'm trying to do," I said. "Thanks, Woz. You've been a big help."

"If you ever find out, let me know," he said. "You're his kid, huh?"

"I was adopted when I was about a week old," I said. "His wife, Judy, died shortly after I was born."

"Yeah, I heard that. That's a shame. She was a pretty little thing."

I bought him another beer and we talked for a little while longer, then Delaney and I went home. I was feeling the effects of all the beer. Delaney had to fly in the morning, and had been surreptitiously passing me her beer after the first one. But he had given me a small insight into Colin McKenzie's character. And added a bit to the mystery of his disappearance.

We lay together on the wide bed, Delaney's head on my shoulder, the faint gleam of city light coming through the pale rectangle of the window.

"I got another flashback today," I told her quietly, marvelling at how calm my voice sounded. "And another one the other day when I met you at the airport. I don't know what it means. The only thing I can think of is that he's closer to me now that I'm here looking for him."

She raised herself on one elbow and looked down at me. She said nothing, but her expression was grave and thoughtful, and perhaps a bit apprehensive in the dim light.

"It's not really scary," I said, thinking about it. "It's just a bit startling, and eerie. Sends shivers down my spine, but that's all."

"Do you think it'll happen again?"

"Yeah, I do. Especially if I stay here in Edmonton. But maybe it's a good sign. Maybe it means we're getting closer to finding out who he really was, and what happened to him."

She lay back again, her breath warm against the side of my throat. "Maybe. We'll see."

The next morning, Delaney dragged me out of bed early and took me down to the airport with her. We caught Rich Duggan in the Canadian Airlines Ops Office and Delaney introduced us before she went scooting off to strap on the G-IV for a flight to Vancouver. I offered to buy Duggan breakfast in the cafeteria in exchange for some information, and he grinned as he accepted.

"Colin McKenzie?" he repeated as we settled ourselves to dig into monstrous breakfasts. "RCMP pilot, wasn't he?"

I was getting more practiced at telling the story now. Duggan frowned thoughtfully as I spoke, then nodded. "Yeah, I think I remember him."

"Anything you can tell me about him would help a lot."

"I didn't know him very well. I was just a kid instructor at the Flying Club then. He and the other pilots used to come over to the cafeteria at the Club for coffee or lunch when they were in town. I had the world's biggest case of hero worship on all of them. Almost figured their wings came out of their backs instead of their airplanes. I don't remember that much about him, really, but I can remember that it was an education to watch him fly that damned Beaver."

"I've been told he was a good pilot."

"You fly, too, do you?"

I nodded. "I'm a captain for Holiday West out of Seattle."

"On the '37?"

"I've been on the '57 for a bit better than a year."

"Like it?"

"It's a great airplane. Maybe not as much fun as the '37."

"So I've heard." He grinned. "Everyone loves the ol' Turbo Football. Loves 'em or hates 'em. Jet age version of the old Dakota."

I grinned back. "Swear by them or at them."

"Yeah." He was busy with his eggs and sausages for a moment. Then he said, "One thing about McKenzie—he always had time for a young pilot who needed help with something. If you asked him something about flying and paid attention, he'd spend any amount of time trying to help. I learned a lot listening him to him talk. But he sure didn't have much patience with people who did anything stupid. I was on the ramp with a student once and somebody came back with one of the Fleets. Left it tail into the wind. McKenzie was out there, just coming for lunch, I think. He lit into the guy and tore a strip about a yard wide off him. Then he helped him turn the airplane into the wind. He collared me and told me I should have been there yelling at the pilot because I worked there and he didn't. Made me feel as if I were about an inch high. Problem was, he was right, of course."

"Ted Wozoleynko called him a hard-nosed bastard."

Duggan laughed. "Yeah, he could be, I guess. I can see how he and Woz could disagree a lot. Woz is a real cowboy pilot in a lot of ways. He quit the Force not long after McKenzie disappeared and went to work for Northern Suppression. Found a home flying those old B-26s. They made him move over into the spotter planes about four years ago before he clipped off one tree top too many. I don't know what he's going to do when they tell him he has to retire. He's over sixty now, and still as wild as ever."

"He must be pretty good if he's still alive."

"Or lucky," Duggan said.

"That, too."

"I don't know what else I can tell you about McKenzie. He was a good pilot. He wasn't maybe the easiest person in the world to get along with, but he had a lot of friends here. I didn't know him all that well, but he was a good friend to me. I remember once I was having a hard time with some silly thing, can't even remember exactly what, and I asked him about it. He sorted it out for me in four words. Fly first, then teach. I've never forgotten it. It was damned good advice."

"Captain Duggan, do you know of anyone else I could talk to if I wanted to find out more about McKenzie?"

He thought for a moment. "I can't think of anyone around here. Thirty years is a long time."

"I know. I'm going around to see a man named Riker tomorrow. He's the one who gave me your name, in fact. But if you could think of anyone, I'd certainly appreciate it." And I handed him my card.

"I'll think about it. If I can come up with anyone, I'll give you a call." Duggan slipped the card into the pocket of his uniform shirt.

I thanked him, and we shook hands. Then just for a second, his face wavered and I caught a glimpse of the young man he must have been thirty years ago. I shivered and turned away.

I went home and called Alan Thurlow.

"You've found out a lot more than I did, Captain Fraser,"

he said. "I haven't been able to come up with a thing. In fact, from what you tell me, it sounds as if you don't need my services at all anymore."

"I'd like to keep you on retainer anyway," I said. "Just in case something comes up."

"Sure. I'll keep the file open. Let me know if you need anything."

Delaney called me at five-thirty to tell me she was back. I went to pick her up and we had something to eat before we went to call on Tom Riker and his wife.

"You don't mind if I come?" Delaney asked.

"I want you there," I said.

Twenty-five minutes later, we pulled up in front of a small white-frame house surrounded by old, full foliaged trees. The hedge bordering the sidewalk was neatly trimmed and marigolds lined the concrete walk leading up to the front steps. As Delaney and I got out of the car, the door opened and a tall old man came out onto the cement porch steps. Tom Riker was probably close to eighty. He looked and carried himself like a man who had once commanded a lot of authority, very much like a retired admiral who was a friend of my father's back in Brindle Falls. Beneath the shaggy white eyebrows, his faded blue eyes still looked sharp and alert. At one time, he must have been a very handsome man, because traces of it were still visible in the deeply lined parchment of his face. Behind him, I caught a glimpse of an old woman in a wheelchair.

"Come in," he said as Delaney and I approached. His voice was deep and firm. "You're the living image of your father, young man. I've been expecting you for a long time."

CHAPTER TWENTY-SIX

WE WERE seated in a comfortably old fashioned living room that might more properly be called a parlour. The sofa and chairs held snow white hand-crocheted antimacassars and arm protectors. It was quiet and cool in the room which smelled pleasantly of lavender and heather.

Some of the shock of Tom Riker's greeting had worn off. He had quickly shepherded Delaney and me, both of us still speechless, into the house and introduced us to his wife, Della. Mrs. Riker was badly crippled with arthritis, her hands twisted and gnarled, an awkward warp in her back. But she had greeted us warmly, then said she was going to get us some tea. Delaney had come out of her trance with a snap and jumped up to offer help. Now, the four of us, fortified with cups of strong India tea, were beginning to relax a little.

"Mr. Riker..." I began.

He smiled and held up a hand. "Please. Call me Tom. We're not related, but we very well could have been."

"Tom, then," I said faintly. "Frankly, I don't know what to say. I'm overwhelmed."

"Tom was never known for his diplomatic tact," Mrs. Riker said with an impish smile. It was easy to see that she had once been a very lovely woman. Despite the distorted body, she retained a great deal of natural charm and poise.

"I owe you an explanation," he said. "And you'll get it very shortly. But first, I'd appreciate you telling me something about yourself. I'm extremely interested in you. What do you do?"

"I'm a captain for an airline out of Seattle," I said. "I fly 757's, sir."

"You're very young to be a captain," he said. "You must be good at what you do."

"He is," Delaney said and smiled. "I was his first officer for two years. I should know."

He nodded and gave her what was almost a fellow conspirator's smile. "I see. Well, it's obvious they did a good job of raising you, Colin. I was sure they would. I saw them come to the hospital to get you. They looked like a very fine pair of young people."

My head was beginning to whirl in confusion again. I looked around for somewhere to put down the delicate tea cup and saucer I held. The only place available seemed to be in the middle of another white doily on a low table beside the sofa. I put the china down before I dropped it, then looked blankly up at Tom Riker. "Sir?" I said. "Tom, just who in the hell are you?"

"I'm sorry," he said. He made impatient gestures with his hands — impatient with himself more than with me. "I do apologize. You must think I'm playing games with you. It's just that I'm so delighted to see you I keep getting ahead of myself. I was Colin McKenzie's godfather. I was with Judy McKenzie when she died. The last thing I promised her was that I'd see to it that you got a good home with people who'd love you."

I remembered what my parents had said about the adoption, and thought for a moment. "Then you must be the guardian who signed the adoption papers." I reached for the cup and saucer to give my hands something to do besides clench into fists.

"I drew them up, too," he said. "Between old Alan Thurlow and myself, we kept all those nosy agency people as far away from it as we could. They would have delayed the adoption for weeks or months, and everyone knows that a small baby needs a mother close to it when it's very tiny. It would have done you no good at all to stay in a hospital until everything could be finalized, or bounced around between foster homes, either. I did what I thought would turn out to be the best thing for you. I trusted Alan to find good people for me, I told him to tell your adoptive parents to take you home and register your birth in their home town because I didn't want any interference from those goddam governmental agencies. I'd seen how they could mess things up. I wanted none of that for you. Not for Colin and Judy's son."

"You said you were Colin McKenzie's godfather.... So that means you must have known him quite well."

"I think I knew him as well as anyone did. His father, Geordie McKenzie, was one of the best friends I ever had. He was a member of the Force, too. We stood as best man for each other's wedding. He was godfather to our first daughter, and Della and I were godparents to his son. I suppose back in those days godparents took their responsibilities a little more seriously. Colin's mother died when he was only twelve. Ellen had never regained all her strength after Colin was born. The doctors could never really tell what was wrong with her. You could almost say she just faded away after that. Geordie took it hard. He died when Colin was seventeen."

As he spoke, I got a flash of a man, stockily built in a uniform I didn't recognize, sandy hair, blue eyes with laugh crinkles around them. It was only a momentary glimpse, but it startled me. I put down the cup and saucer before it rattled in my hand to the point of chipping or breaking.

"We lost track of Colin for a while after that," Mrs. Riker said. If she or Tom had noticed the catch in my breathing, neither of them commented on it. "The next time we saw him was when he showed up in Kamloops, fresh out of training in Regina. Tom was NCO/ic of the detachment there. That must have been in July or August of 1952."

"NCO/ic?"

"Non-commissioned officer in charge of the detachment," Tom said. He laughed. "I was a Sergeant then, and I was Colin's boss and I think it took him back a pace or two. He had always wanted to join the Force. After he finished school, he applied. They didn't take him until he was twenty-two. While he was waiting for acceptance, he'd gone out to Alberta and taken a job in the Turner Valley Oilfields and learned how to fly. When I saw him again in Kamloops, all he wanted was to put in his time so he could get into the Air Detachment, which was just getting started again after the war then, and marry the girl he had met back in Regina. Back then, the Force wouldn't let a man marry until he had served five years."

Before I could speak, Delaney asked the question I wanted to ask next. "What was he like, Mr. Riker?. What kind of a man was he?"

Tom sat back and thought for a moment. "What kind of a man was he," he said thoughtfully. He gazed off into the middle distance for a moment before answering. "Well, he was a hot-headed kid sometimes, Miss Braedon," he said slowly. "Never a discipline problem, but he tended to be a bit of a maverick. A good police officer, though. He had a knack for handling people. He could walk into a bad situation and most of the time, he could simmer things down before it got really bad. If it did go really bad, he was quick and tough enough to calm it down. He did his job well. He could be impatient, too. He had a lot of trouble putting up with stupidity, either in a fellow constable or a superior officer. Let's just say he didn't suffer fools gladly."

I had to laugh. "I heard the same thing from Rich Duggan and Ted Wozoleynko," I said.

The corners of Tom's mouth quirked slightly. "Yes, there was a small matter of a disciplinary action there, I think," he said. "I think that bothered me more than it bothered Colin, though. He wasn't anxious for any kind of a promotion. He was pretty happy just flying that Beaver." He shook his head, still smiling. "He also didn't particularly like all of the rules and regulations and spit and polish and paperwork, but he was proud of the uniform he wore, and he worked as best he could within the system. I guess you could say he was a good man."

"He was certainly keen on flying," Mrs. Riker said. "He once told me it was the only thing he'd ever done that made him feel as if he could get up and out of the world, away from all the stupid little things that dragged a man down. When he talked about flying, I could almost imagine how a bird might feel."

"How long was he in Kamloops?" I asked.

"About two years" Tom said. "He got transferred out in the fall of '54 to a place called Manyberries in Alberta here. It was a two or three-man detachment, so he ended up working on his own a lot. We heard from him occasionally. His fitness reports were always good. He was developing into a fine police officer with a good record. Della and I didn't see him again, though, until he transferred into Edmonton in the winter of '56. By then, he had almost five years in, and he went back to Regina to bring Judy out here. They were planning on getting married in the spring, in April or May."

"She was a pretty little thing, about your size, dear," Mrs. Riker said, smiling at Delaney. "She was very quiet and shy. She found a job as a secretary in a school and she and Colin spent all their spare time together. She didn't much like him flying, though. She said it made her nervous. She was always afraid when he went up in an airplane. She wouldn't go with him. She'd just sit on the ground and clench her hands until her fingernails bit right into them, then smile for him when he came back down."

"Did he know it frightened her?" Delaney asked.

"Oh dear, I hope not," Mrs. Riker said. "She certainly tried her best not to let it show."

"He knew," I said, suddenly certain of it. "He knew but always hoped she'd grow to be okay with it."

Tom and Mrs. Riker stared at me, eyebrows raised. "Do you think so?" she asked.

"I seem to get flashes from him at times," I said. "I can't explain them, or why I know things. It just happens."

Tom and Mrs. Riker exchanged glances. Then Mrs. Riker smiled. "Oddly enough, Colin," she said, "Judy used to say the same thing. Sometimes, she'd just know something. But it didn't seem to work both ways. It would seem that, whatever it is, you come by it honestly."

"She certainly seemed to be able to read him very well,"

Tom said. "More easily than he could read her. But then, women sometimes are puzzles to men. Aren't they, Della?"

She just smiled.

"When did he start flying the Beavers?" I asked.

"Colin transferred into the air detachment in March of '57," Tom said. "They put him onto the Beavers right away and he was out of town a lot"

"Was it on amphib floats?"

He frowned. "I don't think the Force was running anything on amphib floats back then."

Mrs. Riker reached out and touched his arm. "Yes, they were," she said. "Colin's was. Remember? He said it came on amphib floats when they acquired it, and they kept them on because it was less expensive than changing over to straight floats. He said it was an experiment."

"That's right." Tom nodded thoughtfully. "It was the only one in Canada, wasn't it?" He smiled and went on with his story. "They kept the pilots pretty busy. They did a lot of ambulance flights back in those days, what do you call them now?"

"Medevacs," I said. "I did the same thing for a couple of years before I got on with Holiday West."

"Did you? That's interesting. A lot of Colin's flights were bringing First Nations down to the T.B. ward at the Camsell Hospital, or bringing in women who were going to have babies. Accidents. That sort of thing. He also carried medical supplies back and forth a lot—"

"There's a picture of him at Mildred Lake with a plane load of medical supplies," I said. "It's hanging in the Air Harbour Lounge at the airport."

"Is there now?" Tom said. "I didn't know that. Mind you, we don't spend a lot of time there."

"Delaney spotted it," I said. "That's how I finally found out he was an RCMP pilot."

"I'll have to go and take a look at it."

"Sorry, sir. I shouldn't have interrupted you."

He waved it away. "No, that's all right. Now, where was I? Oh, yes... Colin's flying. Well, he was having the time of his life flying like that. But every time he went out, Judy sat home and worried her heart out for him. They were married in April of '57. She asked me if I'd give her away. Her parents were both dead, and she didn't have anyone. I was glad to do the honour."

"She got pregnant almost right away," Mrs. Riker said. "But she lost the baby after only three or four months. Colin was away on a flight at the time. We took her to the hospital, Tom and I did. When Colin finally got there, it was all over. He was beside himself with grief and he was so frightened for her until he found out she was going to be all right. He blamed himself because he wasn't there when she started to miscarry. He told her that he'd give up the flying so he could be home more if she wanted him to. She said he wasn't to give it up because of her. She told him she'd eventually get used to him being away so much, and he was to keep on because it was the only thing he really wanted to do. I think she knew that he was one of those people who just had to fly and that he'd just dry up and get bitter and grim if he didn't, and she didn't want that because it might mean he'd end up resenting her, and she knew that would just about kill her."

"So he kept on flying," I said.

"Yes," Tom said. "He kept on flying. He eventually figured out what it was doing to Judy, but he had to keep on flying. I think the only time the boy was really happy was when he was flying or when he was with his wife. I know it bothered him greatly that Judy was so worried when he flew, and it bothered him that he couldn't give it up. He loved her a great deal, but he loved flying, too. I don't know what would have happened to them if things had gone differently. Perhaps he would have stopped flying for her sake, I don't know. But he would have ended up being miserable if he had to stay on the ground all the time. And as for Judy, she would have been happy to see him stop flying but unhappy because he was."

And he was with me again. I felt the problem tearing him in two, his love for his wife on one side, his love of flying on the other, and sometimes it threatened to overwhelm him. I felt it as sharply as if it were my own dilemma.

"Judy knew she had married a policeman," Mrs. Riker said. "She was prepared to accept all that that entailed. But she hadn't known she had also married a pilot. She tried her best, but she never stopped being afraid for him."

As she spoke, I could again hear that heart-breaking voice in the dream calling my name. No, his name. Not mine. *His* name. I shivered.

"She was in a no-win situation," Delaney said softly. "If he didn't stop flying, she would never stop being frightened, and if he did stop, she'd never stop being unhappy because he was. She must have loved him very much."

"She did," Tom said. "They were good for each other. They were good *to* each other, too. Oh, that's not to say they never disagreed. I can remember a few times when Judy stood nose to nose and toe to toe with Colin over what she called his mule-headed stubbornness. She wasn't very big but she had her share of spirit. And there were times that Colin called her down for some fool thing or another, just like any other married couple. But by and large, they got along very well together. After she lost the first child, she wanted another but it took a long time for her to conceive again. Colin wasn't sure it was a very good idea because of what had happened to the first child, but we knew he wanted children, too. He was against it for a while, but she brought him around eventually."

"Judy wasn't a really strong person," Mrs. Riker said softly. "She was a gentle, loving and trusting girl. She was spirited and independent and coped when Colin was away because he was her strength, and I think he knew that. As long as she had him, she could be as strong as she needed to be. She came to see me in the late winter of 1960. She told me she was pregnant again. She was all excited and happy about it. She said she hadn't told Colin about it and that she was planning to tell him as a surprise on their wedding anniversary. She told me the baby was due around the end of September."

"We know about what happened to him," I said. "A friend of Delaney's dug up the old newspaper articles about it."

"It very nearly destroyed Judy," Mrs. Riker said. "Except for us, she didn't have anyone else in the world. She kept saying she had to carry on because of the baby, but Colin had been her whole life. I think she knew he was dead a long time before anyone else accepted the fact. She knew the search was useless. She tried to keep up a brave face for the rest of us, but she was grieving for him a long time before we let ourselves believe he was dead. She went into labour half an hour after the memorial service. You were born at about five-thirty, Colin. She died about eleven-thirty. The doctors said it was because her heart had been weakened by rheumatic fever when she was a child. I always fancied that she died of grief—a broken heart. I know that's silly of me, but Tom always accused me of being far too romantic and completely impractical."

"They never found the airplane," Tom said. "Colin's still out there somewhere. It would be nice if he could be brought back some day and laid to rest beside her."

"Inspector Murchie told me that there was a faint suspicion that he had skipped out with that ransom money," I said.

"That's pure horse manure," Tom said roundly, his colour rising. "I told Internal Affairs that at the time. I knew that boy as well as anyone did, and I told them that he might have been a maverick, but he certainly wasn't dishonest. And he would never desert Judy like that. But that damned stink of suspicion is still there."

"I'm going to try to do something about that," I said, and knew I was going to do exactly that. I was going to find him and clear his name. I just wasn't sure yet how I was going to go about it.

"It would be nice to find out what happened," Tom said. "Nobody ever knew. All the pilots in the detachment, in fact all the pilots on the field who knew him all said Colin was one of the best pilots around. He was careful, he never took unnecessary chances, never pushed himself or his aircraft past the limits. You'd wonder why a good pilot would crash when the weather was good and there didn't seem to be anything wrong with the airplane."

"We've got a few things you might like to see," Mrs. Riker said. "A few photographs and things. Would you like me to bring them out?"

I looked up at her, startled. It had never occurred to me that there would be photographs. I hadn't prepared myself as well as I had thought, obviously. "Please," I said. "I'd very much like to see them."

"I'll get them, Della," Tom said. "You rest for a moment." He got up and left the room.

He came back a few moments later with a small, round cardboard box tied with a blue ribbon. "One of Della's hat boxes," he said absently as he opened it. "Nice handy size." He peered into the box and stirred the contents with his finger. "Not that much here, Colin. Just a few photographs and odds and end. You might as well take a look at it." He held the box out to me.

For some reason, I was suddenly very reluctant to take it. Tom Riker was handing me mementoes of someone else's life, souvenirs of a life that might have been mine if things had been very different. The people in those old photographs should have been familiar to me, their faces, their expressions, their stances. I should have been able to recall the way they laughed, or the way they sat in a pensive mood, or the way they expressed love or happiness or anger. I should have been able to look at the photos and say which ones were good likenesses, which ones didn't look at all like them. I couldn't because I never knew them. I had been conceived in an act of love between two people I had never known, never really would know. What Tom Riker was offering me now was the only part of them that was still left, and for some reason, I didn't know if I wanted to take it from him. It was as if by taking it, I would be accepting responsibility for them. If I took that box from Tom Riker's hand, I would be acknowledging that Colin and Judy McKenzie were real people, not just part and parcel of my dreams. It would make me forever Colin James *McKenzie* Fraser, and right then, I didn't know if I wanted to be him.

Tom Riker smiled. "Take it, Colin," he said gently. "It won't change anything."

I took the box.

As Tom had said, there wasn't much in it. A photograph

of Colin McKenzie as a young man of about eighteen standing, smiling broadly, under the wing of an old Piper J-3 Cub. I had to take a deep breath to steady myself before I could look further. Bemused, I realized I knew that aircraft. I had seen the underside of the wing while I was practicing steep turns and stalls in a Cessna 150 shortly after my sixteenth birthday. I knew it was the same one I'd seen. That was the first weird and eerie thing my father had sent me.

I picked up another photograph, a studio portrait of a lovely young woman with dark, curling hair in three-quarter profile, smiling with that mysterious, secret smile studio photographers in that era liked to capture on film. I looked at her photograph for a long time, but whatever Colin McKenzie had sent me in my dreams, it contained no images of her at all. There was another studio portrait of him wearing a Stetson and a high-necked tunic, looking very serious and official, but even the levelness of the mouth couldn't hide the glint of laughter in the eyes. It looked like the photograph that had been reproduced in the newspaper to accompany the news story on his disappearance. There were several candid snapshots of them together, self-consciously smiling for the camera. Another studio portrait, a wedding portrait this time. It showed her in a bridal gown, a mist of white veil over her dark hair, and him wearing his dress scarlet as they came out of a church door under an arch of sabres held by a double row of similarly outfitted mounted policemen. They looked very happy. The last photograph was of him dressed in a fur parka, standing in the snow with his hand up against the fuselage of the Beaver, a proprietary gesture. He was again smiling broadly into the camera.

Delaney reached over to pick up the portrait of Judy. She

lightly traced the delicate oval of her face with her finger, her teeth pressing into her lower lip. "She looks so young," she murmured.

"She was only twenty-one when that picture was taken," Tom said. "I think it was taken a month or two before they married."

Delaney looked at the photograph for a moment or two, then put it back into the box with the rest of the things.

"That's all there is," Della Riker said. "They were good people, Colin. Just ordinary people, nothing really special about them, but they were good people. You can keep that box, if you'd like it. If you don't want it, we'll understand."

"They're strangers to me," I said, feeling a little helpless and confused. "I look at pictures of him, and it makes me feel odd because he looks so much like me but I don't know him at all. I don't know who he is."

"Of course you don't," Tom said. Beside him, Mrs. Riker smiled sympathetically and reached out to pat my hand. "I think the best thing you can do right now is spend some time thinking about it. You're more than welcome to come back and talk with Della and me any time you want to. We're usually home, except when Della gets sick of having me around and sends me out fishing for a day or so."

"It's an awful lot to take in for just one afternoon," Mrs. Riker said.

I got to my feet. "I'd like to leave this with you for a while," I said and handed the box back to Tom. "If you could give me a couple of days to mull this through, I'd really like to come back and talk to you again."

"Please do," Tom said. "What are you going to do now?"

I laughed softly and shook my head. "I don't know. But I'm pretty sure I've got to go out there and find him. If I can't, there isn't anybody else who can."

CHAPTER TWENTY-SEVEN

I SLEPT badly that night. I don't remember dreaming but I awoke several times and Colin McKenzie was in my thoughts. At three in the morning, I got up and went to the living room, afraid that my restless tossing around would disturb Delaney. She needed her sleep. She had to fly at seven. I heated a cup of coffee in the microwave and sat at the table with it. All the information that had flooded into my hands in the last couple of days churned through my head like the babble of a busy room. There was just too much there to make sense of all at once. Somehow, I was going to have to sort it out into its component pieces and align it into its proper perspective if I was ever going to assimilate it. But every time I tried to latch on to one fragment, hundreds of others swirled up and I couldn't concentrate on any of them. It was worse than trying to keep track of one raindrop in a hurricane.

Delaney's arms wrapped around my shoulders from behind me and her soft cheek pressed against my temple. "Can't sleep?" she asked.

"My mind is going at nearly mach two," I said. "I can't seem to keep up with it."

She dropped a quick kiss near the corner of my eye. "Come back to bed. Do you think it will help sort it out if you talk about it?"

I shook my head. "Not yet," I said. "It doesn't even make enough sense to think about let alone talk about yet."

"It must be a bit like getting hit across the back of the skull with a length of two by four. Scrambles your circuits."

I laughed without much humour. "That's as good description as any. Delaney, sweetheart, listen, it's not that I don't want to talk about it—"

"Don't be an idiot," she said, squeezing my shoulders. "I know that. I'm not going to get all hurt and upset because I think you don't want to talk to me. I know you will when you can." She kissed my ear, slyly inserted her tongue into it and swirled it around gently, then she sighed and pulled back. "No," she said. "That's probably not what's needed right now. Come to bed. Just hold me until I fall asleep again, then you can get up and prowl all you want."

I reached up and pulled her around so that I could bring her down into my lap. "You are something pretty special, Braedon," I told her. "Until I met you again, I think I was in very real danger of turning all austere and grave and far too serious. Do you know, I don't think I've laughed as much in the last five years as I have this last few days with you. I keep wanting to say thank you. I want to marry you just as soon as we can possibly arrange it."

She shook her head. "No, I don't think so," she said. "I think it should wait until you've finished what you have to do here. Now come to bed. I've got to sleep and you've got a lot of thinking to do, and we both might as well be comfortable while we do it."

Delaney was gone when I woke up. There was a note propped up against the coffee pot. "Home tomorrow night.

You'd better miss me." The coffee was still hot. I poured a cup, took it into the living room and sat on the couch. There was a copy of the latest issue of Aviation Trade on the end table, a picture of a sexy looking Piper Malibu on its cover. I picked it up and idly leafed through it as I drank the coffee, looking at the pictures of all the sleek corporate jets and turboprops for sale. Somebody even had a fully restored old F4U Corsair for sale. The photo made it look terrific, but he wanted over a million for it. That made it one very expensive toy and proved the old adage that you can tell the men from the boys by the price of their toys.

A boxed ad at the bottom of the page near the middle of the paper caught my eye. It contained a list of aircraft for sale by a dealer in a place called Ratchet Lake in Saskatchewan. Canadians seemed to have a penchant for strange names, I mused, then realized I was staring at the line that listed two DHC-2 Beavers for sale, one on Wipline straight floats, one on Edo amphibs. Both also came with hydraulic wheel-skis. The ad said, *Call for prices.* Before I had a chance to think about what I was doing, I had the phone in my hand and there was the harsh buzz of the ringing signal in my ear.

"Lake Air, Barry speaking. Can I help you?"

"I'm calling about a couple of Beavers you had listed for sale in Aviation Trade," I said. "Still have them?"

"The Beavers? Yes, we do. Were you interested in one of them in particular?"

"The one on the Edo amphibs." I said. "What can you tell me about it?"

"Well, frankly, the other one's a better buy. The one on Edos has only got about four hundred hours left on the engine and the other's only done six hundred SMOH." Since major overhaul, technically bringing a tired old engine back to zero time, or brand new. Re-virgining, we call it. "Both are pretty high time airframes, between nine and ten thousand hours. They both flew a lot, hauling cargo mostly."

I didn't think that was really going to be a problem. The very least a high time airframe tells a buyer is that someone took reasonably good care of it. If they were working aircraft, it might also mean they weren't exactly pretty and polished any more.

"How about Certificates of Airworthiness?" I asked.

"Both are current C's of A. The one on Edos just had its annual about two months ago."

"So no major snags?"

"No. The interior's sort of battered, but you have to expect that."

"Of course. If I wanted pretty, I'd buy a Malibu."

He laughed. It sounded like genuine mirth, not a salesman's hunger for a sale. "Nobody would call a Beaver pretty at the best of times," he agreed.

"What else can you tell me?"

"They're pretty well even on avionics. Both have an HF radio, a VHF nav-comm stack and an ADF. The one on Edos has a transponder, the other doesn't, but they're easy to install. Other than that, they're sort of plain vanilla."

"Do the radios work?"

"They bench tested okay."

I nodded. I'd dealt with bench tested avionics before while working on the Stinson. Sometimes they worked fine on the bench, and not at all in the aircraft, and sometimes you got lucky. I wouldn't get my hopes up too high. "How much are you asking for the one on amphibs?"

"Two hundred and two," he said cautiously. "The floats are worth about a hundred."

"Horsepuckey, Barry," I said. I had no idea how much a set of used Edo amphibs for a Beaver was worth, but he sounded far too hopeful, as if he were tossing out a line to see if he could catch himself an unwary fish. "I'd like to come and take a look at it. Where the hell is Ratchet Lake?"

"About a hundred and fifty miles north of La Ronge, sir." My obvious interest had earned me the title of respect.

I didn't know where La Ronge was, either, so I was no further ahead. "I'm in Edmonton," I told him. "What's the quickest and easiest way to get there?"

"Uh, lessee. Probably Time Air to Saskatoon, then to La Ronge, then our Cheyenne to here. We connect with the Dash-8. But you'll probably have to overnight in Saskatoon."

"Okay. Let me sort out the schedules. I'll call you back in about half an hour with the date I'll be up there. My name's Fraser, by the way. Colin Fraser."

"Sure, Mr. Fraser. I'll expect to hear from you."

I called Canadian Airlines. They had Time Air flights from Saskatoon to La Ronge on Tuesdays, Wednesdays and Fridays. The flights from Edmonton to Saskatoon didn't connect. I booked Delaney and myself on the 1815 flight out of Edmonton to Saskatoon on Tuesday, then on the 0815 to La Ronge on Wednesday morning. I hoped she had some holiday time coming. Then I called Barry at Lake Air back and told him I'd be arriving in La Ronge at 0945 Wednesday morning and to reserve space for two on his Cheyenne.

When I hung up again, I sat for a moment and stared

blankly at the wall. Whatever it was I'd done, I'd done before I could think a whole lot about it. Talk about impulse buying. "Fraser, you've fallen right out of your tree," I said aloud.

Which is almost exactly what Delaney said when she got home on Saturday evening.

Before she got home, I spent a busy day and a half. I went to see Alan Thurlow and asked if he could handle all the legal work for the purchase of the aircraft, if I decided to buy it. He had never handled an aircraft sale and purchase before, but he figured it couldn't be too much different than handling a vehicle purchase, or perhaps a house purchase. I could tell him what he had to check out, and he could check with the MoT on their requirements. There would be the standard checks for liens and charges against the aircraft, and he could get someone who knew how to check into the documentation. He said it would be a new experience and he might actually enjoy it.

Then I went to a Royal Bank of Canada and opened an account. I had them cable my bank in Seattle and arrange to forward any funds I might need. Having already purchased one aircraft, I knew that the initial cost of the Beaver was going to be only the first in a long string of expenses. I was going to have to pay an engineer a goodly piece of change to check over the aircraft very thoroughly, and probably pay him an even larger bundle of cash to fix it to the point where I would feel comfortable flying it. There were also going to be a whole slew of other incidental odds and ends that nobody ever counts on. But I had learned of them first hand when I bought the Stinson. Then all the picky little things like transfer and registration fees. I was going to need considerably more capital than just the purchase price of the aircraft.

I found some time Saturday afternoon to visit Tom Riker again. We didn't say much about Colin McKenzie then. He wanted to know more about me. Most of our conversation concerned my childhood, growing up on the edge of the ocean in Brindle Falls. He was interested in my parents, and, when I left him, he looked pleased. And I thought he also looked a little relieved. He had discharged his duty and obligation to Colin and Judy McKenzie as he had promised, and had looked after their son. And in the long run, it had turned out he had made an excellent decision.

Delaney got home at a little after six on Saturday afternoon. I took her out for shrimp and steak. We got home just before ten, and I told her then we were booked through to La Ronge the following Tuesday morning.

"La Ronge?" she repeated blankly. "Colin, are you out of your mind?"

"Quite likely."

"Holy cats. You don't even know where La Ronge is—"

"Hell, I'm not even sure where Saskatoon is either, but I'm sure the Time Air boys know where they're going. We're actually going to Ratchet Lake, a hundred and fifty miles north of La Ronge."

"Ratchet Lake," she said and shook her head. "Dear merciful God in heaven. Why?"

"I'm going to buy a Beaver."

"You're going to buy a Beaver?"

"On Edo amphib floats."

She stared at me, then shook her head again, looking bewildered. "You've lost your marble, haven't you. You've fallen right out of your tree. Do you know how much those things cost? Lordy, it's going to cost about a thousand just to get us to Ratchet Lake." She wasn't angry; just very puzzled.

"Delaney, I've got enough money. I've got more money than I'll ever need in my life. When Glynnis died, I found out her mother had set up a trust fund for her that had matured when she turned thirty-five. It was part of her estate, so it came to me. And there were the proceeds from the sale of that damned house. I'm up to my fuzzy eyebrows in money."

She sat down on the couch with a thump and stared blankly at me for a long moment. Finally, a little breathlessly, she said, "Then I guess you can afford a Beaver, or anything else you want. You never said anything about money before."

"Is it important?"

"Not when I didn't know you had some."

"Does it make a difference because it was mostly Glynnis's money?"

Her expression softened. "Does it make a difference to you, Colin?"

"It bothered me for quite a while," I said. "I didn't want to take it at first. I wanted to give it away or something. Glynnis's father talked me into accepting it and putting it to good use. I didn't stay married to her for her money, because she never told me she had any. Actually, she never told me anything about her personal finances, ever. I knew her father had a lot of money, but I wasn't expecting to get any of it. He told me once that he had made a will leaving most of what he had to Glynnis's two brothers. All he said about her was that he had made some small provisions for her. If there weren't any children, then her share reverted to her brothers. I told him I agreed with setting it up that way, for some pretty obvious reasons."

"You are truly a man of surprises," she said, shaking her head. She began to laugh. "Okay. Okay, so we go to Ratchet Lake on Tuesday and we buy you a Beaver on amphib floats. I've got a couple of weeks' vacation coming. Mark can sit left seat for a while. It'll be good for him."

"Do you have a float endorsement?"

"Yes. Don't you?"

"Nope. So you're going to have to teach me how to fly floats."

"That should be interesting...." Her voice trailed off as the significance struck her. "A Beaver on amphib floats..." She slanted a sharp look up at me, meeting my gaze with a small frown. "Because of Colin McKenzie?"

I nodded. Her eyes were wide, almost startled. I gave her what must have been a slightly mystified smile. "Yes. I think I'm going to retrace his route between Juniper Ridge and Peace River."

"But couldn't you do it just as well in the Stinson?"

I turned away and walked over to the window. It looked out over the city. To the north, I could see the airport. In the late evening sun, the runways looked long and narrow and graceful. Delaney came over to stand beside me. I didn't think I could explain to her logically why it had to be a Beaver, and not only a Beaver, but one on amphibious floats. Hell, I didn't think I could explain it logically to myself.

"Okay," she said. "So it has to be a Beaver on amphib floats. I hope you know what you're doing, Colin."

"So do I. I've never flown a Beaver before."

"That's not what I mean and I think you know it."

"I think I do, but it doesn't seem to make much difference."

"Just remember something. Colin McKenzie died in a Beaver on amphib floats. If he's pushing you this hard, so that you have to go over his last trip as closely as possible, you just be careful that you don't duplicate the very last part of his trip."

Chapter Twenty-Eight

RATCHET LAKE was a bustling, primitive little place, surrounded by boreal forest. It went a long way to shatter my illusions about Saskatchewan being flat, bald prairie covered by grain farms. The airport was right on the lakeshore, a 6,000 foot paved strip with a couple of wood and patch hangars. The busiest part of the place was the seaplane base. I counted no less than a dozen aircraft around it, everything from a Supercub to a Twin Otter on floats.

The flight from La Ronge to Ratchet Lake had been an interesting one. The pilot of the Cheyenne was a gum-popping kid who handled the airplane as if it were a skateboard. He set my teeth on edge twice within the first twenty minutes of the flight, once when he yanked up the gear when the aircraft was maybe six inches off the pavement on the departure from La Ronge, and once when he cranked it into an overly steep turn intercepting his course. Delaney spent a few moments muttering about demerits. The aircraft handling didn't seem to bother the only other passenger, a young woman who never once looked up from the heavy novel she was reading. The approach and landing at Ratchet Lake were a little more conservative. Perhaps it was because the pilot's boss could see him there.

We climbed out of the aircraft and into a cloud of black flies and mosquitoes. As the pilot was pulling our luggage out of the baggage compartment in the nose, Delaney walked over to him, swatting the few mosquitoes that weren't discouraged by the repellent she had smeared over her face and hands before we left La Ronge.

"How long have you been flying?" she asked the pilot pleasantly.

"Nearly five years," he said with a grin.

"Like it?" she asked. "Plan on making a career out of it?"

"Yeah. I've got applications in with a few airlines."

"Then don't ever let them see you fly that Cheyenne, kid."

"What's wrong with the way I fly?" he asked indignantly.

"What's right with it? Do you want an itemized list?"

"Listen, lady, what do you know about it?"

I picked up my duffle bag and Delaney's small suitcase. "Take it easy, kid," I said. "And next time you yank an airplane around like that, you had better make sure you don't have a couple of airline pilots on board."

"Airline pilots?"

Delaney smiled sweetly. "I just fly the 737," she said. "Captain Fraser here flies 757s."

I patted his shoulder. "Don't take it so hard, kid. It's only two possibilities for real jobs you screwed yourself out of today. There are lots of others."

"Where do we find Barry?" Delaney asked.

He pointed to one of the hangars. "Over there." He didn't look happy.

As we walked away, Delaney grinned up at me. "You lied like a trooper, Captain Fraser."

"I know. So did you, Captain Braedon."

"I did, didn't I?"

"No big deal. Corporate flight departments are sort of like airlines. Close enough for government work, anyway."

A man came out of the hangar as we approached. "Colin Fraser?" he said. "I'm Barry Peterson. We spoke on the telephone. I hope you had a good flight up here."

"We survived it," Delaney said dryly.

Peterson shot a quick glance at the pilot, who still stood beside the nose of the Cheyenne, staring after us.

"He'll learn," Delaney assured him. "He's young yet."

"My kid brother," Peterson said. He shrugged. "What can you do? Our father owns the business. He said give him a job. I hired another pilot last week, but he can't start until Friday."

"You'll probably still have a Cheyenne for him to fly then," I said. "Can we take a look at that Beaver now?"

"Sure. If you want to drop your stuff in my office, the airplane's just down at the end of the dock." He pointed to a cluster of aircraft tied to a floating dock thrusting out into the lake. "Come on. I'll show you."

Delany and I stowed our gear then walked together down the undulating wooden dock, past several aircraft that were obviously working hard to earn their keep. He had been honest when he described the Beaver to me. It had certainly seen a lot of hard work. The bare aluminum of the fuselage and leading edges of the wings was visible through the faded brown and cream paint, and years of ploughing through clouds of bugs had left small dents all over. The registration letters, C-FRYN, were dull and bleached from black to nearly grey, the paint crazed with tiny cracks. It wasn't a pretty airplane. It sat high in the water, which indicated the floats were sound and weren't taking much water. Delaney had given me a crash course in what to look for in a float plane and from what I could see, the Beaver was structurally sound even if it wasn't aesthetically pleasing. But I was prepared to ignore cosmetic snags. It sat there with an air of patient, dogged endurance as I climbed all over it. Whatever else it was, it appeared willing to work again.

"You said it was airworthy," I said to Peterson. "Can we fly it?"

"Are you P.P.C.'d on a Beaver?" he asked.

"No, but if you are, I'd like to see how it flies."

He looked at his watch. "I've got a couple of hours now," he said. "We can take it up if you'd like."

"Does it have dual controls?"

"This one does," he said. "The other one has the swing control column."

The Beaver in my dreams, Colin McKenzie's Beaver, had the swing control column. If the pilot wanted to hand control to a co-pilot, he had to undo a pin in the column where it came up out of the floor in front of the instrument panel, then quite literally swing the yoke over and hand it to the co-pilot and reinsert the pin. An arrangement like that made it difficult to check out another pilot on the airplane. I liked the idea of the dual controls a lot better than I liked the idea of the swing control column. I thought about it for a moment or two, then decided the dual controls wouldn't make any difference one way or the other to the success of my mission.

"Got room for one more?" Delaney asked.

"There are only the two seats," Peterson said. "It was used to haul supplies into a fishing camp."

"You can fly me now," I said. "Then you can check her out in it. She's the one with the float endorsement."

"Sure. Why not?"

There's a trick to getting into a Beaver on floats. You have to climb up to where you can reach the door handle, then grab it with your left hand while you swing your body out of the way so you can open the door without giving yourself a concussion or lacerating your skull. I got into that airplane as if I'd been doing it all my life. As I started to get into the right seat, Peterson swung himself aboard and squeezed himself past me to crouch behind the two seats.

"You take the left seat, Mr. Fraser," he said. "You'll get a better feel for the airplane that way."

There was no flashback to the dream or anything even faintly resembling dizziness as I strapped myself into the left seat of the Beaver. Just the strange sensation of letting my mind freewheel in neutral so that my body could perform the familiar, well-known little chores of settling comfortably into the airplane. I knew where to look for all the dials and switches. I looked out the window to where Delaney stood on the float, one arm wrapped around the strut, ready to let go the ropes and push the aircraft away from the dock. I nodded and made a thumbs up motion. She grinned, slipped the lines, and jumped to the dock, then sat down and shoved against the float with both feet. The Beaver drifted free and slowly turned until the nose was into the wind.

Peterson handed me a checklist. "You fire it up," he said. "If you need any help finding anything, just sing out."

I didn't need any help. My hands knew where to reach

for the master switch, the mag switch, the mixture control. The radial engine coughed a few times as the prop kicked over, sputtered reluctantly, then caught and fired. Wasp Junior engines kicking over at slow idle don't ever sound smooth and even. They pop and they snort and they chuff. This one sounded normal.

"Engine instruments look good," Peterson said. "Can you taxi it out into the middle of the lake, or do you want me to do it?"

"Let me give it a try," I said. I pulled the yoke right back and held it securely with my left arm snugged around it while I reached for the throttle. There was no chip in the knurled knob that fit my thumb, and I looked down quickly, startled. But of course there was no chip. Of course there wasn't.

I took a deep breath to hide the shiver down my spine and gradually fed power to the engine. The aircraft started to move, nose high to bring the tips of the floats out of the water so that we wouldn't trip over them and flip over.

"Take it out about a hundred yards," Peterson said. "Then down the lake until you're about even with that outcropping of rock. That'll give us plenty of room for the take off."

Manoeuvring a float plane on water is like a Rube Goldberg cross between taxiing an aircraft with no nose-wheel steering, and sailing a garbage scow with no rudder. At low speeds, the aircraft rudder is not completely effective. The water rudders on the floats help, but it takes a long time to convince the aircraft you really do want to turn after you push on the rudder pedals. We were ploughing through the water sluggishly. Step-taxiing, where you've got enough speed to lift the aircraft slightly out of the water so that you're hydroplaning on the bellies of the floats, gives you a little more control because the higher speed increases rudder effectiveness, but doesn't give you nearly as much time to think about where you're going. We were already facing into the wind, so I didn't have to try the difficult manoeuvre of trying to turn from downwind to crosswind to upwind. I wasn't ready to trust Colin McKenzie's reflexes to that extent yet.

When we came even with the outcropping of rock, Peterson said, "You're doing fine. You should be able to manage the take-off. Just feed in the power easy and slow, and relax the back pressure enough to let the nose down a couple of degrees. You want to find the attitude that'll keep the tips of the floats up a bit but won't put the wing at too high an angle of attack. Once you're up on the step, pull back harder than you do for a land take-off. You have to break the surface tension of the water. It won't be hard today because there's a wind and the water's rippled."

My take-off probably wasn't the most graceful departure in the world, but we made it into the air without causing Peterson to grab for the controls. Once airborne, another difference between float and wheel aircraft became immediately apparent. Those great, heavy things hanging out in the breeze under the airplane affected the feel of it a lot more than I had anticipated. They were like the lead keel of a boat. They made the aircraft slow to turn and made it imperative to use a lot more rudder than I was used to, even after flying the Stinson. It also made it essential to keep the turns reasonably shallow. Turn too steeply in a float plane, and you're all too liable to find yourself on your back and falling out of the sky with all the grace and style of a dropped manhole cover.

We spent twenty minutes just ambling sedately around the sky while I got used to the feel of the aircraft. Peterson sat there with his arms folded across his chest, slumped in his seat, and watched me critically. I felt as if I'd turned right back into a student pilot again. Definitely an odd sensation. But Barry was no Nav Harty. He didn't make me nervous at all.

Finally, he sat up and gestured back toward the lake. "If you want, I'll talk you through a couple of landings," he said. "You handle the airplane very well. More like you're just rusty with it than as if you've never flown one before."

Feeling inordinately pleased with myself, I grinned at him. "I've done a lot of reading on it."

"It must have done a lot of good. Okay, let's go try a few circuits."

I learned the amphib ritual chant. "This is a water landing. Wheels up." The reciprocal was, "This is a land landing. Wheels down." Land an amphib in water with the wheels down and again, you ended up on your back, hanging from your seat belt and scrambling to get out before the airplane sank. Peterson said it was an embarrassing way to ruin your whole day, and I believed him.

My landings worked out quite well. It gave me an eerie feeling to remember that it wasn't all my own experience I was drawing on when I set power and flaps and chose my touchdown point. I felt a little breathless again. This wasn't even something my dreams had shown me because in the dream, I was always in the air. No take-offs. No landings. But I was far too busy to let it bother me then, because things began to happen rather quickly. There was no time to think about anything else but controlling the aircraft, touching down without breaking something, and keeping us right side up.

At the end of an hour, we called it quits. I tried step taxiing and found it worked. But I admitted defeat when it came to getting the Beaver back against the dock. Peterson took control then and very neatly brought us in, running out of momentum just as the floats nudged gently up against the old tires nailed to the side of the dock as bumpers. Delaney had been waiting for us. She stepped onto the float, staying well out of the way of the propeller, and tied the rope to the snubbing ring.

I turned to Peterson. "Is there an engineer I can get to give this thing a good going over before we talk price?" I asked.

"Unless you want to bring one in from La Ronge or Meadow Lake, the only engineer around here is Jock McLeod and he works for me," he said. "He's straight-arrow honest, but I can see how you might not want to take my word for it."

"Let's go take a look at the maintenance logs. Then I'll talk to the engineer."

The maintenance logs showed an aircraft that had been looked after reasonably well. The cosmetic snags went a long time before getting fixed, if ever, but anything serious seemed to have been taken care of quickly and competently. It all looked in order. I spoke with the engineer, who said he'd been looking after the aircraft for the last five years. He'd done the last inspection. He made a point of reminding me that the engine didn't have a whole lot of time left on it, and it was economically unfeasible to put a lot of money into replacing parts that would just have to be replaced again in 400 hours when the airplane had been averaging a little more than a hundred hours a month flying time, so he had repaired rather than replaced in a lot of cases. He admitted there were several things that he would have liked to have replaced if he'd had the time or it was worthwhile. Nothing that affected the mechanical soundness of the airplane, but things that would make it run a little more efficiently and safely. He showed me what he would do if he were going to buy it, gave me a rough estimate of how much it would cost. He told me that for the kind of flying I'd probably be doing, the replacement parts would be worth it because I wasn't going to run off the time as quickly as Lake Air would have worked it off. He said I could probably take it to someone else, maybe in La Ronge or in Saskatoon, or Edmonton for that matter, and get it done quicker, but he didn't think I could get it done any better than he could do it. He said he could have it ready for me in about four days to a week if I wanted him to do the work. I told him if I bought the airplane, I'd give the repairs to him.

I went to find Peterson. It took us a couple of hours to come to an agreement on price and terms. When I left his office, I was the proud owner of a DHC-2 Beaver that was five years older than I was. The Stinson had a baby brother, and I now owned two more airplanes than I had ever thought I would own.

Delaney was in the reception area. She had been talking with the young Cheyenne pilot. She stood up as I came out of Peterson's office.

"Well?" she asked.

"Get out your float instructor hat. You've got yourself a student."

Chapter Twenty-Nine

It was a quiet, peaceful interlude that Delaney and I spent in Ratchet Lake while Jock McLeod, the engineer, had the Beaver in the hangar and worked to his heart's content on it. There was no hotel in the town, but there was a hunting and fishing lodge that had room to take six to twelve guests, depending on whether or not they wanted to double up. It was built more like a big house than a hotel. We rented a room and ate our meals with the owners, Joe and Donna Borden and their son Kev. Joe was a retired Vancouver City cop who had purchased the lodge seven years ago and moved his family out of the city because he was afraid his youngest boy was getting in with the wrong crowd. Kev was now eighteen, a big, strapping, happy kid who was perfectly content to show guests where to catch the biggest walleye or grayling. He planned to attend the University of Saskatchewan at Saskatoon in the fall to take Forestry. Joe and Donna were delighted at how well their plans had worked out.

They treated Delaney and me like family. Donna made a fuss over Delaney and shook her head in bemused amazement over the fact that she was the captain of an aircraft that was as big as the Dash-8's that flew from La Ronge to Saskatoon. "Little bit of a thing like you flying an airplane that size," she would say. She mothered Delaney shamelessly and Delaney simply smiled and enjoyed it.

We made arrangements with Barry Peterson for the use of a Cessna 185 on floats, and he checked Delaney out, pronounced her satisfactorily competent, and signed her off in it. He charged us only his operating costs to use it to get me trained up on float flying, which made me strongly suspicious that, even though I had beaten him down considerably on the price of the Beaver, he had come out well ahead of the game.

It took Jock McLeod ten days to get the Beaver into the shape I wanted it. It was an idyllic time for us. The weather in northern Saskatchewan in early July was usually fairly good I learned, and this week was very good. Delaney and I spent the mornings flying. I learned quickly and she was pleased with my progress. I either had a natural flair for water flying, or I had inherited it. I learned how to handle a float plane in a cross-wind, and I learned how to manage glassy water landings without startling myself or Delaney too badly. I even learned how to get the stubborn, recalcitrant thing back to the dock without causing the people on the dock to dive for safety when they thought we were going to drive right through them, or ending up marooned and dead in the water just out of jumping distance, both of them embarrassing situations.

Our afternoons were mostly spent sitting in the old-fashioned glider swing on the screened verandah, out of the reach of the voracious mosquitoes, black flies, horse flies and no-see-ums. We talked a lot. For the first time, I told somebody how it had been between Glynnis and me, and the talking was like a catharsis. The tenacious and lingering guilt I still carried over her death gradually shredded and dissipated in the clean, fresh air.

Nights were the best times. We made love and discovered all the different tempos and rhythms of each other. Where Glynnis had approached each encounter almost like a production to be scripted and choreographed and timed as precisely and perfectly as one of her commercials, with Delaney, I came to realize that the ritual of the carefully orchestrated mutual orgasm was unimportant. What was essential, though, was loving and being loved. The act of love itself could range from a playful, happy frolic, to a steamy, intense explosion of passion, and any and all areas between, either separately or together. It was something we could do with each other and for each other that was only one more way of saying, *Hey you. I love you.*

One night as I lay holding her, both of us watching a full moon slip across the rectangle of sky framed in the window, I began to laugh softly. She asked me lazily what was so funny.

"Nothing, really," I said. "Actually, it's almost sad. It's a hell of a note, Delaney. I'm going to be thirty-four in a couple of months. You can't call yourself a kid any more at that age, and it's a hell of a time to be learning all the things I should have learned when I was a kid."

"About?"

"About love and loving and being loved."

She snugged contentedly closer. "Better late than never, as they say, whoever *they* are."

"Delaney?"

"Umm?"

"Let's get married tomorrow."

"We can't. It takes four weeks to publish the Banns."

"We'll tell the priest it's an emergency. You're pregnant with triplets."

"It's a little early in the season to find a pumpkin to stuff under my dress, don't you think?"

"We could find a watermelon."

She reached over and snapped on the lamp, then raised herself on one elbow so she could look down at me. Her little gamin face was solemn and grave. "I meant it when I said I wouldn't marry you until you finished what you had to do," she said. "You have to—appease your ghost, maybe—lay him to rest, I guess, before you'll really be free to marry. And I think you know that."

"I haven't had a dream for a long time. And I haven't really had a flash-back since the first time I spoke to Tom Riker, and that wasn't really a flashback. Just a flicker. Maybe just finding out about him was enough." Then I thought about this crazy stuff with the float flying, but that felt different somehow.

She shook her head. "Colin, nobody learns to fly floats as well as you can right now in just a little over a week. Granted, you're a good pilot anyway, but you can fly that thing better than I can now. You fly it better than people I know who've been doing it for ten years. I think Colin McKenzie is still very much with you, and I think you know it as well as I do."

I reached for her, lay her back against the pillow, leaned over her to kiss her. "I love you," I whispered. "I love you so damned much."

"I know. And I love you, too. More than you'll ever know, maybe. That's why everything has to be right. We can't take any chances when our whole lives depend on this."

"You're right. I know you're right. But I can't help

wanting to marry you now. I want every part of us to be together. For always. I want to see you swelling contentedly with our children. I want to watch you grow old with me through all the long years ahead of us. I want to reach out and always know you're there."

"You want for us what Colin and Judy never had."

"Yes. Yes, that's what I want."

"So do I. That's why we have to wait. You're too closely tied to him right now. And I identify with her in every way but one and that scares me sometimes. It really scares me. And I'm so afraid he's getting a stronger grip on you, too. He's closer now than he ever was to you before."

"Delaney, don't..."

"Oh, God, Colin. Hold me. Please just hold me. Sometimes I get so frightened—"

"Why are you frightened now? You weren't before."

"I don't know. I don't know. Just hold me tight. I don't want to be afraid anymore."

I kissed her, and held her, and for a long time, we forgot about everything but each other. But she fell asleep still frightened, and not understanding why she was frightened.

The next morning, when we brought the 185 back, Jock McLeod met us on the dock and told us the Beaver was ready to go.

That afternoon, I went up in the Beaver with Barry Peterson once more. He had me do several landings on the runway. It was an altogether different technique. Every airplane I'd ever landed before touched down in a nose-high attitude, with the possible exception of a wheel landing rather than a three-point landing in the Stinson or Nav Harty's old Stearman. In a seaplane on amphibs, the aircraft is in an almost level attitude when it touches down. The aircraft has to be flown right down onto the runway gently, with a minimum sink rate. It demands carrying extra power into the flare and it demands a delicate touch on the elevator. Come in with the nose too high, and you scrape the heels of the floats on the runway. Come in without the nose high enough and, once again, you trip over the front of the floats and end up in that embarrassing position where you are hanging from the straps.

At the end of an hour, Peterson told me I could fly the airplane as well as he could, and said I shouldn't have any problems with it. I was pleased with the job that McLeod had done, and I told Peterson so. We left the Beaver on the ramp in front of the hangar while I went in to settle up what I owed him for the mechanical work.

Delaney and I left the following morning. It was a Saturday, and she had to be back at work on Monday morning for a flight to Toronto. We took it easy and arrived back in Edmonton about nine-thirty in the evening. Sunday morning, I flew the Beaver out to the float plane base at Cooking Lake, some fifteen miles east of the city. Delaney drove out to pick me up and waited while I made arrangements for the Beaver. We stopped for lunch at a little fish and chip shop on the way back into the city.

"When are you going to do this?" she asked.

"I'll probably take the Beaver up to Juniper Ridge about September 8th or so," I said, skeptically watching her douse her French fries, which she called chips, with vinegar and salt. "I want to do the flight on the tenth or as close to it as I can."

"That's almost a month away. Do you really have to wait until then? Can't you do it now?" She sat back in her chair and watched me closely for a long moment, then shook her head. "No," she said, finally with a sigh. "I guess you can't.

I suppose I understand. I understand, but I can't say that I like it very much." She picked up a French fry soaked in vinegar and salt and popped it into her mouth.

"How can you eat those things like that?" I asked.

She grinned, then shrugged. "It's a Canadian thing, I think. Left over from the Brits."

I called my parents that night and spoke to them for about half an hour. I told them what I had found out, told them what I was going to do. My mother was of the same opinion as Delaney. She thought she understood why I had to do it, but she, too, didn't like it very much. My father was a little more non-committal.

The silence became a bit awkward for a moment, then I laughed. "There's someone here I'd like you to meet," I said. "Her name is Delaney Braedon, but you'd better just call her Delaney. When this is all over, we're going to be married. I'm going to put her on for a few minutes."

Delaney shook her head vehemently, then took the receiver in resignation as I handed it to her. "Hi there, Mr. and Mrs. Fraser," she said. "Your son has some very strange ideas on proper introductions." She turned and made a face at me. I went into the kitchen to make some coffee while she talked to them. I heard her laugh several times. When I came out with two cups of hot coffee, she said, "Yes. Yes, I will. And I'm really glad I had the chance to talk with you." She put the phone down and looked up at me speculatively. "How did two such nice people manage to produce such a horrid kid like you?"

"Nature versus nurture," I said. "Nature won."

"I must say they handled the shock very well. Your mother sounds like a lovely person, and your father has the niftiest sense of humour I've run across for a long time. And then there's you—"

"Ah, but you love me."

"Unfortunately, that's sad but true."

I dreamed that night for the first time in a long time, but it wasn't the same dream as before. Nor was it a nightmare. Not exactly.

I wasn't flying. This dream was full of confused images of aircraft and people, people I didn't recognize, but people I knew. It made perfect sense and it made no sense whatsoever. There was no feeling of cohesiveness. One image flashed and faded into another with no rational logic, no impression of time sequencing.

...I was a small child, reaching out to a big man wearing a uniform who picked me up and swung me high into the air as I laughed with delight and looked down into his smiling face.

...I was a young boy kneeling at a communion rail, looking at a white coffin that was covered with flowers, and felt the tears wash down my cheeks and over my folded hands in the dusty smelling silence of a hot afternoon.

...I was a young man, filled with the elation of fear conquered as I brought the Cub out of a three turn spin and sent it soaring back up into the endless blue of a spring sky, and from there joyfully into another spin, and another, and another.

...I was again a very young child, nestling into the soft and fragrant side of a woman who pointed out letters in an alphabet book and her quiet voice said the names of the letters to me.

...I was a small boy, holding onto the hands of a man and

a woman as we walked up the dusty street of a small prairie town toward a church where the bells pealed to announce the Mass, and I looked down and watched the dust squirt from beneath my shoes in small puffs.

...I was a young boy in a school yard looking up at the flight of Harvards that flew over very low, and I stuck my fingers in my ears and yelled with laughter that even I couldn't hear over the shattering roar of the Pratt & Whitney Wasp engines.

...I was a grown man turning to the woman who stood beside me in the incense-scented shadows and I lifted the frosting of white veil from over her face to fold it back over her dark hair while she smiled radiantly at me from eyes that were wide and nervous and very full of love.

I awoke in the dark, my breathing ragged and uneven. Delaney lay on her stomach, one arm thrown across my chest, her fingers curled in the hollow of my shoulder. The room was very warm. We had forgotten to turn on the air conditioner before we went to bed.

I lay there and stared at the ceiling and remembered things I couldn't possibly remember. How the air had smelled in all those small prairie towns at harvest time when the air was full of chaff and dust and the rain was long overdue. How the sweet, wet smell of the rain always arrived on the wind long before the rain itself began to fall from the monstrous, tumbled heaps of black clouds. How the schoolrooms always smelled of chalk dust and musty coats when it started to get cold out again. How the grain elevators looked so tall and ponderous silhouetted against the pale yellow and blue of the dawn sky. How the gophers, called prairie dogs, sat up and scolded impertinently at each other, then darted back down into their holes at the first threat of danger.

I had not realized Colin McKenzie had been a prairie boy. I had grown up with images of mountains and oceans. He had grown up with images of wheat fields and grain elevators and endless stretches of open space where there was nothing to break the flat, interminable line of horizon but the grain elevators and the telephone poles that stretched along ruler straight lines of roads to infinity.

I didn't know what it meant.

How could I remember so clearly how it felt to be a boy growing up on the prairies? My whole life had been spent among mountains and shores. How was it that I could not only see but *remember* what Colin McKenzie had known. It was different from dreaming. As different from dreaming as actually seeing the Edmonton airport as it was in the late fifties and early sixties was different from dreaming.

Did it mean what Delaney thought it did, that Colin McKenzie was closer to me, that his hold on me was getting stronger now that I knew I had to duplicate his last flight? And if his grip on me was stronger, would he let go once I had done what he wanted me to do?

Or did it mean that I had been closer to the truth when I talked with my mother all those years ago. Had Colin Fraser once been Colin McKenzie? Had I actually lived his life, then died his death to be reborn as his son?

A chill of fear rippled down my spine and I shivered in the warmth of the room.

Would I, too, end up watching the rocks and water and trees spin crazily in the windscreen of the Beaver and call out in pain and terror in my last moments of life?

CHAPTER THIRTY

AUGUST CAME and drew inevitably toward a close. Already, a few poplar trees showed clumps of vibrant, glowing gold foliage among the late summer green. The fields and the sides of the roads around the seaplane base at Cooking Lake misted with purple as the Michaelmas daisies, harbingers of fall, bloomed. I was busy planning the trip, trying to take care of as many details as I could, poring over the maps as I tried to sort out the route I should take. The maps didn't show the detail of trees, rocks and lakes that I saw in my dream. There were several ways to get to or from Juniper Lake, and I wasn't sure which one I wanted.

We were out at the seaplane base, installing a new Emergency Locator Transmitter into the Beaver. Just in case something did go wrong, I wanted the best emergency equipment aboard. We had brought a picnic lunch with us, and ate it sitting on the end of the dock where it was anchored on the grassy shore. Grasses and weeds grew thickly along the strip between the cat tails and reeds of the lake and the gravel road leading onto the dock.

Delaney reached out to a clump of purple Michaelmas daisies, dusty in the warmth of the day. "I always hate to see these come," she said softly. She plucked one and brushed her fingers across the slender, delicate petals. "They always mean summer's just about over. This year, I think I hate it more." She crumpled the fragile bloom in her fist, let it drop to the earth by the dock.

That night, she woke me in the night as she tossed restlessly and muttered in her sleep. She said, "Oh, please. Please, Colin...."

I turned her toward me in the darkness and lay there holding her and didn't know whether she called out to me or to Colin McKenzie.

When I finally slept, I dreamed...

Running...

...Running down a long, endless corridor, the clatter of my boot heels loud on the pale tile in the silence. Hatless, my hair rumpled and tousled because I had raked my hand through it so many times driving at top speed from the airport to the hospital. I didn't care if running in uniform created a bad image. To hell with the uniform....

My wife—

Oh, Jesus, let her be all right—

The baby—

Oh, please, let the baby live. Let them both live. Let them both be all right...

The door of the room ahead opening as I reached it, panting and out of breath...

The grim face of the doctor as he closed the door behind himself....

"She's going to be all right," he said. "She's going to be just fine, son, but we couldn't save the baby. I'm sorry. You can see her now—"

Bursting through the door to see her lying there so pale and worn against the pillow....

Seeing the bruised look around her eyes, the heartbroken way the sweet and gentle mouth drooped....

Watching the tears well up and flood across her lower lashes as her hands went down to press against her now barren belly....

"Oh, Colin..." she whispered. "I'm so sorry...."

Reaching her in two stumbling strides and gathering her into my arms, tears in my own eyes, stroking back the damp, dark hair from her forehead, neither of us knowing exactly who was comforting whom....

Hearing myself say, "It's all right, Judy. Everything is going to be all right. I love you so much...."

I awoke gasping and sweating, tears in my eyes, the sound of my sobs harsh and raw in the room. I put my hands up to cover my face, drew in a long, shuddering breath, held it until I was sure I would not make another of those hopeless, desolate sounds again. I got out of bed and went to the bathroom to splash cold water onto my face, then stood there in front of the sink, leaning hard against the counter.

Dream, I told myself. Nightmare made up of my own memories of the afternoon I had run to the hospital when Glynnis miscarried. My own memories, not Colin McKenzie's.

But I knew it wasn't. I hadn't run like that down the hospital corridor. I had been met by the doctor as I stepped out of the elevator. I had walked with him quickly but had not run to Glynnis's room. I had *not* run. I had wanted to, but I hadn't.

This was *his* memory. It was his, not mine, and the

emotions he felt were still stark and raw in me. I had lived them, I remembered them. It was impossible that I should remember, but I did.

I clenched my fist, slammed it into the hard marble of the countertop. "No," I said aloud. "I didn't live your life. I didn't. I'm not you. Oh, God, I'm not you...."

September brought the first of the heavy morning dewfalls that were the first hint that frost was coming and bringing with it the first threat of winter. My preparations for the flight were nearly complete. I had the maps ready. The long range weather forecast promised me good weather. I purchased camping gear which I took out and stowed aboard the Beaver while Delaney was on a flight to Ottawa. All that remained was to wait for the right time.

As the 8th of September drew nearer, Delaney became quieter, more thoughtful. Her sleep, like mine, became more restless as dreams she couldn't remember disturbed her. If Colin McKenzie stalked my nights, it seemed that the shade of Judy McKenzie walked through Delaney's sleep. Judy was perhaps a gentler ghost than her husband, and didn't wake her victim with nightmares, but Delaney moved fitfully and uneasily during her sleep, and woke tired. A remote expression grew on her face as dark, shadowed circles appeared under her eyes. She tried not to let me see how worried she was becoming as the day I was to leave for Juniper Ridge grew closer, but I knew her too well. She had become the other half of me, and she could no more hide her worry from me than I could hide my feelings from her.

But it was hard to describe what I felt as the days counted down. I was worried, yes. There was anxiety, but there was also a curious elation and anticipation, a subdued excitement that bubbled up at unexpected times and only mildly surprised me. I didn't want to make the flight, yet at the same time I knew I had to and looked forward to it with a mixed sense of trepidation and eagerness. If it was sometimes confusing to me, it must have been far more so for Delaney. But there was nothing that could prevent me from making the flight, nothing I would allow to stop me, not even the growing haunted look around Delaney's eyes. It hurt me to see that look because I didn't want to hurt her. But I was committed. I knew it; she knew it.

The night before I was to leave for Juniper Ridge, Delaney and I made love with an intensity that surprised both of us. She was a heated need in the darkness, a wonder of passion and yielding strength in response to the primitive demand of my own powerful and compelling hunger. We moved together with a tender savagery as it built and grew and overwhelmed us and finally swept us into a blinding vortex where there was no peace or contentment, only satiated desire and exhausted quiescence. When it was over, she clung to me and buried her face in the hollow of my throat.

"I'm coming with you," she said, her voice muffled.

"No," I said. "This is something I have to do alone."

"I'm coming with you," she repeated fiercely.

"Delaney...."

She sat up, eeled around on the bed so she could look at me. "He won't let you go," she cried. "He won't rest until you're with him, you know. He wants his wife with him, and he wants his son." She put her hands to her face and began to cry. "I can't lose you, Colin. Oh, God, I couldn't stand it if I lost you the same way Judy lost him."

"You won't lose me."

"I will. I will. He'll pull you down there with him where

it's all dark and cold— Oh, please. Don't do it. Don't go up there tomorrow."

I drew her down against me, stroked her hair back, kissed her salt-wet cheek and temple. "Nothing's going to happen to me," I promised her. "I'm a good pilot—"

She shook her head violently. "So was he. Don't you see? Everyone says he was an excellent pilot, too, and yet he's out there where nobody can find him and he's lost and alone in the darkness."

"I can find him."

"How? How are you going to find him when they couldn't find him after they looked for all that time?"

"I can do it. I can see what he saw, where he was. I know what he saw on the ground before he crashed. It's something I have to do. You can see that, can't you? I have to do it. If I don't, I'll never have any peace. He won't ever let go of me, and all the nightmares will just get worse and worse until there's nothing left of me at all."

"Oh, no... No—"

"It's okay. It's okay. It's going to be all right. I promise."

"Please. Let me go with you."

"I can't."

"Why? For God's sake, why not?"

"Because he was alone."

"Colin—"

"No. Don't you see?" She didn't understand—maybe couldn't understand—and I was afraid there wasn't any way I could make her see how important it was that she was here, safe in Edmonton. "I need you waiting for me here. I have to know you're here and you need me to come back to you. If I don't know that you're waiting for me, I might not be strong enough—"

She shuddered against me. "I don't want to lose you—"

"You won't. I swear to you, you won't. Because I can't lose you, either. You know that, don't you?"

"I know, I know, I know," she said in a monotonous, grinding little voice. "But I'm scared. I'm so scared, Colin—"

"Why?" I asked. "Why are you so scared? You weren't scared before. Why now?"

"I don't know. I wish I did. Maybe because she was so scared."

"But you're different." I stroked her hair back. "You're not like Judy McKenzie. You know about flying."

"I dream about her, Colin. I keep seeing her sitting by herself at a small kitchen table with her head in her hands, crying where nobody can see her. She's all alone and so scared—"

"But you know I'm not going to push anything I can't handle."

"Neither did Colin McKenzie. And he's dead."

There was no answer to that. I held her and murmured to her until finally, exhausted, she fell asleep, still clinging tightly to me.

In the morning, she was calm and composed and quite pale. She drove me out to Cooking Lake. I filed my flight plan from the airport office, then we drove her car out to the seaplane dock. She helped me load the Beaver. She said very little. As I stowed the last of it in the cabin and put my clipboard with its map and flight planning sheet on the right seat, she waited quietly on the edge of the dock. When there was nothing left to be done, I went to her.

"I'll be back here late on the afternoon of the tenth," I

said. "I'll give you a call from Peace River when I get there."

She nodded.

"Delaney—"

"Kiss me good bye," she said. "Kiss me, and then just go. Don't look back, don't turn and wave or anything silly or sentimental. Just kiss me good bye and go."

She felt so small in my arms. Small and strong and alive and she fit me so well in all the thousands of ways a woman is supposed to fit against a man. Her mouth was sweet and yielding beneath mine, and I tasted the salt from her tears. When I finally let her go, she stepped back and looked up at me for a long moment, as if she were memorizing my face. Then she turned and walked to her car. I got into the Beaver. The last glimpse I had of her was her car moving swiftly down the road from the airport as I climbed off the lake and turned north.

Juniper Ridge was just below the Northwest Territories-Alberta boundary, about seventy-five miles due south of Hay River. It sat on the northern flanks of the Caribou Mountains. They weren't really impressive mountains if you were used to the Rockies—more like rugged and rocky hills—but some of them rose to better than twenty-five hundred feet above the surrounding terrain.

The uranium mine was closed now—had been for more than twenty-five years—and, from what local knowledge I could gather, there was very little left of the town. The seaplane base was still there, an anchor in a blue circle on the map, but the VFR chart supplement showed no facilities and no fuel available.

I had planned my route to take me north through Fort

McMurray, then to Fort Chipewyan, where I could get fuel enough to take me to Juniper Ridge, then from Juniper Ridge south again to Peace River. I would arrive in Peace River with very little left in the tanks but I had brought several five gallon jerry cans with me to use if I needed them. One good thing about a float plane is that it's easy to put it down on almost any decent sized lake to refuel from jerry cans. There's no need to look for a runway.

Below the Beaver, the country changed quickly as we got farther north. The broad checkerboard vista of crop fields gave way to the northern boreal forests. There was a lot more water than I had expected in Alberta, and the lakes became more numerous as I moved north. The lake beds had been gouged out by the glaciers all those eons ago and filled with glacier melt as the ice rivers retreated north. There were literally thousands of them, some not much bigger than puddles, some like the vast stretch of Lesser Slave Lake. There were a lot of narrow, twisting lakes, like lost fragments of rivers, marking old glacier spillways.

I passed Fort McMurray and flew over the tar sands projects, then on farther north to Fort Chipewyan. My Beaver fit right in with the rest of the traffic at Fort Chip. There were far more aircraft on floats than on wheels, many of them older than my Beaver. Lots a whole bunch newer, too. I had something to eat after I refuelled, and rested for a while before taking off again for Juniper Ridge.

The country passing under the wings now was the same kind of country that I saw in my dream, but it wasn't exactly the same. The route Colin McKenzie had flown was farther west. I had purposely avoided going north by the same route as I wanted to use on the flight south again. I wanted to see the country he had flown over the same way he had seen it when I flew over it for the first time. I don't suppose it was really important, but it had seemed to be the right decision at the time.

It was late afternoon when I found Juniper Lake and what was left of the town of Juniper Ridge. I landed on the lake, taxied to shore. There was no dock to tie up to. I'd have to run the Beaver up onto the shingle. The town itself abutted the south shore of the lake, some of the weed-grown streets ending almost at the water's edge. There wasn't a soul around the seaplane base.

One dilapidated hangar, doorless, all the glass gone from the windows, stood on the shore beneath the trees that had almost finished turning gold and pale orange. There had been no aircraft in that hangar for a long time. The roof sagged in the middle and drifts of leaves from the last several decades of autumns littered the floor. I looked around and wondered what it had looked like when Colin McKenzie had been here thirty-four years ago.

I lowered the wheels in the floats. As I ran the Beaver up onto the shingle, a man came around the corner of the old hangar and stood waiting while I shut down the engine. He wore a heavy red-checked flannel shirt, jeans, cowboy boots and a battered cowboy hat. A fringe of white hair escaped below the band of the hat, and hung down curling slightly to brush his shoulders. He might have been anywhere between fifty and seventy. I got out and nodded at him.

"Hey, howdy," he said by way of greeting. A week's growth of white beard bristled his cheeks and chin. He could have posed for the portrait of the typical gold miner from one of Robert Service's poems about the Yukon gold rush. "We don't get much traffic here anymore." He pointed to a pair of concrete-filled ten gallon pails that stood close to the trees. "You can use those to tie that beastie down.

Not that we're expecting much wind, but it doesn't pay to take chances."

He helped me push the Beaver closer to the tie-downs. "I didn't think anyone still lived here," I said.

He grinned, showing a missing eye tooth in his upper jaw. "Not many of us do," he said. "Just me and the wife, really. I'm Jarrod Berenchuk." He thrust out his hand and I took it.

"Colin Fraser."

Berenchuk grinned again. "You're probably wondering what the heck we're doing here," he said. He gestured toward the dilapidated mine structures just barely visible to the east of the town. "The uranium's pretty much gone," he said. "But there's some silver there, too. Frieda and me pull enough out to cover what we need to live. We sorta like it here." He laughed. "We got our pick of places to live. Most of the people left everything they couldn't carry behind when the mine shut down, but the stuff's pretty beat up now. You have to pardon my chatter. I guess I talk a lot, but I don't get a chance to talk so much these days. Nobody but Frieda to talk to, and we've heard just about everything the other has to say after all these years. You come for the fishing? There's still a mess of grayling and lake trout in the lake." He stopped, but only because I think he ran out of breath.

"I didn't come to fish," I said. "My father used to fly out of here when the mine was still active, and I just wanted to see what it looked like. I thought it was a ghost town, or at least that's what they told me back in Edmonton."

He laughed again. "Well Frieda and me ain't no ghosts," he said. "If you're planning on staying overnight, you might want to find somewhere inside. There's still a lot of bears around here. Most of 'em are harmless, but you don't wanna take chances." He gestured toward town. "I could show you a few places in town, if you like. Or you could camp out in the hangar. Probably be just as comfortable there. Most of the houses are falling apart now and some of 'em are full of vermin."

"I think I'll take my chances in the hangar there," I said. "How long have you lived here?"

"Since '70. The mine shut down in '68, and almost everyone was gone by the end of that summer. Frieda and I got here in February of '70."

So he would not have been here when Colin McKenzie was flying in and out of Juniper Ridge. They'd missed each other by ten years. "How do you get supplies in up here?" I asked.

"Fly," he said. "That's my Cub over there."

Until he pointed it out, I hadn't noticed the Supercub on floats in a small bay nearly hidden by the trees farther along the shore.

"Nice little airplane," I said.

"Well, we like it, Frieda and me." He slapped my shoulder companionably. "If you need anything, me and Frieda are squatting in the old mine manager's house." He gestured with his chin. "The big one at the end of the road there. Bottom floor's still in pretty good shape, and we dragged in an old wood stove so we don't freeze and Frieda can make meals."

"Thanks, Mr. Berenchuk," I said. "I should be just fine in the hangar there."

He waved as he turned to go, and I looked at the dilapidated old hangar. If the houses were full of vermin— and I assumed Berenchuk meant squirrels, mice, raccoons, skunks, and maybe even beavers and muskrats because there were no rats in Alberta—then probably several species had taken up residence in the hangar as well. I had a tent, but then, there was a chance a bear or two might wander by.

Bears or vermin? Vermin or bears? Some choice.

Maybe I'd better check out the hangar, just in case. I finished securing the Beaver, fastening the seatbelt around the control column to prevent the ailerons and elevators from flapping because I had no control locks. The sun rode low in the western sky, casting long shadows across the water and the shingle as I pulled open the white painted man door in the wide overhead door.

Door? Had there been a door when I first looked at the hangar?

Light from overhead mercury lamps flooded the interior, nearly blinding me. Half a dozen aircraft stood at odd angles to fit into the space available, some with their cowlings open or removed, and parts of their engines on the concrete floor beside them. In the back crouched an almost new Apache, it's paint gleaming white and red. A tall man in once-white grease stained coveralls looked up from a workbench along the right-side wall.

"Hey, McKenzie," he called. "Long time no see. How the hell are you? That kid arrive yet?"

I laughed. "Not yet, Cal. Soon, though. Maybe this week. I hear you had some excitement up here."

He gave a quick snort of laughter. "Yeah. Anderson's got the kidnappers in the cells. Fortunately, they didn't hurt the kid. She was scared, but she's okay. He's got a parcel for you to take back to Edmonton. We didn't know if it would be you or Wozoleynko came up to take it down."

"Woz is delivering medical supplies," I said. "You're stuck with me this time."

Outside, a vehicle drew up by the hangar door, the gravel crunching beneath its wheels. Cal hooked a thumb toward it. "That'd be your ride into town, I bet. Sergeant's sweating buckets worrying about that parcel he's got locked up in his office. You leaving tomorrow?"

"Probably. Can you see that Papa Echo gets fuelled up either tonight or early tomorrow morning? The pumps are locked up and Barton's gone for the day."

"No sweat," he said. "See you later."

Chapter Thirty-One

I awoke with a start, lying on my air mattress, swathed in my sleeping bag in what had obviously been a parts storage room off the main area of the hangar. Moonlight streamed through the broken glass of the window, so bright it cast shadows on the walls, giving enough light to make out the empty sagging shelves lining the opposite wall. My heart pounded in my chest and sweat streamed down my face and into my eyes, stinging.

I had been dreaming. I could almost remember the dream, but for a moment I couldn't remember bedding down for the night. And I was hungry. Starved, in fact. I couldn't remember eating supper.

I climbed out of the sleeping bag and found my cooler by the parts room door. Around me, the vast, empty cavern of the hangar echoed with my footsteps as I took a packet of sandwiches to the door. I ate a couple of the sandwiches, then went out to stand by the shore, watching the moon path on the water, and lobbed pebbles into the water for a while as I let my mind wander free. After a while, still wondering about the dream, I went back to my sleeping bag.

Sleep brought more dreams. I saw a continually changing montage of aircraft and people and a busy little airport. I heard laughter as pilots talked together while they refuelled and took care of their aircraft. Float planes came and went, everything from tiny little two seater Cubs to an old Beech 18 twin engine commuter aircraft. A constant stream of vehicle traffic moved back and forth on the gravel road that led south to the town. It was at once as familiar to me as Sea-Tac had been, and completely strange and foreign. How very odd.

But then, perhaps it wasn't. This wasn't someplace I knew, but Colin McKenzie knew it intimately.

The next morning, I walked down to the town itself. Except for Jarrod Berenchuk and his wife, there was nobody at all living there now. I saw no sign of either of them this morning. Juniper Ridge truly was a ghost town. Derelict houses slowly crumbled back into the permafrost. It was a sad, quiet place. The skeleton of the mine still stood, abandoned and forsaken, on the hill above the town. I wondered if it was as haunted as I was.

I found the deserted RCMP office. The sign by the door hung askew, held only by one screw in the upper left hand corner. The buffalo head emblem was still discernable, and the letters RCMP-GRC. When I touched the sign, it felt gritty and brittle beneath the pads of my fingers, as if it might crumble to dust at any moment.

Brisk footsteps approached me from behind, and I turned, expecting to see Jarrod Berenchuk. But it was a tall man wearing a Stetson with a pointed crown, a brown tunic and Sam Browne belt over navy blue jodhpur breeches with a yellow stripe down the side seams tucked into tall, highly polished boots. He wore three chevron stripes on the sleeve of the tunic.

"Where have you been, McKenzie?" he asked. "I thought you were going to come to breakfast with us."

"I had to go down to the airport," I said. "I was going to make sure Papa Echo was fuelled, but Cal told me there was oil to hell and gone all over the ground under the engine this morning. He thinks we popped an oil line. It might be tomorrow morning before I can get away with that package of yours."

Sergeant Anderson laughed. "Well, we should be able to keep you busy. Come on in. Coffee will be hot. Millican went out for cinnamon buns and Danishes and should be back in a minute or two, if you haven't had any breakfast."

"I could use something, and coffee and Danish sounds really good."

He laughed again, then stepped past me and opened the door to the detachment office, motioning me in ahead of him.

I blinked as I stepped out of the bright sunlight into the dim interior. Dust and grime caked the counter separating the reception area from the rest of the office, the veneer of the countertop peeling and curling back to reveal rotting plywood. The iron bars in the one cell in the back of the office were nearly rusted through in places and beginning to crumble. It had been many years since they had contained any prisoner. No furniture remained in the office, no desks, no filing cabinets, no chairs. Nothing. Not even a scrap of paper. The living quarters attached to the side of the office were stripped bare and empty. But this was where Colin McKenzie would have come when he arrived in Juniper Ridge. This is where he would have picked up the suitcase he was to carry back to Edmonton where its contents would be used as evidence at a trial. But there was no ghost of him waiting there for me. Just the damp, musty smell of neglect. There was no message, nothing he wanted me to know. I left the derelict office and climbed up the hill to look at the mine.

I saw nothing of Berenchuk there. He and Frieda must be working some part of the old mine out of sight of the office buildings. The crusher house had almost fallen in on itself, all the equipment long gone. The roller mill was more or less in the same shape—dangerous. Nothing remained in the office buildings. The rest of the buildings—machine sheds, garages, workshops, storage units—looked rickety and unsafe, so I gave them a wide berth, and wandered back into town.

It wasn't much of a town. I think the population at its biggest was about 6,000, mostly mine workers and their families, and a few shopkeepers, teachers, clergy, businessmen: people needed to keep a small town running smoothly. The houses had been laid out in neat squares, and the downtown was a short two blocks long. I counted a drug store, a grocery, two churches facing each other across the main street, a hardware store, and a brick-built school, all of them tumbling down. Before long, Juniper Ridge would be completely gone, and the boreal forest would settle down over the land again, swallowing all traces.

Eventually, I went back to the lake, built a fire and heated a can of beans and wieners for my dinner. Sitting with my knees drawn up, my elbows propped on my knees, and my chin resting on my two fists, I watched the sun set across the lake. The water turned luminous turquoise, pink and yellow, then faded to dark blue, then to black. The sky glowed pale red and yellow for a while longer, then all the light was gone.

It was very quiet there. The air was crisp and cool, but not cold enough to be uncomfortable. I thought about him, here at this lake, perhaps laughing and joking with friends in that hangar that was now dilapidated and derelict. Had that been me? Was the jumbled dream I'd had last night just a dream he'd sent, or was it a memory of a previous incarnation? Had I lived before as him?

Again, that chill of misgiving mixed with apprehension shivered down my spine. It was easier to accept the idea of his ghost, his spirit, reaching out from the past to touch me than it was to accept the concept that I had been him once.

Those flashes of him in the hangar, and outside the detachment office—now those felt absolutely real in some ways, but refused to be pinned down when I tried to remember them exactly. The more I thought about those flashes, the more they tended to go fuzzy and blurred around the edges, lose their sharp definition, become confused and imprecise, worse than a half-remembered dream.

In the morning, I gathered up all my camping gear and stowed it back in the Beaver. I was loosening the tie-downs when a dark blue and white cruiser pulled up beside the hangar. Sergeant Anderson got out carrying a leather suitcase wrapped in pliofilm and official seals. He helped me stow it in the back of the Beaver and lock the cabin door on it.

"Take care of that," he said. "It's evidence." He grinned. "No peeking and no heading for Tahiti."

"No worries about that," I said. "This old crate would never make it that far. See you next time."

I took one last look around, then pushed the Beaver back into the lake, climbed onto the float and paddled out far enough into the lake to give me room to manoeuvre before I got in and started the engine.

The take-off was uneventful, as was the first hour of the flight south. Then, very slowly, I began to recognize the country below the Beaver as I flew over the most rugged parts of the Caribou Mountains. He had come this way. The landmarks were familiar. The way a river curved back on itself before flowing into a small lake. The way two lakes had formed so close together there wasn't more than a narrow strip of land only a few metres wide between them. I knew where I was now. I began to smile as the contentment of flying again grew with the knowledge that I would be home tonight. In another hour, I'd be in Peace River, and I could call Judy and tell her I was on my way home. The baby was due sometime this week, and she would be anxious to hear from me.

The air around me shimmered for a second, and I realized what I was thinking.

Oh God. No! That wasn't right. I wasn't going to call Judy. *He* was going to call Judy. It was Delaney who waited for me. Judy had waited for *him*; she had waited almost all the rest of her life for him....

I began to sweat, smelled the sharp unpleasant door of fear in the cabin. I had to keep this straight. I was Colin Fraser. *He* was Colin McKenzie. If I couldn't keep it straight, I would die, too. I would spin into the rocks and the trees exactly as he had.

Chapter Thirty-Two

I WAS in the nightmare again. Beneath the wings of the Beaver, the familiar landscape of rocks and trees and water scrolled past, and there was the strong thread of tension that brushed my mind like a spider web. Something was very wrong. Something threatened everything I loved. There was danger out there. I could feel it now. But where did it come from? Where was it?

The Beaver flew well. The engine note was loud and smooth and confident. The engine cluster proved my ear heard right. There was nothing wrong with the engine. I could feel nothing at the visceral level to tell me there was a fault with the airframe. Everything felt right. Except....

Except what?

Where was the danger?

I reached out, grasped the throttle knob, felt my thumb fit into the worn smooth chip in the black plastic.

No! Dammit, no. The throttle knob of my airplane, of Colin Fraser's airplane, had no chip in it. It was old and worn, but it was whole. Dammit, Fraser, keep it straight!

I was Colin Fraser. Not Colin McKenzie. I was Colin Fraser and Colin McKenzie was over thirty years dead....

My heart pounded in my chest as I frantically searched the panel, then the hard blue of the sky. Where was the danger? The chip in the knob felt deeper beneath the ball of my thumb.

All right. All right, dammit. You can have the chip. Where is the danger? Just tell me where the danger is?

I looked out the left side window. Out under the white wing with the dark blue wingtip, bearing the fore-shortened registration letter. CF-MPE. But there was nothing out there.

Those letters. They weren't right. I rubbed my eyes, shook my head. No. They should be C-FRYN...

The wing shouldn't be white. It should be faded brown, almost tan....

Oh, Christ, what was happening?

I had been sliding in and out of Colin McKenzie's life ever since I landed at Juniper Ridge, I realized. I had lived what he had. I wasn't sure now what had been real, and what had been hallucination, or his memories.

My eyes snapped back to the panel again. I saw my left hand on the control yoke, saw the brown sleeve of my tunic, the gold star on it, saw the wide gold wedding band on the fourth finger of my left hand. For some reason, it startled me. I had forgotten I wore a wedding band.

Why was I so bloody jumpy all of the sudden? Was it Judy? Had something gone wrong as it had gone so tragically wrong with the first pregnancy? Why was I so twitchy? This was just a normal flight. Why was I so damned jittery?

There was something wrong. Something so terribly wrong....

I clenched my fist, pounded it against my knee. *I'm Colin Fraser.* Remember that. I've always been Colin Fraser. Just Colin Fraser....

Colin Fraser? Who the hell is Colin Fraser? My name is McKenzie....

Then I saw the speck against the blue of the sky through the curve in the windscreen. Just a small dot that didn't move in relation to the window post. A late bug splashed against the windscreen I had missed when I polished it before I left Juniper Ridge?

The speck grew suddenly, took on recognizable proportions. No, not a bug. Another aircraft. At my altitude and coming fast. Low wing. Great round snout. Huge barrel shaped body behind the colossal radial engine. A Grumman Avenger water bomber.

I had barely recognized it as another aircraft when I realized it was on a collision course with me. His speed must have been close to 200 knots. Mine was 110. That put our closing speed at over 300 knots, almost half the speed of sound.

Instinctively, I yanked on the control column, pulled it back and to the right. It was the only way I was going to be able to get out of his way. He was slightly below me. I had to try to get over him.

The Beaver's wing came up, but too steeply, too steeply.... I felt it lurch, then shudder. But it was too late. The Avenger filled the windscreen, monstrous and terrifying. I saw the oil stains on its belly as the pilot tried to turn away from the Beaver, saw the horrified eyes of the pilot behind the squared off glass of the canopy. His mouth, like mine, was open in a shout of terror.

The Avenger's right wingtip sliced into the right side of the Beaver's cabin. The outboard end of one of the prop blades broke, spun away. Glass shattered. Wind noise filled the cabin. The engine began to scream in agony.

And the pain. Pain in my back, in my legs, in my head. And blood.... So very much blood.... Where was it all coming from?

The Beaver rolled onto its back. I saw the Avenger again. Incredibly, it still flew, limping away with its truncated left wing. Then it was gone as the Beaver rotated again. Sky and trees changed places crazily.

"No!" I shouted. "Oh Jesus, no..."

Oh God, oh God.... Was this what had happened to him? To Colin McKenzie? Or was it happening to me, to Colin Fraser? Was this now or was it thirty years ago?

Oh Jesus, I didn't know. I didn't know....

I didn't know who I was....

I didn't know when I was....

Which Beaver spun out of control? Was it the white and blue airplane? Or the brown and cream one?

I couldn't tell. I didn't know who I was....

I fought the dead aircraft. Rudder. Elevator. Nothing worked. I kept on fighting. I wanted to live. I had to live. There was Judy and the baby. I had to live for them....

Oh dear Jesus, the baby. Without me, Judy would die and there would be no one to love our son. No one to take care of him. He would be alone.... I had to live. I had to live because of our son....

"No!" I hardly heard my own voice over the screaming engine and the wind noise. "No! I'm not Colin McKenzie. I'm Colin Fraser. Oh God. Let go!"

Judy.... The baby.... I had to live to take care of them....

The rocks, the water, the trees rotating beyond the window.... Too close. Too close now. I could see the exact point where the Beaver would impact, where I would die.

"I'm sorry," I whispered. "Oh, God, Judy, please forgive me. I'm sorry." No, that wasn't me. It was him. It was *him*.

"Let go!" My voice sounded thin and terrified, hoarse and raw in the noisy cabin. I flung my hands up to cover my eyes to block out the terrifying sight of the crazily spinning earth. "I'm not you. I'm not you anymore. I never was."

My son would have no one to look after him, no one to love him. I didn't want to die and leave him. I didn't want to die and leave Judy. My wife...my son...my life....

"No," I shouted. I reached out, grasped the control column with both hands, pulled at it, felt the resistance of a living aircraft. "No. I was conceived of your seed, borne in her body, and I'm not you.... I'm not you!"

Outside the window, the rocks and trees and water blurred as they spun faster, closer....

"I'm not you. I never was you. Let go. I'm Colin Fraser.... Oh, God, I'm Colin Fraser...."

I heard her call out to me. Heard her call my name. "Colin...."

But there were two voices. Two women. One called to me; the other called to him. But one of us was dead, and the other one would die in seconds.

"Oh, please.... I'm not you. Let me go. I'm Colin Fraser and I don't want to die like you did...."

There were two men here, two of us in two Beavers. Both of us were terrified because we were going to die. Both of us heard the women we loved calling to us. But only one of us had to die.

Then I knew. I understood. I was his son, not his

reincarnation. And because I was his son, it all fell into place.

In that oddly timeless instant of understanding, it was as if I moved back and away from what was happening. I could remove myself and watch the confused and overlapping images of the white and blue Beaver and the faded brown and cream Beaver. They weren't the same. They never had been.

"Let go," I said aloud softly. "She'll be with you where you can look after her, and I have someone of my own to look after. You have to let go. It's all right now. Your son is safe. Your wife will be safe with you."

The driving power behind the fear diminished, then faded. I was alone, and the aircraft I flew was the old brown and cream Beaver, my Beaver, Colin Fraser's Beaver.

The world stopped spinning. The wind noise died. The pain vanished.

But the rocks and water still expanded and grew in the windscreen, coming closer with dangerous speed. The Beaver, my faded brown and cream Beaver, was in a steep dive, power on full, aimed directly at an outcropping of rock at the edge of the water. In seconds, I would impact in exactly the same place he had.

But this was something I could understand. This was here and now and it was real and I could do something about it. This was my airplane; my living airplane that was sensitive and responsive.

Calmly, I reached out, pulled back on the throttle knob that had no chip to fit my thumb. Back pressure brought the nose up and only a slight twist to the right curved the Beaver, mine now, not his, up into a climbing turn only a few feet above the water. I circled once, lined up to land on the calm, glassy surface of the water.

We touched down smoothly, and the placid wake arrowed out behind the floats as I taxied toward the shore. The rock rose a sheer twenty feet up out of the water at the south east side of the lake. The last of the Beaver's momentum took us within just a few feet of it. The wingtip nearly brushed against the broken face of the cliff.

I sat there in the quiet airplane, listening to the muted pings and clicks of a cooling engine. I crossed my wrists on the control column, pressed my forehead to my wrists. Rivers of sweat drenched my shirt, made the waistband of my jeans sodden, as I dragged huge, gasping breaths of air into my lungs. My hands trembled and for a long time, all I could do was sit there blankly and blindly while the aircraft rocked gently under me. The fear was gone. It was gone as completely as if it had never been there, and I felt empty and hollow as a blown egg.

Colin McKenzie had been terrified, not so much of his own death, but of what it would do to his wife and his son. He knew his wife as well as I knew Delaney. Judy McKenzie was not strong, either physically or emotionally. Her strength was borrowed from her husband and as long as he lived, she had enough. But without him, she would have nothing, and he knew that. It was his fear for her and for his son, his love and his urgent need to watch over them, which had enabled him to reach out across the gulf and touch me only because I was his son, not a reincarnation. I had said it myself. Conceived of his seed. I was blood of his blood, flesh of his flesh, bone of his bone, bound to him by the genetic coding that passed on his eye colour and his build and even the stamp of his features to me.

And because I was bonded to him so closely, and Delaney was bonded to me, Judy McKenzie had been able to reach out to Delaney and invade her sleep and her dreams. Judy

McKenzie was terrified, sick with worry, when Colin McKenzie flew. He knew that and his guilt for causing that fear, his inability to stop causing her fear, was part of this. Together, they had instilled her fear into Delaney.

But Delaney had not been afraid until that night in Ratchet Lake. Now I understood why, and my dawning understanding had enabled me to detach myself from Colin McKenzie, become Colin Fraser again. We had more in common now, my father and I, but we were at last completely and finally separated.

It was his overwhelming concern for his son that I had felt then. His dread that his son would be alone and lost and uncared for. I had shared that fear. But it was not just his fear alone. It was my own, too. For my own unborn child.

He hadn't known. That vital need to look after his wife and his son was the last conscious thought Colin McKenzie had ever had. That imperative obsession had carried forward, had been the motivating force behind the dreams he had sent to me. He had been so caught up in it that whatever was left of him had been unable to find peace.

Until now. Until I had proved to him that he didn't have to be concerned for me any longer, that he could rest with his wife, my mother, because I needed neither of them as a child needed his parents. Not now.

And Delaney's terror? Even that wasn't entirely hers. Until that night in Ratchet Lake, she had not been frightened. Worried, perhaps, because even though she tried to understand what was happening to me, to us, it was difficult for her. But there was no reason for her to be afraid and she was confused and frightened because she knew she had no reason to be afraid.

Until then, the only bond between Delaney and Judy

McKenzie was Delaney's profound pity and empathy for Judy, that and the consideration that she loved the son as deeply as Judy had loved the father. Then something had changed to give them more in common, something that made Delaney more vulnerable to Judy's fear for her husband's safety.

It was that change that broke Colin McKenzie's hold on me. Broke it irrevocably, because it was that change that finally made the bond between us that of two grown men rather than of father and child.

My son, Delaney's and my son, had been conceived some time during that quiet week in Ratchet Lake. Conceived in love just as I had been conceived in love and Colin McKenzie finally accepted that as validation and the discharge of his responsibility toward me.

I got out of the cabin and climbed down to the float. The air was still and cool. A bright red leaf, cupped and curved like an ancient coracle, rested on the surface of the lake, peacefully rotating above its own reflection.

I lay on my belly, flat on the top of the float, and peered down into the brown-gold water. Sunlight filtered through it in streaks of paler gold and caught bright sparks drifting in the glow.

And I saw it. Saw the shadowy outline of the broken wing, the shattered fuselage, the twisted tail assembly. He was down there. He had been waiting down there for nearly thirty-four years now, but he was no longer lost. He had been found and would be taken home, no longer to lie alone in that still and bitter grave.

I looked down deep into the water to the drowned Beaver. He had not been trying to pull me down there with him. All he had ever really wanted was to know that his son was all right, that I was all right.

"It's okay, Dad," I whispered. "I was loved. I *am* loved. Your grandson will be loved, too."

And as I looked down, the water began to ripple in tiny, spreading rings as my tears dropped into it.

CHAPTER THIRTY-THREE

IT WAS spring again. Holy Cross Cemetery, just north of Edmonton along the St. Albert Trail, lay drowsing in the warm sunshine, oblivious to the hum and clamour of the traffic on the busy highway. The wrought iron gate curved high over the entrance above our heads as we turned off the Trail and entered the gently winding road that wandered among the headstones.

I got out of the car and walked over the newly green grass to where the new single monument stood sheltered by the trees that had just begun to open their leaves to the fresh warmth of the sun. I knelt to place the small spray of flowers by the headstone and the cool dampness of the ground soaked into my knee through my slacks. A soft breeze riffled through my hair as I bent my head in a brief and silent prayer.

The headstone was a polished slab of dark grey marble, unpretentious and unadorned. It contained only his name and her name and the dates of their birth and death, and a simple inscription: *"And while with silent, lifting mind I've trod/The high, untrespassed sanctity of space/Put out my hand and touched the face of God."* John Gillispie Magee's timeless prayer for pilots. Somehow, it had seemed appropriate for both of them.

I had gone to Inspector Murchie's office after they had retrieved and returned the broken wreckage to the city. What he told me confirmed the truth of what I had seen. Colin McKenzie had crashed as the result of a collision between his Beaver and a Grumman Avenger water bomber which had been on its way from Peace River to investigate a sighting of smoke near Fort Vermilion. The wreckage of the Avenger had been found all those years ago nearly twenty-five miles from the lake where the RCMP Beaver had finally come to rest and been lost. Since I could never tell him how I knew of the collision, I told him about how I had seen a mention of the Avenger crash in the photocopied newspaper account that Delaney's friend had provided, and had made a shrewd guess. He had accepted that, perhaps with a trace of skepticism, but he had little other choice.

I had not been there when they lifted the old Beaver out of the water and searched through the sodden, decaying cabin. Nor had I been there when they took what was left of him out of the disintegrated and crumbling pilot's seat where he rested with his seat belt still latched, and brought him back to Edmonton. They told me they had recovered the suitcase; it had been filled with nothing but a pulpy, soupy, unidentifiable mass, but it was enough to close his record cleanly and with honour.

But I had been there at the funeral home where they completed the final services that needed to be performed for Colin McKenzie. Tom Riker had been there with me. He had chosen the plain, varnished casket adorned only with a simple bronze cross that would hold his godson's remains, and had made the arrangements to place Colin

McKenzie beside his wife, Judy, after thirty-four years' separation.

And I had been there with Delaney when we came here to lay him beside his wife under the bright, golden leaves that drifted down from the trees. There had been a scarlet-clad honour guard standing with bare heads bowed as the priest said the final words. My parents had come up from Oregon, and my mother shed silent tears for him. Tom Riker and his wife, Della, faces calm and composed, stood beside me at the graveside, and even Ted Wozoleynko had come to pay his respects. Inspector Murchie was there, remote and thoughtful, dressed in his scarlet serge.

When it was all said and done and over, I remained there for a long time, looking down at the raw turf that covered the mound where they now lay together. It was almost finished then. There was only one more thing that I had to do for them, and that would be done in spring, when the warmth and the light returned, when new life began.

I had looked up when I felt a hand on my shoulder. Tom Riker stood there beside me, and we were alone by the graveside. I smiled and reached up to put my hand briefly over his, then we both made our final leave-taking and turned together, his hand still on my shoulder, to go to where our families waited for us by the cars.

As we walked away, I caught a glimpse of the image from the dream, of him lifting the veil back from her face and looking down into her eyes that were filled with love for him. Then I saw him—him, not me—running up the stairs to the small apartment, taking them two and three at a time, flinging open the door and calling to her. "Judy! I'm home. I'm home." And I saw her rise from her chair by the kitchen table and rush to meet him, laughing.

I smiled again, but I didn't look back.

There was nothing more I could do for them then; nothing they needed from me, except one thing.

I had come back today to say good bye for the last time. I most likely would not ever return here to this quiet corner. It was time to take up my life again in the place I belonged, a life where Colin and Judy McKenzie had no part.

But he would not be forgotten. I got to my feet and turned to where Delaney stood waiting behind me. The baby in her arms was asleep, nestled quietly and snugly into his blankets. I went to them, put my arms around them, and kissed her before we walked slowly back to the car and got into it to drive away for the last time. In his infant carrier between us, Colin McKenzie Fraser slept on, undisturbed and untroubled.

Afterword

I have used the call letters CF-MPE for the half-ghostly aircraft in this story. There really was an RCMP aircraft with those call letters. In fact, there were two. The first was a Norseman Noorduyn originally registered as CF-BFS, but re-registered as CF-MPE when the RCMP purchased it in August, 1938. It was written off in October, 1939, when a defective oleo strut collapsed. (Oddly enough, the wreck was shipped to Noorduyn where the wings were attached to a new fuselage to become CF-MPF.) The second aircraft, registered as C-FMPE was a deHavilland of Canada DH2 Beaver registered in October of 1963 and written off in B.C. in March, 1990, after nearly thirty years of service.

The aircraft in the story bears no resemblance to either of these aircraft, other than the fact that one of them really was a Beaver. I chose the letters randomly, but indeed any registration with the MP letters in it is, or was, a real aircraft owned and operated by the Royal Canadian Mounted Police Air Services.

I am grateful to S/Sgt. Jerry Klammer, Chief Pilot of the Edmonton RCMP Air Services Division, for clearing up some points for me. Any mistakes are strictly my own. Thank you, Jerry.

c/n 16 CF-MPE RCMP

C-FMPE at Edmonton in the early 1970's.

I'd like to take this opportunity to thank the members of my writers' group, The Cult of Pain, for all the helpful advice they've given me over the years. It's difficult to write in a void, and the support of other writers is a boon every writer needs and appreciates.

Thank you, too, to Lorina Stephens of Five Rivers Publishers, my publisher, my editor and, I hope, my friend. She never lets me get away with anything and has therefore made my books become a good as they can be. Thanks, Lorina.

About the Author

Ann Marston has worked as a teacher, a flight instructor, an airline pilot, airport manager and literacy coordinator, and several other odd and assorted careers in between. While maintaining this weird schedule, she has also been writing most of her adult life.

Together with her friend Barb Galler-Smith, she teaches writing fantasy at Grant McEwan University in Edmonton, and mentors up-and-coming writers in a writers' group that grew out of the writing classes. She lives in Edmonton with her daughter and their floppy eared dog.

BOOKS BY FIVE RIVERS

NON-FICTION

Annotated Henry Butte's Dry Dinner, by Michelle Enzinas

Al Capone: Chicago's King of Crime, by Nate Hendley

Crystal Death: North America's Most Dangerous Drug, by Nate Hendley

Dutch Schultz: Brazen Beer Baron of New York, by Nate Hendley

John Lennon: Music, Myth and Madness, by Nate Hendley

Motivate to Create: a guide for writers, by Nate Hendley

Stephen Truscott, Decades of Injustice by Nate Hendley

King Kwong: Larry Kwong, the China Clipper Who Broke the NHL Colour Barrier, by Paula Johanson

Shakespeare for Slackers: by Aaron Kite, et al

Romeo and Juliet

  Hamlet

  Macbeth

The Organic Home Gardener, by Patrick Lima and John Scanlan

Canadian Police Heroes, by Dorothy Pedersen

Canadian Convoys of World War II, by Dorothy Pedersen

Shakespeare for Readers' Theatre: Hamlet, Romeo & Juliet, Midsummer Night's Dream, by John Poulson

Shakespeare for Reader's Theatre, Book 2: Shakespeare's Greatest Villains, The Merry Wives of Windsor; Othello, the Moor of Venice; Richard III; King Lear, by John Poulsen

Beyond Media Literacy: New Paradigms in Media Education, by Colin Scheyen

Stonehouse Cooks, by Lorina Stephens

FICTION

Black Wine, by Candas Jane Dorsey

Eocene Station, by Dave Duncan

88, by M.E. Fletcher

Immunity to Strange Tales, by Susan J. Forest

The Legend of Sarah, by Leslie Gadallah
Cat's Pawn, by Leslie Gadallah
Growing Up Bronx, by H.A. Hargreaves
North by 2000+, a collection of short, speculative fiction, by H.A. Hargreaves
A Subtle Thing, by Alicia Hendley
Sid Rafferty Thrillers, by Matt Hughes
  Downshift
  Old Growth
The Tattooed Witch Trilogy, by Susan MacGregor
  The Tattooed Witch
  The Tattooed Seer
  The Tattooed Queen, by Susan MacGregor
The Rune Blades of Celi, by Ann Marston
  Kingmaker's Sword, Book 1
  Western King, Book 2
  Broken Blade, Book 3
  Cloudbearer's Shadow, Book 4
  King of Shadows, Book 5
  Sword and Shadow, Book 6
A Still and Bitter Grave, by Ann Marston
Indigo Time, by Sally McBride
Wasps at the Speed of Sound, by Derryl Murphy
A Quiet Place, by J.W. Schnarr
Things Falling Apart, by J.W. Schnarr
And the Angels Sang: a collection of short speculative fiction, by Lorina Stephens
From Mountains of Ice, by Lorina Stephens
Memories, Mother and a Christmas Addiction, by Lorina Stephens
Shadow Song, by Lorina Stephens
The Mermaid's Tale, by D. G. Valdron

YA FICTION

My Life as a Troll, by Susan Bohnet
Eye of Strife, by Dave Duncan
Ivor of Glenbroch, by Dave Duncan
  The Runner and the Wizard
  The Runner and the Saint
  The Runner and the Kelpie

Type, by Alicia Hendley
Type 2, by Alicia Hendley
Tower in the Crooked Wood, by Paula Johanson
A Touch of Poison, by Aaron Kite
The Great Sky, by D.G. Laderoute
Out of Time, by D.G. Laderoute
Hawk, by Marie Powell

YA NON-FICTION

The Prime Ministers of Canada Series:
  Sir John A. Macdonald
  Alexander Mackenzie
  Sir John Abbott
  Sir John Thompson
  Sir Mackenzie Bowell
  Sir Charles Tupper
  Sir Wilfred Laurier
  Sir Robert Borden
  Arthur Meighen
  William Lyon Mackenzie King
  R. B. Bennett
  Louis St. Laurent
  John Diefenbaker
  Lester B. Pearson
  Pierre Trudeau
  Joe Clark
  John Turner
  Brian Mulroney
  Kim Campbell
  Jean Chretien
  Paul Martin

WWW.FIVERIVERSPUBLISHING.COM

Hunter's Daughter
ISBN 9781927400777
eISBN 9781927400784
by Nowick Gray
Trade Paperback 6 x 9,
302 pages
March 1, 2015

Northern Quebec, 1964: Mountie Jack McLain, baffled by a series of unsolved murders, knows the latest case will make or break his career. Eighteen-year-old Nilliq, chafing under the sullen power of her father in a remote hunting camp, risks flight with a headstrong shaman bent on a mission of his own. Their paths intersect in this tense mystery charting a journey of personal and cultural transformation.

Growing Up Bronx
ISBN 9781927400005
eISBN 9781927400012
by H. A. Hargreaves
Trade Paperback 6 x 9,
144 pages
April 1, 2012

Growing Up Bronx allows readers a poignant insight into the mentors and influences that shaped one of Canada's brilliant writers of science fiction. Hargreaves takes you through the Great Depression and WWII, in his native Bronx neighbourhood, into the lives of shopkeepers and family, heartache and triumph.

This is definitely a must-have collection of short stories to complete the canon of H.A. Hargreaves' work.

A Subtle Thing

A DEBUT NOVEL
BY ALICIA HENDLEY

A Subtle Thing
ISBN 9780986542701
eISBN 9780986642326
by Alicia Hendley
Trade Paperback 6 x 9,
200 pages
July 1, 2010

Raw, honest and relentless, Alicia's debut novel is a heartbreaking and uplifting journey into one woman's battle with clinical depression. Drawing on her experience as a clinical psychologist, Alicia has created a compelling portrait of what life looks like through the eyes of someone whose actions may otherwise appear inexplicable.

A Subtle Thing is a must read for anyone trying to understand what it's like for the friend, family member, colleague or employee who suffers from this debilitating condition.

CPSIA information can be obtained
at www.ICGtesting.com
Printed in the USA
LVOW12s0855281016
510685LV00001BA/4/P